THE PEEPAL TREE BOOK

OF CONTEMPORARY

CARIBBEAN SHORT STORIES

THE PEEPAL TREE BOOK

OF CONTEMPORARY

CARIBBEAN SHORT STORIES

PEEPAL TREE

First published in Great Britain in 2018
Peepal Tree Press Ltd
17 King's Avenue
Leeds LS6 1QS
England

ISBN13: 9781845234102

Supported using public funding by
ARTS COUNCIL
ENGLAND

CONTENTS

INTRODUCTION 7

INTRODUCTION

Peepal Tree has published over fifty collections of short stories since its beginnings in 1985. *The Caribbean Short Story: Critical Perspectives,* a collection of essays we published in 2011, makes a strong case for regarding the short story as the pre-eminent Caribbean literary form – for a combination of both practical and cultural reasons. The small magazine and the newspaper have historically been the most available spaces for literary publication, and they naturally place a premium on brevity. And one can argue that even in a digital age, Caribbean societies still have strong oral dimensions. The urge to tell stories remains.

There have been good anthologies of Caribbean short stories dating back to the 1940s, but whilst more recent ones such as the *Penguin Book of Caribbean Short Stories*, edited by E.A. Markham and published in 1998, or the *Oxford Book of Caribbean Short Stories* edited by Stewart Brown and John Wickham, published in 2001, are strong surveys and still have their value, there has been a further flowering of Caribbean short story writing over the past twenty years that warrants collection and exposure.

It is no accident, though, that those two collections came from big publishers. The business of putting together anthologies of that kind is very expensive. The fees for rights that we and our authors received from those two volumes were very welcome additions to our struggling income. Our anthology has more modest aims. Unlike the Oxford Book (which I believe had a fees budget of £30,000), we make no attempt to survey the region as a whole, across its four main languages. Unlike the Penguin Book, we don't have the resources to buy the rights for work we haven't published ourselves. Nevertheless, the stories we have chosen from our list offer an unrivalled representation of the very best Anglophone Caribbean short fiction since the turn of the century.

We chose the stories collected here because of their quality and because they fairly represented the work of each writer. Our dearest hope is that the anthology will encourage readers to explore the collections from which the stories here are drawn. Each story in the anthology offers a complete and satisfying reading experience, but many are drawn from collections in which individual stories are part of a careful architecture that builds to a coherent whole.

Again, whilst the stories in this anthology do offer powerful images of the contemporary Caribbean, we have not chosen stories because they fitted some predetermined picture of the region we wanted to give, nor have we sought balance in geographic or ethnic representation. We know, for instance, that the anthology underrepresents Indo-Caribbean voices, though these are far from underrepresented in our catalogue as a whole, only in the short story list – a fact from which we draw no conclusions. In any case, readers will not find it hard to see that much of the writing here comes from those whom education has shifted, whatever their origins, into positions of relative social privilege. That is a Caribbean reality. If there are working-class voices here, they are chiefly voices that draw on childhood memory. Even so, it is not hard to see divisions and contrasts of perception between the stories collected here that draw on the writer's sense of social location. And whilst this may be writing *about* the social majority that rarely speaks for itself in literature, there are many stories here that empathy and imagination carry beyond the sharp social divides found in Caribbean societies. Equally, there are some excellent stories here that dwell very honestly on their character's social separation from the wider world, such as Elizabeth Walcott-Hackshaw's "Here", or Keith Jardim's "Beyond Open Water".

What is not underrepresented here is the voice of women, and this is undoubtedly one of the dominant characteristics of the post millennial short story. Over three-quarters of the stories collected here are by women. Another of the post-millennial extensions of the range of Caribbean writing has been the work of writers who espouse LGBTI identities. The work here of Anton Nimblett and Helen Klonaris is part of that growth. Equally, as the story here by Raymond Ramcharitar shows, the issues of gay sexuality and homophobia have become part of non LGBTI-identifying writer's concerns.

As noted above, we made no artificial effort to represent all Caribbean territories in this anthology. Jamaican authors make up almost half, Trinidadians well over a quarter, the rest from Guyana, Barbados and the Bahamas, in that order. This of course says something both about sheer population size (Jamaica's 2.5 million to Grenada's 104,000), but also about the writing cultures of different countries. St Lucia, for instance, has a strong and very publishable community of poets, but is much less well represented by prose fiction. And, of course, to indicate where writers came from and where they write about is not the same as saying that this is from where they write. Well over half of the writers represented here are resident in the Caribbean's main diasporas, North America and the UK (57%), but the fact that 43% are still writing about the countries in which they live is also a new feature of post-millennial Caribbean writing where, particularly in larger territories, the growth of middle-class and professional occupations (and the increasing hostility to immigration of those once diasporic destinations) has made it more likely for writers to stay resident in the region. The current location of writers is noted in the section on contributors at the end of the book. We leave it to readers to come to their own conclusions.

These stories are contemporary in the sense that almost all have been written since 2000. Where a few outside that parameter have been included, it has been because of their quality and contemporary feel. We could not leave out Hazel Campbell's long-short story (verging on a novella) "Jacob Bubbles" for those reasons, though it was published in 1992. Of course, contemporary stories are not necessarily about the post-millennial Caribbean world, though the stories about childhoods and earlier times are inevitably filtered through the present. In the context of the collections from which they have been drawn, many such "looking-back" stories often point, by contrast, to the difficult and confusing directions that Caribbean societies appear to be taking. This is at a point in time when many Caribbean states have been contemplating (celebrating would be the wrong word) the achievement of fifty years of postcolonial independence. As a significant number of stories suggest, the nationalist hopes of rapid decolonisation have given way to reflections on how deeply the centuries of colonial history remain embedded in culture, mentalities and the connections between race and class structures, and how much remains to be done to realise true sovereignty and the kind of social justice that would unpick the harsh inequalities inherited from colonialism. We are conscious that many of the stories chosen here would hardly win the endorsement of Caribbean tourist boards as invitations to enjoy the delusions of sun, sand and blue skies. Indeed, we rather hope that the anthology contributes to undermining the remnants of that kind of false consciousness. As Ifeona Fulani's story "Fevergrass Tea" shows, the experience of return even for Caribbean persons who have lived outside the region may be beset with illusions and complications.

If the stories here tend to the dark, the alarmed, the sorrowful and the serious, that is a faithful representation of what has driven the writers included here to turn to the short story form as a way of trying to make sense of their societies. This is not to say that the reader won't find rich humour in several of these stories, such as those by Rhoda Bharath, Geoffrey Philp and Leone Ross; though perhaps a more characteristic tone might be the bitter-sweetness of many stories or the subversive humour that surfaces in Hazel Campbell's and Sharon Millar's stories; whilst the cathartic pleasures of Breanne McIvor's "The Course" reminds us that the boundaries between the horrific and the comic are very permeable.

As editors, the issue of the length of the stories we had to choose from was an issue, and sometimes compromises had to be made to keep the book to bindable proportions. There were other stories by Opal Palmer Adisa and Raymond Ramcharitar, for instance, that got nudged out by sheer length. This is another good reason for exploring the collections from which the selections were made. Even so, we remain convinced that there is much to be said for an anthology that contains stories of variable length – illustrating that, as a form, the short story can do very different but equally valid things with length.

We resisted the temptation to order the stories in some thematic plan. We know this is foolish anyway – readers will dip in and read for their own reasons. Even so, we have attempted to describe some of the salient features of the stories in terms of themes, approaches and formal styles that readers may find helpful.

The Caribbean short story has always done childhood well, and there are few individual collections that don't have at least one story that focuses on childhood. Here, several deal with that moment when the child comes to consciousness or reaches an awareness of the complexity of the adult world surrounding them. Merle Collins' "Mapping" and Alecia McKenzie's "Planes in the Distance" both focus (one movingly, the other ironically) on the differences between the world as seen by adult and child, whilst Barbara Jenkins' "I Never Heard Pappy Play the Hawaiian Guitar" explores how a child, sent to extract maintenance money from an absent father, has to come to terms with the different ways her father is seen: as the home abandoner and the man with gifts among other men. Geoffrey Philp's "My Brother's Keeper" throws lights on both the phenomenon of the jacket, the outside child, and way the narrating half-brother has to adjust to this unwelcome cuckoo in his nest. In Leone Ross's "President Daisy", a story about a train journey, the travelling child learns about mindless homophobia and human gaiety, and comes out with an enhanced understanding. Whilst all these stories deal with aspects of the child's vulnerability, their child figures emerge unscathed. Other stories remind that this is not always the case. Velma Pollard's "Ruthless" and Olive Senior's "Silent" both put children into positions where they witness what they should not have seen. In "Ruthless" the child sees the local pastor sexually abusing his servant, whilst in "Silent" the child is present at the murder of his gangster father – in a story that is masterly in conveying the physicality of the child's perceptions. In Jennifer Rahim's "Stranger", the child discovers too late that sexual danger comes not from the eccentric stranger her family recoils from, but from much closer to home. Kwame Dawes' "The Gully" brings us close to a child who is subsequently raped and murdered. Perhaps most powerfully of all, Hazel Campbell's "Jacob Bubbles" traces the career of the abandoned child who becomes the ruthless leader of one of the posses who fought out the turf wars on behalf of Jamaican politicians in the 1970s and 80s.

If, in general, the short story is about the moment, there are several stories here in which the passage of time is an important dimension. Jacqueline Crooks' "Cool Burn" is one instalment in a set of connected stories that move through space and time, from rural Jamaica at the turn of the 20th century to Britain much later in the century. The story reminds that the situations of class and racial oppression that emigrants to the UK tried to extricate themselves from are rooted in a past that is, in fact, relatively recent. Here, the wife of an Indian indentured labourer (only 100 years ago) tries to free her imprisoned husband by surrendering herself sexually to the white plantation manager. The depth of memory that shapes the continuing tensions within a migrated family is also brilliantly caught in Valda Jackson's "An Age of Reason (Coming Here)", a story that explores how a family in Britain remains deeply and differently shaped by their experience of leaving Jamaica and arriving in Britain at different times – the way, for instance, the eldest sister feels wounded by the responsibilities loaded onto her, whilst the younger sisters remember the experience quite differently. The different perceptions of those who left and those who stayed in the Caribbean is also shrewdly caught in Jan Lowe Shinebourne's story, "The Godmother".

However, we have called these contemporary stories not just because they were written over the past twenty years but because many of them address the difficult realities of the contemporary Caribbean. This includes the widening gulf between elites and masses graphically noted in Elizabeth Walcott-Hackshaw's "Here", of societies marked by the private affluence of gated communities remote from contact with the lives of the mass of people – an element, too, of Christine Barrow's "Three, Two, One", though this uncovers the reality that ladies who lunch can also be covering-up their own experience of gendered violence and unhappiness. Stories address the reality of societies that have become trans-shipment zones for the narcotics trade, where addiction to cocaine has supplanted the milder pleasures of ganja, and local dealing results in violent turf wars. This is a feature of Caribbean life caught in Jacob Ross's ironically named "Rum an Coke", and as the alarming background to Keith Jardim's "Near Open Water". Stories focus on locally developed specialities in criminality, such as Sharon Millar's "The Hat", a darkly comic story of tables turned in the Trinidadian kidnap industry. We could have included several stories from Rhoda Bharath's collection, *The Ten Days Executive and Other Stories*, that indicate how enmeshed political corruption has become with other kinds of criminality. Nor did we include any stories from Jennifer Rahim's 2018 Bocas prize-winning *Curfew Chronicles* (on the grounds that taking out individual stories from the context of the whole does too much damage to their artful interlinking) in which the big fish who order assassinations, whose activities lie behind the abused street boys who run drugs, are a menacing presence just off the page. Hazel Campbell's "Jacob Bubbles" is set at the time in the 1980s when garrison dons did the politicians' dirty work; Olive Senior's "Silent", is set decades later when the inheritors of those dons still have the guns – and their own agendas outside political control.

Elsewhere, the contemporary may be seen as the bizarre collision of present and past, as in Raymond Ramcharitar's satirical "The Abduction of Sita", where he mashes together a narrative about prosperous, modernistic Indo-Trinidadians seized with pieties about the indentured past, and a narrative of unexpected sexual identities. Other aspects of the contemporary may be seen in the frankness of a story such as Sharon Leach's "Mortals" (from her powerful collection, *Love It When You Come, Hate It When You Go*) which portrays the mother of a child dying of cancer engaging in utterly random sex with a stranger in the hospital grounds as a desperate attempt to assert her connection to life. Leach's short stories are also contemporary in the sense that they feature people from backgrounds that, previously, have scarcely featured in Caribbean fiction. They are not the urban poor inherited from the fiction of Mais or Patterson, or the urban middle and upper class who exist in contrast to them (as in Diana McCaulay's novel *Dog-Heart*), but the black urban salariat of the unstable lands in between, of the new housing developments, people struggling for their place in the world, eager for entry into the middle class but always anxious that their hold on security is precarious. These are people wondering who they are – Jamaicans, of course, but part of a global cultural world dominated by American material and celebrity culture.

What we see emerging as a powerful expression of writers' attempts to make sense of the confusing reality of the contemporary Caribbean is a re-investment in the potential of the gothic. Of course, this is not new. Edgar Mittelholzer, whose fiction we have been republishing, and whose short stories are collected together for the first time in the compendium, *Creole Chips and Other Writings* (2018), had seen the potential of the gothic as a way of addressing Caribbean realities in the 1940s and 1950s.

The genres of the gothic and of what Karen Lord describes as speculative fiction (we recommend the anthology from our former imprint, Peekash Press, *New Worlds, Old Ways, Speculative Fiction from the Caribbean*, edited by Karen Lord) and before that marvellous realism, have both become distinctively Caribbean forms and offer interesting alternatives to the dominant genre of an often autobiographical realism. In the case of the gothic, here are societies displaying all the features of global modernity – in shopping malls, the (costly) availability of consumer goods, skyscrapers and ruling elites that remain almost wholly enmeshed in the culture inherited from European, Western colonialism. On the other hand, powerful elements of the "folk" cultures brought from Africa and India have been creolised in the region and survive amongst the poorest. The Trinidadian poet and high court judge, James C. Aboud, recounts in the introduction to his *Lagahoo Poems* how the defendant to a wounding charge was acquitted on the grounds that he believed that his victim was a lagahoo, a werewolf. In Breanne Mc Ivor's "The Course", there is a chilling and satisfyingly gory return to that figure of folklore in a contemporary setting – a fascination with the uncanny also present in Jacqueline Bishop's "Oleander" and Meiling Jin's "The Tall Shadow". In stories not included here, we'd point to the presence of the gothic in Sharon Millar's *The Whale House and Other Stories*. Since the gothic emerged from the Caribbean connections of William Beckford, author of *Vathek* (1786), who inherited a massive fortune, slaves and Jamaican estates from his father, and also from the slave-owner and author of *The Monk* (1796), Matthew G. Lewis (who did visit and write about his estates, also in Jamaica), this seems a most appropriate return.

These are stories chosen, in the first place, because they offer pleasurable reading, but we also had an eye on the potential of the anthology as a source of profitable study – both in academic contexts and by would-be writers keen to develop an awareness of the range of generic forms, styles and narrative devices available to the short story. Stylistically, there are – among others – examples of the conte, satire, the uncanny, marvellous realism and the gothic. A few can be read as cautionary or morality tales; others are graphic, open-ended snapshots of humans under stress or confronted with implacable dilemmas. The variety of strategies each writer uses to position their narrators will make for fascinating study. In Rhoda Barath's "Redemption" for example, the narrator is an observer, on the periphery of the action. On the other hand, in Kevin Jared Hosein's "King of Settlement 4", his character is both protagonist and narrator whose personal unfolding drama *is* the story. Mark McWatt's story, from his collection *Suspended Sentences: Fictions of Atonement*, in addition to the ingenuity of inventing multiple supposed authors, here provides a story that is cunningly ambivalent in its supposed author's reliability. Is this a story of attonement, or a narrative of achieved revenge?

While the majority of stories here adopt the classic singular point of view, several interrogate and subvert this "singularity" by presenting us with multiple points of view, shifting perspectives and conflicting perceptions. Some are notable for their explicit deployment of the authorial "god voice" – a strategy that allows the writer a more sweeping, panoramic view of the reality they are examining. In contrast, several succeed precisely because the authorial presence is so effectively eliminated.

It's all here, crafted stories that brilliantly exploit and/or subvert the classic western short form, invariably presenting us with something new and refreshing; they sit alongside narratives that draw powerfully on the tropes, language and Caribbean's unique *ways of telling*.

We have enjoyed revisiting the stories collected here. We trust the pleasure will be shared.

Jacob Ross
Jeremy Poynting

OPAL PALMER ADISA

TRYING WORDS

The words galloped out of his mouth and landed like corpses at his feet. His temples throbbed. He quickly glanced around to see if anyone had witnessed his dilemma. This had never happened in public before. A woman to the right of his peripheral vision, wearing thick lenses and hair pulled back tight, caught his eye. She gave him a sheepish smile and, only bending her fingers to pat her palm, waved to him. Had she seen the words *Beguile*, *Amuse* and *Agitate*, leap to their death? And if so, was she going to report him? Sheldon Jerome Bowen glanced at the dead words at his feet, then decided to turn around and face the woman, but she had gone, as quickly as a mosquito. Angry at the lack of protocol, at this complete exposure, he decided to step over the words and leave them right there. Let them bury their melodramatic selves, he grumbled, as he made his way out the store and into the street. The cool air greeted him, and he felt the sweat drip from his forehead and realized that his shirt, especially under the armpits, was pasted to his body. Damn blasted words, he sputtered, almost colliding with a woman, who glared at him before scampering out of his way.

Forgetting his plans to shop, he made his way to the bus stop, trying to erase all ideas from his head. Ever since his fight with the verbs, they have been attacking him. He knew the nouns were the instigators, but of course they denied everything. The verbs would surely be awaiting him, once they found out that three of their associates had died. He knew it was futile to try and convince them that he had nothing to do with their members' deaths. He could almost see them gathered, strident and persistent as ever, not caring if anyone overheard. The bus pulled up, and he stepped out to allow two elders to get off. Just as he was about to step back into the bus, a group of nouns whizzed by his cheeks and buzzed in his ears.

"You saw them, didn't you?" he turned to the bus driver, who looked at him with a blank stare, except for his knitted brow. "They are instigators," he insisted, showing his bus pass.

"Man, if you drunk, you can't get on my bus," the bus-driver eyeballed him.

Dr. Bowen heard the nouns, *Content* and *Ancestors*, chortling in his ear and decided to ignore the bus-driver and find a seat at the back. Because of the blasted verbs he had been given administrative leave, and now the nouns were trying to make him appear drunk or mad. He didn't know what he'd done to make them hate him so. He was becoming a recluse, afraid to go out or speak to anyone, in case a word decided to debate with him, or worse, jump to its death so he could be blamed. Dr. Bowen walked to the back of the bus, his head bowed, eyes to his feet, jacket hanging from his dwindling frame and found a seat by a window.

He refused to look at anyone on the bus because, if he did and something about them provoked a thought, then the words would collide in his head, he would start to speak in tongues, and get thrown off the bus, like the last time, when he had to walk home five miles in the pouring rain, only to be greeted at his door by a chorus of words, taunting him. He cracked open the window and allowed himself to look out. The gentle breeze melted away his agitation, and soothed the throbbing in his head. If only he was a little boy again, living with his grandmother in Jamaica. He recalled riding the bus with her from the market, sitting in the back, both of them munching on the treats she always bought for them. Distracted by his childhood memory, Dr. Bowen's mind was like a freshly polished mahogany table, and his face, fully relaxed, was handsome.

"You're enjoying the breeze, aren't you?"

He hadn't noticed that the bus had stopped, nor that the same woman with thick lenses now sat beside him, but the moment, she spoke, he felt her shoulder pressed against his and his skin goosebumped. Suddenly he was afraid, and something told him not to look at her. Perhaps it was the nouns, disguising themselves as a woman. They had tried to trap him before, although never camouflaged as a human. Normally he didn't have any problem with them, except lately some had become traitors and were working undercover for the verbs, trying to implicate him, tricking him to confess crimes he didn't commit. He continued to look out the window and pretended he hadn't heard her. He could feel her leaning closer to him and trembling.

"Professor, listen." Her voice was crackly in his ear, like a poor long-distance telephone connection. "I am no longer the person you wanted me to be. I saw *Beguile* and *Amuse* jump to their deaths from your mouth and *Forget* and *Run* did the same thing a few days ago. I have been trying to catch up…"

"Get away from me, get away from me," he hollered, springing up, sweat glistening on his face and spreading over his body. "You're an agitator! I do not know who you are. You can't fool me." He hopped over her as if she was contagious, almost falling on the man in the seat in front of him, who shoved him to the floor, with a dismissive, "Fool, what's wrong with you!"

"They're trying to trick me, get me to confess to crimes I didn't commit," Dr. Bowen offered to the passengers who were looking at him as if he had lost more than one of his marbles.

"I'm not that person any more," the woman who had been sitting beside him said. "You have no business treating me like I am one of them. I tried to follow the programme you outlined for me, but I kept getting lost, unable to find myself."

"Keep her away from me," Dr. Bowen continued to sputter, as the woman rose from her seat, his hands raised as if to ward off blows to his body. The bus came to a screeching halt. He tried to stand up, but each effort only made him slip and stumble. He felt as if his muscles were conspiring against him too. Then the bus grew quiet and he heard feet walking towards him, and the passengers parted. He imagined this is how it must have been when the Red Sea parted for Moses; this is how he had hoped words would part for him, but instead he looked up at the bulky frame of the bus-driver. The woman stepped forward, and touched the bus-driver's hand.

"He doesn't know who I am either. He thinks I'm one of them.

How could he not recognize me? I was one of his most diligent students. I saw how it happened. It wasn't his fault."

"Ma'am, I don't care whose fault it was; you all can't be making confusion on my bus." The driver's words were slow and deliberate. "Now you have two choices as I see it. First," and the bus-driver looked deliberately at the woman, whose fingers still rested lightly on his arm, "you best remove your hand and step off my bus and maintain some dignity, or I will lift you off myself. Now which will it be?" he asked, pointing to the back door. The woman looked around her, and could not find a sympathetic pair of eyes, so she squared her shoulders and stepped off the bus, protesting, "No wonder they are killing themselves; he refuses to heed the truth."

"You did the right thing," Dr. Bowen said to the bus-driver as he rose to his feet.

"I know I did," the driver replied. "But you getting off, too. I knew from the moment you got on you would be trouble. Now get!"

Dr. Bowen managed to hoist himself up, and cowered off the bus, feeling whipped and wronged again.

When he looked around the woman was nowhere to be seen. Nonetheless, he felt her sting as sore as a mosquito bite.

In less than an hour he made it home by staying off the main streets and hugging the buildings when he had to pass by someone.

His relief was great when he turned into the yard where the grass and weeds had overtaken the walkway and were working their way to the front steps and door. Inside, all the drapes and blinds were drawn. For some time he'd shied from turning on any lights, as that would just be an invitation to the nouns. They had taken over his sanctuary; they had caused him to be banished from his only place of refuge, his office in the beloved university where he had taught successfully for the last thirty years; they had also helped to isolate him from the few associates he had. Even more devastating was their invasion of his home so that, quite literally, he had to hide out from them, sitting in a tub of water to keep them at bay. He had tried to smoke them out, but had set the house on fire. The fireman told him he should seek counselling. He had sneaked into a Catholic church in the middle of the day and filled a gallon bottle with water from the font and had tried to drown them, but that only made them more furious. Now they were all over his house, except for the bathroom, the only place where he felt free from them. He wasn't sure why the bathroom was off limits, or why they feared water, but on these two small points he had the upper hand.

Although hunger gnawed at his stomach, he knew that if he ventured into the kitchen they would be there, perched on the knives, sprawled in the pots, meeting on the plates, waylaying him on the rim of a cup or glass, eager to condemn him for deaths he did not cause. He tiptoed across the living room in the darkness, stubbing his toe on a stack of books he had been intending to read and, ignoring the pain, gingerly made his way to the bathroom. He could hear the nouns singing out of tune, "Come we go down, Come we go down to Linstead Market." He wanted to shout at them to shut up, tell them what awful singers they were, and that he was very, very far from Linstead Market, had not graced it for over seventeen years since his grandmother died, but he was hoping to get some sleep, and if they knew he was home, they would be relentless, singing dirges throughout the night.

What abominable hooligans they are, he thought.

At the bathroom door he held his breath as the singing quieted, then he pushed open the door with force, and sprang in, shouting over his shoulder, "This is my house damn it." Slamming the door behind him, he turned on the cold faucet, shouting at the top of his lungs, "You dirty, nasty words. I will drown you yet." Instantly there was quiet and he sighed, too weary to enjoy his small victory.

He stripped down and got in the tub and, as always, the fatigue peeled from his body like the skin of a guava. He let his body relax and for a moment forgot his quarrel with words. He felt normal, as he did as a boy, taking his ritual Saturday herbal bath in his grandmother's house, as she sang loudly in the kitchen as she prepared the ingredients for the pastries that she would rise to bake before dawn on Monday to sell from her little stall at Crossroads.

Sheldon Jerome Bowen loved living with his grandmother because she was never cross with him. No matter what he did, she never sucked her teeth in vexation or told him to "just clear out from me sight", as his mother did. His mother would punch him whenever he did something that made her angry, or when she was upset with his father. His father was often stone silent, moving about the house like a shadow. What Sheldon Jerome liked best about living with his grandmother (she always called him by both names, although she often shortened it by calling him SJ), was his soothing Saturday evening baths, made from a concoction of leaves and herbs she purchased from the small obeah stores tucked in a corner downtown, near Parade Square. Bath was always followed by a light supper that would often include fresh pineapple. But even better than his Saturday bath was Monday morning, which he always recalled as an endless dream – waking to the aroma of sugar and spices infusing the house, and knowing full well that in his lunch box would be a variety of little cakes, made especially for him. His mouth watered from the memory, and he sat up in the tub, and reached over to the shelf he had installed in the bathroom for cans of food for those times when the words were especially aggressive. He grasped the can of pineapple and smiled. He had not known until he was almost fifteen that pineapple and other fruits could be canned, accustomed as he was to eat all fruits and food fresh. But when at fifteen, on June 3, 1957, he joined his parents in Canada, who had relocated about five years earlier, and his father took him to the supermarket, he could not reconcile the pictures of the fruit contained in the can with the fruits he knew. Befuddled, Sheldon Jerome didn't eat for almost a week, until his mother called his grandmother in Jamaica and told her to tell him to eat before he starved to death or the authorities would arrest her for neglect. Sheldon Jerome could still hear his grandmother's words, her voice soft, but firm.

"Don't mind. You mama and papa can't help but give you false food. Is foreign you is now. Eat it for Granny so you don't get sick. Eat it and pretend like it fresh-fresh and I just peel it for you." When he got off the phone, his mother gave him slices of pineapple that were perfectly even, round slices, without a trace of moles (as his grandmother called the dots that patterned all pineapples). Sheldon Jerome had bitten at the edges gingerly, tasting what he suspected were traces from the metal can. He forced himself to eat it, although it tasted very little like the pineapple he loved. Over time, he grew to like the taste, and now, without foods that he could eat directly from cans, he would probably have starved because of the conspiracy of words to do away with him.

Dr. Bowen reclined further into the tub and ate the entire can of pineapple cubes, then dozed, but not for long as he jerked awake when he heard the verbs banging on the door and shouting, "Murderer! Murderer!" He turned on the faucets to drown them out, but they kept up their strident accusation, until he filled the empty pineapple can with water and tossed it under the door. He couldn't help but laugh when he heard their hasty retreat. As always, his happiness was short lived, as the nouns started their mournful songs. Enough was enough; it was time to face his accusers. He unplugged, stepped out the tub and, still wet, pulled on his robe. Armed with two bottles of water, just in case the darned words tried to get physical – he could put up with obstreperous behaviour, he could put up with shouting and unfounded accusations, but he would not countenance being physically attacked. The memory was still raw, almost twenty-seven years later, of being beaten by three young white men one night when he took the wrong exit off the freeway in Utah and decided that he wanted a beer before finding his way back to his hotel. Once he had stepped out of his rented car, he could tell they were tipsy, and he tried to stay clear of them, but one of them almost tripped, and instinctively he reached out to help the drunk man regain his balance. All he remembered after that was feeling their fists and boots connecting to his body. It was in a daze, while in the hospital, that the first word, *Kindness* jumped to its death from his mouth. But then he was so consumed by pain, he didn't give it much thought. Ever since, he avoided physical pain at all costs.

Dr. Bowen flung open the bathroom door and bellowed, "This is my house and I am declaring peace." An adjective fizzed by him. That was so uncalled for. He knew adjectives were colleagues with nouns, but normally they were cheerful and without guile. He just didn't understand what had caused words, which he was very fond of, to turn against him like that. He'd had enough. He squared his shoulders and even though his body trembled, he blew out a full breath and marched into the living room, where the words had been sitting-in for the last three months, barring his entrance. As he stepped onto the blue Persian rug, he almost lost his resolve. They had made a mess of things: the rug was covered with crumbs and grime, his prized leather sofa was ripped in places, cushions were on the floor, books, gutted and mangled, were strewn all over. Tears sprang to Dr. Bowen's eyes, but he blinked them in. He would never give them the satisfaction of seeing him cry. They were assembled everywhere, like an army on alert. Why had he not gathered a similar army? Who would come to his defence? He had no friends. *Friend* was a word he killed long, long ago, when he was only nine years old and still in Jamaica.

When he was a boy, living with his grandmother, a group of children from the neighbourhood took to taunting him each day as he walked home from school, chanting as they trailed him, "Cry-Cry Baby, Moonshine darling, take off your shoes and run on home." They used sticks to beat near his feet and force him to run. By the time he got to his grandmother's gate, he was in tears and all the other children had disappeared. The first few times, his grandmother took him onto her lap, wiped his tears with her large, warm palms, and pressed him to her bosom.

"Hush, don't mind, is jealous dem jealous dat me love you more dan all de world." Then she would tickle him until he laughed, and then take him into the kitchen for a sugar-bun and a cold glass of cherry or guava juice.

After the fifth time, however, she didn't wait for him to come through the gate and run and hide his head in the folds of her skirt. Instead, she met him outside.

"Don't come in here wid you long face. Defend youself. Same way dem hurl words at you, you dash some back at them. Use words to pelt dem, so dem leave you alone."

She refused him entrance, took his book-bag, then sent him running after the children who had been chasing him. SJ ran after them, and words he didn't know he knew spilled from his mouth. Even grown-ups stopped in their tracks. Still he ran, flinging words at the backs of the retreating children until he was exhausted and they had all taken refuge inside their respective homes.

That was the last time they bothered him; it was also the beginning of his public speaking. People came to his granny and asked her to let him speak because he was so eloquent and used big words, such as *erudite*, *mollycoddle* and *casuistry*, the meaning of which they didn't even know. Each word had a specific smell and taste and he knew them, not by their meaning, but by their action. He didn't study the dictionary, yet he knew words, and daily more words came into his head and leapt from his tongue, amazing and astounding everyone, most of all himself. Every evening after school several people would gather in his grandmother's yard and listen to him read the *Daily Gleaner*. As SJ's confidence grew and he saw the pleased and pleasing approval in his grandmother's eyes, he began to comment on the news after he read it. Soon, more and more people came for him to read letters from relatives abroad, or even documents from the government about their land. SJ was solemn at the beginning, basking in the attention, but then he started to use the information he learned about people to criticize and even make fun of them. His grandmother admonished him, saying, "Horse never know the ground is dry until he's hungry." Although SJ didn't understand quite what she meant, he knew it was a warning. It was only after he entered high school at ten years old that Sheldon Jerome realized that not only was the word *Friend* lost to him, but its very essence, and that although admired, he was completely and utterly friendless.

Now as Dr. Sheldon Jerome Bowen stood face-to-face with the jury of words that formed a tight circle in his living room, he wondered whether all of this was a result of what his grandmother and others had said. "You getting too boasty, too full of yourself. Seems like you think you and words are equals." He had gotten to think that he owned words, and that no one was beyond his reach; all he had to do was hurl words at them, and they couldn't hide from him. But now he, Sheldon Jerome Bowen was the one hiding out, afraid to speak or think, afraid and silenced by the very power of words. Dr. Bowen smiled just as *Dictate*, Grandfather Verb, pounced on him.

"You are smiling as if the charges we have brought before you are not serious, as if we are mere words to be ignored or discarded. Need I remind you we have no tongues to clip. You will be tried here tonight."

Instantly Dr. Bowen's head throbbed and he felt as if someone was inside it, pounding with a jackhammer. He was at a loss for words, and that scared him; he heard himself spluttering, but no coherent words would form in his head and find freedom on his tongue. Had the words succeeded in clipping his tongue? He knew, although he didn't know how he knew this, that this had been the fate of a maternal ancestor who had tried, three times, succeeding the fourth time, to run away and seek haven with Nannie of the Maroons. This was only after they had clipped her tongue and amputated her right big toe, yet still she made it to Nannie's camp in the mountains. His grandmother had told him this story, saying she was a direct descendant of the clipped-tongue woman, and had tried to impress upon SJ that his gift of speech had surely come from this ancestor, her endowment to ensure that her line continued and her story was not forgotten. Sheldon Jerome had never told anyone about her life. In fact, that was one tale his grandmother told that he did not believe. He always asked her why they clipped his great, great, great maternal grandmother's tongue since it was her feet that allowed her to escape her enslavement, not her tongue, but always his grandmother would reply with a deep guttural clicking in her throat:

"Is not only feet know path. Tongue does climb tree too."

What she said never made any sense to Sheldon Jerome, but now it did. He cleared his throat.

"Noname, my maternal great, great, great grandmother, refused to be a slave. She berated the slave master and the overseer. Weary of her nagging, they clipped her tongue, but still her story reached us here." Dr. Bowen did not recognize the sound of his own voice, but he had succeeded in silencing the words. He could hear his own breath, and sweat like blood from a new wound oozed from his body and cooled him down. *Dictate* nodded at him, then asked, "Why are you telling us this story now? Why have you kept concealed every essential thing about who you are? Why should we listen now? How do we know this is not a ploy or academic manoeuvring to throw us off or an attempt to win our sympathy?"

"Noname was seven months pregnant when she finally ran safely to the Maroon camp." Dr. Bowen spoke as if he didn't hear what *Dictate* said. "She had seven children, six boys and one girl. My grandmother was her only granddaughter." He paused, amazed at his own penchant for lying. His grandmother had never told him this about Noname. He didn't know how his grandmother was related to her, yet he felt that what he had just said was not a lie, but the truth come to him now. He couldn't know what this ex-slave looked like, but an image of a woman the colour of sandalwood, with three plaits, small round eyes, a braided scar by her upper left cheek and wearing a crocus-sack dress, with a piece of colourful African fabric in the shape of a diamond sown over her right breast, came into view. Dr. Bowen swayed as if he was on a boat navigating rough waves. He saw the woman step out of his head, touch him on his shoulder, and just as she walked away from him, he heard her say very clearly, "Now you talking!" but it wasn't her mouth that spoke, rather her heart. Sheldon Jerome heard her, heard every syllable loud and clear and he knew and understood what she meant. Now his talking had to have a purpose other than its own indulgence in hearing itself.

Dr. Bowen held on to the wall, ready now to listen to the words' accusation, ready to accept his just punishment. He was indeed a murderer. He would not ask for mercy, or plead innocent. He had consciously used words like weapons to hurt others and had in fact been delighted when he witnessed the pain he was able to inflict. Still leaning against the wall, he raised his head, looked into *Dictate's* eyes and said, "Read the charges."

At that very instant, there was a banging on the door.

"Open up! Open up!" a female's voice demanded.

The words shuffled, and Dr. Bowen wondered who it could be. Perhaps it was the new faculty member, Dr. Roseth Smalling, who was now the darling of the department, the very one who was being groomed to take his place. The same woman, with her unapologetic common speech and dreadlock hairstyle, who flaunted her island ways, as if where she came from was somehow on par with the US or even Europe; the same woman whose first book had won a prestigious award that he had coveted and had thought his third book should have received – in fact everyone had said as much – but there she was with a first book that focused, no less, on the culture of the island. It was even being touted as seminal and ground-breaking scholarship. This was the same woman who, at the reception they held for all shortlisted faculty, had come over to him the first day they met, after she interviewed for the associate position (he had voted against her outright) to say she had read his work, but was perplexed why he, a man of such sound scholarship, (*What audacity to feel she had the right, the qualifications to assess his research projects!*) should continue to write about Europeans rather than his own people (*Which people were these?*), and besides, she felt his last book was redundant (*The impertinence!*), and wondered if, after the party, which she said was boring and full of white people's pretence (*Who was she to assume that just by the virtue of colour or misfortune of birth that they had anything in common?*), if he would like to join her for a drink and give her the scoop on the department. All this she said to him forthrightly, and Dr. Bowen had wondered if she was also about to proposition him, he a respectable man of letters, who had never stooped to such things. He was well aware, or rather had heard through the grapevine, that several of his male colleagues and even one female faculty had engaged in sexual politics to get ahead, as well as dabbling in student liaisons in the bullying manner of the weak. He was above such indulgent acts, and had an unblemished record – at least until they hired that woman, Dr. Smalling, despite his threats to leave the department rather than be associated with the likes of her. So imagine his chagrin, when about five months ago, he turned up his pathway after a long day at his office, to find Dr. Smalling camping on his steps as if she belonged there. She'd smiled up at him as if they were friends, and spoken to him in that laconic, familiar tone. He was so aghast at such presumptuous familiarity that he stopped in his tracks.

"They said you didn't teach today. I knocked on your office

door when I was on campus, but you weren't there. I called too, but they told me in the department that you seldom answered your phone, so I decided to drop by. I was just about to leave, but let me get up so you can get in." At which point, Roseth stood up, brushing off the shirtdress she wore that showed, to his disgust, her unshaven legs.

Dr. Bowen had disdained to speak to her. The unmitigated nerve! One didn't just drop in at another's house unless specifically invited. That was why he did not associate with island people, with their lack of social protocol, their insistence on assuming a commonality where none existed, their disregard for personal space, their predilection for speaking their minds, regardless of the audience's disposition to hear their story; their effrontery in inserting themselves in places where they were not welcome. Dr. Bowen stepped around the woman, without so much as a word, and slammed the door in her face. Even so, whenever she saw him on campus, she greeted him. He was sure it was merely to rile him, to make him lose his composure and descend to her level by engaging her in some heated quarrel. He had a reputation to preserve. It was well known on campus that he openly snubbed anyone, students and even administrators, whom he felt beneath him. As the years went by, more fell into that category.

"Is stalkin me, de damn woman, stalkin me." The words sprang from his mouth, awakening a memory of another tongue Dr. Bowen was sure he had long buried.

"Open the damn door, Professor, I know you're in there." A female's voice interrupted his reflection. He peered through the peephole and recognized the woman with thick-lenses from the bus. Her eyes were puffy and drooping as if she were tired. It was not Dr. Smalling, but who was this woman, and what did she want? Too weary to make sense of the muddle that his life had become, one water bottle slipped from Dr. Bowen's hand, wetting his feet and spreading on the floor. He opened the door and the woman pushed past him. He slammed the door shut quickly, hoping no neighbour had seen the woman enter. Should he ascertain who this woman was and what she wanted? Or should he just let the words deal with her. As if answering his thoughts, *Dictate* said, "Now that she has come, let's hear what you have to say to her."

"I know what you are trying to do and I only wish that you had intervened years ago before…" the woman shouted in a hoarse voice.

"Meddler!" *Dictate* shouted. "The esteemed doctor has wronged us, abused and misused us. Used us against the very people we wanted as allies. He is loathsome. He is a traitor, even to himself," *Dictate* ended, clasping his fingers and using the index fingers to tap his chin.

"But Professor Bowen did not murder those verbs. I saw them jump. They committed suicide," the woman insisted.

Dr. Bowen wondered why she was so determined to defend him. He didn't know her; at least, he didn't think he knew her. "Would you care to introduce yourself, Miss."

"How can you not recognize me? I am Sheri Washington Pringly, your first graduate student. I wanted to be just like you." Spittle flew from her mouth and sprayed Dr. Bowen's face. Her breath was hot and he saw her chest heaving. "I became you, until the day I looked into the mirror and could not see my own face, and didn't like or recognize the person whose face I was wearing. You told me *that* was the ticket to my success," she said, pointing her index finger at his chest.

Dr. Bowen gazed into the woman's face and still did not recognize her, although he well remembered Sheri, his first graduate student. He had groomed her for a professorship, had allowed her to practice on him, taken her through the process step-by-step, had helped her to peel away all of who and what she was that he thought was common and ordinary, criticizing her whenever she reverted to her former self. He had secretly desired her. And he had been successful. She had earned a prestigious position at one of the top ten universities in the country, her scholarship had been cited, she had made the circuit tour, and had even married – alas, her first error – one of them – and was doing well. This he knew from the occasional, concise notes she sent him yearly, or from reading the journals. Then he hadn't heard from her for a while, and was told – she never informed him of this – that she had a child – her most tragic and egregious act. The news was like a stab in his chest (so many times he had wanted to caress her, to feel their bodies pressed

together; she had stirred in him a desire he had not known he had)
and he had banged on his desk and shook his head thinking *Black
folks always go and mess up a good thing by wanting to reproduce
themselves; they just can't leave well enough alone.* He knew that
nothing good could come of this and lamented the wasted time: all
his encouragement, reading and editing her articles, suggesting
journals for publication, writing to the editors – all of his effort for
naught. He prayed she would stop at one child, and hoped that
perhaps it wouldn't be so bad since, after all, her husband was
white. But alas, three years later her heard about another child. She
had not sent him one article to critique and he heard nothing of her
on the circuit, so he had washed his hands of her, erased her from
his mind, as he did with everyone and everything that displeased
him. Now she stood before him, unrecognizable.

"I heard you had a mental breakdown," Dr. Bowen said flatly.

The woman shook her head as if to deny the facts.

"You strayed from the well thought-out plan I had put in place
for you. Noname took the freedom route." Dr. Bowen realized
that Noname was inside his head again, and she was in control.
"You must take the freedom route too. Be a runaway."

The words applauded and Sheri Washington Pringly gulped
for breath.

"Dr. Bowen, you said that for us – you and I and a few selected
others – freedom came through the manipulation of words, that
the newest and most malleable plantation was the academy and
we could garner coveted places in the Big House by gaining
tenure and through publishing." Her voice was calmer now.

"Nonsense," interjected *Opulence*, Grandmother Noun, who
had sat quietly throughout the entire proceeding, knitting a
Rasta-colours cap for her grandson. "Freedom can never be
gained through words, but rather with words. You need us as
much as we need you to give us life, not drown us because you are
too afraid of who you are. There can never be any freedom in
someone else's house."

"You sure right," interrupted *Dictate*, Grandfather Verb. "If you
want to live on a plantation – though for the likes of me I can't
understand why anyone would want to – but if you do, you'd best

go and build it yourself rather than work to get a place on someone else's. That's just squatting. Seems to me, all that education should teach you the importance of owning your own house."

"You don't understand," Dr. Bowen finally boomed.

"What don't we understand?" the words chorused.

Dr. Bowen felt as if someone was hammering a nail into his forehead. He closed his eyes, massaged his temples and Noname stepped forward.

"Me always did know words had power. When me was enslave, it was the only thing dat was free. It was words that led me to de path of freedom. It was words that kept me running, even when me did tired and blister cover me feet. And every time de overseer say how we no good, how we lazy, how we is savage, me pepper him wid me mouth; me use words fi give de others faith; me use words fi remind meself me free, always free. Dat's why him have dem tie me to a pole, then him pry open me mouth wid sticks, pull out me tongue and chop off de tip wid him knife. Me blood spray him face and stain him permanently. Him go to him grave wid me blood still pan him face. And it still pan him people's face, as long as dem continue in him ways. But what de overseer don't know is dat clipped tongue have memory, and words and me is blood sister. We done made dat pack long time now, and some of us only have life in words."

The words listened to Noname in silent awe. Dr. Bowen kept massaging his temple and Sheri Washington Pringly fanned herself. Noname turned to her great, great, great grandson, and spoke a soft, but penetrating warning to him.

"You must do betta than that. Handle youself betta. Maybe me didn't prepare you well enough. But handle youself betta. Words are not de enemy, words are our friends." Sheldon Jerome cringed. He had not heard or used that word *Friend* since he was a boy wearing short pants. After he found words, and the children stopped teasing him, and the adults started to admire him, and come to sit and listen to him talk, he had wanted nothing else but to be friends with Delvine, the boy who lived in the house directly behind his and who was the same age. He remembered clearly now that Saturday afternoon, so unusually hot that even with his shirt off, sweat covered his body. He was sitting in the backyard, twirling a small ball on the ground, and he could see Delvine in his own backyard, directly behind his, doodling with a stick on the ground, while two puppies rested on his feet. SJ wanted to go over to Delvine's yard and play with him and his puppies, but he was afraid that if he asked he would be rebuffed, so instead he began to make up and recite out loud a poem about Delvine. Dr. Bowen laughs now recalling the nonsense of it:

"He who doodles doodles alone
He who idles, idles alone
Separated by a margin of space
An indolent boy sits, puppies at his feet
With nothing to do but doodle."

At which point, Delvine had looked over to Sheldon Jerome and asked, "Heah boy! Is who you a talk bout now? Mek you always talk like you have hot yam in you mouth a burn you tongue?"

At which point, Delvine stood up, sucked his teeth in a dismissive stretched-out sound, brushed off the bottom of his pants, picked up his puppies, one in each hand, and went inside, slamming the door so loud his mother shouted at him. It was that Saturday afternoon, fifty-two years ago that the word *Friend*, with all its attendant identification, intimacy and sense of belonging, evaporated from SJ. The tears trickled down Dr. Bowen's cheeks, before he wiped at them. He wanted to bawl for the missed friendships, for all that he lost, all that was stolen from him. He realized now that Delvine probably thought he was making fun of him rather than trying to befriend him. Sobs wracked his body.

Sheri touched his arm lightly. "I wanted to be your friend, Sheldon. For a long time, that was all I wanted. I would fantasize about us being together, but it seems that whenever you felt we were getting too relaxed with each other, you erected a higher wall to immure any threat of closeness."

"I never felt you saw me as a man, a man other than a mentor, or someone who knew how to navigate the system – someone to help you get over." Dr. Bowen slumped to the floor, his entire body flaccid. He did not notice that some of the words had begun creeping out and, more boldly, that the adverbs and conjunctions were skipping out the door and climbing through the windows. Sheri sat on the floor beside him.

"I spent twenty years of my life trying to be like someone who didn't exist. I don't know or even like the man who is my husband. My children are angry with me and I don't want to live this way any more. What do I do?" Sheri turned to Dr. Bowen who was gazing into space. "What do I do now that I've discovered that the path you sketched out for me was a maze whose exit is very carefully hidden." Again, anger crept into her voice.

"You must stop asking me and others, and find the way for yourself," Dr. Bowen said, taking her hand into his. "You have to find the way for yourself. I have been lost to myself too."

"We are done here," *Dictate*, Grandfather Verb declared.

"What says you, the jury?" inquired *Opulence*, Grandmother Noun.

"Case dismissed," pronounced *Outdated*, Adjective Juror.

The words looked around at the mess. This had been the longest and hardest case to date. They were tired and anxious to return to their rightful places. Those that were still there quietly dusted themselves off and made a hasty exit.

Dr. Bowen and Sheri Washington Pringly sat on the floor until their legs cramped and the half-moon was slanted in the sky. She stood and helped him to his feet. She realized he was an old man now, and she was middle-aged. Although the words had led her back to the story of her ancestors, just as they had led Dr. Bowen to Noname, no new path was yet clear to her. She felt trepidation, but hope too, to start again, to invent who she would become. She looked around, found a piece of paper and a pen, wrote her address and phone number, and put it by the phone. As she walked to the door, she turned to see that Dr. Bowen had shuffled over to the easy chair and sat slumped in it. She knew he had a lot to think about and make right – if it was still possible at this late stage, but she was hopeful. However, she was not willing to stay and help him; she had two children and an estranged husband to try and make amends to, not to mention her family who had made great sacrifices to send her to college, whose love she had dismissed and ignored. She rubbed memory into her eyes, opened her mouth wide and stretched out her tongue.

"I wrote my number and address and left it by the phone," she said, looking at Dr. Bowen. "You may call me if you are prepared to talk. I must admit I am still somewhat angry at you, and at myself for allowing you to convince me, and for believing that the machinery of the academy was more important than me, than us. I am going now because there are things I must say to my children and my parents. There is an ancestor story I still must tell." She turned and grasped the door handle, then looked back at the man, her mentor. How flabbily he sat in the chair, yet she glimpsed the man whom she once desired. "Sheldon," she said with compassion, "Call me. Maybe now we can work at being friends."

Dr. Bowen looked up at Sheri and managed a faint smile before she stepped over the threshold and closed the door softly behind her.

The gracious light of dawn stole through the closed blinds. Dr. Bowen stood up, shuffled to the window, lifted the blinds softly and peeped out. He recollected that his grandmother would rise at dawn to begin baking. Often he awoke when she did, but almost always would fall back asleep to wake up later to find the house perfumed with the sweet aroma of pastries. Dr. Bowen jerked the blinds open and Noname entered his head again.

"You ever wonder what happen to you granny's house now dat you mammy and pappy dead? You ever wonder what is happening to dat place dat give you life? Maybe is time you go and see," and just as suddenly and noiselessly Noname vanished. Dr. Bowen panicked. He felt certain he would not see the school of words again, at least not for a long time he hoped, and for that he was relieved. But he needed Noname; she was the life-thread back to himself.

CHRISTINE BARROW

THREE, TWO, ONE

Eleanor's long shadow is sharply outlined on the concrete ahead of her as she strides along the Careenage, swinging her string bag and humming a reggae tune. She's running late. But there's no one at their table. She huffs; it wasn't her idea that the three friends should meet at the Waterfront Café, every Saturday.

She slips onto one of the three upright seats under the green awning. They have elegantly curved, wrought-iron backs, painted a lighter green. The man behind her, inside the café, watches as she arranges her strands of ebony and silver beads threaded on strips of leather and pats the braids coiled around her head. She lifts the hem of her ankle-length black dress to just above her knees and stretches her legs and arms, like a dancer embracing the day. Men are attracted, and challenged, by her style. Alan, though, seems to enjoy simply being with her. He lets her be herself, and she lets him know when it's time to leave. She needs her space.

A message from Tamara appears on her cellphone. What now?

————

"Hi, Ellie. Sorry, yoga finished late." Michelle is decked out like a frangipani flower – bright yellow Capris and a white top with cap sleeves. She kisses Eleanor on both cheeks and points to the copper wire ring with a jade-coloured stone on her left thumb. "Oh, I do love that."

"Oh, no, you don't. You've seen it before and you know it's not real."

"Right. Sorry." Michelle fluffs up her damp curls. "I'll just go and freshen up."

Eleanor sighs and looks out at the row of white boats at the water's edge. *Fancy Free* and *Sunshine Girl* bob and bump against one another in a tipsy dance. She sways her shoulders in rhythm.

Michelle returns and sits opposite with her hair perfect, make-up on, and her brave-face smile. Eleanor knows it well and shifts to their schoolgirl talk. "So, chile, you goin' good?"

"Fine," says Michelle, but she's replaced her smile with a downward-facing yoga-dog look.

"And you?"

"I here – hangin' in."

"And flirting, as usual."

Eleanor's eyebrows shoot up. "Me? No way. Guide's honour." She holds up the three middle fingers of her right hand in salute. "The man looking good, dough, nuh? Check the biceps."

Michelle refuses to look. "How is Alan? It's him we need to check, Tammy and me. She's coming?"

"On her way. And it's only been two months. I don't know him myself yet."

"So?"

"So, he came over last night."

"And?"

"And nothing." Yet not nothing. Last night, Alan sitting on the broad coral-stone windowsill of her studio, with the rum and water and slice of lime she'd made the way he likes it, pretending to read the newspaper, but glancing across at her, at her thighs gripping the wheel, her right food pedalling, her tongue over her top lip, her hands around the lump of soft, slimy clay, slender fingers stroking, squeezing and lifting, thumbs pressing down inside. Shaping the pot – a slight wobble, then perfect symmetry.

He'd raised his eyebrows in mock-fear as she pulled a piece of wire taut between her fists. She slid it under and cupped the pot in both hands, laid it on the workbench as if it were as fragile as a bubble. She gave him an elaborate bow, holding up her hands, dripping clay.

"Come here," he said, but it was he who went to her, opening his arms, muscled like those of a man who lifts weights, not one to hook up with a string bean like her. She knows that he won't wait too much longer.

But Eleanor is not ready to share this, even with her best friend. So she asks, "Where's Zoe? I thought you were bringing her."

"Confirmation classes."

"But it's Saturday."

"Extra…"

"What?"

"…early start."

"She's five years old, for Christ's sake!"

"Richard insists."

"Ah, Richard. Pillar of the law and now the church. What would this country do without…"

"Ellie, stop. Please." Michelle is blinking rapidly. "I'll go and get the waitress."

Eleanor blows out her cheeks. Shite.

———

The three have been friends since primary school. Each an only child, they were not the cleverest, nor the prettiest, just together like fledglings in a nest, covering up for each other with fingers crossed behind their backs, sharing every one of their little secrets, and the coconut bread, tamarind balls and sugar-cakes in their lunch boxes. When they all passed for Queen's College, the best secondary school for girls, they held hands and shrieked.

"We did it," said Eleanor.

"Unbelievable," said Tamara.

"Together forever," said Michelle, "like sisters."

They'd held tight, the only three to go to school by bus, country bookies up against town-girl sophistication. Tamara was chubby and flatfooted, hopeless at netball, and struggled with proper English; Michelle was shy, with freckles and a lisp. But Eleanor was the tallest girl in the class, shoe size six. No one dared mess with her and her friends.

They cried together through monthly cramps and acne zits; invented their own secret code of knowing looks and hand signals, and often fell about in helpless giggles, like the time they imitated their science teacher's toothy outburst – "This one takes the biscuit" – after Tamara blew up and burst a paper bag during an experiment. They were Girl Guides together, though Michelle chose the Cook badge, and Eleanor the Craft one, but they both did First Aid. Tamara's was something to do with conservation. One badge, she said, was good for her, a green one. Michelle always liked yellow best, and Eleanor the deep tones of mahogany and indigo. "We're like a rainbow," Michelle said.

They didn't really notice when they no longer caught the same bus home.

———

"She's coming," says Michelle.

"Who?"

"The waitress – made me feel like a real nuisance."

Eleanor shrugs and passes her phone across the table, showing Michelle the message from Tamara – st andrew bus late c u soon.

"What's she doing out in St. Andrew?"

"Me nah know. Mussee a next man." Eleanor's voice softens. "Miche, what is it?"

"Nothing… nothing I can't cope with. It's just every day. You wouldn't…"

"Try me."

"Every day, school runs, karate and piano lessons, tennis and ballet…"

And confirmation classes, Eleanor thinks.

"…and maids and gardeners and plumbers."

Collecting his wigs from the dry cleaners.

"Tempers and tantrums, every day. And Zoe's crying a lot and wetting her bed again. And the boys don't speak to me unless Richard's there… Sorry."

"And Richard?" Richard, above it all, another bewildered man wondering what could be the matter with his wife. What more could she want?

"He's really busy at work." Michelle's voice rises. "Ellie, I keep telling you, Richard is a decent man. He's never cheated on me." She looks down.

Richard – his very name triggers recoil in Eleanor. Big-shot lawyer. Queen's Counsel at thirty-something. The world his courtroom. 'Absolutely' – his favourite word. SMS, Eleanor thinks, small man syndrome. She'd met him just before the wedding, but already knew too much about him – how he'd wangled custody of the twin boys from his first marriage, bewitched Michelle with diamonds around her finger and neck, got her to put her career as a going-places auditor on hold, gave her permission to have one child, and made her wear flat shoes. Could I, Eleanor asks herself, have found something to like in him if he'd married someone else?

He has it all planned. He will rise to become a high court judge, receive a knighthood – Sir and Lady Richard Harding. His power play; her sell out – that's how Eleanor sees the set-up. And Michelle knows it.

Eleanor knows that whatever's upsetting her friend is not children or chores.

"There she is," Michelle says. "Look, or rather, don't. And I'm alright. Don't say anything." Eleanor groans as Tamara waves, trips and grabs the edge of a table. She hugs Michelle who wrinkles up her nose, and puts her arm around Eleanor's shoulders for a quick squeeze before slumping onto the seat between them, facing the Careenage. She taps her fingers on the table. "Made it. Have you ordered?" Typical, Eleanor thinks. Over an hour late and no sorry; nothing so.

Michelle tries not to look at the new tattoo of a scarlet heart with barbed wire around it on the back of Tamara's left hand. Eleanor sees that two of the fingernails on her right hand are broken – one black, the other green. Why is she wearing a plain white shirt, buttoned right up, so unlike her usual plunge necklines? And why the large, black lens sunglasses?

Michelle smiles her hyped-up smile as she reaches to tuck in the label at the back of her shirt. "What were you doing in St. Andrew?"

Tamara flinches.

Michelle sits back, but chatters on. "Remember when we went there on that school outing, and I sat on those turnovers…"

"He beat me," Tamara says.

"…cherry jam all over the seat of the bus, what a sticky… What?"

"Who?" Eleanor asks.

"Dwayne, last night. He laughed, like he would never stop. He said if he didn't laugh, he'd have to beat me some more."

"Who's Dwayne?"

"No matter. We done, finished. I need a lawyer." Tamara looks towards Michelle.

"Oh, um, but Richard doesn't do…"

"I've got to get a restraining order."

"Tammy, are you hurt?" Michelle holds her hand – the hand without the tattoo. "You saw a doctor? Called the police?"

The waitress's high heels clack as she approaches. She places cut-glass salt and pepper shakers and three white paper napkins on the table. "Hi, guys, how y'all enjoying this beautiful day?"

"Like hell," Tamara grunts.

"At last," Michelle murmurs.

Eleanor cringes. She won't be here for long; too much attitude. And those heels.

"We got fresh juices – mango, guava, golden apple."

"Three coffees, please. One decaf, two regular," Michelle says. "And bring the bill."

Eleanor points her finger at Tamara. "You can't expect Michelle to get Richard involved. She's got enough on her plate." She feels a kick under the table. "Anyway, you need a female lawyer."

"It's alright, I'll ask him." Michelle takes hold of Eleanor's finger. "But where will you stay? You're not going back there?"

"Where else can I go?"

Michelle looks down and shuffles the salt and pepper shakers around the table. Eleanor is focused on removing a speck of clay from under her thumbnail. Tamara stares out over the water. She's still wearing the sunglasses, but flicks her head as if she's trying to shake something out of her eye. "Ugh, I wish those boats would stop moving. I need to sit where you are," she says to Michelle. She stands and her seat tips over, wrought-iron clanging on concrete. She grabs one of the napkins, holds it to her mouth and stumbles into the café. The man inside half stands as if to help.

"Oh, sugar, what are we going to do this time?" Michelle says as she pulls the seat upright. "Her breath smells stink."

"Call a taxi for her." Eleanor twists her ring around her thumb. "Listen, I don't want to meet here anymore."

"How can you say that?" Michelle pauses. "There's something I should tell you." Eleanor leans forward. "About when her mother died and she stayed with me." Eleanor closes her eyes. She thought Michelle was going to talk about what really has her upset.

"It was awful, like she couldn't cry. Locked herself in the bathroom, always bathing, bathing, as if she was trying to scrub herself away." Michelle's eyes fill. "The man her mother was seeing abused her. They never found him."

"Jeez, I never knew."

"She made me promise not to say anything. Anyway, you were away."

I was away, Eleanor thinks, in Jamaica. Off to Art College, finding myself, and never looking back. I'd mastered the art of sidestepping Tammy and her problems.

"Ellie, she only has us. That's why I thought we should meet on Saturdays."

"Haven't we done enough for her? Are there no limits?"

"Right. Bad idea. Sorry, sorry. OK?"

They are silent as the waitress places three coffees, milk, sugar and the bill on the table. Michelle is fiddling with something in her bag, probably her phone or her watch. Eleanor lifts her gaze across the shimmering water to the Chamberlain Bridge and the Parliament Buildings. She stirs sugar into her black coffee. "Miche, I know how you feel, but…"

"You know nothing, Madam Got-It-All-Under-Control." Michelle looks down and a fat tear drops onto the table. She sniffs back the rest. "I'll go," she says.

Eleanor reaches out and touches Michelle's arm. "My turn."

———

Eleanor remembers the time at school when she told Tamara, "Go ahead, mess up your life, see if I care," though she can't recall exactly what it was about. She herself was busy reasoning with the Debating Club girls, spurning prescribed topics, like "A Good

Education is a Passport for Life," in favour of "The Bussa Slave Rebellion" and "Back to Africa with Garvey." Michelle hung on longer, as best friends should, not giving up on Tamara, but staying clear of her force-ripe group with their foolishness about cute boys – "who going wid who and who get dump" – and their disgusting sex talk. Michelle spent hours in the library, studying really hard; and her new friends initiated her into the posh QC walk and talk, their two-cheek pecks, mwa-mwa.

She blossomed into the special kind of girl the school was designed to create. So they both lost track of Tamara's detentions for rudeness and her suspension for truancy – though she was given a second chance, "on account of issues at home." They couldn't believe it when she hissed, "I hate you two," and dropped out of school the week before her sixteenth birthday.

After years of drifting from shop-assistant to waitress to babysitter, Tamara found her voice, her soul voice. She wore locks, head-ties and earrings with beads and feathers that dangled to her shoulders; lost weight and changed her name to Folami. Her audiences at open-air concerts were mesmerized as she darted like a firefly against the night sky. With picnic baskets of canapés and rosé and arms draped around each other's shoulders, they swayed to her beat, moved to tears by her songs of solitude and betrayal, loving her.

Loving her, until one night her emaciated body, dripping bling under multicoloured lights, could take no more. She fumbled her words, lost her way across the stage and fell, leaving her fans transfixed between shock and applause. Those in the back rows cheered, thinking it was all part of her act.

Eleanor and Michelle agreed they should have been there. She'd sent them free tickets, as always. Guilt followed them like a shadow, bloated with the endless gossip they heard delivered with malicious glee. "I hear you friend gone and get sheself in trouble again." They dried her out and revived her spirit as best they could.

But there was no persuading her to return to the spotlight. Tamara quit – her own light snuffed out.

———

Eleanor stands inside the café, trying to steady her breathing as she watches Michelle finish her decaf; she's put saucers over the other two cups. She answers her cellphone, retrieves her watch from her bag and looks at its oval face with four Gucci diamonds. Eleanor knows she keeps it hidden to avoid her comment.

The man is still there. He catches her eye, but Eleanor turns and rejoins Michelle. She puts her elbows on the table and covers her mouth with both hands. A braid falls across her cheek. Michelle moves next to her, to the seat Tamara had occupied.

"She was slumped on the floor," Eleanor says, "hugging the toilet. Her foot was blocking the door. I couldn't get it open."

"Oh, God, I should have come with you."

"I had to call the barman. We got her up, out the back door, into a taxi. He said they'd clean up the mess."

"Mess?"

Eleanor mimes vomiting with her hands. "Her shirt buttons were undone. I saw the bruises on her neck. She kept calling for her mom." Eleanor wipes her eyes with the second napkin. "She's gone to pack her things. I told her she can stay with me."

"Oh, Ellie." Michelle uncovers Eleanor's coffee and slides it towards her.

Eleanor holds up her hands. "For a week." Only a week, but would Alan understand?

Almost a year ago, Eleanor had surprised herself by renting a building in the plantation yard of a Great House, owned and occupied by a family that could probably trace its roots back to slavery. But it was ideal with two storeys – three bedrooms upstairs and plenty space for a studio below. Whitewashed coral-stone walls, cool with high ceilings, and a view of the sea across the cane fields. She was determined to keep herself to herself and declined the family's invitations to sundowner cocktails, until the three little grandchildren, two girls and a boy, peeped in at the jalousie window, inched through the door, and charmed her. She arranged seats for them next to her workbench.

Eleanor's ceramics have won awards, but she keeps her trophies stashed in a cupboard and likes to tell people that she just potters about. There's nothing she enjoys more than to have Zoe come over and watch the four children play together, rolling out clay and coiling pots, or folding coloured paper into humming birds and flying fish to thread on strings and twirl around. With little hands covered in clay, paint and glue, they stroke each other's arms and hair with curiosity and delight. The easy way all children make friends, Eleanor muses.

———

"Ellie," Michelle clutches her bag and rocks forward. "Ellie, I putht him off me, last night." Her lisp is back.

Eleanor clamps her lips between her teeth to stop the shout bursting out of her: Yes, finally, you told him. No!

"I told him I had a terrible tummy ache. He knows I was lying. He's never looked at me like that before… like judgment." Michelle strips the cuticle off her index finger with her teeth. "I don't know what made me do it. God, what's wrong with me?" A small bead of blood appears. She dabs it with the third napkin, licks her finger and dabs again. "What will I do if he leaves me? And takes Zoe?" She folds the napkin over the two red spots and puts it in her bag.

Eleanor clasps Michelle's hand. "He'd never do that," she hears herself say. But he's done it before.

"I can't live on my own. I'm not like you."

Like me? Eleanor freezes. She lets go of Michelle's hand.

"And I was going to ask him about going back to work, now Zoe's at school."

Eleanor doesn't trust herself to say anything. She makes herself think about Zoe. Only last Saturday, the three of them had hunched over her first report: *A good term's work. Zoe tries hard, but must concentrate more.*

Michelle had beamed.

"Why them always puttin' down children?" Tamara said.

And Eleanor nodded. "They have no idea how bright she is."

They'd shared the joy of Zoe's first steps, her first words, her ballet – all elbows and knees, but adorable. Just to look makes Eleanor want to hug her up, clap hands and sing lullabies. She was thrilled, and speechless, when Michelle asked her to be a godmother. "You and Tammy, my best friends. I haven't asked Richard yet, but...."

Eleanor has an idea – a long shot, but it might cheer up Michelle. "Hey, why don't you come, too, you and Zoe. We'll make lots of pots." She is about to add that they could meet Alan, but stops herself. This is no light-hearted, meet-my-friends fling. Alan has said he wants to know all of her; his eyes probe as if he reads her soul. But she holds back, and flirts. Michelle is right.

Michelle shakes her head, her smile is sad. "I have to go. He just called, to remind me to pick up Zoe. Well, that's what he said."

"But he knows you're here, with me."

Michelle flicks open her compact and checks her face. "Ellie, about Tammy, I can't ask Richard, not now. I'll keep praying for her. Call you tomorrow."

"I'm sorry," Eleanor says.

"Sorry? You? What for?"

"Me, my big mouth... about Richard."

Michelle's sunshine-girl smile is back in place. "I do love him, you know," she says. "Love you, too."

Eleanor waves her fingers as Michelle leaves. Miche, she thinks, with boundless love in her heart, despite the pain; Tammy who can't even love herself; and me, only now learning how.

———

The sky is overcast now. The shadows have blurred; the boats hold still. Across the Careenage, the buildings look bleak. Eleanor can't make out the clock tower, but hears the midday chimes, echoing Big Ben's solemn tune. Nor can she see the life-size, metallic statue of Lord Nelson, but she remembers it well, prominent as ever on a platform of concrete and marble, one armless sleeve tucked into his jacket. Her voice had been among the loudest petitioning to have him removed after Trafalgar Square was renamed National Heroes Square. But the government of the day caved in under conservative pressure and proclaimed, "Like it or not, he is part of our heroic history," and rotated him one hundred and eighty degrees further to the right. Back then, she was feisty; she said what she was thinking.

Her napkin is still damp from her tears, but she folds and refolds it into a bird, one with a long egret neck.

Four young-looking women arrive at a table on the other side of the café, flapping their hands and cackling like crazed chickens. Eleanor wonders what they're on about – zumba, pedicures, liposuction? They're not listening, not touching, not even looking at one another. Not like us, the three of us, with our three late nights – me playing with Alan in a plantation outhouse, Miche trapped by Richard in his mansion, and Tammy beaten up by whoever he was, wherever she was. So different, yet bound together, year after year, like the rings on a tree trunk. Sisters, rainbow sisters.

Eleanor stifles a yawn. She feels as if she hasn't slept for a week. She sips her coffee and grimaces. It's cold.

The man from inside the café comes over. "Hi, everything OK?"

"Yes, thank you."

"I'm Adrian."

"Eleanor." His handshake is firm, comforting.

He points to her coffee. "Allow me to get you another one."

She smiles, her own warmest smile, "Thanks, but I'm just leaving," and watches him saunter away from her along the Careenage, hips swaying, hands free. She tucks the paper bird, a new one for Zoe, into her string bag and lifts the strap over her shoulder. She hands a twenty-dollar note with the bill to the waitress who quips, "Them leave you one to pay?"

Eleanor blinks. "Their turn next Saturday."

RHODA BHARATH

REDEMPTION

New Testament Revival Tabernacle was only ten houses away from the Sunrise Palace Hotel and Bar. Redemption, the village in which these two places are situated, is really small. If you lived in Port of Spain you would say Redemption is pure bush, and the people there are country bookies who ain't exposed to much, and life have a sameness to it that could stifle you. So it's not surprising that the closeness of these two places is a constant source of talk. Even people who are just passing through talk about how these two places are positioned. The men talk about it and smile that kind of cunning smile they have when sex is the subject matter. The women talk about it, too, or complain rather, with shock in their voices, as if sex and God don't mix. But their real problem with these two buildings is that they know precisely who the patrons are.

You might also think it made sense for these establishments to be so close to each other because they had plenty in common. Both places were fully air-conditioned and serviced almost the same set of clients. The cars you saw parked at Sunrise on Friday and Saturday nights were the same ones parked at New Testament on a Sunday morning – their occupants now making a joyful noise unto the Lord. So it was nothing strange to hear cries like "Sweet Jesus!" or "Oh God!" in both buildings as folk raised their voices in a crescendo of praise to the gifts of life given by their Maker.

The owners of the cars paid their tithes at both places, religiously. It was either $40 an hour or one-tenth of their monthly earnings. Either way, they felt it was a small contribution to make for the joy that came into their lives. Neither place really discriminated against the customers of the other. The

New Testament pastor, Winston Duncan, had learnt a long time ago the wisdom of judging not, lest he be judged, especially when his judgments started to affect the amount of money offered at collection. Those in the flock who were willing to throw a crisp hundred dollar bill in the collection plate at the end of the Sunday morning service expected and got the indulgence of a blind eye turned to at least one of their faults. Similarly, in his role as caretaker for his own particular flock of sinners, Mr Faustin, the owner of Sunrise, never turned anybody away unless all of the rooms were filled, and even then, once you were a regular customer, he would organize to clean up a back room quickly for you.

It's easy to understand why Sunrise was so popular. Redemption village is not a place with too much recreation. You could drink, play cricket or football, lime by the corner or run women. If you were able to do all three comfortably, then you became a hero in the village. It meant that as a man your business was in order and you had everything under control. You were a god among mortals.

Women, though, had rather less recreation allowed to them. There were the occasional church bazaars or harvests; sometimes the football or cricket club would host a family day; or there would be the informal gathering in someone's yard to exchange gossip. But mostly it was the routine of domestic chores that kept the women occupied.

Today though, the worlds at both ends of the street were coming together to celebrate the passing of one of their own. Stanton Crewley, one of the most respected men in Redemption village had died at Sunrise and now, three days later, was being buried at New Testament.

If there was a man in the village whom the younger men looked up to and tried to emulate it was Stanton. He was big and strapping and had a good job working as an installation technician for a telecommunications company. His wife, Sylvia, had been the catch of the day in her time. All the men had secretly or openly lusted after her, but Stanton had been the only one to stir real interest, the only young man to make it to her front porch and not only survive, but find favour with the village princess. As a boy he was the crowned prince. As a man he became the King. And now the monarch lay dead.

The way Stanton died gave the whole process of mourning a rare kind of excitement that lasted until the day he was buried. It was almost like a mini-series for Redemption. The incident was, of course, too trivial to require actual television cameras and reporters, but in its own way, Redemption afforded the key players in the tragedy their fifteen minutes of fame, though some were reluctant to accept it. From the morning he died to the day of the funeral, everybody had either a new piece of information to add to the story, or something to speculate about. Everybody waited patiently to see how things would play themselves out.

Mrs. Stanton, ever the lady, remained quiet and dignified throughout the affair. She knew that the mourners were there more to observe how she was dealing with the shame and strain than to offer any real condolences. Even the well-meaning ones, the ones she could usually rely on, were there carefully searching her face for the slightest flicker or change in expression to add to their stories. But Sylvia disappointed them. She served her Crix, coffee and sweetbread with the same expression she wore in New Testament on a Sunday: serene and poised. Eventually people got fed up of shoo shooing in the yard and went out into the road where they could voice their thoughts more openly and relish the gossip like a well-seasoned stew-chicken leg.

Down in Sunrise, the whole yard was lit up with flambeaux; even Room 12, where the ambulance had picked him up. Downstairs in the bar, men were ordering a Heart Attack, the new drink they had concocted since Stanton's passing. The village was like that; every occasion had to be marked with a name. If a flu virus had been going around at the time, they might have called it the "Stanton".

All five of the rumshops in Redemption were hot with talk about what lead up to his death.

"But boy, for a strapping fella like Stanton to get a heart attack, she had was to be real good!"

This was quickly followed by, "You ain't know if he heart was okay. Suppose he had a weak heart."

This was followed by a wave of sceptical laughter.

"Stanton weak?"

"You have to be joking! A big strapping man like Stanton? Who never feel sick a day in he life? Who had woman from since he old enough to make thing with them? All you have to be joking."

"Men like Stanton does live until they ninety. With children, grandchildren and great-grandchildren all over the damn place."

"Boy, men like Stanton does just get up good good one day and drop down dead just so."

For a moment there was silence. Men started to think about their health, their lives, the families they would be leaving behind. But as the next round of drinks arrived, the talk went back to Room 12 and the level of exertion that must have taken place for Stanton to die so scandalously.

In spite of all the talk, there was one name people hardly mentioned and when they did, they lowered their voices in an almost reverential way, the way a Catholic might make the sign of the cross when discussing something particularly sacred or evil. But this death, had turned Precious, who was already a legend in Redemption, into something almost mythical.

Precious's story had a kind of magic to it that thrilled the villagers. She'd arrived in Redemption at the age of fourteen, from Venezuela via Cedros. The owners at Sunrise had secured a forged birth certificate to say she was eighteen, in case the police ever made a raid on the premises and asked uncomfortable questions. The issue of her age caused heated arguments in the village. Sometimes even the midday television soap opera the women watched religiously was forgotten for a discussion about her age. Even Pastor Duncan raised it as a sermon in his pulpit. But when the Sunday after that saw a decline in the male attendance, Pastor called a halt to the fire and brimstone he was calling down on Sunrise and its owners. The women, though, still had plenty to say about Precious and her youth, because they knew their husbands had been with her.

It was difficult to say what Precious was. She looked Spanish, which was what everyone in Redemption assumed she was, but not quite Spanish. The men speculated that perhaps she had Amerindian blood. Whatever, it was the first time that anyone as exotic had been to Redemption.

"Snake oil waist" was what the men called her. Faustin organized things at the club with flair. He had seen how the clubs in the city did things and tried to copy them. Precious used to do a kind of pre-show whose purpose was to demonstrate not only that she was young, but also extremely flexible. Faustin would walk around while she was performing, asking the men if their wives could do any of the things Precious did. She would whip the men into a frenzy and would go to the highest bidder. Rumours flew about her insatiability.

Precious's stock was high. Men were lining up to conquer her or simply be able to say that they had possessed her. Stanton had not been one of them, though. His pleasure was the live show and once in a while, after a few drinks he might have fun with one of the girls. He never stayed overnight at the hotel. In his mind it was a big insult to his wife to be coming from another woman's bed in the early hours of the morning. Sylvia knew all of this. There was a quiet understanding between them. No public shame or embarrassment and all would be well. She understood her duty to him and he to her. Many times she would cross paths with one of the women from the hotel at the market and ignore her, back straight, nose held high. They borrowed her husband from time to time, but she was secure in her position as wife.

That was until the night Stanton decided that Precious was going to be his. His sudden passion for her caught him off guard. It was Faustin who explained it to the men.

"Boy, one night he bounce she up by the bar and buy she a drink and sit down in one long conversation, and then went upstairs with she. Then he was back the next night, then the next night, then the next night again. Like he had a fever and she was the bush tea."

At first, Mrs. Stanton gave no hint that she'd noticed a change in his habits. She felt that, given time, things would settle and return to routine. Her mother had often told her, "Men does like to do their thing and have their own way. You just be patient. They does always come back. You is he married wife. He bound to come back."

The first time, on a Friday, when Stanton returned at daybreak instead of his customary midnight, she took note but remained quiet. He also managed to return just after midnight on Saturday, more than enough time to sleep and prepare for church the next day. By the following weekend, Stanton's behaviour was under scrutiny not just from his wife but the macos on the street.

Celestine John and Miss Agnes lived on either side of the Stantons. They had started their own surveillance, meeting at least twice in the day, just after *The Young and The Restless* and before *Santa Barbara*, to discuss the latest developments. They were waiting for Sylvia to open up and make some kind of a distress signal before they jumped in to console her. They didn't want to appear pushy and nosy. They noted that, on Sunday, Mrs. Stanton's amens in church did seem a little louder and to have more meaning than usual. But they were disappointed. Not once did Mrs Stanton ever discuss Precious with them, even when it was obvious that everybody else was talking about what was going on.

If ever a man was under a spell, it was Stanton. He went from spending all weekend to all week long at Sunrise. The more nights he spent there, the colder and tighter Mrs. Stanton got, but still not a word. She couldn't be faulted on her role as mother and wife. The children and the house were in immaculate order, and she only stopped being a *complete* wife to Stanton from the moment he went to Sunrise one Friday night and only came home midday the following Saturday. Stanton made no comment, but his hours and behaviour became even more erratic. All he could be relied on to do was to take the family to church on Sunday.

While his status as husband was in peril, his position as village hero remained intact. The men were only too anxious to have him around, hungry to understand his madness even though they never spoke directly to him about Precious. That was not how it was done. Stanton was, after all, married. His wife was to be respected. But when he had finished his last drink with them, or got up to leave at the end of a card game, they didn't press him to stay; they understand that he had an agenda and needed to attend to it.

He never used the word love in the presence of his closest friends, but it was there all over his face on the few occasions he mentioned her name. At first it was only the sex he talked about. Her softness and flexibility and eagerness to please him. Never any headaches or tiredness. But after a while his obsession became plain. The way he talked, it was as if he was the only man she had been with, ever. The men were shocked.

"The man mashing up he good good living for a piece of skin!" was Boboy's comment. "I never know Stanton to be getting on tootoolbay so! The man does usually have heself in order."

The others in the bar silently agreed, happy that though they had tasted of Precious, they weren't infected with the same madness.

And while Stanton was hot and sweaty with Precious, some of the more enterprising men had begun to pursue Mrs. Stanton. They were ignored. She treated them to a cold, unseeing stare when they approached her at the market or the shop or even on the side of the road, pretending to want to help her and then propositioning her in their sly way. They took their rebuffs quietly. To protest would draw attention to themselves, especially from Stanton. As occupied as he was with Precious, Sylvia was still his property.

For a time, it appeared as if Stanton had recovered control of himself. One of his sons fell ill. Stanton was back at the house, no longer frequenting Sunrise as he made regular trips to the hospital in the city to visit his son. Weeks passed in this way until one night a drunken rumshop customer hailed him out saying, "Boy, I woulda say Precious mighta dry up and dead after you stop coming round Sunrise, but the girl bloomin man. Business swinging!"

If Stanton's skin had been lighter, he might have paled. That night he and Precious fought in public like a regular married couple. Faustin had to put him out and Stanton became the first customer to be refused access to Sunrise. The story went that he had rushed into the place and gone straight up to Room 12, interrupting Precious and a client. He had dragged Precious out, with only a sheet protecting her, even roughed her up a bit, all the while shouting, "You promise me! You promise me!"

The news spread like bush fire that night. By the time neighbours started sweeping their yards next morning, everyone on Stanton's street had the score. Mrs. Stanton pretended she didn't notice how people were watching and whispering as she sent her other son off to school and prepared to go to the hospital.

Stanton began to lose his position in Redemption. At work he became the butt of malicious jokes and endless picong. Men would randomly begin conversations about fighting in public or how stupid some men behaved over women. To Stanton's credit he took the talk, but even he realized that he had fallen from grace. The men around him had found their hero was weak: a woman had conquered him.

"Poom poom rule, boy!" men called in the rumshops. They didn't bother to lower their voices if Stanton was around. In fact, if anything, they talked louder, relishing the effects of their comments. Things got so bad that one evening Stanton threw a cuff behind Boboy; they scuffled in the rumshop and had to be parted. But Stanton had fought only to save face. Now when he entered any of the rumshops he would walk straight to a corner table and sit only with his closest friends. The days of him walking into a bar to loud greetings and calling for a round of drinks were over.

About two weeks after the fight at Sunrise, Stanton moved Precious into an apartment. That raised so much talk, even the Pastor preached on it. Stanton wasn't present for that sermon. Still Mrs. Stanton said and did nothing. Her quietness became quite alarming. People started speculating that the pressure of staying quiet over something so shameful must be sending her mad.

Stanton barely went home anymore. He visited on weekends, cleaned the yard and spent awkward time with his children. The boys either ignored him or sat down and watched him with sour faces because their mother told them they had to spend time with him.

The women were waiting in their own agony for a showdown between Mrs. Stanton and Precious. Miss Agnes got so impatient she asked Mrs. Stanton point blank what she was going to do. The women in Redemption began to feel let down. Not only had she lost her man – which could happen to any of them – she had lain down and taken it – no fight, no struggle.

One Saturday their paths finally crossed at the market; Mrs. Stanton moved quietly towards a heap of cucumbers while Precious continued to haggle over the price of yams. The whole market waited on tenterhooks wondering what would happen next. When they realized that nothing would happen, that in fact, Mrs. Stanton was quietly skittering away while Precious held her ground, a dam burst.

"But she is a blasted fool. Any woman could just take my man and get away so?"

"Me is one woulda mash up their apartment long time and buss up she ass!"

"Imagine, a good-looking woman like Sylvia eh, is not to say she is any old fowl, a nice red woman like Sylvia have this mix-up Spanish bitch mashing up she living so!"

"Me, I woulda done dead from shame. But look how Sylvia just taking this cool. Like she ain't even noticing what going on. If she ain't mad I ain't know what wrong."

"Poor thing, though. To have to deal with all this in such a short space of time. In less than a year she gone from queen of the village to a damned fool. Everybody laughing at she behind she back, some even laughing in she face and still not a peep from she. She don't even try to defend she reputation. Playing Miss High and Mighty. She feel she too good to touch all this nastiness, when the nastiness coming from she own house. She have to deal with this whether she want to or not. The time will come when she ain't have no choice but to face it."

"Sylvia ain't moving like a woman there at all, she moving like a damned cunumunu, bébé bébé like she is a damned child. She allowing the two of them to set she pace. She moving scared, scared."

"And you believe she still referring to the man as husband? I hear that when Sunday come she does still set the table with a place for him! She saying she doing it for the children. Children! Children, my ass! Them children ain't have time for he, they ain't want to see their father, 'cause he hurt them. Sylvia know in she heart of hearts she still want him. She still waiting for him to give up the woman and come back. I does feel sorry for woman who grow up like Sylvia, because she have a mother who tell she it okay to take all this shit from a man and stay quiet."

"You give she wrong, Celestine. Stanton is she man. Look how much years she give him before this woman come in the picture? Eh? You think is just so you does give up a husband? And say what you want, he still minding she and the children. Bill still paying and food still reaching on the table. In he own way he still loyal to the family."

"But just so, the man practically shack up with this next woman. You woulda take that quiet so in your young days, Miss Agnes? Mr Bertille coulda ever come back home after he do you something like that?"

Then just as quickly as the affair started, it ended. It didn't make any sense. People were confused. One Monday evening, after work, Stanton turned up at his house instead of going to the apartment that he and Precious shared, parked his pick-up in its usual position under the mango tree and went into his house. Precious returned to Sunrise. The news ran as fast as it could up and down the street. By the following Sunday morning, New Testament Tabernacle could barely contain itself with all the talk.

There was a noticeable shifting and nudging in the pews when the family arrived, Stanton in front, head high, leading his pride down the aisle towards the Lord. Pastor had a hard time getting the murmuring down as he started the service. The first song he chose was clearly a test for Stanton: "Yield Not to Temptation". The congregation tittered through the organ's opening bars, waiting for the verse to start. All eyes were on Stanton and he didn't disappoint. With his eyes looking at the rafters, he belted out the chorus: "Yield not to temptation, for yielding is sin...

Look ever to Jesus, He will carry you through." His voice led the congregation for the entire song. With the closing bars he looked around, challenging the congregation to mock him or continue to titter. The king had returned.

The men were the first to seal the unspoken truce, seeking him out in the courtyard to shake his hand and say a respectful hello to Mrs. Stanton, who stood quietly next to Stanton with her children. The women, less ready to forgive but having no choice, followed suit, though from the looks they exchanged and the couyou mouths they were making, you knew they would meet later to chew over the story.

Life went back to normal. Stanton was at home with his wife and children and Precious was making money for Faustin. The men who visited her were careful not to mention her name in front of Stanton. Once or twice they slipped and his face would go still. There would be a rush of conversation to cover the awkwardness. The only change was that Stanton never returned to Sunrise. Not even for a round of drinks with the boys. Until the night he died.

Nobody saw it coming. The men had settled at Sugar's Rumshop after an impromptu cricket game. The match fell apart after Boboy got run-out and refused to accept it. Stanton had made a violent pelt towards the stumps and long after the match had ended was complaining about cramps running up and down his left arm.

A noisy group made their way off the field, by turns complimenting and criticizing each other's performance. Eventually the conversation turned to more philosophical talk about life and family. Boboy started it after a deep pull on a bottle of beer.

"Boy, you think after marriage and children you go feel settled, eh? I married bout fifteen years now, have two children and it does still feel like it supposed to have something else. Something more."

"I know what you mean," chimed in Clement. "When I was in school I used to think that to be a policeman had to be the best thing in the world. It couldn't have nothing better than that. To walk down the street in your uniform, swinging your baton, gun hook in your side, people watching you with respect. I have all of that and it come like nothing. Then I say to myself, 'Clement boy, you need to get a wife, settle down, make some children. I do all of that and still... still I don't feel..." he paused as if searching for his thoughts, "I don't feel like my life full up. I don't feel full up. Sometimes I does think maybe is a promotion I need. A change of pace. But after that, then what?"

"Boy, sometimes I think it ain't have a thing like satisfied and happy. I think we could only *make do* with what we have, and once in a while, when we having a good lime, or we and we woman enjoying weself and things good and the talk nice, maybe then we could think we happy. But I don't think it possible to really be satisfied one hundred percent and be happy all the time. If I happy, really happy, three, four times in a year I glad for that. What you say there, Stanton?"

Stanton sat quietly, almost as if unaware a question had been asked, his right arm still massaging his left shoulder while he stared at the drink in front him. His face looked funny, a cross between sadness and pain. Clement tried to prompt him again, but Stanton got up and left, mumbling an excuse. There was a awkward silence until the conversation resumed, but this time the men talked of minor things, conscious that somehow they had rubbed Stanton the wrong way.

The wail of an ambulance siren in the wee hours of the morning warned people that somewhere in Redemption things were bad for somebody. Some turned long enough in their beds to wonder who in the village was sick enough to need an ambulance at this hour of the morning, then fell back to sleep, confident that the news would get to them later in the morning.

The following night the men heard the details from Faustin.

"The man come in here drunk and kind of desperate looking, calling for Precious. I did always feel he woulda come back for she, you know. I had to beg him to quiet down, because she was with a customer. I call she, without telling she who it is asking for she. When she reach downstairs and see him, the two of them just watching each other quiet. He open he mouth like he was going to start to say something and quiet quiet she tell him, 'Hush, we could talk upstairs.' They went upstairs – mind you he ain't pay down nothing eh – and the next time I hear bout him is when she tell me we need an ambulance."

"He look sick at all?"

"No, he look normal. Just a little drunk and sad. But he didn't look sick. Precious say he was complaining about he shoulder cramping, but that was about it."

Stanton's funeral was a holiday for Redemption. Hardly anybody went to work because it was scheduled for 11 am, and those who went to work signed their time sheets and left early. From Mrs. Stanton's living room to under the trees in her yard was packed with people who had come to get a glimpse of the body and see if he looked any different. Some came away from staring at him in his powder-blue suit, swearing he had a smile on his face. Outside in the yard, far away from the women, the young men joked that he probably still had an erection and that was probably why only half the casket was open.

The crowd walked along with the hearse the two streets from Stanton's house to New Testament. Some of them were hoping the car would have passed in front of Sunrise. Rumour had it that Precious was planning to attend, but the driver, sensitive to the scandal, had taken a different route.

In the church, everybody was united in their grief, singing, swaying and praying for Stanton's spirit to reach heaven safely. Mrs. Stanton leaned on her sons, singing and dabbing her eyes. That was when Precious and a few others from Sunrise came in at the back of the church. Their outfits alone told you they were not accustomed to grieving. People tangled their heads to see, some staring openly as the news made its way to the front of the church that Precious was present.

Pastor Duncan was inviting people to come up and say a word or two of remembrance for Stanton, or even to sing a song. Stanton's last remaining aunt, Miss Evey, came and talked about his childhood. How he had really loved cricket, breadfruit oil-down and life, and how saddened she was to see him cut down in his prime. Clement, who nominated himself as best friend that day, talked about their schooldays, their weddings, their lives as grown men. Stanton's boss came and acknowledged him as a real leader among the men. The eldest son maintained that in spite of everything, Daddy had taken good care of them and their mother loved him and missed him. It was as he spoke about his mother's enduring love for his father that Mrs. Stanton let loose a long, hoarse wail. It was what the women had been waiting for. At last they could do what they had wanted to do for so long – give Sylvia comfort and collectively absorb her misery. They knew that it was not grief at Stanton's passing that caused the tears; if anything it was relief from the burden of his horning ways. Their hands reached forward, handkerchiefs and bottles of Limacol and smelling salts at the ready.

In all the commotion, no one noticed when Precious left her seat and took the microphone away from Miss Evey who was leading the choir in a rendition of "Are You Washed in the Blood of the Lamb".

Her voice was tentative at first.

"I want to say something about Stanton." Then she stopped as if she wasn't sure if she should continue or even be there. The congregation watched in a menacing way, as if they wanted to beat her. Some mothers covered their children's faces, as if watching Precious was a sin in itself.

"I hear all of you talk bout Stanton. About how you know him, and love him and really miss him." She paused again looking at the casket in front of her. "I know what all of you here think of me. But in spite of all of that, I want to stand here and say that I miss and I love Stanton, too."

A chorus of steups followed the statement and a murmur started up.

"Who the hell she think she is? Love! Love! She live with the man for a few months and she could talk about love. Try living with him for twenty years, making he children, living with him everyday, taking the pressure and taking horn whenever he feel like it."

But Precious remained strong.

"I not here for your approval. I just want to say that in spite of everything Stanton was a good man. The best man I know. He was the only man who ever, in all the time I living here in Redemption, see me as a person. All you see me only as a whore. Something to use or to hate from a distance.

The congregation nearly collapsed at her boldness. The murmuring got louder. The women were angry that what was supposed to be Mrs. Stanton's moment was being upstaged. Here was Precious getting on more like the grieving widow than the widow herself.

"But with Stanton I wasn't just a whore. He see... saw me as a person. He know I had hopes and dreams. I know he had hopes and dreams too. I know all the things he wanted to do with his life. He helped me to realise I could have goals too."

Sensing just how vexed people were getting she sped up.

"I just wanted all of you, well really Stanton, to know, that I love him and I really appreciate all he was to me."

She walked down the aisle to the casket and kissed Stanton's cheek.

There was a low groan, followed by a slight scuffle, as Precious stood bent over Stanton. Mrs Stanton broke loose from the cocoon of women and headed straight for her, arms arcing wide. As Precious raised up, she let loose a slap on her. Women screamed and the prostitutes at the back stepped out of their pew ready to defend their own. But Precious motioned them back.

Mrs Stanton was heaving from the effort of the slap and watching Precious like she wasn't sure what to do next.

"I know you hate me and I understand why. But I want you to ask yourself something? In all the time you was married to Stanton, you was ever happy to see him? So happy that as soon as you hear his voice you feel you could burst? If he wasn't the king of this village, if he wasn't the man that every other woman wanted, if he wasn't a good provider, if he was just some poor ketch-ass man with the same hopes and dreams, would you been happy to see him when he came home? You woulda love him at all? Because Stanton tell me that you never love him. He tell me he never feel like it was love. He tell me you love what he represent to you, but you don't love him. He wasn't happy with you. He was never happy with you. He say so. But he tried to make it with you. All he wanted you to do was to cherish him a little. Instead you treat him like he was some kind of plaque to put on display. He leave because he was fed up being a plaque on the wall of the house. It ever occur to you that it take more than a wedding ceremony and having children to make him happy? It ever occur to you that when he come home from work on evenings he wanted more than some food? That sometimes he wanted to talk about he and you, and not just the house and the children? You feel beating me in public will make you look like a good wife? Try it! But as much as I is a whore, I was more Stanton's woman than you ever could be!"

And that was the hardest slap right there. That lash was the one that Revival heard the loudest. Even after Precious and the rest of the prostitutes walked out the door, it left a ringing sound in people's ears. The women tried to comfort Mrs. Stanton but it was half hearted. She was a weakened woman. All of her practised poise and self-possession was gone. At the graveside behind New Testament, Stanton's sons threw in the first handfuls of dirt on his casket while his wife leaned up, crying on Celestine.

At the other end of the street, in Room 12, the candle that had remained lit for three days was blown out and a picture taken down from the dressing table. Life had to go on.

JACQUELINE BISHOP

OLEANDER

It started with one tattoo. A tattoo of a flower. Or part of a flower. She came with a photograph, but it was no flower he had ever seen before. She wanted it here, she said, pointing to her navel; she wanted it surrounding what she considered the most important part of her body. She also wanted the exact same shade of colour. Since she was chocolate brown, he, the tattooist, had to play a little bit with the mixture. When they were both satisfied with what he came up with, the tattooist wrote the combination of inks and dyes into a book, so he would always remember. He knew that she would be coming back many times thereafter.

As he readied the electric machine, the tattooist explained that the ink would be inserted into her skin through a series of fine needles, that it would be over before she knew what was happening. Still, there would be some stinging and burning and a slight swelling. He made sure that she saw the gloves that he was wearing, that he opened a brand new pack of needles and wet disposable napkins. There were no risks of any kind of infection.

To make small talk as she took her clothes off, the tattooist told the young woman that though it was hard to tell, he knew she was a foreigner. Well, not a foreigner exactly, for who could really claim to be a native New Yorker? But there was a soft lilt to her voice, an accent that was somewhat muffled. Such thick dark hair, he thought, admiring the young woman. The dark-almost-to-violet eyes. As she lay back on the raised narrow bed, he gave her what he thought was the beginning or the very centre of a flower. He noticed how, after they were finished, she stared at herself for the longest time in front of the mirror.

She came back a few weeks later with another photo. This one showed even more parts of the pale pink flower. Though he could not see all the plant, he instinctively knew that this was a flower that bloomed profusely. He saw the five petals that were beginning to flare from a yellowish centre. Could he do this, she had asked, softly, could he enlarge her flower? She lifted up her blouse so he could admire the work he had already done, that first tattoo forming a ring around the rumpled dark spot of her navel. How well everything had healed! Such vibrant colours! As he mixed a new batch of colours, she told him that she was from Jamaica, that she hadn't been home for such a long time that she could barely remember the outline and contours of the island, and she didn't really feel right in still calling the island her home. The tattooist smiled to himself. He remembered the time, years before, when he'd fallen hard for an island beauty. Every time he thought of that woman, she was conflated into a vividly coloured flower. That day he extended the pale pink colour halfway across the young woman's belly.

The next time the young woman came she wanted to round out the edges of the petals to a magenta colour. She wanted the sepals curving slightly. She wanted streaks of white mixed in with the magenta. The flower was now extending upwards to cover almost half of her body. When he was done, she kept looking at herself in the mirror, all the while mumbling, "Larger. No, larger!" He would keep working on her until the image started touching a rigid dark nipple.

The tattooist liked working on this woman's body. How effortlessly the needle sank into her skin. As if it were the very best crushed velvet. How she sighed each time she felt the piercings, almost as if it were a release to have something enter her body painfully. She wanted him to tell her all he knew about the custom of tattooing. Something of what he said about "modification" and, especially, "branding" seemed to please her immensely. Then she asked him if it was true that the ink might fade one day, in the far away future? She seemed overly relieved at his answer. That, yes, the tattoo would fade, but no one could ever totally remove it from her body. When he said this, a calm relaxed look came over her.

The next time she came she wanted lance-like, dark-green

leaves to go with the flower. She had done some research, she said, had found out that many people erroneously believed the flower to be a member of the olive family. She could understand why; the leaves they grew looked so much like each other. Indeed, the night before, she had dreamt that she was applying olive oil all over her body. But, no, this wasn't some olive plant imitation flower. Anyone with any kind of sense would know that just because two things, two people, looked alike, that did not necessarily make them family. Family. In the soft lilt of her voice, she repeated the word over and over, even as he worked on the soft velvety canvas of her body, extending the flower to her back and then down her arms and legs.

But then the woman with the burnt-sienna hair had taken him aback when she told him she was working as a helper. He'd had her pinned down as someone's spoilt, rebellious daughter. But, no, she told him; the work she was doing was as a housekeeper. Still, she must be paid handsomely, this woman who kept adding more and more parts of the strange and exotic flower to her body, for she never had any problem paying him what he charged – and he knew that he charged more than any of the other tattooists in the city. They must be some very rich people she worked for.

A couple of weeks later she told him that the couple she worked for looked just like her. Had, in fact, the same warm brown colour. Did he remember what she had said before about people looking exactly like you not necessarily being your family? They were both lawyers, this couple who she worked for, with a thriving practice somewhere in midtown Manhattan. She was lying on the flat narrow bed, and this time she wanted even more branches and leaves added to the now gigantic flower that was consuming, it seemed to the tattooist, her slim young body. After a while, it did not seem right to him that this flower just kept growing and growing, up and down her arms and legs, her back, breasts, belly and even surrounding her pubic area. Was the flower sucking the life out of this once-vibrant young woman? She seemed weak and tired when she came to see him. It was then that she told him. She was but a child when she had left – had been taken – from Jamaica. And never, not once, had she set foot on or been allowed to go back to the island. Yes, she said, in a hiss of a voice that could not hide her anger, there had been a few letters over the years from a woman who claimed to be her mother, but this woman only ever wrote her when she wanted something; only ever wrote to beg her money. But she was finished with that now, the young woman busy turning herself into a flower was saying, all she cared about these days, was the style and the stigma of her flower, it's filaments and anthers.

Another day she started telling the tattooist a new story, which at first seemed to him a far-fetched, hallucinatory tale, except that she told it with so much detail and vigour. Of a little girl who had been given away by her mother. How this eight-year-old girl had just been handed over. The tourists, whom she called terrorists, had come to the island on a "visit", but had ended up taking the frightened little girl with them back to America. All the promises they made to this little girl's mother! How they would send her to school in America. How she would grow up to be a big-time doctor. The young woman told the tattooist how her mother had whispered in her ear that she was to go with these people, these strangers, and the little girl was to do what these people told her to do. They were her parents now. When the little girl started crying, her mother shushed her and told her to think of the other children. The little girl would never forget the thick wad of American dollars handed over to her mother by her new tourist/ terrorist parents, and that her mother barely had time to say goodbye to her because she was so busy counting the money.

The things this couple did to the little girl-child from Jamaica! How for years she was never allowed to leave the house without one parent or the other with her. Even as she got much older. How it was that they, her "parents" – who kept handing her the begging-letters from Jamaica – also kept insisting there was no such place as Jamaica. The couple told her that her memory of a life on an island so many years before was all part of an overblown imagination, the same imagination that had landed her on the psych ward one time after another for *making-up-stories-about-such-good-people*. For years she could not sort out the truth of one story from the fiction of another.

The tattooist listened without saying a word when she told how one, then the other, and sometimes both together, the couple enjoyed her; not only enjoyed her but made of her a cardboard character, filming and photographing her; sharing her with friends who eagerly came over. Calling her this horrible name – Lolita. And when the tired weakened girl left him that day, the tattooist had no choice but to trawl the Internet until he found a picture of a hardy pink plant called the oleander – a plant that the young woman said grew in abandon in the yard of a lean-to, tin-roofed house of a bedraggled woman with too many children around her. After he found the plant he sat looking at it for a long time, the tattooist, knowing, instinctively, that this would be the last time he would see her.

HAZEL CAMPBELL

JACOB BUBBLES

I

The year that Jacob was born, it rained so generously during January and February that the sugarcane grew fat with water and it took twice as much to produce a hogshead of sugar, so the masters worked the slaves twice as hard and twice as many attempted to escape, only to be recaptured and severely punished as an example to the others.

Later that year the ratoons came out weak, just like the puny babies the slave women bore, and many fields had to be replanted before schedule and the masters, pressured by heavy debts and their colicky dispositions, turned into larger demons, whipping, swearing, maiming, and killing.

The owner backra on Jacob's plantation got sick and returned to England, leaving the slaves to the mercy of the overseer who drove them beyond endurance, for the more sugar they made, the more profits he could skim off into his own pockets.

Many of them died that year, and the backra swore at the miserable rascals for the finality of their escape and the depletion of hands; the slave trade had been abolished, the price of replacement was high, and the birthrate was low.

The year that Bubbles was born, the city fathers decided that they had had enough of Back-o-Wall, the shanty town which too many people thought was the womb of all the criminal activity in the city.

So they served eviction notices on the squatters. Everybody ignored them. Nobody believed the promises of modern, decent shelter to take the place of shanty town at prices that they could afford. And meanwhile? Where would they go? How would they live? When the bulldozers arrived to raze their makeshift shacks, they screamed and threatened and stoned and resisted. Some bullet wounds and one death later, they gave up in despair and left the bulldozers to do their work.

★

In Jacob's birth year, Na Pearl began to dream many strange dreams. On a Sunday evening, when her neighbours from the slave barracks gathered around her doorstep, too tired even to complete domestic chores, she would entertain them with her visionary stories.

"All a we was a live into a village. Not like this ya hell hole barracks we living in now. Everybody have him owna hut, nice nice, an de village surroun wid a fence mek outa de tall bamboo dem. An no backra no de deh; an no canepiece no de deh, an no slave no de deh. All a we plant out one big field wid coco an such de like an we feed we one anoder, nice nice. An in de middle a we village was one great big stool. It tall, it tall, it tall so tell! So das is only a giant coulda siddung pan it. It mek out a guango an carve pretty pretty like how Jabez can mek a tree trunk tell you a story.

"An a big tall king come fi siddung pan de stool. Him dress up! Plenty big gold chain roun him neck. Him have on a long hat mek outa fedda an it follow him like massa dress-up flyway coat tail. An a whole heap a people wid spear an such de like a follow him an all a dem dress up too. An him hol up him head so gran jus like when Benjie cock a crow, an so much man a follow him dat when dem come de groun jus a grumble "blooma bolucha, blooma tiga. Blooma bolucha, blooma tiga". Lord de dream sweet so till!"

"An when him siddung everybady start fi dance. All de young gal dem wid dem bubby outa door, a jump an a prance, an de man dem only have one piece a cloth cover dem private. An den de king get up an start fi dance too, an him mek one almighty leap, an same time de fedder hat drop off, braps, flat a grung. An de whole place get quiet an everybody frighten, for is death fi see de king bald head. An all a we jus a trimble, an me so frighten me jump up out a de sleep."

And the next Sunday:

"Me dream bout one hilltop, high, high up. But is more dan a hilltop. A really plenty little hill pon top a odder hill, till you ketch dis one. De hill top dem look like young gal bubby pinting straight up fore man start fi trouble har an pickney mek dem drop. An pon top a di high, high hilltop is a village same like de village me tell you bout las time. Everyting nice an clean up dere so, an we plant fi weself and everybody belly full an peaceful. An in de middle a de village is a stool fi de ruler fi siddung pan. Him is a very tall, good lookin man, black an shine, an him wear a hat mek outa yellow snake skin wid a tail a swish behin him neck back. An him call we togeder fi mek a proclamation an as him start fi tell we wha fi do, him two front teet drop out, an me so frighten, me wake up same time."

The third Sunday after Na Pearl started her dream telling, even more slaves gathered before her door, for word had spread and many were trying to interpret her dreams. Some thought that they promised better days, while others said they were just an old woman's foolishness. Others just liked to share the thought of the freedom in those dreams.

As they settled on the dirt to hear the current dream, the overseer backra and three drivers appeared. They whipped and scattered the crowd and Na Pearl was dragged off to be tied to the guango tree at the entrance to Hogsfield where everybody would see her in the morning. She contracted a bad cold from the exposure to the night dew and never recovered her strength. She died two months later.

★

In Bubbles' birth year, his father, who disowned him before he was born, and his uncle were both killed in a fight which started in a bar on Lindy Way. Bubbles' father, Papa Tee, and another man had a quarrel and Papa Tee had gone for his friends to help him discipline the man. When he returned the other man was waiting for him with his friends. When it was all over, Papa Tee, his brother Charlie and three from the other side were left face down in the dust. They said that this incident marked the beginning of gang warfare in the city when men and women had to stop walking alone for fear of ambush; when people began to exchange residences according to their loyalties, so that a whole community would be one in defending itself against the enemy; when crossing the border into enemy territory could mean one's death. It also marked the beginning of the time when, if you were a young man and hoped to survive in the ghetto, you had to get hold of a gun; and target practice for young boys was more regular than attendance at school.

In that same year Mother Osbourne got a vision one night and left home to become a *warner* woman. Dressed up in a long white robe with a red sash at the waist and a matching turban, she warned up and down the streets of Kingston. She warned about drought and she warned about flood. She warned about pestilence and famine. But her favourite topic was the sea of blood which would wash the streets of the city if the inhabitants did not repent and turn to God.

They said that she was mad and her children tried to get her put away, until the night she appeared at her daughter Ida's gate and warned of the destruction about to visit the yard. The next night Ida's manfriend came home and found her in the bed of another man who lived in the yard. Before they could subdue him, he had chopped up Ida and the man, and three other people. They left Mother Osbourne alone after that and she continued to walk the streets and warn the wicked city of hell and damnation and blood running in the gullies like angry rivers.

★

The night that Jacob was born they say that his mother's screams kept the slave quarters awake for several hours. They say her screams could be heard all the way up at the Great House. The nanas boiled woman piaba and thyme-leaf tea. They gave her pennyroyal and strong-back to drink, but none of the potions could ease the pain or hasten the birth. Jacob entered the world as big as a three month old baby. In a world of puny infants who often died at birth, the old people regarded his great size and his lusty crying as an omen.

The backra's comment was: "Good breeding stock. Tell the mother to give me more like that. Who's the father?"

But even as they approved of his size, they disapproved of his fearlessness. While the slave toddlers learned very early to move out of the way of the horses and mules of the masters as they came trotting by field or quarters, Jacob would stand up, eyes round with wonder, staring as though he were equal. It took several years of flicks from the masters' whips and scoldings by the women to teach him to turn aside or lower his eyes when the backras passed or spoke.

But though he bore the scars of their displeasure, they couldn't quite tame the sureness with which he walked, hotstepping and proud like the fantail peacocks in the backra's garden. Nor could they completely stunt his quick intelligence. The old women fed him with kon-konte, the dried plantain porridge he liked so much, and saved titbits from the pot specially for him, and looked at him and remembered Na Pearl's dreams.

The night Bubbles was born was the same night the bulldozers moved in on Back-o-Wall. His mother felt the first pains as she struggled to save her possessions: a stool and rickety table, a coal stove and a mattress. There was nobody to help her and no money for a taxi fare and by the time she reached the nearest police station to ask for help, it was already too late.

The sergeant on duty helped with the delivery and said with disgust that it was the third one that week. The lady constable who usually dealt with such matters was on leave, but all of them had basic training in midwifery because of the frequency with which the surrounding squatter communities needed this kind of help. So, although he knew what to do, Sergeant Brown was annoyed and the first thing Bubbles heard when he came into the world was the sergeant cursing, "These damn careless people who drop them pickney like cow." His mother named him Brown after the sergeant. Nobody knew Papa Tee's real name anyway.

A number of Back-o-Wall squatters gathered their scattered pieces of board and zinc and hastily put together shelters in the old part of the city cemetery; the living retrieving space from the dead. It was to one of these shacks that Bubbles went home after he was born. A male acquaintance of his mother, Manatee, had offered her a cotch with him. His previous woman had gone back to her country home rather than "tek box from duppy" in the cemetery. By the time his brother was born eleven months later, Bubbles was learning to walk from tombstone to tombstone. He lived off the generosity of neighbours during his mother's brief absence; Manatee would not care for him; he was not his child. They called him Bubbles because he would amuse himself for hours by blowing bubbles with his spittle. Nobody had any dreams for him.

II

Jacob liked the feeling of danger he got from dangling his legs beneath the dray as it dipped and rose and clattered over the rocky surface, flattened grass or lumpy bare earth of the narrow road. It took skill to know when to pull up his legs to prevent his toes from being scraped.

The girl Miriam had gone to sleep. At first she had leaned against him until he shifted her body away and rested her head on one of the sacks. Asleep, she looked even more mawga, almost as bad as the skin and bone puppies he had seen wandering in the streets of Falmouth. She said that she had not had the flux, but even though it had nearly killed him, he was much bigger and stronger. He could not believe that she was eleven years old as the auctioneer had announced.

He had seen her once before on the plantation when her mother had brought her from the great house where they lived to visit with the old nana in the barracks. She had attracted a lot of attention and admiration because of her long wavy hair and smooth brown skin. Jacob had not liked her. She was only a puny girl who worked in Massa's kitchen. The girls who worked in the second gang with him were strong and playful and when the driver wasn't looking it was always possible to play brief games of hide and seek in the tall cane or to feel up their femaleness when they allowed it.

On top of everything she was a cry baby. Ever since the new bacra had bought them and left them in the care of the man driving the cart, she had not stopped crying. When he tried to talk to her, she only shook her head as if she was dumb.

He too was feeling sad at the breakup of their old life; and he too was fearful of the new life waiting for them on the new plantation. Femus, the driver, had told them that it was a coffee plantation called Mount Plenty.

Cross at being saddled with the newcomers as well as his other duties of collecting and loading the dray with tools and barrels and sacks of produce for the plantation, Femus had wondered aloud about what the Massa was going to do with the "lil kench a gal pickney, and the ole fowl", meaning the old woman who had been thrown in to make a bargain sale of eighty pounds for the three.

They had been travelling for a long time. When they left Falmouth, the sun was high in the sky; not long after the noon break, Jacob thought. Now the sun was almost down; about the time when the second gang would have been collecting machetes and hoes to bring back grass to the pens and finishing their daily routine before the land grew black.

Jacob hoped that the new plantation was not far away. He did not like the night, especially in a strange country.

Abruptly, Femus began to shout, "Whoa! Whoa!" and to pull up the mules. The dray came to a halt. He jumped down and steered the mules into a large grassy clearing beside the road. The girl and the woman woke up and they all came off and stretched.

"We a stop little fi res de mule dem and eat sinting," Femus announced.

"Please, sar," Jacob said, minding his manners to his elders as he had been taught. "We is close?"

"Close nuff," was the unaccommodating reply.

"Me wan pee pee," the girl said timidly. The woman took her hand and they went off into the bushes.

Femus went to relieve himself against a tree, and Jacob did the same close by.

"Night gwine ketch we?"

"What a bwoy fi chat! You nyam fowl batty? When we ketch, we ketch."

Femus took a large enamel carrier off the dray. From it he extracted a couple of boiled dumplings and pieces of yam. He shared the food onto the leaves of the nearby trumpet tree and passed it around. The food was not fresh, but Jacob ate greedily.

The girl took only a few bites from a dumpling and the old woman nothing at all. She asked for some water and Femus pointed to a covered jar and a tin cup.

"The wuk hard, Mass Femus?" Jacob asked. He was curious about life on a coffee plantation, never having seen anything else but sugarcane.

"No wuk?" Femus answered gruffly. "You ever hear say wuk no hard?"

"Come bwoy," Femus said when he had finished eating. "Help me set up the lantern. Night a come, an me na stop again."

Jacob did as he was instructed. As they were about to move off he shouted, "Wait little, Mass Femus! Mek a pick two guava." He dashed off into the nearby cluster of trees and returned shortly with two green fruit.

"Me couldn't see no more and them pan grung a rotten."

"Lawd bwoy!" the old woman exclaimed, suddenly excited. "You no know say you no fi pick sinthing affa tree a night! Dash it way, less the tree duppy a go follow we!"

"Stupidness!" Femus sucked his teeth.

"Dash it way!" she insisted.

"Oonu hurry up," Femus said impatiently, pulling at the reins. The mules began to move off slowly.

The woman sounded so frightened and was so insistent that Jacob reluctantly threw the fruits back into the bushes.

"You fi spin roun tree time and say, 'Ask pardin! Me no wa none!'."

Jacob sucked his teeth and jumped on to the moving dray.

"Tree duppy a go follow you," the old woman warned. "You an all you generation. Bad luck all you days," she ended as if saying a benediction.

They rode on into the darkness, lit only by the lantern swaying at the rear of the cart and the kitchen bitch near the driver. Sometimes they had to dismount to lighten the load for the mules in places where it was particularly steep or the road too difficult. In spite of his bravado, Jacob was glad when Miriam sought his hand to keep company in the darkness as they hustled to keep up with the dray. At such times the old woman clutched an old torn-

up blanket over her head and shoulders to keep off the night air
and ignored them.

Eventually, far into the night, they made out lights on a hill and
knew that they were near the end of the journey.

Femus asked them to dismount again, then he hooted twice,
so loudly and unexpectedly that his passengers shivered with
fright. Their fright increased as he was answered first by one then
another voice, the shouts echoing eerily through the night. Two
figures appeared out of the darkness and walked beside the mules
as they climbed the steep hill towards the great house. Midway,
they stopped beside a building, and by the light of the kitchen
bitches, unloaded most of the sacks and barrels.

"Tell Busha me come, an Massa buy tree new one," Femus said
and signalled the weary trio to follow him.

Years later, when he remembered that night, Jacob would
wonder why he had been so frightened.

The plantation was a new one, just settling into the rhythm of
growing coffee. Until their numbers increased, the twenty slaves,
including Jacob, cleared the land, planted the fields, tended the
nurseries, collected sand and clay for making buildings, made
lime kilns, cut wood, tended the animals and worked at all the
jobs necessary to establish a plantation.

They were fortunate to have a conscientious and compassionate owner, unusual in those harsh times. There were few whip-
pings on his estate and he kept in check the wanton cruelty which
came so easily to the other white men on the estate.

Very early, Jacob showed a liking and aptitude for mason work,
so, as the slave population on the estate grew, he was allowed to
develop this skill under the tuition of the head mason, himself a
slave, an intelligent man, skilled in his craft.

Now, as he moved about the plantation with the freedom
granted those with special skills, Jacob felt a sense of pride in the
many buildings which he had helped to erect. There was the mill
house which had given them so much trouble: the cisterns to
catch water, the channels into the mill house; the first drying
platform and the barbecue which had crumbled under the first
heavy rains. They had discovered then that the gravel stones they

had used were too soft and therefore wrong for that kind of structure. So much of their building had been trial and error, a constant struggle of discovery and invention. Jacob had also helped to erect the cut-stone foundation to the great house, only recently completed.

It was while he was working on the great house that he had met Miriam again, grown, but still frail with a perpetually sad face beautifully framed by the long braids twisted around her head.

He had been working on the foundations for a week before he spoke to her. In fact she'd looked so aloof that he might not have had the courage to speak, had she not, one day, in a very impersonal manner, brought him a duckunoo wrapped in its banana leaf, resting in a small packi.

"Mama Leah sey fi gi you dis an she say if you like it she have more."

Like ducknoo! he thought with amusement, and his mouth watered for a bite, but he merely nodded his thanks and told her to put the packi on a pile of nearby stones.

"Hi massa!" the headman teased him. "Smady ready fi start carry straw!"

Miriam rubbed one foot against the other nervously as she delivered her message to the older slave.

"Mama Leah say fi tell you say she leave sinting up a kitchen fi you, sar. She say you fi come fi it."

They all understood. Mama Leah was looking with favour on Jacob for Miriam. She wanted to discuss the matter with the man in charge of him.

Mama Leah had mothered Miriam from the moment she had arrived at the plantation. She had protected the girl from the attentions of both white and black men by keeping her almost hidden in the kitchen and under her eye all the time. The girl's frailty worried her. Since she wasn't sure how much longer she could continue to hide her, she had looked around and chosen a protector in Jacob. The next day Miriam turned up at the mid morning break with a carrier of food.

"Nice!" Jacob said, licking his fingers free of pork fat. She had stood patiently waiting for him to finish so she could retrieve the carrier.

"A you cook?"

Miriam shook her head. "Mama Leah say me fi tell you say a me cook, but me can't cook so good yet."

Jacob nearly laughed out loud at her awkwardness. Her lack of guile was quite unlike the easy flirtatious ways of the other girls on the plantation. To him they appeared saucy, teasing, daring, tempting: easily available. Miriam seemed special.

But in spite of his youth, flesh was not the most important thing to Jacob just then. Like all the other slaves, he hated his bondage even though his skills earned him more leniency than others – he was even sent to work on neighbouring estates. The last time he had done this he had been given two shillings to keep. At the back of his head was the idea of buying himself from his master. The more he thought about freedom the more he liked the idea. As a mason he could earn enough money to live comfortably. So the older ones said. It would take him a very long time to get enough money, but he was determined to do it.

Then there was the satisfaction of building things: watching lime and stone and clay and dirt come together under his hands to form sturdy, useful structures, like the stone wall which he had helped to erect to protect the long steep driveway to the great house.

And he had a dream. He ached to be able to talk to the busha about it, or if he was very, very lucky, to the owner bacra himself. He wanted to plan and build a stone bridge across the river which ran through the main road on the property, and which was often impassable for long stretches during the rainy season. The bridges they had erected out of planks and iron had never lasted more than two seasons. Jacob was convinced that only one of stone and mortar, reinforced with bricks, could be strong enough to withstand the flooded river.

Shortly before his work on the great house ended, Mama Leah summoned him one evening.

"You like the food Miriam give you?"

He nodded.

"She cook good. Nearly good like me," she said with a smile.

He nodded again, not revealing that Miriam had already confessed.

"She a nice gal. Nobody no touch har yet. But that no gwine las. Me anxious fi smady good tek her."

Jacob said nothing.

"Well?"

"Yes mam," he said stupidly.

"Whey you a go do?" Mama Leah asked impatiently. "She good an obedient. You is a strapping, good-looking prosperous young man an you na keep smady. Me talk to Massa aready."

Jacob waited for Miriam until she had finished her kitchen duties.

They walked out for two weeks before he took her to his hut. But the first time, awed by her frail beauty and innocence so different from the women he had known, he could do nothing with her. When the consummation finally occurred, he entered her with the knowledge that she was very special and that he would kill for her if necessary.

One rainy season, the busha, in a rash moment, tried to cross the river when it was in spate and nearly drowned. The owner backra, who was in England, sent out a man who was said to be a great bridge builder. He was very tall, very thin and very pale with hair so blonde he was quickly nicknamed "the duppy backra".

Animosity flared between himself and the mason gang from the beginning. In the absence of the owner he began to introduce punishments hitherto unknown on that plantation. He was especially venomous against Jacob who had unwisely criticised his plan to build yet another wooden bridge. The fact that the bridge did not survive the first rainy season made the bridge-builder's temper even worse. The owner backra sent instructions for a stone and mortar bridge and, knowing little about local materials, the duppy backra had to rely on the local gang's experience. Jacob saw a few of his ideas put to use.

One day Jacob was scouting the property for stones of the particular kind they needed. He was almost at the edge of the property where it joined the hilly forest land when he heard "pst! pst!" He peered into the bushes but saw no one. He dismounted and stood beside the mule, puzzled.

Suddenly two men appeared beside him. He hadn't heard them approaching. Two short, black men. Maroons, he thought immediately. He was a little afraid of them. They got money for capturing and returning runaway slaves according to their treaty with the white men. Not that he was a runaway, but he had heard many bad things about them.

"You a run way?"

Jacob was annoyed. "How me fi a run way wid de Backra mule? Me is a mason. Me a look fi stone."

To his surprise they were able to tell him that he would find the kinds of stones he described in an old river bed "We coulda use a mason up so," one of them said.

"But onoo suppose fi ketch runway," Jacob answered in surprise.

"That a fi we business. Tink bout it. Up so you free!"

From that day Jacob's life became a torment between the urge for freedom, the desire to see the bridge finished, and caring about Miriam, for the maroons had made it clear that he could not bring his woman. He tried not to think what would happen to her if he ran away. She would be punished for his escape, he knew. What form that punishment would now take, made him break out into cold sweat.

On the other hand, if he were free, perhaps he could convince the maroons to allow him to rescue her, especially if they liked his work.

Many times he met the two maroons at the foot of the hill. They became his friends, sharing their jerk pork, spicier and sweeter than anything Jacob had ever tasted, and the coffee which he had started to steal for them. They talked so much about freedom and the deeds of the maroons and how a man could be a man up in the mountains that sometimes Jacob could hardly swallow, but still he could not make up his mind.

Eventually the decision was made for him. One day he met his friends at the edge of the forest, as usual. They were talking when suddenly the two men vanished. One moment he was talking to them, the next they weren't there. Jacob looked about him in bewilderment. It was a few minutes before the approach of the duppy backra on horseback made him realise why they had disappeared. Jacob was accused of plotting to run away and whipped all the way back to the busha's house. He was flogged till there was no more skin on his back, and in an almost unconscious state tied to a tree for all to see his disgrace. But that night, even as Miriam shivered and wept for him in their hut, his maroon friends came for him.

III

Bubbles was a puny child; undernourished, bang-bellied, nose running from a constant cold; miserable in the early years before he learned to fend for himself. At ten, he could barely pass for seven or eight.

He had smooth mid-brown skin and Papa Tee's naturally jherri-curled, really black hair; the kind of person they call "coolie royal"; and though his mother and the women in the graveyard loved him for his pretty looks and his air of helplessness, their struggles to keep life going for themselves and other numerous offspring meant that there was little that they could do for him.

His pretty face helped when he went begging downtown, mostly outside restaurants. Which woman leaving the dining room satiated with a company or man-paid-for meal could resist the appeal in those large eyes?

Every year he was enrolled in the primary school, but he rarely attended for more than six weeks in a year. He had no shoes, no clothes, no money to buy lunch. In any case, he hated school. Nobody insisted that he attend.

Instead of school he spent his time swimming with other unclaimed urchins in the warm currents released into the harbour from the power station. One summer, when he was twelve years old, he attended a special camp for underprivileged boys like himself where he learned the rudiments of reading and writing and the beginnings of an exciting theory which taught him that all men were brothers, equal under the law and entitled to a fair share of all the world's wealth; that he was a unit of labour and therefore of immense value to the state. He was given a whole set of rights which he had never thought about. It was intriguing but it didn't change anything for him, and when the boys were invited to enrol for evening classes, he lost interest.

Besides, it was time for him to join his community gang. Feared throughout the city, the gang known as Suckdust made sure that all males, twelve and over, living in the Coalyard area were fully committed and knew how to protect themselves and the community. It was the only way to survive. The more enterprising youths were chosen as official members of the gang.

At fourteen, after months of clandestine practice, Bubbles could handle a "dog" or a beretta or any of the small weapons which fell into his hands better than the police with their formal training. He had two ambitions: to own a gun, and to get his hands on an M16, the king of the underground weapons, but his gang had only two of these and only the top ranking could touch them.

At fourteen he left his graveyard home for good after a fight one night with his stepfather, Manatee, who had just given his mother another beating. Bubbles hated this man who kept everyone around him in constant fear of his temper, threats and assaults.

One night, while carrying ganja to a ship outside the harbour, some members of the gang came across an abandoned canoe. When they examined it they found that it was half full of a variety of hand guns and paint cans full of bullets. Somebody had either missed or was late for a rendezvous. The windfall was later distributed to everyone's satisfaction. The event sparked a whole week of celebration.

It was during this week that Bubbles, armed with his new strength, went to visit his mother. She was sitting on a tree stump in the yard and tried to hide her face when she saw him coming.

"A the dutty man do you so?" he asked angrily, when he saw the bruises on her arms and her swollen face.

"Is all right," she said. "No bother."

"Whey him de?"

She didn't answer. Her eyes showed her fright. "You ongle gwine mek it worse," she pleaded with him.

"Dutty man!" he shouted. "Whey you is! Come out an face real man if you bad! Is the las time you beat har up."

"Lawd Jesus!" his mother exclaimed when she saw the gun in his hand. "No, Bubbles. No!" she begged. "Bubbles! Bubbles!"

"Dutty man!" he shouted again, ignoring her. He fired a shot into the flimsy wood of the door.

The noise attracted several people, so there were many who saw Manatee emerge from his doorway, a sharp machete in his hand.

"Because you get gun you tink say me fraid a you? You stinking little pissin tail bwoy! You a go dead bad, jus like you puppa. A who you a call dutty man?"

He rushed towards Bubbles, machete raised to chop, but never had time even to feel the three bullets which ended his life.

The police arrested Bubbles. No witness came forward so there was no real case against him. If you wanted to continue living in Coalyard, if you wanted to continue living, you didn't see most of the things that happened. However, the judge sent him to reform school. He was still under legal age, and there was widespread alarm in the country at the growing violence and the involvement of young boys in criminal activity. Bubbles stayed at the school for two days, mostly out of curiosity.

Coalyard covered several acres in the northern section of the city. As well as the coalyard from which the area got its name, it included the city's main burial ground, which gave its protectors the alternate name of "Duppy Gang".

People said that the coal yard had been selling wood and coal, produce and small stock since the days of slavery. But, with the increasing popularity of kerosene stoves, and the emergence of other more comfortable markets, the actual area used for these purposes had shrunken. The drays and donkey carts laden with crocus bags of coal no longer came in from the country parts; people no longer came with their paper bags to buy a chamber pot of coal; the trucks of goats and pigs appeared only at Christmas time now. Only the sooty residue of coal now reminded of its former use.

On the side furthest away from the cemetery, Coalyard shared a road boundary with another ghetto community known as Slow Town. Nobody knew why it had this name. In an area of

extremely scarce resources but numerous people, a natural rivalry
had sprung up between the two communities. Perhaps it had
started when they both shared the single standpipe which had
been situated on the boundary line before the authorities put in
a network of standpipes to serve the fast-growing communities.
Perhaps it had started when people from Slow Town got more of
the jobs when the slum upgrading and road-building projects
began. Slow Town had supported the party which was then in
power. Slow Town's gang was known as Superduper Posse.

By the time Bubbles was nineteen, he was deputy leader of the
Suckdust gang. Police bullets and ambushes by other gangs
reduced leaders rapidly. If one was competent and ambitious, one
could quickly achieve authority.

That was the year when a police bullet ripped through his
groin while he was on a mission one night. The doctors patched
him up so that he was able to pass water, but Bubbles had lost his
balls.

For technical reasons, the court dismissed all the charges
brought against him. Bubbles went a little crazy after he was
freed. If you wanted a quick death, all you had to do was to hint
that he had been emasculated. Two policemen paid for his loss
with their lives. A few people who uttered the word eunuch in his
presence disappeared. A dance in another community was shot
up because Bubbles heard that people there were calling Suckdust
the "ballsless posse". Everybody walked in fear of Bubbles. He
was angry, fast and never missed.

Finally, the leader of Suckdust ordered him eliminated. He
was too crazy. He was drawing too much official attention to the
area. Bubbles heard about the order and went straight to the
leader's yard, called him out and beat him to the draw. Nobody
disputed his right to succeed. You had to respect a man so fearless.

After that he calmed down a little. The claims of leadership
were too demanding for craziness if he was to survive. A little of
the desire for revenge had been satisfied, but the bitterness never
left him.

As time passed, Bubbles created a small court around himself.
For his personal protection he had with him only one man, a

friend from childhood whom he trusted. No other adult male lived in his compound. Five women and their dependents lived in various units in the yard. They cooked and washed and carried out other domestic chores for him. It was whispered, very softly, that he had paid two of them to name him as their "baby father". They were also his watchmen and his spies, keepers of bullets and concealers of ganja, guns and stolen goods when the police chose to raid the area. They were well taken care of.

The rest of the community protected him too, for he came to be regarded as a fair leader provided you didn't cross him. He was generous with money, particularly to women in need. They said he had a soft spot for women and would be very hard on any of his men who abused women in Coalyard. Growing in wisdom as a leader, he did not, however, chastise them for abuses outside the community, but it was known that he disapproved of wanton cruelty to women and legend had it that if Bubbles was present on a mission, women would not be molested.

He was also a good negotiator with the community's political bosses, and since the party which Suckdust supported was now in power, he was able to get improvements like a community centre for the youths, equipment for sports and additional standpipes. His growing notoriety in the city as a marksman, feared alike by enemy and authority, also gave the community reason to be proud. No other gang dared touch anyone from Coalyard without expecting quick reprisal. Coalyard respected him as much as it feared him. It was proud of him inasmuch as it wished for peace.

One morning, getting up late as was his custom, Bubbles was greeted by the news that one of his informants wanted to see him.

"What!" he exclaimed when he heard the news. "Man if a joke you a joke, you know say me no like them kinda joke!"

"But is true, Bubbles," the informant protested, and hastened to fill in the details.

"Superduper go pan a mission las night cross the waters. But them run ina one patrol, two jeep; an the police an soldier bwoy dem clap dem. Hotfoot dead. You know him sista, the one dem call Pantyhose, whey always a falla dem bout the place? Well, a she lead dem outa the trap for she know de place good. Dem say a she tun back an lif the M16 affa Hotfoot body. Dis morning dem have a meeting an she still a hol on pon the sixteen an fore dem know what a' clock a strike, Pantyhose a de leader!"

"Rahtid!" Bubbles exploded. "Then we no gwine have fi change them name to Panty Posse!"

He was amused but also insulted. The ghetto gangs were tough. Many people had been outraged that Hotfoot had allowed Pantyhose to run with the gang so freely. She was said to be tough too but she was still a woman. She was Hotfoot's half-sister and they said that he had been sweet on her from they were small, but to allow her such liberties! She had sometimes been used as a decoy and distraction for the posse's activities, but to be gang leader! Impossible! That wouldn't last long, Bubbles thought.

Bubbles sat over his late morning breakfast of fried dumplings and callaloo washed down with beer and thought about this twist.

"Hold a Stripe, no," he invited the bearer of the news. "So, how them man tek it?"

"Some a dem a screw, but a she hol de sixteen an dem say she know how fi use it. Hotfoot did teach her every ting."

"So whey Quicksilver? Me woulda think a him woulda turn chief."

"The police bwoy dem hol him. Him in a KPH. Dem say him well bad. Dem shoot him an Tie-tongue and Lesley."

"Rahtid! Is a big haul that! Rahtid!" he said again. "The police bwoy them must be feel good enh!"

He thought for a while. "So, Slow Town man them unda panty rule. Raas!" He stretched out the exclamation into a laugh.

He leaned over his now empty plate stroking his chin and thinking hard. His face would not grow a beard, only a few strands of hair which he kept shaved. The clean face had served him well on occasion. Who would suspect a nice, clean-faced, coolie-royal man in a crisp three-piece suit of intention to rob a bank?

He was picking his teeth with a matchstick when he heard a slight commotion at his gate. He was curious but knew that the women would deal with the situation and tell him what he needed to know.

Soon one of them approached with the news that Panty hose had sent a message.

"She wan talk to you," a slightly out-of-breath youth who was with the woman explained.

"Say what?"

"She de pan fi dem side a No Man's Lan, say she want a meeting."

"Who wid her?"

"Bout four man. Police lash dem las night."

"Raas! Tell her me soon come."

For some time an uneasy truce had existed between Suckdust and Superduper for the practical reason that both Coalyard and Slow Town shared the same entrance from the main road into their communities – the road and the roundabout now called No Man's Land. During previous war times between them barricades had been erected blocking the roads which gave direct access to the communities and a line of shacks burnt out so that the boundary was very clear. Either side caught lingering in this area was regarded as the legitimate target of a mugging, rape or shooting.

Gradually, however, they came to realise that the hostilities not only cut them off from each other, but from services which they needed. A broken main needed to be fixed, the fire brigade needed access, food needed to be delivered, midwives needed to deliver babies, but nobody of sound mind, no taxi, no bus, not even a handcart man would voluntarily enter the area, so they had had a formal meeting and called a truce. Violence in the immediate communities got less; the barricades were removed, and they turned their destructive energies against other enemies. People from either side were still cautious when using No Man's Land, but at least they could do so without being used for instant target practice.

Bubbles took his time about putting on his shirt and his Clarke's booty. He was not about to allow a woman to take the lead in any negotiations, so he deliberately dawdled for nearly an hour. When he thought that enough time had passed for Pantyhose to get the message, he chose five of his men to accompany him.

They checked their guns before leaving, uneasy diplomats going to a hostile conference. Not that they expected any direct hostility, but they had heard that Pantyhose was still wearing the M16.

Protocol demanded that Bubbles wear his too. He also gave his bodyguard one of the other M16s that his gang possessed. It helped to show the superior strength of his armoury. The Superduper Posse was known to have only one. Perhaps that was why Pantyhose had risked her life to rescue it from the police. Bubbles knew that Superduper's arsenal consisted only of 45s and some 22s and some homemade items from bicycle parts. He had mainly handguns too, but he had six more M16s broken down in a trunk hidden in an old latrine in his yard. This was not the time for them to be used. To bring them out would attract too much attention. The security patrols would step up their harassment.

Bubbles walked down his street toward the meeting ground. Behind him were his deputies and a crowd of the curious who knew that they had to keep a respectful distance.

The gangs would meet in the dusty roundabout which separated the road into their two communities. They didn't need to fear the patrols for the various itinerant sellers of food, cigarettes and other commodities on the sidewalks for a mile in either direction would pass on the word of any approaching problem in time for them to cover themselves.

"You call me?" Bubbles shouted to Pantyhose who was waiting in the shade of a duppy cherry tree on Slow Town's side of the road.

"We can talk?" she replied using the rifle to point to the island in the roundabout.

Bubbles noted that Pantyhose carried the rifle with the ease of familiarity and immediately felt a grudging respect for her. She was dressed in the dark green fatigues which was standard night mission costume for the gangs. It confused people. Made them think that they were soldiers.

She was sweating freely in the hot midday sun. Her shirt was torn at the tail and Bubbles saw blood stains on her right shoulder. He realised that she had not changed since the gang's disaster the previous night; that in true leadership fashion she was organising her posse, putting them back together on some path before allowing herself any rest, and his respect grew. Her eyes were red. He wondered if she had been crying for Hotfoot. His death must be hard for her, Bubbles thought.

"So what happen?" he said when they faced each other. He was deliberately, insultingly casual, his curiosity concealed behind his dark sunshades.

"Me know say you hear already say that the raas claat police and soldier bwoy them kill Hotfoot last night."

She was a strapping woman in her early twenties, not fat, but big-boned and at least three inches taller than Bubbles.

"So?"

"Three man ina KPH, an three missing."

"So?" he asked again.

"Me jus wan tell unoo, official like, say that we have a meeting this morning an from now on a me a rule."

"You a mek joke!" Bubbles said with a laugh.

"No. Me well serious. An don't think say that because me is a woman the posse get sof. We badder than ever." She adjusted the shoulder strap of the M16 as if to prove her point. "Me did jus wan fi tell oonu meself, so every body know what's what."

She moved away as if to depart, then turned back swiftly to face Bubbles again.

"An a nex thing. Me know say oonu gwine want fi call we Panty Posse, Pussy Posse and all them kind a name deh. Me know how oonu man think, but no bother with that. Seen? The man them na go like it. Me name is Inez. Memba that. Figet bout the Pantyhose business. The posse still name Superduper. Me na call oonu Duppy Gang."

Bubbles stared at her, one hand casually on his rifle, the other stroking his chin.

"That's all?" he asked as if surprised. He was in fact a little puzzled. He had thought that she might have summoned him to ask for help. Instead, here she was issuing a challenge.

"Enh, enh! Jus memba say me can shoot better than all a oonu put together. A Hotfoot teach me an him was the bes."

Again Bubbles felt growing respect for her. There was no hint of sadness in her voice when she mentioned Hotfoot.

She pulled herself up appearing even taller than she really was and turned away to be followed by her scowling lieutenants.

Bubbles also turned around. Scratching his head he said to his men, "Oonu hear the lady!"

They all laughed loudly and started walking towards home. But before Pantyhose was fully out of hearing, someone in Bubbles' crowd shouted, "Go way! Panty Posse!"

There was an instant reply of four shots. Suckdust's followers scattered, hugging zinc fences or lying on the ground. All except Bubbles and his immediate party. They knew that there was no real danger; that the Panty Posse had fired in the air; a warning only.

"Cease! No bother!" Bubbles restrained his followers. It was a minor incident, not worth a waste of bullets.

The uneasy truce might have held while people waited to see how the Panty Posse developed – in spite of her warning, that was the name that stuck – but suddenly the party in power announced elections and the political bosses called for serious action from both gangs. Coalyard and Slow Town were one voting district and heavily populated. Both parties wanted all the votes possible, but the area was unpredictable. The side which could intimidate most usually decided victory.

"Mek sure the votes swing my way," both gangs were told by their faceless bosses. "Anybody not fi we, can't stay."

Pantyhose laid the first ambush. Some Coalyard youths returning from a dance hall session and moving carelessly through No Man's Land were shot at. The only casualty was a finger on the right hand of one of the youths. It was an announcement rather than a killing spree.

The barricades at the entrances to both communities went up immediately: old tyres; a twisted rusted bus chassis; tree stumps; the only way to enter was by a slow climb if not given passage by the watchmen. Footpaths at scattered points of the areas were the only other entrances. The audacity of the ambush shook Bubbles. The following night two shops in Slow Town were the target of gasoline bombs thrown by a daredevil rider on a Honda 750 who couldn't be stopped. The fire brigade turned back when it met the barricade.

Next two girls from Coalyard were raped by ten men.

All of Suckdust's M16s were brought out for that reply. A dance was raided: two dead, several wounded.

People began to move out in fear of their lives, but now the order came "Nobody is to move". Too many moves meant lost votes. The gangs began to threaten those who wanted to move. The really timid and desperate left everything behind and ran away. The bosses were not happy. The gun population increased. Fear spread beyond Coalyard and Slow Town as the increased supply of guns began to be used all over the country for purposes other than political intimidation.

The really big explosion came on the night that some Slow Town men and women were at the cinema which served both communities. They had taken to going to the cinema on alternate nights.

The show was a horror movie about monsters from space eating up earth people. Three youths hoping for a free show climbed the wall at the back of the premises and followed a well-worn path across the ceiling where a large hole allowed easy viewing. The ceiling tiles, weakened by many such excursions, chose that night to give way, depositing the three on the heads of the frightened patrons. Their descent showed up grotesquely as large shadows on the screen as they passed through the projector's beam, adding to the audience's terror.

In a minute the Slow Town inhabitants were breaking down the exits and running for their lives. Instinctively they ran towards the nearest entrance to home and safety – No Man's Land. Sanity, however, returned when they remembered the danger of using that road, especially at night.

It was while they were milling around, some fifty-odd of them, embarrassed but trying to discover what had happened in the cinema, that the only plausible explanation began to take shape. There was instant anger when they confirmed for each other that the incident in the cinema was really an attack by Suckdust.

Anger grew as they discussed the matter. A quick decision was reached; several figures melted into the darkness. The rest turned away to take the longer route through the footpaths which led home.

Suddenly the darkness was lit by several burning shacks and cries of alarm spread through Coalyard. Then the guns started playing question and answer games; sweeping for targets, dollying in crazy bursts of excitement.

Flames shot up in Slow Town. The combustion was so great that many people outside the area feared that the whole city was on fire. The police and the army were brought in to try to get the fire engines through the constant sniper activity which kept them out.

They could not pass the barricades. Even the security helicopter, with its bright searchlight hovering to help the ground troops, was ineffective; whenever it came too close, the M16s were turned against it. It was a warning to the authorities. This was their fight. They wanted no interference.

Nobody ever knew the full count of those killed that night. Next day the combined police and military patrols removed five bodies off the streets and out of the burnt-out buildings. There was speculation that some were given secret burials. The police carried out a thorough search of the unburnt buildings, took some people off to jail, beat up others, discovered small amounts of ammunition, but were unable to pacify the area.

As news of the war spread throughout the city, as the strength of the gun power became known, as the impotence of the authorities to contain the battle and its companion criminal activity was discussed, public opinion became so strident that even the faceless bosses became afraid. The monsters they had created had emancipated themselves. Orders were given to contain the gangs. They had outlived their usefulness once they could not be controlled.

While Coalyard mourned and Slow Town wept over their dead, a permanent patrol of soldiers and police was installed in a tent on the roundabout's island.

Bubbles was humiliated. He had led his gang through a previous election and there had been nothing as vicious as this. Superduper had not had such firing power and Suckdust had been largely unchallenged.

But this Pantyhose woman was deadly. She was determined to prove herself better than any man. That his gang should be held in check by one led by a woman! It was unthinkable. The hitherto cringing men of the Pantyhose Gang were now holding up their heads and boasting. Now it was Suckdust who walked around on the defensive.

Bubbles thought hard. Too much loss of face would cause his gang to want a change in leadership. This could mean his life. He began to plan a major manoeuvre to boost morale. The target would be the patrol post at the roundabout. He chose three experienced men for the diversion; Cubal, Bolo and Shanty. Himself and Sharpus, the only one he really trusted, would carry out the main action backed by Pablo and Redwood.

Like most overt military operations, the post's routine had quickly become well known. If there was no trouble they drove through the streets of Slow Town and Coalyard at three hourly intervals. At nights they used the tank backed by the helicopter, or travelled in three jeeps, well-armed and shooting at the slightest suspicious movement. Both communities were under curfew from seven in the evening to six in the morning. If there was trouble, all the vehicles converged on the spot and at such times only two men were left to guard the camp.

It was a simple matter for Cubal, Bolo and Shanty to start a shooting spree about two miles from the camp. While the jeeps were rushing to the spot, Bubbles and Sharpus would divert the attention of the guards by throwing a gasoline bomb which would set fire to the shed they used as a latrine. While the men were busy with this they would enter the tent and pass out the boxes of tear gas grenades and ammunition to Pablo and Redwood who would be waiting to transport the booty to a safe place.

It was a quick, smooth operation. Bubbles was proud of his men. They gathered at the agreed hiding place, an old hut far from the scene of the diversion, to count their gains and gloat over the ease of the operation.

Bubbles and Sharpus showed off the magazines for the automatic rifles that they had captured. They couldn't use them but it would be a severe embarrassment to the authorities. They waited for Pablo and Redwood to appear with the boxes. One hour later they were still waiting. Bubbles began to worry. The patrols would have started their search. The helicopter had arrived and had already made one pass over the hut. It was time for them to move out of the area. More worrying minutes passed. Bubbles began to suspect that something had gone wrong. He gave orders and they melted into the darkness to search for Pablo and Redwood; in spite of the curfew experienced fighters had no difficulty moving around.

Sometime later some Suckdust searchers came across Pablo and Redwood tied up in the shell of one of the burnt-out buildings. They had started moving towards the meeting place as agreed but had been jumped on by Pantyhose herself and a couple of her men. They had been tied up and the boxes taken away. It had been a quiet, efficient, totally unexpected operation by the Panty Posse.

None of Bubbles' men had ever seen him so angry. His spittle frothed as he cursed some of the vilest badwords even the most seasoned among them had heard. He was so angry that the caution essential to good leadership deserted him. He wanted immediate and total confrontation. All his firing power against hers, but Sharpus begged him to be sensible. Not only would Pantyhose be prepared for an attack, but the police and military would soon be swarming all over the place and would be only too happy to wipe them all out. In fact they would have to go into hiding immediately.

It was during the hiding period that another plan was made. If Pantyhose had not humiliated him, Bubbles would not have agreed, but she had proven herself to be more man than woman. No punishment was too harsh for her. No abuse too great.

One week later Pantyhose and three of her men: Bedward, Teddy and Three-finger Jack, who had lost two fingers when a homemade gun exploded in his hand, were returning from a small uptown mission. They were pleased at their take, thirty thousand Jamaican dollars and six thousand US without even a shot fired. The donors had been very co-operative. It had been a very good tip-off from their contact. Drunk with their success they stopped to celebrate at a friendly bar a little outside their neighbourhood. While the men were drinking stout and sharing a spliff, Pantyhose excused herself to use the toilet at the back of the premises. She was always meticulous about her privacy, never flaunting her sexuality before her men, a little prudish even.

Five minutes later the men heard her calling out to them to go on without her. She had some business, she said. They were surprised but she insisted that she was all right and would make her own way home. Since they had learned not to question her decisions, they finished their drinks and left.

What they couldn't see was that she was being held by two Suckdust men, a gun at her head and one in her back.

She didn't go with them willingly. They had to push and drag her through the yard behind the bar, into the gully and up the other side to a waiting car which sped away to the rendezvous.

There was no furniture in the hut except for a small stool on which Bubbles sat waiting, gun in hand, both judge and executioner. He would be the guard while his men took multiple revenge and disciplined Pantyhose with the ultimate insult a man could offer a woman.

They pushed Pantyhose onto the floor, Bolo ripping off her shirt in the process. She fell without resistance, sizing up the situation. Instinctively she knew that they were not planning to kill her; would not kill her unless they became frightened; that the plan was humiliation and that the best way to survive was to take the punishment as best she could.

Indeed she was not even really afraid of them. Her feelings were more of anger and contempt. She had beaten them and this was the only way they could handle it.

"Stay cool! Stay cool!" she kept telling herself, but as she watched them fumbling with zippers and underwear, awkward in their anxiety, each wanting to be first, anger exploded.

"So, the woman them a Coalyard dry-up, mek oonu have fi a tek it by force outside now?"

"Shut up!" Pablo warned as he tore at her pants. Cubal and Sharpus were still pointing their guns at her. She drew up her knees and kicked Pablo across the room. He came back, knife in hand, slashing at her pants and tearing it off.

"Bitch!" he screamed. "Try that again and you dead."

She realised that resistance was only making them hotter so she changed her tactics. As he forced her legs apart, she said in as threatening as voice as she could manage, "The man them have them orders you know. When them ketch oonu, them gwine chop off oonu buddy, piece by piece. The woman them a go do it."

The hot organ which had been forcing entry into her suddenly began to lose its power.

"Bitch! Bitch! Fuckin bitch!" Pablo screamed, grabbing the knife which he had abandoned, but Sharpus held his hand, and the cold, deadly voice of Bubbles stopped him.

"Mek a nex man go on. An oonu hurry up."

"Gag her!" Pablo said, his voice was hysterical as he stuffed his shame into his trousers. Sharpus took up her torn shirt to carry out the order but she bit him and cried out, "None a oonu no ha no mother? Oonu no ha no sister?"

It was then that Bubbles, the point of his gun shifting around his men, suddenly got up and said: "Enough! Cease! Oonu can't manage her. Me wi fix her business."

They looked at him in surprise. They couldn't imagine what he was planning to do.

"Me say fi stop!" he raised his voice at Cubal who had taken Pablo's place and was preparing to thrust. He pulled Cubal by the neck of his shirt and pointed the gun at him.

"Me will handle this," he repeated. They said that Bubbles' angry voice could put a chill in hell. His men recognised that voice. When he spoke like that you obeyed or you died.

They looked at each other in bewilderment.

"Get up!" he ordered Pantyhose.

She scrambled to her feet, trying in vain to pull up the shreds of her pants. Her breasts were bruised and there was blood on her belly where the knife had cut her.

"Wait!" he ordered his crestfallen men, and pointing the gun at Pantyhose he said, "Outside."

Now she was truly frightened because she didn't know what he had in mind. Perhaps, after all, he would be foolish enough to kill her. Neither side would survive the bloodletting that would follow. They both knew this.

But when they were outside, he took off his shirt and gave it to her. She put it on, wordless now. It fitted closely and was barely long enough to cover her naked bottom.

"Me woulda len you me pants but you too big, it not gwine fit you," he said. "Here." He gave her the gun in his hand. "You mighta need this fi reach home. But no bodder use it less you mus."

"You mad!" she exclaimed as she fitted the gun into her expert hand. "Mek you think say me won't use it pon you?"

He shrugged. His life was no longer safe. There were four disappointed and shamed men waiting for answers that would make sense of his actions. He had no sensible answers for them. He had forfeited their trust. Now he could only rule by added force and terror and he knew that could last only for a time.

"Get out!" he said, showing her another gun in his left hand. She hadn't seen the movement which had brought out the second gun. "You never hear say that me lef han badder than me right?" he asked. "Me a go bus two shot, but no notice it. Gwan."

Creature of the criminal night she melted into the darkness, and he heard her voice saying, "Me gwine member this." But he couldn't tell whether she meant the abduction or his attempts to help her.

After that night, Bubbles lived as if he was a marked man. He expected treachery from any source. The women guardians were told to be even more careful. Nobody could enter the compound without first surrendering their weapons. Among his men he was always tense and, even as they whispered rebellion among themselves, they knew that he wouldn't hesitate to shoot the minute he suspected any of plotting against him.

The urgent need to abandon the hut that night had prevented any discussion. His men were not fooled by his brief explanation that he had shot at Pantyhose but missed. Bubbles never missed. He was right in supposing that his days of leadership were numbered. The threat would come from Pablo who since that shameful night had assumed an especially boastful attitude.

Bubbles rarely went on missions with them any longer. A man could easily get shot in the back or be set up for capture by the law. They began to make mistakes. One night, they were caught breaking into a supermarket and Pablo was shot dead. The rebellion, temporarily leaderless, lost its momentum.

Although he had suspected Pablo's intention, and would not have hesitated to shoot him, Bubbles was sad when he heard of his death. He sat for a long time contemplating the futility of the game they were playing; directed and controlled by the big bosses, who were faceless like ghosts, who risked nothing at all. Not even their names could be called, for who would believe or give evidence?

Nomination day came and both communities were heavily involved in a show of strength: intimidating, threatening, booing, and promising the better life that their particular bossman had sold them.

But it wasn't only Bubbles who kept out of direct action.

Pantyhose too, who, before the rape attempt had never sent her men on a mission unaccompanied, was now scarcely seen on the streets.

A kind of wait-and-see attitude set in among the gangs, so that the area that was expected to go up in flames showed only a few smoke signals. Nobody could understand what had happened, though the security officials praised themselves for having at last brought the gangs under control. There were still some minor skirmishes and some missions, for people had to eat, but the scale of violence was so reduced that the bossmen became alarmed. How could their side ensure victory if the gangs had stopped doing their work?

Election day came and though there were threats from diehard party followers and several ballot boxes were stolen and electoral officers intimidated, the only shots fired in Coalyard or Slow Town were by a policeman alarmed at the size of the crowd which had descended on the polling station he was guarding.

When the results for the island were known, Slow Town's party had won.

Bubbles sat in the front room of his house listening to the sounds of celebration coming from Slow Town that night. Two of the women and his mother were with him. The room had no light, reflecting their gloom. It wasn't just that their side had lost, but that he had a sense of the futility of all their efforts. He was twenty-four and he had a strong feeling that he wouldn't live to see twenty-five.

His mother, mistaking the cause of his sadness, said:

"Them can gwan mek noise. Tidday fi you, tomorrow fi me. By a morning the bossman them figet say them help them get in. Wait and see."

Bubbles nodded. It was true. Life would not improve for the majority of the ghetto people, no matter which side won. A little more talk; a little more work for some, perhaps; but never enough to make a real difference. The only way was for the ghetto people to help themselves. He recalled the lessons when he was twelve. But how could they help themselves when they spent all their time fighting one another? The recent campaign had created so much bitterness; there had been so much loss of life; could they ever forget? And if the gangs gave up their guns and the war and lost the support of the bosses, how would the communities survive? This kind of thinking confused him.

The very next day, the new power ordered peace in the ghettos and declared amnesty for all gunmen provided they turned in their guns. The word went out that if they didn't obey, the full wrath of the security forces would be turned against them.

Tired from the battle and lacking the forceful leadership they had once enjoyed, a fair number of gunholders did turn in their guns and when the new boss declared that he wanted a peace ceremony, the communities agreed without protest.

Immediately the organisers went to work. It would be a spectacular event to show the world that what had been almost a civil war had truly come to an end. The acknowledged gang leaders would be there; the clergy would be there; reggae stars would be there; and since Slow Town and Coalyard had been among the worst offenders, the party would be held on the roundabout and roads in that area.

There were some in the gangs who wanted to maintain the badman image; who wanted the war to continue, but they reluctantly had to agree that the time was no longer right and that it would be better for them to keep a low profile, for the time being, anyway.

Celebration day arrived. The women from both sides cooked kerosene tins of mannish water, curried goat, boiled bananas, rice and peas and chicken. Donations for the feast poured in from the business places, glad that the gangs had decided on peace. One firm donated a truckful of drinks; and the boxes housing the amplifiers were so big it seemed as if all of Kingston would be sharing the musical part of the celebration.

The next day's papers would show the climactic moment when four of the leaders of the ghetto gangs held hands on the stage while the crowd cheered. There was another picture of Bubbles and Pantyhose in a symbolic embrace of peace.

The next day's papers would carry another story also.

As Bubbles and Pantyhose embraced and their followers cheered, she said to him, "Me have something me want show you up a yard."

"What?" he asked suspiciously, from habit. He had not seen her since the night they had tried to discipline her.

"Jus something," she replied.

In the spirit of the new peace he agreed to accompany her, so they left the celebrations in full swing and walked up the street which led to her home. Only the henchmen noted this.

"You know," Bubbles said as he looked around, "Is the first time me come over Slow Town bout five year now."

"Me know," she replied. "Is really time we stop the foolishness. Is only the big man a profit anyway. Is like duppy a follow the res a we."

"Me did want fi wear a dress," she said, irrelevantly, "but me did think say nobody never see me in a dress so long, them wouldn't know me."

He smiled politely.

"So me put on this outfit instead. You like it?"

He looked at her white shirt and pants stuffed into blue boots and wondered why it was important whether he liked it or not.

"Me wear white fi show the peace. Battle time done."

Bubbles looked around him curiously as he walked with Pantyhose. Slow Town had suffered the same scarring and destruction as Coalyard. They were both war-torn and desolate with burnt-out shells of houses, abandoned huts, junk and debris everywhere. Some sections looked like the ghost towns of a western movie.

He wondered again how they could be so foolish as to destroy each other solely for somebody else's benefit. People who didn't care about them. When war suited them they declared it. When peace suited them they demanded it.

"Puppets on a string": a phrase from a popular song jumped into his head.

"Puppets!" he said aloud. "That's all."

"Come in no," Pantyhose invited him. They had stopped before a neat concrete nog house with a short walkway, red and shining from a recent polish.

"You house nice," he said, as she opened the door with her key.

"Everybody out a street," she said unnecessarily.

He wondered what it was she wanted to show him so urgently, and why she was behaving so strangely.

"Me a give up the posse," she said. "Me a go settle down. Open a shop at the corner and turn respectable." She laughed loudly. "Me might even start go a church. New Converts a open back them church since the violence stop."

He smiled. He wasn't very interested in her plans. He didn't know what plans to make.

"What bout you?"

"Me don't think bout it yet," he lied.

"Come in here," she said, leading him into a small bedroom. There was a dresser with bottles neatly arranged and a vase with gerberas in the centre. The bed had on a heavy pink chenille spread. It didn't look like the headquarters of a tough gang leader, he thought.

"Me have drinks, if you want some."

He noticed that she seemed to be getting more and more nervous.

"You did want to show me something?"

She laughed.

"Me kinda nervous, you know. Is long time me no have no man. Not since Hotfoot dead. Him wasn't me real brother, you know. We did only grow in the same yard."

"Anyway me never did get fi say thanks that night when you stop the man them from rape me. Me no know what woulda happen if them did get them way. All now we wouldn't de ya. Me never tell nobody you know. You was a real gentleman. Me did think say that maybe we coulda jus figet everything."

Bubbles backed away from the outstretched hand in amazement. He knew that woman's look. The look which said that she was ready to offer herself, the most precious gift she owned. It was so unexpected that he nearly laughed out loud.

She got up from the bed, pulled back the spread, settled the pillows and started to take off her clothes.

"Jus as cheap we tek the little privacy while them all outa street." She was sure of a positive response.

Bubbles collected himself He wasn't sure why, but in his new mood of uncertainty he felt he might as well play the game with her. He had no interest but perhaps she could be of use to him in the future. Long ago he had learned how to cope with similar situations: with women who felt that they had to have intimate contact with him and who for one reason or the other it suited him to accommodate.

He went over to the bed and sat on the edge. Pantyhose pulled him down. Suddenly transformed into a trembling animal, she unbuttoned his shirt and forced him to take it off. In order to prevent her taking off anything else he went to work on her immediately, kneading her breasts, touching all the right places expertly.

It was funny, he thought, almost with contempt, how all women were reduced to animals at times like this. He could never have imagined that this was the powerful woman who had so frustrated him; mocked him. He could hardly believe that this was the same woman now wetting his fingers and writhing and moaning at his touch. Assaulted, yes; forced, yes; but never this giving, this yielding, this complete abandonment of self to another.

"Me no do this so long, me hungry," she panted, pulling his head down and kissing him wildly.

After a while she whispered. "Come we do it now, no." He didn't respond except to increase the pressure of hand and the rhythm of his fingers.

"Me can't discharge like this," she moaned, so he moved his head downward.

"No! Do it now!" she exclaimed and grabbed at his trousers. There was nothing to feel. He shifted away and continued stroking her but she had stopped responding and when he looked at her she was staring at him.

"Jesus Christ! Me never did believe them. Is true what them say. Them eunuchize you! Me never wan believe them." Her eyes were a little wet; there were tears close by, but he didn't see them.

What he thought he heard was contempt and suddenly his old mad reaction surfaced. He got up abruptly and went to stare through the small window, his back to her. She wanted to hold him close like a mother, to comfort him, to tell him that it was all right, but she read his reaction as rejection and her mood suddenly changed to anger.

"Cho! you shoulda tell me say you couldn't do it, and me wouldn't bother waste me time!"

The tensing of his shoulder muscles warned her a second before he turned around, animal rage on his face, gun in hand.

"Stop it!" he shouted and fired hitting her in the belly.

She was almost as quick. There was a gun under her pillow. Her first shot went through his right arm and the gun fell but in one motion he retrieved it with his left. He fired again and the bullet, jerking her body as it entered, caused her return shot to lodge in his heart. He cracked his head against the bedpost as he fell.

"Hell!" he thought. That he had survived so many battles only to be killed by a woman!

In his waning consciousness he thought he heard her calling him, weakly, "Bubbles! Bubbles!" But then it could have been his mother. It sounded like his mother's voice calling him that day he had shot Manatee.

The crack on his head opened a memory path leading back through his life and the lives of all the ancestors: to Papa Tee, a regular bullbucker and duppy conqueror chopping at human flesh; swearing at mothers with babies he had no intention of supporting; swearing in frustration in the line at the docks – no work this week, again! The blood leaking from him belonged to all of them – to Johnson, Papa Tee's father working the piece of land on the hillside which barely gave him enough to eat; to Cris-Cris, digging earth and coughing blood in a strange Spanish-speaking country; to Maas Sam, the obeah man at whom ghosts laughed; to William, chased off the estate because he asked for more wages; to all of them passing swiftly back into time; back to Jacob, the runaway slave pausing under a tree to rearrange his human burdens so that he could make a faster escape into the forest, up into the mountains to freedom.

Jacob realised that Miriam would not be able to walk any further. In fact she seemed to have fainted away. Her eyes were closed and she was barely holding the infant. Any moment it would roll out of her hands. He would have to carry her. They could not stay there. It was too close to the plantation. He did not doubt his strength but what would he do with the infant? He was still too far away from the first lookout to expect to run into a patrol which would help him carry them up to the town. He cursed his stupidity for not bringing a companion, but he didn't want them to know lest they objected and he hadn't expected to find Miriam with a baby and so weak. What could he do?

The faint moonlight and his nose led him to a guava tree close by. As he reached up to pick the fruit, a distant memory flared for a moment. "You fi spin roun tree time." He shrugged it away, picked a fruit and rubbed it with his fingers as he thought about his problem.

Suddenly the image of women working in the field floated into his head. They had babies safely tied in slings on their backs.

That is what he would do. Make a sling for the pickney, put it on his back and carry the mother in his arms.

He looked around. What could he use for a sling? It had to be cloth. His shirt was too short. He couldn't use the blanket as he needed to keep Miriam sheltered from the cold mountain night air. He looked at her clothing. He would have to use her under-skirt. Lucky that she still dressed as if she was a privileged kitchen slave.

He lifted her frock and fumbled for the string which he knew tied the petticoat at the waist. How many times had he done this under different circumstances. He half-expected her to slap away his hand in mock dismissal, as she used to do, but she remained in her faint. He would have to go fast. She needed help; woman help.

His nose wrinkled in disgust as he pulled off the petticoat and smelled the unpleasantness of a bleeding woman, but he couldn't afford to be finicky now.

He tied the petticoat this way and that over his shoulder, trying to get it right before putting the baby in. Eventually he felt that he had a satisfactory hammock and, putting the still sleeping infant in it, he carefully put his arms through, trying to remember that it wasn't ground provisions that he was carrying. He hoped the child would not suffocate. Then he bent down, lifted Miriam and started his arduous climb.

MERLE COLLINS

MAPPING

When Mr Moses shows them the map of Paz, she thinks the island looks like a leaf, a long, scraggly leaf, drifting to the right-hand side when you hold it up in your hand. Her friend Sharpey says the island is like a yam. It does look a bit like a long yam when you pull it out of the ground, before you peel it and cut it up to put in the pot. But yam makes her think brown, and the map Mr Moses shows them is all green, with place names written in black all around, and a black PAZ in the middle.

When Mr Moses brought out the map to talk about the geography of Paz, what she thought of was the way her mother said, when she was talking to herself sometimes, "Nothing to show for it, but I map this country with my work. I walk from stem to stern, working for high-up people and dragging my children with me. Name the place in this Paz, I work there!"

Where they are now, Providence, is just below the word Paz, under the middle on the right-hand side. She can't find the exact name of the place where her grandmother lives, Hideout Hill, but she knows it is right near that place called Leaping Lift, at the top of the map. Leaping Lift is the capital of St Camillus, and that is her grandmother's parish. The capital of the country, Paz City, is on the left-hand side near the bottom, near the squiggly part where you could put your fingers to hold up the leaf, or grip the yam. She has never been to Paz City, but she knows that the high-up people live there, the Governor and people like that. Her mother says that she used to work with a family in Paz City once, before Doux was born. "Nothing to show for it, non, but I map this country with my sweat and my tears. You never know how life will meet you."

Doux looks at the spot named Providence, the place her mother is mapping with her work now. Her mother goes to wash their clothes in Providence River and sometimes, when her mother can't go, she, Doux, takes them there. For some reason, her grandmother, Mama, won't keep her in the house in Hideout Hill like she keeps the other two sometimes. So wherever her mother works, she is like a dress-band dragging behind. That is what her mother says. "Wherever I go, you like a dressband dragging behind me." Doux looks at the map of Paz and imagines her mother walking across it, with a dress-band trailing behind her. Mr Moses pulls the map to one side, and begins to talk about something else. About goats, and a ledge.

Doux is big for Standard Two. Most of the other children in the class are eight, or some even nine. Her best friend, Sharpey, is nine. Sharpey was born in 1922, two years after Doux.

For a change, this time, her mother has all her children living with her. She is a baker for Mr Jimmy's shop right here in Providence, just down the road from the school, and she has a whole house to stay in, so all of them can stay together. Her mother, Mr Jimmy's baker, sells bread to all the shops in the area, and sometimes, on a Saturday, she and Sister carry baskets of bread on their heads to the other shops. One good thing this time is that she, her sister and her brother go to school every day. Sometimes her mother can't manage to buy the books, but she thinks children must go to school, so she doesn't keep them at home. Her mother says, "You have to show me real evidence that you dying, for me to tell you stay home. And if you dying," she says, "we could call somebody to make the coffin. I want you children to go to school and see if you could find out how to put money in your pocket! It have a secret there, and I want you to get it!" So now, even on Monday and Friday, Doux is at school. Trying to find out secrets about how to put money in her pocket.

"Doux! Doux Thibaut! You with us?" Mr Moses is standing over her desk, tapping in the palm of his left hand with the long ruler he holds in his right. Doux sits up and glances across at her friend, Sharpey. Mr Moses is asking a question. Sharpey's finger lingers under the title of the lesson. Mr Moses asks, "What did I say the homework is?" Sharpey's finger is right under a sentence.

"Two goats met on a narrow ledge, sir!"

"Good!" Mr Moses swings away, looking for another victim. Over his shoulder, he says, "Pay attention, Doux!"

"Yes, sir." Doux smiles gratefully at Sharpey.

Mr Moses is the Standard Two teacher. Today he gives the class reading to do for homework, reading and spelling, because usually the spelling goes with the reading. Doux doesn't have *Royal Reader Book Two*, the book with the homework, but Sharpey has the book. The lesson is about two goats. Two cabrit, one child giggles, because that is what they call the children from the Catholic school, *français cabrit*, french goat. And the Catholic children call them *cochon*, pig. *Anglais cochon*, they say, English pig. In the first part of the story, Sharpey explains, the two goats meet on a narrow ledge over a high cliff, and there isn't enough room for them to either turn back or go on together. But they are nice to each other. One of them lies down to let the other one pass, and then that one gets up and goes over, so that both goats end up bounding about the meadow and enjoying the sweet grass. Two Catholic goats, they giggle, enjoying the sweet grass. They have to read the second part of the lesson and learn to spell the words for Monday. Right after school, Sharpey lets Doux write down the homework from her book. In exchange, because she is good at plaiting hair, Doux promises Sharpey that she will ask her mother to let her go up the road to Sharpey's aunt's house this Saturday, in the evening, after she carries the bread to the shops. She will plait Sharpey's hair in cornrow. She writes down the lesson on both sides of her slate.

> Two other goats had left the valley, and climbed far up the mountain. At length they met on the banks of a wild, rushing stream. A tree had fallen across the stream, and formed a bridge from the one side to the other.
>
> The goats looked at each other, and each wished to pass over first.
>
> They stood for a moment with one foot on the tree, each thinking that the other would draw back. But neither of them would give way, and they met at last on the middle of the narrow bridge!

Even though she is writing small on her slate for the homework to fit, Doux has no more room after that, but Gift, her brother, is waiting, and she borrows his slate to write the rest.

> They then began to push and fight with their horns,
> till at last their feet slipped, and both the goats fell into
> the swift flowing stream, and were lost in the waters!
> Both might have been saved, if either of them had
> known how to yield at the right time.

On Saturday morning, Doux doesn't have to wash in the river. Her mother says she will have Monday off from the shop, so she will wash then. After Doux and her sister Selma finish cleaning the house and helping Gift to sweep up the leaves in the yard, all the children do their homework. Their mother believes that children must always have enough time to do their homework, so she doesn't mind. That is another thing Doux likes about staying with her mother. Her mother understands things that other people she stayed with couldn't understand. Her mother doesn't think Doux is idle just because she isn't doing something in the house or cleaning up the yard.

Doux learns to spell the words Mr Moses told them to underline – "stream", "length", "bridge", "horns" and "ledge". If Mr Moses calls her to read, or to spell, she will be ready. She has to give Gift his slate for school on Monday morning, so she learns by heart the part of the lesson that she wrote on Gift's slate.

> They then began to push and fight with their horns,
> till at last their feet slipped, and both the goats fell into
> the swift flowing stream, and were lost in the waters!
> Both might have been saved, if either of them had
> known how to yield at the right time.

When she is done, Doux goes up the trace to Sharpey's aunt's house and keeps her promise to plait Sharpey's hair. Later that evening, she and Selma help make up the baskets and carry bread to shops in the area. Selma makes two trips, but then she is tired, so Doux continues alone for two more trips, one to a shop on the

Providence Main Road, and another one to a shop just lower down, off the Providence Road and along a track.

First thing when it is time for Reading and Spelling on Monday morning, Mr Moses calls on Doux to read. She picks up her slate, relieved because the part he has asked her to read is the part she has on her slate, and not the one that was on the slate she has returned to Gift. She learned that part off by heart, it's true, but at least she has this one here on her slate to read.

Mr Moses says, "Child, put down the slate and read the lesson."

Doux stands with her mouth open and the slate in her hand.

Mr Moses says, "Young lady, I'm waiting."

Doux lifts the slate again and stands looking at it. She opens her mouth. Mr Moses says, "Put down the slate, child, and pick up your book." If Sharpey weren't at home sick today, she would just pick up Sharpey's book and read from it. Mr Moses is walking towards her. Doux can see him out of the corners of her eyes, but she doesn't look up. She stands there, still, looking down at her slate. She is suddenly feeling very tall, very big and stupid, with all the little children turned around in their seats, looking back at her, waiting to see what will happen. The cut of the whip across her back surprises her. She jumps and cries out because it hurt through her thin dress and because she is surprised. Mr Moses always threatens, but he is not a teacher who beats much. And besides, she has done the homework. Doux puts the slate down on the desk, puts her hands up to her face, and begins to cry.

Mr Moses picks up the slate and stands looking at it. He looks for a long time, as if he can only read slowly. He turns the slate over and reads the other side. He pulls a breath deep into his lungs, holds it, and stands there with his eyes closed. He opens his eyes and stands for a moment looking down at the head of the sobbing girl, at the two big plaits, the print dress, the hands held to the face in shame. He looks up at the eyes fixed on them, around at the silent, waiting faces, at the apprehensive looks that say, *I hope is not me next.*

Mr Moses says, "Come, child, come outside." He touches her arm to guide her, and then turns away, walking toward the door. Her hands still up to her face, the child follows him, sobbing, walking slowly. The slate still in his hand, Mr Moses walks to the door at the right-hand side in front of the class. He walks through the door, watches her follow him through, leans back inside and says, "Learn your spelling. Kenneth, you're in charge. Make sure there's no noise while I'm out here." Mr Moses pulls the door almost closed behind him, and then he goes to stand by the railing. He looks at the little girl still sobbing with her hands to her face, and he pulls in his lips, biting the bottom one as if he, too, will start crying. He puts the slate under his arm, puts both hands on the railing and stands looking down into the empty schoolyard. When he looks back, she is wiping her eyes with the palms of her hands. She jumps and takes a step back as he turns.

Mr Moses says, "I won't beat you. I shouldn't have hit you. I didn't know you had done the homework." She sniffs, stands looking at him.

He is looking down at the slate, turns it over and reads. He asks, "When did you write this?"

"Friday, sir. I borrow Sharpey book and I write out the lesson."

"Where is your book?"

"Sorry, sir. My mother say when she get some money, when Mr Jimmy pay her, she will buy a book for me, but she don't have it yet."

Mr Moses looks at the child for a long time. He looks at the faded red and white print dress with one band trailing, at the four big plaits of hair arranged neatly on her head, down at her bare feet, back at the face streaked with tears. He puts up his hand and seems to be trying to loosen the knot of the red, white and blue tie lying against his white, short-sleeved shirt. He turns away and stands looking away into the distance, the slate under his arm and his hands in the pockets of his dark brown pants. He turns back, clears his throat and says, "Child, I would not have hit you if I knew you had the lesson on your slate. I thought it was just defiance why you weren't answering. And I remember that last week you weren't paying attention. Why didn't you tell me?"

"I didn't have a book, sir," she tells him, as if this explains everything. The tears are in her eyes again.

Mr Moses says, "It's alright. After school today, come to the staff room and I will give you a book that you can use for the rest of the term. Okay? Tell your mother that she won't have to buy a book for you. And – Doux – child, I'm very sorry. I didn't know." And then he asks, gently, "You know the spelling words?"

"Yes, sir."

"Okay. Stop crying. Go back to your seat now."

"Yes, sir."

When she goes back into the class, heads turn. The children watch Doux's face to see what they can read there. There is a general murmur and Kenneth, the little Indian boy sitting at the front of the class, lifts his voice and says, "Sir say stay quiet!" The noise dies down. Doux goes to her desk, sits down, puts her head on her hands and sits looking at her slate.

Mr Moses actually said he was sorry, and teachers supposed to beat, so they don't tell children they are sorry! Mr. Moses said he was sorry!

When he comes back into the class, he doesn't ask her to spell a word right away. But before the bell rings, he asks her to spell "ledge". Doux doesn't even stumble over the spelling like some of the other children have done. She just spells it right out, one letter after the other, her voice confident and strong. Mr Moses says, "Very good." And then he says to the whole class, "I made a mistake when I hit Doux. I realise now that she really knows her homework." And all the other children turn around and look at her. Mr Moses tells them strange things sometimes, like when he said he doesn't really like to beat, but this is the strangest of the strange. Mr Moses seems to be saying he was wrong, and they don't know what to do with that news. It is a good thing the bell rings right at that time. Doux runs out to go and find Selma and get something for break.

She cannot forget that Mr Moses said he was sorry. She wonders now if she should tell him that every time he brings out his map and talks to them about what the country looks like, she thinks about her mother. She wonders if she should tell Mr Moses that her mother says she maps the whole country with her work, from stem to stern. She tells Selma and the two of them use the dictionary Mr Moses leaves on his desk to find out what "stem" and "stern" mean.

Doux says, "From just how she say it, I know it was two different end, but I didn't realise it had to do with boat." Selma says, "I thought it had to do with a flower, but Paz in the middle of the sea, so is like a boat in truth!"

Mr Moses finds them there, laughing at their discovery, leaning on the desk during the break, looking at his dictionary. They jump when they see him, and look ready to run away, but Mr Moses says, "It's alright, it's okay. That's why I have the dictionary there, so you can find out the meaning of words."

JACQUELINE CROOKS

COOL BURN

Roaring River 1908

Mrs Lulla is sitting on the steps of the barracks. It is harvesting time, and the north wind has set in. There is blackness in her heart. Blackness blooming across the cane fields. Long-time-back smoke rising.

The overseer's bell rings out across the plantation. Five more hours loading trash onto the carts. Five more days burning cane. Three more weeks before her husband will be freed. She squinches her eyes against the black smoke and looks at the labourers sharpening their machetes. They are standing under the extended roof of the labourers' barracks. From the moment their feet touched the island they were not the same.

Nor was she.

"Accha! Let them sharpen." Nothing was sharp and dark as the kohl around her eyes, which flicked up at the corners like horns.

She *aiiiee-aiiieee's* to the dancing girls squatting by the chulah, rolling chapattis. They twirl wrists, jangle their beaded necks in response.

She slurps ganja tea from a bowl. Smacks her lips, clenches her eyes as the ganja lights her gut.

She is taken back to the cold of another lifetime. And there he is, the same husband.

"Why does he follow me through lifetimes?" she asks aloud. "With that long face of his, hollowed-out like a begging bowl!"

She cannot remember her name in that lifetime of creaking ice islands, but she thinks she was the same as she is now – tiny, wire-waist; bead-eyed. Holding out a piece of charred wood, she tells her same-husband, "Put protection around your eyes."

They are standing at the edge of the ice-jumbled Chukchi Sea. Blue sun. Indigo sky. In the distance, black fur-covered specks walk on the smoking ice, loading canoas with blubber and chaga.

"Wife, listen to me," the same-husband says. He pushes the charred wood from his face.

"Fire protection for mind," she says.

He grabs the stick, throws it onto the ice. "We will be cursed if we leave."

"Spirit can go anywhere," she says. She looks beyond at the ice floes floating south, glinting with the promise of unknown worlds. Behind them lie the wet-sedge meadows and shallow ponds of their Siberian village. Some of their people refused to leave. They lit peat fires and prayed for the souls of those departed. Watched as the Katabatic wind covered their tracks.

She cannot feel what happened next in that lifetime. They must have boarded the canoas because the next thing she sees are storms in the sky. The hollow of her same-husband's face becomes the night-sky filled with star dust.

He did not make it to the new world.

Mrs Lulla drains the ganja tea, takes a handful of roasted cashews from her lehenga and shakes them in her hands like dice. "If I bury same-husband again we will meet in next lifetime. Again, again," she thinks. She knows she must save her same-husband if she is to be free of him in lifetimes to come.

She knows, too, that the tin roof prison that he is in will boil out the little life that is left in his bones.

She throws the dregs of the ganja on the ground and twists her small bare feet into the damp earth. The labourers walk past, their machetes glinting. Staring at her, black juice seeping from their burning eyes.

Later in the night, when all the men are sleeping, it is safe for her to climb into her cot, but not safe to sleep. She keeps her small lantern burning. Nothing more than a rotting partition board separates her from the labourers in the barracks. She hears their chests rattling; smells their breaths and overheated bodies.

Her same-husband is in prison for running away.

He'd chopped his way downriver, trying to get back to the sea, to India. To Hariharpur.

His chiggoe feet and hookworm belly hadn't taken him far.

She dreams far and wide with her eyes open. Dreams her dead, wart-riddled mother is throwing scalding cane juice into her face, screaming about the shame of prison.

Mrs Lulla gets out of her cot, her face burning.

"Who are you to say this?" she hisses to her dead mother. "You had no shame."

She remembers how, as a small child, she ran away, trying to get beyond the vermillion dust of Hariharpur. Her mother would drag her back by her hair, shouting: "Worthless girl. You bring shame!"

Her mother – henna-haired, nose-ringed and bull-headed – was the most shameless woman she had known. There was no one her mother would not bribe. Nothing and no one she would not sell.

Nothing too small to avenge.

Mrs Lulla leaves the barracks, goes out into the foggy night air of the mountains. One or two fires are still burning in the cane fields. White egrets fly close, swooping and pecking at the insects that fly out of the flames.

With quick, small steps, past the boiling house, the mill and trash houses, she drags the angry face of her mother behind her.

She comes to the Big House. She believes that Massah Sleifer is one kind of man in the cool comforts of the plantation house and another in the accounting barracks where he spends his evenings during the burning time, close to the smoke and stench. And why not? Hadn't she been another person in her mother's mud hut in the village of Hariharpur?

Who was she now?

She can no longer see her dead mother's face, but she can smell her cardamom-and-amla-oil spirit in the smoldering air. "Go!" she hisses.

She goes up the wooden steps of the accounting barracks and steps inside. An old-time plantation whip hangs on the door, its cowhide tail swinging.

Massah Sleifer looks up from the dim light of the desk lamp. He sees her and his mouth turns up like a sugar bowl. The accounting books are open in front of him. Half a bottle of white rum, a plate of gizadas.

She stays close to the door.

"Too many men in the barracks, Mrs Lulla?"

"I cannot sleep without my husband, and with the sour breath of men in my face."

He stands up. "Plantations need women, not wives."

She holds out her hands, palms upwards. "You have taken my husband. I am in the hands of God."

Massah Sleifer gets up, walks away from the pool of lamplight by the desk and his squat shadow rises up and follows. He points to fireflies hovering inside the room by the open jalousies. "Look there, they take refuge from the cane fires. In my father's time, life here was different for our women. We held great dances in the Big House. Our women wore fireflies – alive. Living jewels of fire and light. All women are fire, I think."

Mrs Lulla takes the whip off the door. Runs a section through her fingers as if she is assessing the finest silk. She imagines the burn of it against skin. "You are the one turning day to night with black snow," she says.

"Mrs Lulla, you are not a preacher and I am not the converted. I know what you want. You people think I am hard, but the authorities don't want crimes to go unpunished. Your husband stays in his prison."

She wonders whether with one-two-three *lassshhh*, like a Goddess, she can transform the room. But there is no fire in her, only smoke.

Massah Sleifer gives her a glass of the rum and she drinks it.

"Ganja better for my spirit," she says.

"Rum keeps the ghosts away," he replies. He puts his glass on the side table.

She knows he will not speak of the thing that all the labourers are talking about: the strike on the Seaford estate, on the other side of the island. The plantation manager had been killed trying to stop a riot. His skull had been broken. His eyes taken out.

She squinches her kohl protected eyes on Massah Sleifer. If she takes out his grey eyes with the tail of the whip he would stop staring at her. He would stop saying, "You people!"

She walks towards the jalousies, looks at the living jewels weaving trails of light in the smoky air. Like the lighted ghats on the river near Hariharpur.

She left Hariharpur with her same-husband two years ago. They travelled by bullock cart to Calcutta in the summer, through saffron dust storms and thunder. Spent three weeks inside the walled New Garden Depot where she hawked and spat from her dry throat, afraid to drink the globby water that was drawn from tanks.

"Everything has the hand of God in it," she said to her husband as they went into the agent's room. The recruiters in the yard below were shouting, "No dwarfs. No scarecrows!"

She felt sure her same-husband would be told he was a scarecrow. Her mother had called him worse, even though she had promised her to him, an old-man Dholi, when she was eight.

The agent sized her same-husband up with an east-to-west shake of his head. "Wiry-tough is good. Go to your fortune."

Mrs Lulla pressed her thumbprint on the indenture warrant. Her husband was as still as a votive figure.

She lashed her hawker's tongue at him, "Bhains ki aulad boot-nee ka."

"Chup! Chup!" He shouted. He did not look at her as he pressed his thumbprint on the warrant that neither of them could read.

A week later they boarded the SS Ganges, a steamship loaded with scribes and weavers, soldiers and dancing girls.

Four months later they arrived on the island. A truck ride through forested mountains, before the final ridge from where they looked down at a flat valley. A twisting, silver river. Massah Sleifer's sugar plantation.

Massah Sleifer pulls her back, tugs her onto the day bed beside him. He takes the whip from her hand and places it on the pillow as if he is putting it to sleep.

She hears the cries of crickets and cicadas escaping their burrows in the bush of the lowlands.

Massah Sleifer takes her face between his hands and squeezes until her black-protected eyes bulge.

She sees that his eyes are filled with the numbers of his accounting books. She holds his stare and the numbers fall from his eyes and she is able to see the darkness of his own journey, the migration of his German people a hundred years ago from their land. The same tin tickets, rations. Crowded steamships with rotten partitions that did nothing to protect their women.

Massah Sleifer pushes her onto her back.

She thinks, "This grinding season. All cutlass thrash and thrust. Breaking my body for land. What have I become?" She remembers her mother's hawker tongue.

"Grinding season hard," she says. "Plenty cane to cut, Massah Sleifer."

He is on top of her. "Two hundred and eighty acres," he whispers in her ear, "seventeen point one a piece. I will give you two days holiday when all is done."

"Strong hands not easy to find in these times," she says. "And we Indians good at strike."

"What is that you are saying?"

"We can strike good, like the Indians on Seaford plantation."

Massah Sleifer rolls over, sits up, clicks his wrists. "Woman, don't play with me tonight."

"It is bad when an honest Indian is put in prison like a criminal. It is a great shame for our people. The Indians say they will strike." The Indians had not said this, but she decided she could play with numbers too. "If Indians strike, you have to hire Creoles for harvesting, and them is more shillings than a Coolie."

Massah Sleifer takes the whip and lashes it at the fireflies, breaking up their trail of light. "Madam Lulla, take your husband tomorrow. But be careful. Plantations can be dangerous places for wives."

"God is good."

She does not go back past the Big House, or the cane fields. She walks towards Roaring River village and crosses the old Spanish bridge to the river.

Women stooping at the shore, lighting votive boats, placing them on the river where they sail south into darkness.

She is not sure what lifetime she is seeing.

KWAME DAWES

IN THE GULLY

I

She scrambled down the gravel path, her bag bouncing against her bottom. The path was dusty and her shoes lost their sheen as she skidded on the steeper slopes. Near the bottom of the path she slowed herself down by grabbing onto a hanging branch. Her feet gave way and she sat down suddenly on her bag. She laughed to herself, then looked up the hillside to see if anyone was watching. She saw no one, just a haze of slowly falling dust particles landing on the thick clumps of bush that barely survived on this stony slope. To her left, the sound of traffic was faint above her.

Carefully, she regained her footing and continued to move down slowly, keeping as close to the wall as possible and trying not to look over the edge until she was almost at the gully bottom. As she got closer, she increased her pace until she was sprinting at full speed onto the cracked concrete floor. Her footsteps echoed in the empty space. She stopped in the middle and then looked around. From where she stood she could see the line of the gully for a few chains until it vanished around a sharp corner. She knew that it stretched for miles until it came to the sea. Just above the corner was a bridge. People walked across it like tiny insects.

The walls rose fifteen feet above her. There were huge cracks where shrubs and large trees had pushed their way through the concrete. Enough silt and topsoil had accumulated from decades of rains to sustain a series of small forests. At the sides of the gully larger clumps of thick bush grew, some with vines that crawled up the sides of the grey walls. These had so weathered that their surface was pocked with holes big enough to take the toe of a man's shoe. Grass poked out of these holes. In the middle of the

gully was a smaller canal that ran its entire length, also disappearing around the corner. It too was filled with debris and sand, in
which more trees had started to grow.

She moved quickly to the clump of bushes on the side where
there was a huge boulder, about her height. Under it she found
her books, hidden there on her way to school. She read them as
she walked to and from school but couldn't take them in with her
because it was a Catholic school and they did not encourage that
kind of literature.

She might have defied the school and taken the books to class
had she not been working to impress her new form mistress that
she was a good student. This teacher had said that such books
were silly and only filled your mind with nonsense, ideas about
love that were not true. She agreed with the teacher, but still
enjoyed reading her true romances. As long as the teacher did not
know, all would be well.

She picked up the books and stuffed all but one in her bag,
opened this at the right page and began reading as she walked
along the gully towards the hills. She rarely looked up because she
knew her way so well – where to stop reading and watch the path
so as not to step into black balls of goat droppings. Then she
would continue reading.

Whenever she came near the police station, she would always
stop reading. She had heard that the high wall that loomed just
above the gully with barred windows was the back wall of the
police lock-up. Sometimes she saw hands hanging from the
windows but the holes were too dark to make out faces. Here, on
the stretch of concrete above the wall, was a thick mass of barbed-
wire that rose almost as high as the windows. The wall was a faded
orange colour, with patches where raw concrete had been smeared
as if to fill holes in it.

She walked quickly past the police station and where the post
office had been before it was burnt to the ground. She walked past
the wall that protected the horses in the paddock beside the post
office from falling into the gully. Next, it bisected a small housing
district. She had to walk under a footbridge which hung over a
roadway that ran through the gully. Usually this area was busy

and quite a few cars used this roadway, uneven as it was, as a short-cut from the main road on the police station side to the residential area on the other side. She would sometimes walk into this district and buy sweets. She had a few friends from school who lived there and whenever she did not have swimming practice they would walk there together. She would continue along the gully while they went home via the roadway.

She knew quite a few people in the district. There was Caddy, and the gardener who looked after their yard; he lived in a small hut just beyond the footbridge. He had the reputation for being wild and violent, but she knew him as a friendly and gentle man. He would sit by himself on the gully wall, smoking herb. When he saw her, he would smile and nod. She was always afraid he would fall off. He never did. Sometimes he would come down to talk to her. She also knew some of the "rude" boys who hung around the bars and the side shops in the area or played cricket in the gully. They had been her schoolmates in primary school; the ones who failed the Common Entrance and were not bothering with school again. She was amazed at the way they suddenly seemed to mature. Some were growing moustaches and beards and their voices were deeper, more manly. They had been friends with whom she had stolen golf balls from the golf course and eaten unripe mangoes. Sometimes they greeted her, sometimes they didn't. She never tried to understand why; it was quite normal. She knew she was more fortunate than them and that some of them thought she was just a spoilt girl. But then they had always felt that way so it didn't bother her. Caddy, though, was always glad to see her.

After passing through this district, the gully was narrowed by thick forests on both sides for a few hundred yards. She enjoyed this area most because it was the quietest and most isolated. It was the only place where she felt safe to pee by the concrete wall without anyone seeing. Doing this in the wide open was somehow exciting, even though she only did it when she felt she couldn't wait until she got home.

She would read along this stretch, occasionally looking up to watch the dart of birds from one side to the other. She walked under another bridge that was never used by cars and then she came to the tributary that passed just behind her backyard. She climbed up the thick concrete slope, walked along the edge of the tributary for a few yards and then turned up the path that led through the short patch of bush onto an open lot. This was owned by the people who had built the house in the lot beside it. It was the largest and most elaborate house on the avenue, and the houses in the avenue were all quite large. The owners of this particular house were rich. The man was a politician and his sons all worked in the family business. All except one: Felix. Felix stayed at home.

She put her books in her bag and began to run through the open lot to the avenue. A dog from the politician's house began to bark and to paw at the fence. Felix looked out through the grill. His face was red and full of pimples and sores.

"What you doing in there?" he shouted over the dog barking.

"Nothing," she said, slowing down. She was frightened.

"I will set the dog on you, you know," he shouted back.

"Sorry," she said, moving slowly towards the avenue.

"I will set Charles on you, you know," he shouted again.

"Sorry," she said as she reached the road.

She began to run up the road. The dog chased her along the fence, jumping, barking, with a mouth full of foam.

"Get her, Charles, get her, get her!" Felix stood behind the fence screaming.

She hesitated a little near the gate. She wasn't sure if the dog could jump the gate. She started to move and it was there snarling. Soon dogs from the other houses had joined in the noise. She was terrified. She stood still, almost in tears.

"Get her, Charles. He can jump the fence, you know!" Felix was still screaming at the top of his voice.

"Call your dog, please," she said, still unable to move. "Please."

"Felix! Felix!" A woman's voice came from the back of the house. "Felix! Felix!"

"Yes, Ma."

The woman was on the verandah now. "What are you doing? What kind of nonsense is this?"

"She was trespassing. I set Charles on her. He can jump the fence." Felix was much taller than his mother. He looked down at her, his face glowing with great intensity.

"Oh, God. Felix..." She saw the girl in the white uniform standing transfixed in the road.

"Go on, little girl, the dog won't trouble you... go on. Come, Charles... Come..."

The dog stopped barking and moved towards the girl, wagging its tail. As the girl moved for the first time it suddenly barked again, but this time it was at the woman. The bark became a playful whine as the dog wagged its tail so aggressively that it seemed about to dislocate its spine. The girl did not wait. She ran at full speed towards her home. She did not look back.

That night she promised herself never to walk though the gully again. She would walk along the road and hope that Felix did not see her. She told no one about it.

But the problem with Felix and the dog did not happen again, and soon she began walking her usual way, waving to the gardener and Caddy and watching the crazy crows circle dizzily above the dry gully walls.

II

They said he was mad. He had heard that all his life and while he didn't believe it, he grew to live it. He wasn't mad. He was slow. He was different, he knew that. He was the only person who dared to kill john-crows with his catapult. Most boys said it was illegal to kill the sleek black buzzards but Caddy wanted a close-up look at this huge crow so he shot one and showed it to his friends. They were all amazed at its size and the smooth texture of the pink bald head that had buried itself in so many carcasses, but they were even more convinced that he was mad.

He was aggressive; he knew that.

The other boys expected it from him. He played cricket aggressively. He never learnt to bowl properly but he flung the ball with more force than anyone else. He batted well and so very often he spent most of the recess time batting. Few boys dared to go after a ball while he was going after it. He threw his size around and kicked, pushed and punched while trying to get the ball to bowl. His greatest pleasure was to hear the loud bang of ball on the metal desk which was their makeshift wicket.

Caddy was a black child with half-brothers and sisters who could pass for white. They, more than he, with their tattered clothing, skins reddened from walking miles in the sun, and the thick patois they spoke, were targets for bullying and abuse. They were self-evidently a worthless lot, squandering the advantage of their skin, so useless that even with their whiteness they remained hopelessly poor. There was a more deep-seated reason for their targeting for persecution. Their poverty was a threat to the almost comforting article of faith among their black neighbours that race and race alone was the cause of their poverty. If the poverty of Caddy's family was the result of their hopelessness, what then of theirs?

The bullying, though, was more intended than carried out. Caddy saw to that. He worked hard to protect his siblings, took great pains to ensure that they lived a remarkably spoilt life at school. They would complain to him and he would punish those of their friends who were unwilling to comply with their wishes.

He wasn't always called Caddy. He was called a lot of other things like 'Blacka', 'Last Night', 'Midnight', 'Bigga', 'Tar Baby', 'Maddix', 'Toughas', and a variety of other names referring either to his size, his colour or his temperament. He fought his way out of all of them. He selected 'Caddy' because he wanted to play golf himself one day and the little girl who used to walk home with them everyday said the boys walking with the golfers were called caddies. So he named himself Caddy and soon it became clear that Caddy was the only safe name to call him.

Caddy knew he wasn't very bright. He liked to read, though he read very slowly, but he hated maths and really made no effort to understand. His mother said that his father was like that too. He knew everything about his father because his mother was not the type to hide those things from her children. His father was dead. He died in jail in America, she said. He was a big construction worker who did not speak much but could fight. She was a higgler in front of the building this man was working on. They got along well, she said. She was the only person who could control him. They never lived together, but he used to visit her. When she was pregnant he went to Montego Bay to work. Then he went away to America. He got into some dark deals up there and they caught him. He died in jail. She said he was a very black man and she should have known that anything too black was worthless. Caddy, she said, was just like his father and he was going to get into the same mess if he wasn't careful. She hoped, though, that the other children would take after their father. He was white – a successful businessman who gave her money now and then. She had been a servant in his house. He did not care about his outside children. He was quite clear about that.

But she didn't dislike Caddy. In fact he knew that she loved him and depended on him. She used to beat him a lot because, according to her, his skin could take it. He didn't mind that. She didn't expect him to do very well in school and so when he repeated a few grades she did not punish him much. She just forced him to find work cutting lawns and painting houses in the afternoons. She argued with him a lot but she was rarely surprised by the things he did. Even when he said he wanted to go to extension school downtown, she said it would be okay as long as he still worked.

She heard about all the things he was supposed to have done. She knew half of them were stories – though some were true.

It was true he used to sneak into the paddock at night, lead one of the horses out and spend a good portion of the night riding it on the golf course. He stopped doing it when the owners got complaints that their horses were causing girls in the convent, which was beside the golf course, difficulty sleeping at night. He found out that most of the girls in the school had heard about his cowboy stunts on the golf course. The little girl who walked through the gully mentioned it to him one day. He was pleased that she was amused. She just laughed and said: "Boy, Caddy, you are something else."

It was also true that he was the most remarkable mango thief in the district. He went to places that most boys dared not enter.

He went into the most affluent residential areas where the dogs were the fiercest, the yards the largest. But mangoes were most abundant and sweet in those areas. He picked only pedigree mangoes: Julies with their blandly sweet, subtly aromatic but large, chunky fruit; Bombays with their tangy, fleshy fruit, and the hood-ended East Indians that that were the sweetest, juiciest mango anyone knew of. It was also true that he had killed a few dogs with stones and had gotten in trouble with the police because of this.

It was also true that Caddy was one of the boys who had burnt down the post office. When he heard that the boys wanted to cause some trouble as close to the police station as possible he was happy to join them. They wanted his help because he was daring, not to say crazy. He was the last person to leave the scene. He was impressed with the blaze. He had been pleased with himself for being a part of it, because the little girl had complained to him that the post office was inefficient and she wasn't getting her letters on time. She wasn't pleased when it had burnt down and that had upset him.

He made friends with some of the golfers, the richer older men. He became caddy for Mr. Ernest, the politician, who hired Caddy to do his lawn and garden as well as be his caddy. He encouraged Caddy to play golf and gave him his first two clubs. They were old and Mr. Ernest had gotten a new set. Caddy thought Mr. Ernest was a good man though he never allowed Caddy to get familiar. He knew Mr Ernest was also a very powerful man, not afraid to walk through the district and talk to the people because he had men there who looked after his interests. Caddy hoped that Mr. Ernest would make him one of those men soon. The men lived in Mr. Ernest's yard. They came from the district but he insisted that they stay in the small house behind the big house. They were guards for the house and they got along well with the dogs that were always chained to the twelve-foot chain-link fence behind it.

Mr. Ernest asked Caddy to befriend his son, Felix. Felix was retarded. He was the only one of Mr. Ernest's sons who was not working in his garment factory. Felix said he wasn't born that way, but the pressure was too much for him. Felix said his mother and father were wicked and ever since he was a boy they had tried to dump him. He wanted Caddy to understand this. Felix talked a lot about his family. He claimed he only told these things to Caddy but Caddy doubted it.

He would watch Caddy mowing the lawn from the grilled veranda as he squeezed his pimples and wiped the little worms that curled out of his face onto his clothes. He would call Caddy over to talk.

"My father," he began, "my father said you are a dangerous guy."

"Your father say that?" Caddy asked, after emptying a bottle of water in a few long gulps.

"Yes."

"Uhmm." Caddy looked into the sun, squinting his eyes. "Hot."

"Daddy, my father… he had another woman, you know…" He waited for a response. Caddy said nothing.

"You don' believe me? Ask mummy, my mother. She knows. It's a woman who works at the factory. A young girl. He have more than one woman but my mother only knows about her. And guess what?"

Caddy looked into the sun again. He said nothing. Felix pushed his shoulder.

"Guess what?"

"What?" Caddy said without conviction.

"Sherlock screwing that same woman too…" He laughed a very strange and loud laugh that was too sudden and too energetic. He kept laughing until water filled his eyes. Caddy smiled because he did not know what else to do.

"Yes Sherlock screwing her too. And Shane used to screw her. You know that? The men in this family love women. We love women too much. Like Daddy. He's like that. We love women. Me too… I love women."

Caddy chuckled slightly.

"You don' believe me? You think I am a battyman, nuh, like you?" He said stepping back and laughing.

"Daddy said you are a battyman, you know."

"You better mind your mout', you hear?" Caddy was not amused and did not really care if he found himself punching the little fool in the mouth.

"What happen? Is lie?" Felix said, still laughing.

"Shut yuh mout'! You hear me?" Caddy turned sharply on Felix. "Don' call me no battyman, you hear?"

"Aright, aright… is jus' a joke." Felix was noticeably shaken. "So you like girls then. Me too, I like girls. I screw that woman already: Myrtle, the helper. I screw her right in the living room. She never want to do it, but I screw her and I know she like it. And I tell her if she tell mummy, my mother, she would lose the work. Screw her right on the sofa."

Caddy got up and started towards the lawn. Felix followed.

"You ever screw yet?"

Caddy did not answer.

"You know who I want to screw now? You know who? I want to screw Mrs. Marshall, Shirley, who live next door and that same woman in the factory. I want to screw all of them."

Caddy went to work on the lawn again. He started the mower and drowned out Felix's fantasies. Felix went back to the verandah and sat there watching Caddy. His eyes slowly glazed over and his mind drifted far from the verandah. He continued to squeeze the huge red blotches on his face. His other hand rubbed the thin red hairs on his chest. Caddy continued to mow.

The girl came up the gully path and walked quickly through the open lot. She saw Caddy. He saw her too. He figured it was her by the uniform and as she came closer he was sure of it. She waved to him and he waved back, watching as she moved past the verandah, then by the front gate and disappeared up the road. Felix saw this. He walked to the front gate looking after her until she turned into her yard. Then he walked over to Caddy and shouted.

"I want to screw her too!"

Caddy wanted to ignore him, but he continued:

"You don' want to screw her too? Nice girl, you know. Nice little girl. She like me, I know that. Hey, you know how you can screw her? Well, she walk there everyday, jus' wait for her and…"

He did not get the chance to finish. Caddy slapped him across the face with such force that it threw him to the ground, then he punched him in the face with both fists. Felix struggled to get away, screaming at the top of his voice. One of the guards came from behind the house and pulled Caddy off. Felix was still screaming at the top of his voice.

"I gwine screw her. I gwine screw her, you watch, you watch, battyman, battyman!" He went into the house and returned with a gun.

"You wan' me shoot you, you wan' me shoot you? I will shoot you, you hear, you little battyman!"

He pointed the gun but didn't fire it. He just stood there looking around distractedly as if waiting for someone to stop him. The helper came out and took the gun from him and then guided him into the house. He threw his body on her and started to bawl loudly. The door shut on the noise of his screaming. The guard told Caddy to go home. He asked no questions, he just said, "Go home."

III

Five john-crows circled, each on a different level, swooping and swerving under slowly moving white clouds in a still and strangely peaceful blue sky. From afar the black crows looked glorious.

Faint smoke from a fire in the forest beside the gully slowly drifted upwards and then vanished in the still sky. The sun was directly overhead and it beat down relentlessly.

One of the john-crows swooped down gracefully just below the tree-line and then just as languidly flapped its wings twice as it swayed back into the sky, joining the circle dance. They waited for stillness before they would land.

The forest was silent.

In the gully a strong stench of rotting flesh filled the air. It was so intense that it seemed visible.

Three men, two in uniform, stood in a triangle around a clump of bushes. At a distance, a woman, plump, with shining skin, stood holding the edge of her dress to her face. The policemen were continually spitting and waving flies away with their hands. One of them moved towards the clump and disappeared behind the thick bushes. He came back out stumbling somewhat and dragging a rope behind him. The rope was taut for a while, then suddenly became slack. He dropped the rope and turned away from the clump with his handkerchief over his mouth. He walked quickly to the opposite wall, leaned on it and began to vomit violently. The other two policemen, one in uniform, the other in white short sleeves and black trousers, held their stomachs and watched their friend with grim faces. Suddenly the plainclothes officer was retching just where he stood.

"Jesus Christ! Jesus Christ! Man!" the third policeman said. "I tell you, I tell you, man… Jesus Christ, man!"

"Where them guys with the masks, man?" the plain-clothes officer said, wiping his mouth with the handkerchief and putting it to his nose.

"You radio them?"

"Yes sir." The third policeman watched his companion leaning on the wall.

"What I tell you? You see what them do to her? You see it? Jesus Christ man, I never see nothing like that yet? Jesus Christ, man?" He spat.

"Stop it!" the officer said. "We have to bring her out of there."

"Not me sah! No way. That is… Oh God, is only a little girl," he said shaking his head.

"I cyaan tek the smell, sah. When the mask them come. You want to see her?"

"I have seen her. You alright, Jones?" he asked the officer who was sweating by the wall.

"Is not the first dead body you see. Or is the firs' one you never shoot?" The officer laughed nervously.

"Is wickedness… wickedness… poor ting." The woman standing afar off still held the skirt to her face. "I never know it was somebody t'row down here, but when I look… the john-crow them pick out her eye them… Oh Lord, have mercy, why them do dat to this lickle girl. It is a nice girl, yuh know… nice girl."

"You know her?" the officer in plain clothes asked.

"She live up the hill," the woman said. "She walk this way everyday. She just go to that school up so…"

"I see the uniform…" The officer turned away.

"Come, Jones, come man, pull the body out here so, come man."

"No sir," Jones said, leaning on the wall. "Cyann look at that, sir. Is a lickle girl."

"Jesus Christ man, Jesus Christ!" the third officer was muttering. Then he put his handkerchief over his face and moved to the clump of bushes. He picked up the rope and began to pull…

"Maggots, you wan' see maggots…" he said, his voice muffled by the handkerchief.

The woman gave a small scream when she saw the black shoes and the blue socks with the rope tied to it.

The officer dragged the burden onto the clear concrete area leaving a trail of moisture and white worms where the head bobbed.

The girl's hair was splattered with blood, but the thick plaits were still somehow intact. The crows had made craters where her eyes should have been, dark holes with red lining and worms crawling around. Her skin had darkened in death. In her forehead was a huge hole. Her mouth was still clearly formed and her teeth stuck out under the tight lips. Her right arm was twisted behind her back and the navy-blue ribbon was hanging loosely on her neck, and under it her white belt was pulled tightly around her neck, embedded in her flesh. Her white dress was dirty with mud and dust. There were black and red holes across her chest. Four of them. The dress was torn where the wounds were. Her dress was lifted above her waist. She had on no underwear. The area that was her vagina was a massive wound lined with a slippery dryness that was cracked like the dry blood around the wound. Her thighs were marked with black bruises, round blotches of black. Her knees were dry and cracking with the same slippery dryness. Her bag was still around her shoulders but it dragged through the lines of moisture and maggots coming from her head.

The flies danced around and inside her body.

The plain-clothes officer moved forward to look and stood still for a few seconds. Slowly he began to shake his head. He spat as fluid began to gather in his mouth. He wiped his lips and covered his nostrils, standing very still. Fluid filled his mouth again and he spat to his side. He tried to distance himself from the child, but the wounds glared back at him.

Stab wounds... strangled to death with her belt... gagged with the ribbon, her mouth sore at the edges; those flies, why don't they leave her alone...? John-crows ate her eyes. They eat the eyes first. Why? Why not the largest wound, like the small mouth torn open. Strangled to death perhaps. Stab wounds. Stabbed to death. Bleeding: insignificant. Did they rape her before or after? Approximate age 14 years, maybe 13. She hasn't got breasts. No hair. Who the hell could do a thing like that? She is about Clarissa's age. Haven't ever seen Clarissa's stomach, not since she was two. We should cover her body. Those flies. Flies give birth to maggots who in turn become flies. They eat the eyes first.

Jesus Christ!

He turned to move from the body and his stomach twisted violently. He moved towards the woman, holding his mouth. She turned away as he began to vomit again.

The third officer watched, almost wanting to gloat but feeling absolutely sickened by the sight and the stench.

"You have the sheet?" the plain-clothes officer asked, his mouth sour with vomit.

"Yes sir." The third officer said.

"Cover her up," he said. "Blow away the flies firs'..."

The third officer moved to the pile of folders and briefcases and took out a stained white sheet. He walked up to the body and waved away the flies with the sheet as much as he could. Then he picked up a small stick and moved it towards the hem of the girl's dress.

"Don't touch it... her..." the plain-clothes man said sharply.

"But, officer... she..." The policeman still kept the stick on the dress.

"Alright, alright," the plain-clothes man said. They had already moved the corpse, disturbing the crime scene. They had taken the photos. That was enough. It would make no difference. The position of the body did not matter in these cases. Someone would come forward' someone would know. It was just a matter of time.

"Cover her," he said. *Cover the poor child*, he said in his head.

The officer pulled the dress over her stomach and legs. Then he covered the body with a sheet. Climbing over the body he walked behind the clumps of bushes grunting through his nose and spitting. He came back out with two books and an immaculately white pair of panties. He held the panties on the stick while keeping the books between a folded piece of brown paper.

"Put them there…" the plainclothes man said pointing to the briefcase and folder. "Nothing else?"

"Cyaan see nothing else, sir." The officer said. "But we coulda look."

"Yes… Jones…Jones."

"Yes sir?" Jones straightened up and moved towards the officer.

"Jesus Christ, man. Jesus Christ! How man coulda be so sick, so damn wicked. What she coulda do…?" The third officer was moving through the bushes looking for evidence.

"You said you know her?" the plain-clothes man said to the woman.

"Yes sir. I think she live up on Radial Drive. That is jus' up so and she normally walk this way and she use to go to school with my daughter… my daughter…" She was crying.

The crows circled, hanging above them. The sun was relentless in the blue plate of sky and the clouds hardly moved or changed their shape.

IV

When Caddy heard that the girl was dead he knew who had done it. He said nothing. He just disappeared for a week. He ran away to his grandmother in the country because he was hurting. But the story followed him on the radio and in the newspapers. If he had stayed he would have killed Felix because he knew that Felix had done it.

He spent a week hiding out in the woods during the day, only coming in late at nights to sleep. He did not eat much and he did not explain what the problem was to his grandmother. She knew

Caddy was strange and she assumed he had fought with her daughter again. She suspected that if Caddy couldn't run away to her little house in Mandeville, there was a risk he could do something dangerous. Here it was cooler and he did not have to deal with so many people, so it was less dangerous. She asked him no questions. She moved slowly about her business, cooking for him, washing his dirty clothes and sometimes singing hymns in the hope that he would hear and be transformed. She knew that only one thing could help him but she didn't know whether she had the strength to confront his demons.

After a week Caddy knew what he was going to do.

v

He ran. He always ran. Sometimes they caught him, sometimes they didn't, but he always took the chance and ran. He knew the area better than any of them so he knew he could lose them. So he ran when he heard them.

"Hey bwoy, stop! stop!" a policeman shouted from the car parked in front of one of the shops that overlooked the roadway that traversed the gully.

He ran.

The two policemen jumped out of the car, slamming the doors. The plain-clothes officer in shirtsleeves stepped out of the back door with a pistol in his hand. He followed the other two officers, who carried a submachine and a shotgun, along with their revolvers.

"Don' shoot him, you hear!" he shouted after them as they took off down the gully after the short black man in khaki shorts and a red singlet.

The plain-clothes man stopped running and went back to the police car. Two women stood beside the car.

"Is him, officer. Is a little bad boy. I know is him do it," one said.

"Wicked, wicked. A girl say him rape her already," the other said.

"Which girl?" the first woman asked.

"Elsie… you know Elsie…?" the other woman said.

"That is a little bitch. Anybody can rape her!" The first woman laughed.

"Well, she say him rape her." The other woman laughed too.

The officer was doubtful about these two women, but the old man who lived on the edge of the gully and a few other people said they had seen this short black fellow in red singlet and khaki shorts walking through the gully towards the hills on the day that the girl must have been killed. They said he was carrying a long pole with a wire hook at the end and a huge bag. He was probably going to pick ackees, but he also carried a very sharp-looking machete. They said the girl walked by there a few minutes after and so he must have done it. He was the kind of fellow to do something like that. The officer wasn't sure, he just wanted to question the man. He was looking for someone who was insane, not a hardened thief like this short black fellow.

He was breathing heavily now. He could hear their footsteps on the cement floor not far behind. He knew that he did not have to stop because they were not supposed to shoot him and they wouldn't catch him at the rate things were going. He was sweating. He had reasons to run. Normally, he would have stopped if he heard instructions not to shoot, but this time he would have gotten into trouble. He reluctantly pulled out the lump of newspaper filled with dried ganja leaves and tossed it into the bushes to one side. He noted where he had thrown it. Then he discarded his knife, a huge two-edged weapon that he claimed he used to peel oranges. Then he threw out the four gold chains in the other pocket. He couldn't see where they'd gone, but he'd return and find them later. He was still running as he reached for the gold watch at the bottom of his pocket. He had to discard all these things because the helper must have suspected him of taking them and told the police. She had not seen him, but if she did not point at somebody, she would lose the job. He hadn't been back to the house for a few days after the girl's body was found, and they hadn't tried to find him to ask him back or pay him after he'd spent most of the week cutting the hedge around the house. So he had slipped back gotten something from work. A few small items.

He kept running.

The policeman caught sight of the red singlet bobbing its way up one of the concrete slopes and about to disappear into the thick bushes just above the gully. He was sure that this was the guy who did it. He knew this boy. He was a tough and wicked fellow and he would rape a girl and do that to her. He stopped suddenly and lifted the revolver. The other policeman stopped and looked at him.

"I gwine kill the dog. Jesus Christ, man. I gwine shoot the dog," he said slowly, aiming at the bobbing red patch.

"He say don' kill…" The other police was suddenly silent. He couldn't do anything.

The shot echoed. Birds rose above the trees. The red patch stopped suddenly and the short black man fell over the gully wall landing heavily on his shoulder.

"Bitch!" The policeman smiled with the gun still pointed. "Bitch!"

They walked up slowly. The short black man was groaning loudly on the ground. The bullet had disfigured his head. It was lodged in his brain somewhere. He was dead but unwilling to die. He was groaning and clawing at the concrete as if reaching for something. They found the gold watch in his pocket. It was the same watch described by the girl's mother.

"Stinking dog!" The policeman said, spitting.

"I don't give a rass. This dog fe dead."

They dragged the body by the feet to the bridge, leaving a trail of blood on the concrete. It was all very untidy.

VI

"Felix not here," the helper said, through the grill. Her face was shining with sweat. Her head was covered with a floral scarf. "Felix gone weh from las' week."

"Mr. Ernest there?" Caddy shouted from the gate because the other dogs were unchained and lying in the driveway. The three vicious ones were lying harmlessly looking at him. The less ferocious, Charles, was barking himself hoarse and spewing foam all over the concrete.

KWAME DAWES . THE GULLY

"Him say him don' need you to work today; the grass cut two day now." She kept looking behind her.

"Mr. Ernest in there?" Caddy shouted again.

"Him say him don' need you today." She was almost pleading with him. "Come back nex' week. Alright?"

"I wan' see Mr. Ernest," Caddy shouted. "If him in dere tell him I have to see him. Is about Felix."

Mr. Ernest stood in the doorway. He wore white pants and a white shirt carefully tucked into the pants. He wore a pair of white brogues and a black belt. His hair was slick against his head. He had a fresh, clean look about him, as if he had just showered and shaved. He said something to the helper that Caddy could not hear. She bowed her head and walked into the house. Mr. Ernest walked into the light on the veranda. His clothes glowed in the sunlight.

He unlocked the grill and walked slowly towards the gate. The three sleeping dogs got up and followed him to the gate, growling.

"Sit down, sit down, man!" Mr. Ernest said. They hesitated. "You don' hear. Sit down. Go back, go back!"

The three dogs moved back to almost the exact same spots they were in before. They circled the area slowly, their paws clicking on the concrete ground. Then they lay down and watched. Charles was silent but he kept prancing about.

"What you want?" Mr. Ernest asked, standing a few yards from the gate. One of the guards had come from behind the house. His waist bulged with a gun. Caddy could see a black object sticking out under the shirt. He stood at the end of the driveway, watching as if he just happened to be passing by. Mr. Ernest did not seem to notice him.

"Sir... sorry..." Caddy started.

"Jus' talk man, come talk." Mr. Ernest used the same tone that had used on the dogs. "What you want?"

Caddy began to have doubts about what he intended to say, but he thought about the girl and decided to go ahead.

"Is Felix, sir," he began.

"Felix not here," Mr. Ernest said. He sucked his teeth trying to dislodge a piece of beef. Then he stuck his finger into his mouth to pick it out.

"I know, but… Mr. Ernest, is Felix kill that girl, Mr. Ernest," Caddy said quickly.

Mr. Ernest barely reacted. He stopped poking at the tooth for a split second and then continued. He pulled the finger from his mouth and sucked the tooth again while wiping the finger with a handkerchief. Then he pulled the dark glasses from his breast pocket and began to wipe them slowly with the handkerchief. He looked down at his hands as he spoke.

"Who tell you that?"

"Him say him was going to do it, Mr. Ernest. Ask Myrtle, she hear him," Caddy said quickly. He wasn't sure whether Mr. Ernest was upset or not.

"Yesterday they kill the man who do it. You never hear?" Mr. Ernest put on the silver-framed dark glasses. His nose twitched a bit.

"Is not that man do it, sir. Is not him, is Felix…" Caddy said.

"How you know?" Mr. Ernest spoke slowly and calmly.

Caddy felt awkward. He was sure it was Felix but he wasn't sure he could convince Mr. Ernest if Mr Ernest was intent on not being convinced. In an odd way, Caddy had expected Mr Ernest to find a solution based on the simple truth that Felix had done it. But now it was clear that Mr Ernest had made up his mind. He would demand evidence from Caddy. Mr. Ernest always wanted facts. Immediately. He always asked Caddy to give his own estimate of what he should be paid for any work he did. He knew Mr. Ernest did this to ensure that the payment was low. Mr. Ernest knew that people would underestimate the cost of their services when they were dealing with him. Caddy knew what Mr. Ernest was doing, yet he always charged less than he deserved. He always felt cheated. Mr. Ernest always wanted the estimate on the spot.

"He said so," Caddy said uncertainly. "Right here so."

"That's how you know?" Mr. Ernest asked, looking directly at Caddy. Caddy could not see his eyes.

If Mr. Ernest had been there that day he would understand why, he would believe, Caddy thought, but he couldn't prove it. He began to feel it was a bad idea to tell the man.

"So tha's how you know?" Mr. Ernest said a little louder than before. Caddy knew he was getting upset.

"Yes sir…"

"Hmmm." Mr. Ernest shook his head. Then he waited, still looking at Caddy. The sky and earth were evenly divided in black and white in the reflection of his dark glasses. "So what you going to do?"

"Well… I was goin' tell the police, sir," Caddy said quietly. He looked at his hands.

"Police?" Mr. Ernest said, in a tone that seemed to sneer at the absurdity of Caddy's statement "You going to tell the police that my son murder that lickle girl who live up the road from us. You going to tell the police that…"

Caddy was silent.

"Eh?" Mr. Ernest shouted.

"Yes, sir," Caddy said quickly.

"Go home and sleep, boy, you hear me? Go home and sleep, you hear?"

"I have to tell them, sir. I cyaan do no better, sir." Caddy now realized what he was doing. He realized that Mr. Ernest was very angry. "You ask Felix, sir? You ask him if is him, Mr. Ernest? Ask him, sir, jus' ask him an' see…"

"You hear what I say, Caddy?" Mr. Ernest stepped closer. "You hear what I say?"

"But…" Caddy started.

"Go home," Mr. Ernest said.

"I have to tell the police den, sir." Caddy was stammering. His heart was sounding through his entire body.

"Oh," Mr. Ernest said calmly, "oh…" as if he had received a pleasant revelation and had arrived at some simple conclusion.

"Yes sir." Caddy pulled back from the gate. "I gone, sir… But you mus' ask him."

Mr. Ernest said nothing. He watched Caddy walk down the road into the open lot. Charles chased the boy along the fence barking madly. Caddy was unnerved by the barking. He walked unsteadily along the path into the gully. As he disappeared past that sign that read "No trespassing. Trespassers Will Be Prosecuted' and into the bush just above the forest, Mr. Ernest called the guard to him. They stood talking for a while, then

Mr. Ernest went inside and the guard disappeared behind the house.

VII

Above the gully, five john-crows circled, swooping down occasionally and soaring upwards, flapping noiselessly in the very still sky. Caddy smelt the residual stench of rotting flesh in the air. As he reached nearer to the area lined with the thickest trees the stench increased. The crows circled again closer to his head and he remembered the peculiar texture of the crows' bald head and rough feathers. He kept walking, the stench thick in his nostrils and heavy in his stomach.

He heard footsteps behind him, but he didn't look back.

The crows dipped and circled in the still blue sky. The sun was relentless on the cracked cement of the gully.

CURDELLA FORBES

SAY

From the moment she get off the taxi I know something wrong. Is the Monday she phone me, say Gan Gan, I coming Wednesday. I send Jew Boy taxi to pick her up at the airport, I couldn't go myself much as I long to see my darling because the arthritis was on me worse than usual. I sit on the verandah whole day straining my eyes to see as far as I can see, till at last I see when the taxi breast the bump in the road and drive up in the yard and Jew Boy come out with her suitcase and bring it in the verandah.

Him is a mannersly young man and he give me good evening and say, "Mammy, I bring her safe. Where to put the suitcase?"

But I not hearing him for my eyes on my darling as she come up the step looking so big young lady I can hardly believe is the little scrawny something I bring back to life from three months premature when the mother thought she would died. She say, "Gan Gan", and I hold out my two arms and she walk in them and hold on to me with her face hide in my shoulder, and is then I know something really wrong. You see, I live on this earth by the grace of Massa God eighty-three year now, and I practically grow that little girl, for every Augas holiday the mother uses to send her to me, put her on the plane from Castries to Bridgetown and from Bridgetown to Montego Bay, from she small till she big and they go away to America. So I have a good understanding, and that little girl especially, much as she go away from me to foreign when she twelve years old, I know her through and through. So from that minute, I knew. Oh yes, I knew.

But I don't say anything. I leave it to her to tell me.

She ask for her old room and she don't even look surprise to see I keep it just the way she leave it all those years, like it waiting for her to come back. She sit in that room for three days looking out the window. What she seeing I don't know, for all that is outside there is the same banana tree with beard like old man wanting a trim, and the canepiece and the hill-and-gully ride and Moutamassy Liza housetop at the bottom of the gully where is only Jesus know how Liza climb up from it every day to mind people business and trace them. Nothing new that she don't know already, but she looking out like she searching for something that her heart break from losing.

But I don't say anything. I leave it to her to tell me. But I pray. I go down on my knee inspiten the arthritis because I realize is principalities and powers not flesh and blood, and I going have to storm Massa God throne, hold on to the horns of the altar.

I cook all her favourite food to tempt her appetite: corn pone, duckunoo, roast breadfruit and gumma, ackee and saltfish with hardough bread and avocado, rundung and salt mackerel with green banana. I make toto and bammy and drops and grater cake with the red colouring just how she like it. I even call Jew Boy to make mannish water as only he can make it, but though she try hard she don't eat much, she jus sit in the room searching the window for thing that lost. Finally I can't stand it no more, for is flesh and blood, so I go to the room door and I say, Dou dou? Mi binny? and she come out of the room and stannup there looking at me with her eyes far and her body naked as the day she born, and I see that she black and blue all over like tie-and-dye.

I cry out, Lawd Jesus, mi pickni! and I feel somebody shaking me and is Jew Boy stanning over me on the verandah where I doze off in the sun. He shaking me and saying "Mammy, you awright? Mammy you awright?" and I realize was dreaming I dreaming and is a terrible dream.

But this time, as I wake so, I get down on my knee in truth, for of a surety I know is not dream, is vision, and my one darling in trouble.

I can't manage the phone thing, but I give Jew Boy the number and ask him to call her but him don't get any answer, so I ask him to call her madda and fadda and they say she alright as far as they know; she in school in Iowa and she keep in touch with them every two week. Jew Boy try plenty time but don't get her. "Mammy, I think she awright you know," he say. "Maybe her phone just out of order or maybe she don't feel to answer. Dem American young people very different you know. Dem have mood."

"My granddaughter not no Amurcan young people, you hear me," I tell him. "She wouldn't not answer her Gan Gan phone call. Something wrong."

Next day Jew Boy come running like him mad cross my yard. "Mammy, Mammy, she call, she lef metches," he shouting pon the top of him voice.

I say, "Jew Boy, stop mekking up dat ruckus in my yard," but I so glad to hear she answer, I don't really vex with him. He do whatever he to do with the phone to make it talk and put it in my ears and I hear my darling, "Gan Gan, I can't write now. But write me, please. I soon come."

I play the metches over and over to see if I can catch anything in her voice but all I catch is the foreboding of my own heart that know trouble, but I say I give everything to my God, Massa Jesus take the case and on top of that I give you the pillow.

I write her. I write, I say, My dou dou I don't know what happening to you I trying not to worry, I say to myself maybe you busy with school work for I know how it go sometimes, I hope you are drinking plenty carrot juice for the eyes so you can see to read the words sharp and I hope you are taking your cod liver oil to keep your pretty skin smooth like how it used to be when you stay here with me when you was a little girl and bathe in the river. Your cousin Celeste say to tell you howdy, you remember Celeste? The jokify one. She uses was to go town to buy and sell but now she stop and gone back to her sewing, for the other day when she go to town big riot, and police tear-gas her and some other people and she lose all her goods. Celeste say ascorden to how it happen, a sewer main burst on King Street, and the vendors had was to heap up their goods on sidewalk so they wouldn't get soaked in the sewer water. One woman name Corpie who Celeste say is some kind of joker sit up on her mountain of goods with big placard telling everybody who pass, "Danger! Filth ahead!" Filth is not the word she use, she use another word but my dou dou I shame to write the word, that is to show you how big people disrespect themselves these days.

Things not what they uses to be. Jamaica change a whole heap since you gone. Anyway as I was saying, this Corpie woman there with her out-of-order announcement and some uptown young people pass and see it and start to laugh. The long and the short is the vendor dem get vex for they say the uptown young people disrespecting them, laughing when they in such a plight, so they make to attack the young people with stick and stone and is so police come and scatter them with tear-gas and rescue the young people dem. You see the sort of hooganeering? That is what is happening here these days, Lord have mercy on us. So now Celeste catch her fraid, for she say it could have been real gun the police shoot and nobody to tell the tale or perhaps the young people could have got hurt and murder commit. So Celeste staying at home now doing a little sewing, and Massa God is good for as I pray for her I see that she making it, not as much as the buying and selling but she making enough to send the children to school and buy book for Junior. My dou dou I telling you this to let you know that no matter how a situation hard, God find a way to work it out, so you must carry on and have faith. Your loving Gan Gan, Mimma Barclay.

Yesterday Jew Boy come and help me in my field and we plant a new row of tomato for her. I water it and I say the Lord's prayer over it. Jew Boy say, "Mammy, if you so concern bout her, why you don't go out? Madda Penny can read her up and tell you what wrong. Is plenty people I know go to her and she help them."

That Jew Boy is a nice mannersly boy, a God-bless boy, really helpful to me a old lady that he don't have to bother with for he young and have him taxi to run to make a living. He is not my relative but every week as God send, if is even two hour on Thursday, he come and help me, whether him bring my groceries in him taxi from Browns Town or help me weed out the field. I give him a smalls for him time, is true, for reward sweeten labour, but he don't have to do it so I thank him. Yes, a God-bless boy, I pray for him every day. But sometime he talk nonsense just like a lot of the heathen people around here. I say, "Jew Boy, shut you foolishness. I not going to no guzzum wukker, you hear me? I pray to my God and Him wi take care. If my mouth bruk and I cannot say to God what I wants to say, I know who to call upon to travail with me."

The boy look in my face and tell me, "But Mammy, Madda Penny is not guzzum wukker. She say the Lord's prayer same like you and when you enter her balmyard you have to spin three time and say the Lord's prayer to show you is not a evil wukker. And anybody who don't do it, you hear Madda Penny start trump, "Hu-hum, hu-hum, hu-hum, somebody in here not clean. Come outa mi yard!""

"Ah say stop the foolishness." I rebuke him strong for I don't want my God to vex with me that I don't warn the young people when they going astray. "All that is obeah wukking – why you want to spin three time to say the Lord prayer, ehn?"

"What it matter if you spin one time or three, Mammy?" He looking innocent but I know he trying to make fun of me. I tell him you not suppose to spin no time at all, let your communication be yea and nay, no spinning, for whatsoever cometh of more than these is evil, and I stop the conversation right there before he blaspheme and is I who encourage idle chatter.

In the night I write her name on a piece of paper and I spread it out before my God, just like how Nehemiah did spread out wicked Sanballat letter and God destroy Sanballat evil plan – *Nehemiah* Chapter 6 verses 14, 15 and 16 – so I plead with my God to destroy any evil plan that plan against my darling. I bow myself to the earth three time like David bow and I call out her name and I see when my God hear for lightning flash and thunder roll and the rain come down that night. Is long time we waiting for the rain for the fields well dry.

I write her. I write, I say, My dou dou how you manage with the bad food over there. You mustn't eat too much of it, don't make them kill you off. Take your cod liver oil and drink salt physic once every three weeks. If you can't get salt physic, take castor oil with plenty plenty water. I wish you was here so I could fix you some strong cerasee and noint you down with olive oil, give you some good ground food and some fresh fish to eat. When you coming to look for your Gan Gan? But I know you have to finish your studying first.

I write and I tell her everything that going on in the district, just to keep up conversation, but I don't hear from her. In Almighty God name I just keep on praying and saying my psalms.

I don't hear from her but I don't call the parents again for I don't want them to say I harassing them, especially the father for he and me don't get on. He say I don't like him for he come from St Lucia, and I think only Jamaica man good enough for my daughter. What a big woman like me doing disliking people because of they race? Some people is just like children, talk foolishness when they don't want to face they own fault. He don't treat my daughter good and when I talk to him about it he say I don't like him. But I a woman who talk plain. I say is not only your wife, is your daughter you damaging with you foolishness. You is her father, you is the first man she learn to trust or not trust, and if you don't set her a good example she won't know who to trust and not trust.

Two nights now I dream her, I see her standing in the river bed with the moon in her eyes. I say Dou Dou why the moon in your eyes. She say Gan Gan my soul gone in hiding. Is a lantern I holding to take it out. I say why you skin black and blue? You not using the olive oil I tell you to use? She say something that I don't hear, but in my dream and when I get up in the morning I putting her name before God.

I don't hear from her but I keep on writing, for I says sometimes when you down and out and you hear a voice, a voice of somebody who love you, even if is from far, it hold you up like a rope that somebody string cross a precipice, and you begging Massa Jesus not to let them pull the rope up before you cross, though you not saying anything with words. I know how it happen when you can't speak but you hope somebody speaking for you. So I write her a letter every week. Can't do more because the arthritis, it on me real bad now.

Grandma, my mouth is broken. My mouth is full of sores. Gan Gan, I fraid of my own mouth, my own body. A stranger come in there and invade it and I feel so unclean. Grandma, I running fast from myself, I am running on a long white road to come to you but there is this thing running inside of me, I am inside it. They say it is my body, that is what the counsellor says. She says this thing running behind me catching up with me, so dreadful and horrible, is my body. But that thing is so dirty and ugly, Gan Gan, I don't know it from anywhere.

Grandma, do you remember the story you used to tell me when I was a little girl, about an old man called Hungry? He would look at you pitiful in the market and beg you to take him home, but he wants you to take him on your back because he is so thin and hungry he cannot walk. And when you feel sorry for him and take him on your back, you cannot get rid of him because he grows heavier and heavier and eats more and more and will not get down off your back.

Grandma I am going to be well. I was glad to get your letter yesterday. But I can't write you now.

My dou dou, why you don't write. Even a little card to let me know you alright.

I write, I say, all sort of things happening in the district now. Hattie gone, take the plane yesterday, and Missa Miller and Totol finally married, after living in sin so long. Forty-three years, till people all forget they not married. Their grandchildren was bridesmaid and flowers girl. Say they want to get in the church and make their way right with God. Well, it is never too late for a shower of rain, and those who are laughing had better stop laughing for they have not made their own way right, and while they are laughing, the opportunity might pass them by, though God forbid, for the Saviour is merciful unto all. But if He call and they don't come, what can He do? All I say is dry stump a cane piece mustn't laugh when cane piece catch afire. Two of the little children in the district, you might remember they parents, Sam and Louise Lue, pass examination with the highest marks in the region. Not just Jamaica but the whole Caribbean region. I praise God, for the parents poor and humble and is try they try. God is good and the whole district proud. As if they was we own.

My dou dou, I dream I see you again standing in the river with the moon in your eyes and your body looking black and blue. This time I noint you with olive oil and I sing the songs of Zion over you and you lay down in my hands and I let the river water run over you. And I see where you fall asleep with the river singing over you. I goes on my knees and I says to my God, Massa God, is life or is death? She fall asleep to come to you or she fall asleep for she find peace in this life? My dou dou, I cannot even say these things to you, I has to ponder them in my heart like the blessed mother of the Saviour, for I don't want to make you fret. Some things I write, some things I only say, and I says them to myself and I pray.

Grandma, I don't go to school three days now. The counsellor says I am improving and she thinks it is her skills. But it isn't. I am getting better since I get your letters. But sometimes when I am inside a building I hear funny sounds in my head, bell a-ring, cement a-mix, like an election calling (Do they still ring bells at election time, Grandma?) or a cement mixer churning up inside my head. I go to sit in the park sometimes. I don't do anything. I just look at people walking their dogs and leaves falling and the way ears look funny coming out of the sides of faces – Gan Gan an ear is a really funny thing. I laugh both because it's funny and because I can imagine telling you this when I was little and you understanding exactly what I meant and laughing. I thank you for the letters and for planting the tomato row for me.

She sits in the park and she rocks herself and she rocks herself until her body feels wound round in a tight cocoon, and she is a little girl again crawling into her grandmother's lap in the rocking chair or hiding from her friends, laughing in a hollowed rock by the sea at Anse La Raye.

Grandma, I wish I could tell you the truth. But it cannot pass the sores in my mouth. I don't know how to tell. I told the counsellor but mostly it was she telling me, she made up the words when I nodded in answer to her questions. Grandma, can you imagine someone could look at you and think you were nothing, and smile with you and lie to you when all the time they were planning to cut you down, to tear you apart like you were a piece of rag, as if you were nothing and did not come from anywhere? At first, after it happened, I wrote a lot of poems, but I can't write poems any more. I had to throw them away. The counsellor says I should not have thrown them away but she says it was good that I wrote them because they probably saved my life, getting the poison out. But Grandma, I still feel poisoned, I feel as though my flesh has rotted. I do not even like to touch my own self. Grandma, just hold me tight with your rope of letters across this precipice, till I get over. Grandma, I would like to come to you, or go to walk on the beach at Anse, but I have nobody left in Anse. Everybody is here.

My dou dou, I write, I say, Celeste happy as a lark. She have it hard, especially since she stop selling the goods and the sewing slow because of the competition from Half Price Depot, you know people go there and buy things cheap that come down from America, so they don't too wait for the tailor and dressmaker any more, so plenty tailor and dressmaker gone out of business, but those who selling the foreign goods, they prospering. Ah, my dou dou, the falling of a old mule is the rising of a john crow. Up to yesterday I see Mr Vassell Forbes, who they say was the best tailor on the ridge here, catching bus to go to his security guard work in Montego Bay, for that is what he doing now to make a living, had was to give up the tailoring. But God is good and He hold strain with Celeste and she able to send the children out to school in them new khaki this bright September morning, and the best of all is Junior, he pass the GSAT and going to high school. You should see the boy, bright as a new quattie. The boy say, Gan Gan, Mama, I go work hard in school and make you proud of me. Watch me and see. When I see him my heart full. I say Massa God, praises be to you, You give me not just the bare seventy years that You promise Moses but you give me thirteen years reason of strength to see my great grandchild come out to something. And you let me still be able write letter to my dou dou in foreign, though the wicked arthritis trying to hold me down.

I write, I say, Your granduncle, I forget to tell you about him, he here boasting up himself same way as he used to do when you was a child. Old age on the man and he still carrying on like he is a child. He going around telling everybody how Junior pass the highest in the country and is his family side of blood Junior inherit why he so bright. Well you see, the Almighty have a sense of humour for he was there telling that to the man whose daughter come first in the class, beat Junior, but he don't know is the man daughter, so the man just let him talk and then he laugh behind his back. I say, Cecil, you talk too much and you talking embarrass the children, that's why they don't like to go anywhere with you. I say your enjoyment is their grief, what feed him wife, kill Jack Sprat. You must stop it. But he don't pay me any mind. The boasting just in him like that. You remember the time when you were little and your other cousin Manfred get the teaching assistant job at the primary school and he went around telling people how Manfred get job as headmaster at the school? Some people did believe him and come to tell me congratulations. I had was to pray for Cecil same time. You would think a big man would sit down and talk to his God and prepare himself for when his time come, but no, not Cecil. Jus like a child. Ah my child, it take all sorts to make up this world.

I remember Uncle Cecil. I used to be vexed with him but when I got older and understood him a little better he used to make me laugh. I think he was just living out his own unfulfilled dreams through our success. But once he was cruel to Celeste. I remember one summer when I was there, he had to take her to the doctor. Celeste didn't want to go because she said he was always saying things to embarrass us in public.

"Lie, lie, lie dem a-tell pon mi," Uncle Cecil protested, and Celeste's mother Aunt Vie counselled him very strongly, hushed Celeste and sent her off with him.

They were standing at the bus stop and getting along just fine, until a lady came along, who Celeste said was looking very smart, dressed like she was going to a wedding. Celeste notices after a while that Uncle Cecil is looking at her, Celeste, and looking at her and looking at her and his eyes are narrowing and becoming critical as he looks her up and down.

Feeling uncomfortable, Celeste says, "Uncle why you looking at me like that?"

"Why you comb you hair in that ugly style to make yourself look so ugly?" Uncle Cecil says. "Don't I tell you not to comb your hair like that? It don't look good."

Celeste said the ground just opened up at her feet and took her in. But the dressed-up lady looked around and said, "But I think she looks lovely! I always do my daughter's hair like that."

Celeste was wearing corn rows, which Uncle Cecil hated, and that was the whole trouble. But from the lady opened her mouth, Uncle Cecil changed his tune. The lady was not only well dressed, she was brown and spoke English. Uncle Cecil saw the chance to social climb, even if it was only for a few minutes till the bus came. All of a sudden Celeste hears, "Yes is a nice hair style, fit her, but she don't do it good this time. See some strands hanging out the side there."

Celeste said she was so shocked and angry she couldn't speak.

"Oh no," the lady exclaimed, "Not at all. Just a strand or two, and it makes her look so cute." Celeste didn't like cute, but she was so glad for the lady, she wasn't quibbling.

Before she knew it, Uncle Cecil and the lady were in big conversation which continued till the bus came, Uncle Cecil boasting about all his nieces and nephews, including Celeste, who had become the mayor's daughter by the time the bus reached its destination. But the best part was when after they got off the bus and Uncle Cecil and the lady waved goodbye, Uncle Cecil went in his pocket and gave Celeste a hundred dollars to spend for herself for creating the opportunity for him to talk to "that nice brown lady." He was always doing things like that. He would make us feel bad because of the ways he used us to make himself look good, and then he would feel awful and try to make it up to us by giving us presents.

I understood afterwards what was wrong with Uncle Cecil. He would do anything to reach the moon. Celeste told me in a letter, when we used to write, before I got used to being in America, that he mellowed with age and stopped embarrassing people with rude remarks in public, though he has never stopped boasting. The world as it is has never been good enough for Uncle Cecil, so he makes it up as he goes along.

Today, Gan Gan, your letter made me smile. It hurt to smile, my mouth is so full of sores, but at least I did. Smile. The therapist says it's a good sign.

But Gan Gan, it comes and goes. Some nights I dream I see you in the river, holding out your arms to me and smiling, the river running so sweet and free, and other times I dream like I dreamt last night the terrible dream that I cannot tell you. It is like touching my body that I don't want to touch any more.

The dream she don't want to tell Gan Gan is the one where she wake up to find herself heaving and humping on the bed like she lifting weight, her face wet with sweat and tears from her eyes squeeze catatonic shut, one grotesque caricature of the act of love, one desperate bid to heave herself out from under the flood of sewage that pouring on her head. Somebody open a sluice gate in a silo of filth and the nasty water pouring out on top her like Joseph in Egypt pouring grain. She say, Gan Gan, the sewer-water washed out Celeste's goods on King Street, and it is washing me out same way in America now.

But she is dreaming that dreadful dream less and less these days now. More and more, it is the river dream that she dreams.

And Gan Gan, last night when I wake from that dream I read your letter about Maisie buck down the big bull cow, and I laugh till I cry.

And after she has finished laughing, she says she will go to her grandmother, she will walk through the district on glass nails till she comes to the tree where her navel string is buried, she will make lightning flash from her wounds. Miss Mimma will give her peas soup and beverage with lime, will noint her down with oil.

"See I wash you in the river."

"Yes, Gan Gan."

"I noint you."

"Yes, Gan Gan."
"Drink the peas soup."
"Yes, Gan Gan."
"You revive now."
"Yes, Gan Gan."
"Try your tongue, don't you feel the silence breaking?"

This morning Jew Boy come in my yard asking me if I going to Curly funeral and I don't know if is because of that why I see what I see in the dream where, as I lay you in the river, a big black man looking just like Curly standing on the bank, watching and looking dead. When I wake up from the dream I don't feel good. Who is that man, is Curly or who?

I say, I write, My dou dou, I hope you well, in the Saviour precious name. I longs to hear your voice, hope you write me soon. My binny, all kind of wickedness going on. In these enlightened modern times, when people should look to their God, you still have people practising back-o-wall wickedness. You remember Maas Curly, the deacon that work as overseer at Hampden sugar factory when you was a little girl? He die yesterday. Strange and sudden death. Ascorden to how Jew Boy tell me, he pay D Lawrence to tell him how to hold on to his position at the factory till he die. And the D Lawrence man tell him he must throw the big Bible off the church podium into Pan Swamp and as long as it in there, nobody can take him out of the overseer job. And all these years Curly is in the church preaching from the pulpit, and all these years at the factory disadvantaging the young girls that come to look work, and everybody know, yet nobody do anything about it for Curly put spell on them. And Curly never need to do it for he have a wife. But he do it because he feel he have the power. Dog have money, buy cheese. Yesterday a cow fall in Pan Swamp so they had was to dredge the swamp to get it out so it don't stay in there to rotten an pollute the atmosphere. Jew Boy was there. Jew Boy say people stannup on the bank looking to see the cow come up and instead what come up is a big black leather case cover over with weed and slime, eh, eh, then is what? They zip it down and lo and behold, Satan is the father of all wickedness. My dou dou, not the Bible that missing from the church pulpit all these years? That was what was in the case!

All this time I in the house sweeping out as best as I can with the wicked arthritis riding me, and sudden so I hear a mighty scream, as if all the demons of hell let loose, and when I run outside, what that? What that? Is Curly drop dead in him house at the same exact moment that the Bible raise up out of the swamp, never to rise again. Dead as dead can be. The scream I hear is the sound that Curly make as he see the pit of hell open at his feet and himself falling down in it. Now all the church people, who should have rebuke him long time, gone on fasting and praying, sweeping out and repenting. Massa God is merciful but sometimes I wonder how people take chance with Him and call themselves Christian, and who to blame, if is only Curly or is the whole of them.

Grandma, your letter cut me like a knife. Gan Gan, I think I am going to hell. I prayed against a man and he died. He killed himself. It was on the news this morning. He was an important man. It came on the international news. Grandma, he hurt me so bad, so bad, I didn't do anything to him and he hurt me so bad. I prayed to God to do him something bad in return, and he died. Gan Gan, he hurt me in a place I cannot tell you where.

My dou dou, I have a strange dream in which I see you crying crying crying, saying Gan Gan I make a man die. A man that hurt me and I pray to God to do him something bad and he take his own life. I see you bend in two like a thing that break and when I grab you suddenly I see you in the river and your body slip through my hand and I fall in the water with you and I swim with all my strength gainst the current till you reach a culvert where your body can't go through. I don't know where the culvert come from in the river but I thank God I grab on to you and I hold you and I wake up from my dream. Sweet dou dou my binny, what kind of thing is happening to you? You don't know that you can't make God follow you to do bad thing? God make up His mind

what He will do. No prayer you pray make Him do evil or change
His mind. It only change you. Man kill heself, is not God or you.
Man do such a thing to himself is a man have more pain inside of
him than Job read bout, is a man that turn his face away from his
own self in folly. Every dankey have him own cubby, every tub
pan sit down pon him own bottom. Man deal with him own life,
you have to deal with fi you. My dou dou, rise up and live. Come
let I noint you with olive oil and wash your batter-batter in salt
and rub you down with blue.

Eighty-three year now I eating salt on this God's earth and never,
I tell you, I know pain till now. I see clear clear now that my dou
dou in trouble, I see it, Lawd. I see at last what the man do to her
and I bawl. I hold my womb and I bawl. I ban my belly and I bawl.
I hold her bend-in-two body under the river water and I bawl. I
travail in the spirit three night and day, I call upon the sisters to
travail with me, forty days and nights seven times round I spin, I
groan, I trump – Madda Penny couldn't show me nothing how I
trump. I say hu-hum, hu-hum, hu-hum, hu-hum, mercy Jesus,
mercy Lawd. I flat on the ground, I see nothing, I eat nothing, I
cannot talk. I lie on the ground like Saul.

All night she vomits, she sweats; rolled tight in a ball, she moans,
as if in the morning she will die. When the pale sun falls in the
room, the counsellor looks at the doctor and says, "She has passed
the worst. She will recover."

The doctor smiles. "I commend your skills."

The counsellor gives a modest answering smile.

Grandma, I see myself on a minibus driving to come to you. It is
day but the moon is shining. Apocalypse in the sky. The road is
long and white and you are a tiny dot at the end of the road. It
seems that I will never get to you, but I know I will and I say to
the driver "Faster! Faster!" and he speeds up the bus until it is
flying. I can see ahead of me what is going to happen. I will step
off the minibus when it reaches the district square, right in front
of Mr Wycliffe's shop (Does Mr Wycliffe still have that shop, Gan

Gan?) People in the piazza, sitting on the stone wall, will call to me and say, "Miss Mimma granddaughter, pretty girl, you come to look for the old people? But you look nice, how nice you look, foreign gree with you!"

I will be glad to hear their voices, even though I know it is not true. Foreign don't 'gree with me.

They will look at me funny because I came in a minibus and not in a Bimmer, they will say (but not so I can hear) that I am not supposed to be coming from foreign and riding a minibus instead of driving a Bimmer, they will say I must travel in a way that will lift up my grandmother. Grandma, I would not be able to explain to them that I came in the bus because I want to ride with real, with glory, with judgement, with the smell of kerosene oil in pan in the minibus-back and yam, patty, cocobread, skellion, thyme, life and red peas, sun smell and people cussing, mercy Jesus! That I come that way because I want to ride with body self.

They will whisper and then they will say, when I call out good evening, some brazen boy will say, "Hail sister. So what you bring for the poor?"

And I will say, "Ha! The poor – don't you know I am the poor? What you have to give me?" and they will say, "Nah, man, you is not the poor, you is the rich, you coming from foreign, you must have something to give."

I will pass them, the boys on the corner, complaining, "Cha, she too mean." They will kiss their teeth in disgust, and I will be laughing in my sleeve, because I am so glad to be home and hear their foolishness.

Grandma, I get excited thinking how I will walk fast past them to come to you, and I get back in the minibus and say to the driver "Faster! Faster, don't stop!" and Gan Gan, when I look it is me alone in the minibus. There is no driver and no market people, only the wind driving through a blackness in the trees. I see myself and I am not a real person, but only a ghost that the wind driving through. I calling out for you and I calling out for Anse La Raye, and is not my voice I hear, what I hear is a wind off a overturn boat in Castries.

Gan Gan, I fraid, I so fraid. I turn right and left for help and instead I see a big duppy man laughing at me and I realize is the wind I hear passing through his bones. And just as I am about to die a second time, I hear your voice calling me, Gysette, Gysette! I look up and I see you clear clear at the end of the road and a whole set of other women holding their bellies like coalpots full of sacrifice standing up straight behind you. They look like a wall, and I don't know where the words come out of my mouth but I hear my self say, "Retro me, Sathanas!" and I cross my two hands "Pow Pow!" and the man disappear and I see that he and the wild wind was a lie. When I look again I see a girl walking naked into a green river and her skin shine and I see an old lady looking at her with deep smile and I cry out, "Gan Gan! It's me, Gysette!" And I go in the girl and the girl go in the river to the old lady, and is me, Gysette.

She strike her two hands sudden so, "Pow Pow!" and the man disappear. She cry out "Gan Gan! Is me, Gysette!" and she wake up.
    She feel weak weak weak and she don't know what it mean. She put her head between her knee. She say, Gan Gan, what does it mean?

Late in the night she see a funny thing in the sky. She standing up at her window with the lights out, for she like to watch the night in the dark. That way she can almost see heaven behind the electric light. She see a big stain like a sheet in the sky, and while she watch, the stain shift shape and resettle and turn into two big angel wing, spread out. She see things write on it like rune, and she straining her eye to see what the writing say but the cloud reshuffle itself so fast, it disappear, and she find herself watching a rainbow like a arc in the sky. She say to herself, I am really hallucinating now. This is the kind of thing that used to happen to people who went to England in the old days – you know England is a place that used to make black people mad. But I am not in England, I am in America, and this is not a dream, so I must be mad. I am standing at this window going mad, after coming through hell in such wringing wet dreams, quietly stark staring mad, for where does a rainbow come from in the night?

But see ya, sah. Big shining rainbow, colour of the sun just set, or rising. Blue green yellow orange red, look it there, it stain the sky. And sudden so, she feel the weirdest hope taking wing in her heart. That is how she know prayer answer, benediction come. She decide that she going to find back her body, live in it again, and she hanging on to the navel string that connecting her 'cross the rainbow to Gan Gan, Mammy, Miss Mimma Barclay letter dem. In a funny moment, she feel to say after all she could fly.

She will write to her grandmother in the morning.

The one Jew Boy is a real Godsend. He cheer up my spirit. This morning he come in the yard looking at me and smiling. Not saying anything, just smiling.

"What you looking so please with youself so for, Jew Boy?" I ask him.

"Is you looking please with yourself, Mammy," he say. "I here looking at you looking please. Is days now I don't see you looking so please. So don't I also mus please?"

I just look at him and laugh, I don't answer him.

"So, Mammy. Tell me the truth. You go to Madda Penny?" That boy don't stop.

"Madda Penny? What I have to do with Madda Penny?"

"But you granddaughter awright. I feel it."

"Yes, my granddaughter awright, praise God," I tells him.

"So how you know? You get letter?"

"No, but I dream her. And I see where she don't black and blue any more."

He don't say anything, but I can see he think I don't get enough surety, I should still go to Madda Penny. I pick up the watering can and I says to him, "Son, you coming to help me weed the tomato this morning?" For I done with this conversation.

He stannup there a good while studying me before he smile and say, "I hear you, Mammy."

I singing serene and he walking behind me. Nice God-bless boy.

IFEONA FULANI

FEVERGRASS TEA

When she first moved into the house, she used to lounge on the verandah at sundown, sipping pineapple soda while the sun slid behind the mountains in a haze of purple flames. But in a matter of days her evening idyll was disrupted by one destitute woman, the first of a steady trickle of needy locals who, sighting her on the verandah, pushed at the rusty iron gate, braving the overgrowth of thorny bougainvillea, to bang on her door and beg.

Tell me, Yvonne, who's to blame? Margie her cousin and neighbour demanded when Yvonne complained. Who in their right mind would put their hand in their pocket and give that old drunken wretch Isilda *ten whole dollars* for no reason at all? Privately, Margie had thought Yvonne's charity typical of the show-off behaviour of returnees who came home from America with dollars flowing from their pockets. Three months after her arrival and many supplicants later, Yvonne was less generous. These days, as soon as she heard the creak of the gate she would call out: Sorry! Nothing to give away today!

The day Donovan pushed at her gate and entered her yard she did not call out. Something about his height, the muscular arms, the way his thick hair sprang back from his forehead, stilled her tongue.

Mornin, ma'am. He paused by the step and greeted her with a courteous nod. I'm Donovan. I live down the road, just past Chin shop. I pass here often, you know, and I can't help noticin that this yard need some attention. His voice was soft, his speech deliberate, and he looked her in the eye.

I do yard work. I can clear up this mess for you.

Oh. Yvonne raised a hand to smooth her braided hair. Well, yes, it really is a mess. She wished she were wearing something more stylish than baggy cotton pants.

I've been thinking of hiring someone to cut the grass.

I figure three days' work go fix it. His glance took in the drooping mango trees and the unkempt hedge of crotons with branches that waved in the breeze.

For a moment she pondered the wisdom of hiring a total stranger. She took in the bright white T-shirt and well-fitting jeans.

You don't look like a gardener. Her eyes narrowed.

Don't worry yourself, miss, he said with a lopsided smile. I been chopping yards from I was a little youth. This is nothing. I live in this district for years. Everybody know me. Ask Margie next door. She'll tell you.

So you know Margie? Ah. OK, then. What's your fee?

He named a sum she thought pitifully small. He was asking less for three days' labour than she charged to cut and sew a simple blouse, but that was how it was in that part of the island. Men and women chopped cane or tended fields, from dawn to sundown, for a few dollars a day. It was backwards, yes, but nothing she alone could do about it. She accepted his price. They agreed he would start work the next day, and with the briefest of nods he turned on his heel and strode away.

Yvonne went back indoors, intending to start work on a wedding dress for the daughter of a local politician, but her mind was racing too fast to concentrate, buzzing almost. This couldn't have anything to do with the yard man. Maybe she had made her morning coffee too strong. She sank into an easy chair beside the wide window overlooking the miniature forest that passed for a front garden. When Donovan finished clearing it she would be able to see beyond the head-high hedge of crotons, across the valley to the panoramic stretch of the Blue Mountain ridge. She eased back in the chair, one hand travelling under her T-shirt to finger the crescent-shaped scar in the crease beneath her left breast. The scar was raised and still tender to touch, though the breast that covered it was numb. The scar would heal completely, in time, the specialist had said, and she would quickly grow accustomed to the saline-filled sac that had replaced her diseased breast.

Yvonne thought of Leyla, her mother, who had taken time off

from her job to nurse her through the weeks of chemotherapy. Now that she was well again, Yvonne felt ashamed at how completely illness had robbed her of adulthood, of how abjectly she had depended on her mother's care, a scared, needy child again. Leaving New York was as much about getting away from Leyla's coddling as about recuperating in the sun. Margie had come up with that idea . She had made all the arrangements; found the house, helped Yvonne to settle in, even found custom- ers in the village, so Yvonne could earn a little money as a dressmaker. The small house was cheap to rent, and close to Margie's much larger home. It suited Yvonne, even the riot of plant life overtaking its grounds. Nature's vitality was every- where. She heard it in the day-long noises of restless crickets, in the nighttime warbling of contented blackbirds. She saw it in the fluttering blue swarms of morning glories, measured it in the exuberant growth of every flower, shrub and tree. It was like food taken in through the senses. Yet at night she was lonely. She still ached for Martin, her ex-lover. He had promised he would visit, but she doubted he could face her after their long-distance break- up. She missed her girlfriends, going out for a pizza and a movie, the morning banter of colleagues at the studio over coffee and a bagel. There was Margie, of course, and she was lively company, but she was married, with three children and a teaching job. She had little time for entertaining her cousin.

Donovan came the next morning, before sunrise, while Yvonne was still asleep. She woke to the rhythmic *chop, chop* of his machete, and dressing quickly in shorts and a ribbed cotton top, she went outside to watch for a while. He was cutting back grass that had grown shoulder high, wielding the machete with fluid motions of arm and torso. In the pale grey light of early morning, he was a graceful, almost ethereal figure, absorbed in the work, unaware of her gaze.

She breakfasted on grapefruit, papaya and Earl Grey tea. She offered him a cup, calling out from the front window. The steady rise and fall of his cutting arm paused. He looked up, mopped the sweat from his face with a piece of old towel.

No Miss, no thanks, he said, and returned to work. She drew back from the window, piqued by his refusal, and wondered at his curtness: had she violated some local code of conduct with an offer of tea?

She took her mug into the tiny room at the back of the house where she had constructed a makeshift work table from an old door covered with a plastic sheet, and stacked-up wooden crates. A portable sewing machine took up one end of the table; the other was swathed in white satin, marked up and ready for cutting. She picked up the scissors, but the view from the window distracted her: a gently sloping hillside clad in coconut palms, their branches shimmered by the wind, their leaves refracting light. After New York's concrete grey congestion, the aquamarine sky and rich greens had a sweetly narcotic effect. How could she possibly miss the bustle of Seventh Avenue and the studio where she had pored over a drawing board for ten, twelve hours a day, six, sometimes seven days a week? She didn't miss those interminable hours. Had those long working days lowered her resistance to disease? Had stress made her ill? Had she been weakened by a diet of coffee, fast food and exhaust fumes?

She'd been happy enough in her tiny apartment on 8th Street. She stayed there twelve years, the last with Martin. Martin. His face interrupted her reverie, a quiet ache taking shape in her head. His forehead seemed always creased with worry: worry about problems at work, about money, and later on, about her health. In the end she had asked him to move out. She couldn't bear him to see her so altered, so weakened by surgery and medication. Till you get well, he had said, and she agreed. He had driven her to the airport, had held her and kissed her face. He'd promised to fly down for a few days soon, real soon. He called the morning after she landed, and every evening for a week after, then less and less frequently. It hurt that she could see his face so clearly, yet he felt remote and somehow irretrievable, part of a past unblemished by disease. Tears pricked her eyes. She blinked and shook her head, forced her attention back to the fabric on the table, took a firm grasp of the scissors and resumed cutting.

At 4 o'clock, as she was pinning sections of the dress

together, she was summoned to the verandah door by a tap on the grille.

I finish for today, Miss. Donovan had changed into his regular clothes, jeans and a T-shirt. He gestured towards the now neat lawn. I'll be back Thursday, same time. He nodded and walked away.

On Thursday Donovan worked late into the evening, pushing himself to complete the job until darkness stopped him. Yvonne had downed tools at sunset. She was stretched out on a lounger, a novel open on her lap. As he approached the verandah to take his leave she noticed with a twinge of conscience that he walked with a tired droop.

Donovan, she said, rising to meet him, why not rest a minute and have a cool drink? Or some tea?

Abruptly, without a word, he turned and retraced his steps down the path, the mashed-down backs of his work-shoes flip-flapping against his heels. He stopped near the gate beside what looked like a huge clump of long, coarse grass and cut a fistful of blades with his machete.

What's this? she said when he handed them to her.

You don't know fevergrass? His eyebrows rose. Don't you know how to make fevergrass tea?

I don't. It doesn't grow in New York. Yvonne laughed.

Leaving his shoes by the doorway, Donovan followed her through the living room to the sparsely equipped kitchen at the back of the house. She sensed him taking in the freshly painted walls and polished floor tiles, and noticed he trod gingerly, almost on tiptoe, as though he were trespassing.

In the kitchen, she reached for the shiny new kettle which sat on the stove, but he stopped her.

You make this tea in a pot, he said.

Feeling ignorant, she took an enamel pan from the cupboard and handed it to him. He half-filled it with water and set it on the stove to boil.

I probably had fevergrass tea as a child, before my parents took me to the States, she said. I'll probably remember when I taste it.

He rinsed the leaves, twisted them into a thick coil and immersed it in boiling water. A rich, delicious aroma rose, filling the kitchen with a perfume of lemon and roses.

It smells good, she sighed, inhaling the fragrance. She handed him sugar, which he spooned into the pot, and two mugs which he filled with the pale, green-gold liquid.

And it will do you good. Donovan handed her the mug with a slight bow, as if it were a gift.

Good in what way? she asked, leading him back to the verandah.

In every way. This tea good for the head, good for the heart.

Yvonne threw back her head and laughed.

Is not lyrics, trust me. Ask anybody, ask Margie, she will tell you. Fevergrass cure for all kind of ache and pain.

Then it's just what I need, she said, raising the mug to her lips.

They sat silent for a while, sipping tea in the dark to a syncopated chorus of croaking lizards.

Tell me, Miss, Donovan suddenly asked, how come you leave America and come to live alone up here in this lonely old house, in this lifeless place?

Why do you want to know?

It seem strange…

I… I'm taking a break from New York, she said. I was… overworking. I needed a break. I can rest here. It's so peaceful, so beautiful. And hardly lifeless! Listen to the croakers! Look how everything grows so fast; it's uncontrollable!

That's not the kind of life I meant, he said. I wondering, where is your husband? He leaned closer and Yvonne caught the odour of sweat, damp earth, cut limes and decomposing leaves.

I don't have a husband.

What, a pretty lady like you with no husband? What's wrong with men in New York? He smiled, revealing large, yellowing teeth. She began to regret offering him tea.

I used to live with someone…

Ha, I knew…

We broke up over a year ago.

Oh, he said, looking grave. Then he nodded, as though all at once, he knew everything worth knowing about her. It rough when things mash up like that. Believe me, I know. Best make a fresh start... if you can, eh?

Yvonne didn't respond. In the silence that followed, the piercing song of a solo bird trilled above the hum of insect noises.

I use to live in town, in Kingston, Donovan announced suddenly. When I finish high school I moved to Kingston to work for my uncle. He own a lumber yard in Meadowfield and I go to learn the business from him.

Meadowfield! The place where they're having all that gang violence? I saw a report about it on the news just the other night. That must have been tough!

The violence wasn't so bad in those days. People had jobs, a young man could make a decent living. I stay by my uncle five years, learnin the business and savin money. My plan was to get away from Kingston, to come back here and start my own business. I wanted to be my own boss, and not work to make some other man rich.

He fell silent, gazing off into the dark.

So what happened to your plan? She scanned the wide set of his eyes, the curve of his jaw, as though these features could reveal whether a man was honest or a cheat.

He hesitated, then took a mouthful of tea.

Go on, she urged. You can't stop halfway through the story!

Well, he sighed. I come back and rent a small yard, a space near the market. I start tradin and business go well at first but then – you know how it goes. People mash up everythin. People takin things on credit and never payin. People stealin your goods when you're not lookin, your money when you not lookin. Before long the business crash and I in debt up to my eyes.

What do you do now?

Any work I can get. Yard work, farm work, any work... His mouth twisted in a bitter smile. There's no money here. A man can barely make a livin, barely feed his children. It can kill a man's soul.

Yvonne noticed the deep grooves on either side of his mouth, and realized he was older than she'd thought.

How old are your children? she asked, gently.

Ten and twelve. Two fine boys. They're in foreign, gone with their mother.

There was not enough light to read his expression.

Is five years now since I last saw them.

That must be hard…

Is a whole lot easier than havin them here and not havin food to give them.

So why didn't you go with them? She frowned. Was he a delinquent father, a negligent spouse?

I didn't have papers.

Then why doesn't their mother send them to visit you? Or why don't you go just for a visit?

He laughed and his teeth glistened in the dark.

Why don't I visit? He laughed again, a harsh sound. My wife send me money for the fare over a year ago. She send invitation, bank statement, everythin. I took everythin to the US Embassy, stand in line one whole day, fill out form, go back next day, go back the next week and what happen? No visa. Up till now, no visa.

Yvonne sank deeper into her chair, drawing back from his bitterness. She wished he would finish his tea and leave. She had enough sorrow of her own, she didn't need to share his.

Just last week I went back there and fill out new forms. I don't know why I bother, though. Is just a waste of time. But a man have to try, eh? He picked up his mug and drained it in one long quaff.

Is time I go home, he said, looking around for his shoes. I should finish up the back yard next Tuesday, easy. It will only take an hour or two more.

Yvonne got up to open the grille and switch on the verandah light so he could see his way out of the yard.

Within minutes of Donovan's departure, she heard the gate creak open.

Good evenin, good evenin! Margie's voice preceded her slender form up the garden path. Margie! Hey, girl!

Yvonne felt herself flushing, as if she had been caught misbehaving. She wondered how long Margie had been concealed in the yard.

Come on up, come take a seat!

I'm not sitting down for long. Donald soon come home for dinner, and I soon have to put the boys to bed. Margie flopped into the chair facing Yvonne. I see you met Donovan.

He says he knows you.

Margie crossed her slim legs. Her figure and face were youthful, almost girlish, in contrast to the thick, purplish veins curving across her calves, the legacy of three pregnancies.

Everybody here knows Donovan! He's a decent enough fellow… but I hear he love women too much.

Is there a man on this island who doesn't? Yvonne shrugged.

True… but he have a wife and some family problem… you know the kind of thing.

Actually, I don't.

What I'm trying to say is, you don't want to get too involved!

I'm not getting involved, I'm giving him work.

Maybe so, but… one thing can easily lead to another, eh? You didn't grow up around here; you wouldn't understand how a man like Donovan operates.

I don't understand what you're hinting at, Margie.

All I'm trying to tell you is, you have to be careful of people around here. Margie's voice dropped to a whisper. All of them looking for something, especially from somebody like you, coming from foreign.

What's *really* bothering you? The fact that he does manual work? That people around here will disapprove of me drinking tea with a yardman? Folks round here sure are backward!

I only mention it cause you're not… Margie faltered under her cousin's glare. Never mind. I done say what I come to say. Donald must be home by now, waiting for his dinner. I gone. She sprang to her feet, patted Yvonne's shoulder and hurried away, leaving her cousin fulminating at this fresh invasion of her privacy.

Around sundown on his third day in the yard, Donovan summoned Yvonne to inspect his handiwork.

You didn't know you had so much hiding under all that bush, eh? He had chopped back the croton hedge, pruned the bougainvillea and cut away the mango tree's overhanging branches. Yvonne trod gingerly over the spiky brownish crabgrass, making politely appreciative noises as Donovan pointed out a bed of stunted Easter lilies, the remains of a small rockery and, at the centre of the newly-made lawn, a cluster of straggly poinsettias.

Hmm. She looked around, not sure that she liked the yard now it was shorn of its lush overgrowth. I suppose it *is* a lot neater.

Donovan glanced at her face.

You miss the flowers, don't you? Don't worry, I'll make them bloom again for you.

That's quite a promise, Yvonne said, laughing.

Just a few hours a week, and you won't believe how everything will thrive!

I should have seen this coming.

Don't feel obliged –

Half a day, once a week, you say?

If you can afford it."

Oh… I suppose I can, she sighed. OK. She offered him her hand. "It's a deal.

He squeezed her hand in both his, thanking her repeatedly. She pulled away, embarrassed, saying it was nothing, really. She headed towards the back yard to see what changes he had made there.

On the afternoons he came to work, Yvonne sat on the verandah, tacking segments of dresses together or taking up hems. Sometimes when he was done, he rested on the step and they discussed the garden's progress. She discovered that Donovan was a mine of information about people in the village, most of whom he'd known since childhood. He was knowledgeable about the parish as a whole: its characters, its history, its places of danger, its beauty spots.

He must have sensed that Yvonne enjoyed his conversations, for he fell into the habit of stopping by just to wish her good day. Once, when she was out, he left a sack of jelly coconuts, husked and ready for piercing, propped up against the verandah door. Another time he left a bag of luscious, crimson otaheiti apples.

The next time he arrived for work he was cradling a bunch of tiny apple bananas. He offered her the fruit with a small, solemn bow, and she warmed with pleasure at the delicacy of the gift.

One Friday morning as she was loading her dusty VW beetle in preparation for a trip into Kingston, Donovan appeared at her gate dressed in neatly pressed slacks and a short-sleeved white cotton shirt. He asked for a ride into town. He had an appointment at the US Embassy: more visa matters, he explained. Of course, she said, she could use some company on the road.

They climbed into the ancient car and set off on the road to Kingston. The road wound steeply into the valley, past acres of orderly banana groves, through dense emerald woods, levelling out alongside the glistening waters of a sweeping, sleepy river. The morning air retained a hint of the night's coolness, and though the sun was not yet high, its light played on the river's surface in a quivering, dazzling dance.

Do people here know how lucky they are, surrounded by all this beauty? Yvonne said.

Lucky? Donovan frowned. He had been deep in thought, as if inwardly rehearsing for the interview at the Embassy. Lucky? I call winning the Lotto lucky! Or getting through with a visa first time… He paused, looking wistful, contemplating the unlikely possibility of such luck passing his way. Then he shrugged and said:

There are places close to your house prettier than this. You ever swim at Strawberry Fields?

I haven't, but I'd like to, she said, thinking how seldom she went to the beach, how much she'd like to go someplace new. She felt Donovan's gaze on her face.

I need to see more of the island.

But you need company?

I guess so. She caught his glance for a second, then looked away.

Nothing more was said until they approached the outskirts of Kingston and hit a cloud of exhaust fumes from an unexpectedly long and sluggish line of traffic. All thought of beaches vanished from Yvonne's mind, replaced by the need to concentrate on the line of vehicles stretching as far as she could see.

Sunday morning, Donovan tapped on the verandah grille at eight o'clock. He wore a sky-blue shirt and beige polyester pants, a rolled-up towel under one arm, a bulging plastic bag in his hand.

Is a perfect morning for Strawberry Fields, he said as Yvonne unbolted the grille. What you think?

I'm sorry – I have a *pile* of work to do.

The day's perfect for the beach. The sun not too hot and the breeze just right. You could do your sewing this evening.

Yvonne fingered the strands of an unravelling braid. Then she laughed and threw up her hands. Yes! It *is* the perfect day! She hurried into the bedroom to rummage for a bathing suit.

Could she get away with a bikini? She pulled a favourite black two-piece from a drawer. Would he notice that one of her breasts was smaller than the other? She pulled on the bikini bra and scrutinized her reflection in the mirror, turning left, then right, and grunted, satisfied with what she saw. She pulled denim cut-offs and a white lawn shirt over the bikini, wrapped an Indian cotton scarf around her braids and stuffed sunscreen and oil into a Bloomingdale's beach bag, snatched her sunglasses from the dresser and hastened back to the verandah.

I have jelly coconuts. Donovan held up the plastic bag to show her.

But we need something to eat! Yvonne hurried to the kitchen, threw two mangos, two avocados and a packet of plain crackers into the beach bag, then hurried back to the verandah, ready.

As she started the VW, Margie's face popped up in Yvonne's head. The engine stalled. Should she be doing this? Then: Why not? *Why not?* She re-ignited the engine. What harm could come from an outing to the beach? She turned to flash a smile at Donovan, who settled back in his seat and strapped on his seat belt.

The road to the coast was punctuated with holes the size of trenches and sudden, sharp bends. Donovan attempted to start a conversation, but gave up, silenced by Yvonne's absorption in

manoeuvring the car away from potholes. He spoke only to give
her directions. They'd get to Strawberry Fields by a sharp turn off
the main road, he explained, but the first turn they took led to the
high, wrought-iron gates of a private house. The track was too
narrow to turn; Yvonne had to reverse back to the main road.

Are you sure you know the way? If you're not, we should
probably turn back.

Is only one wrong turn, Donovan said. You always give up so
easy?

Yvonne bit her lip so as not to snap a sharp retort.

Anyway, there's the turn. Yes, that is it.

Yvonne was relieved to see a faded wooden sign pointing the
way down a narrow turning, but as the aged car bumped and
rattled along a seemingly endless, rock-strewn dirt track, what
remained of her good spirits faded. By the time she pulled up
under a clump of sea almonds, her head ached, her nerves were
frazzled and she wished she were back on her verandah, alone.
She stepped out of the beetle, slammed the door shut and leaned
against it, trying to calm down. Donovan eased out of the car and
reached into the back seat for their bags.

You look like you need a swim, he said, and frowned when
Yvonne did not reply.

Yvonne followed behind as he led the way through a grove of
sea pines to a tiny cove that was no more than a fringe of trees and
a horseshoe of white sand embracing an expanse of sparkling
azure water.

Tell me if you ever see any place as pretty as this, he said, with
a proud gesture of his arm.

Yeah, it's pretty, she said offhandedly, and watched his face fall.

She spread her towel in the dappled shade of a palm tree,
settled herself on the towel and began smoothing oil on her legs.
Donovan spread his towel a cautious yard or so away. He sat fully
clothed, knees drawn up, staring at the sea.

Their silence was disturbed by the sudden arrival of a youth.
He jogged out of nowhere and halted in front of Yvonne, one
hand buried in the pocket of torn-off nylon sweatpants, the other
outstretched, palm facing the sky.

Mornin, Miss, I'm hungry Miss, beg you a few dollars to buy breakfast?

Donovan jumped to his feet in a flurry of sand and lunged towards the boy, a stream of curses spewing from his mouth. The boy fled, disappearing through the trees.

Did you have to react like that? Yvonne jumped to her feet. Did you have to be so aggressive? The sudden, hostile outburst alarmed her: did he have a violent streak? Had he beaten his wife? Was that why she left him?

You don't understand these youths around here. Donovan kissed his teeth and sat again. They're good for nothin but beggin and stealin. Not one of them would consider doin a decent day's work for their money.

That's a bit harsh, isn't it? Yvonne loomed over him, hands on hips. Aren't you the one who's always saying how hard it is to survive around here, how there's no work, no money? She glared down at him. For a moment he glared back.

Besides, she continued, it's annoying when they beg, but it's not a crime. All they want is a few dollars. I don't mind handing out a few dollars now and then. It's the least I can do.

The least you can do?

Yes, the least I can do! To make up for having so much more than them.

He laughed at her, a hard, incredulous bark. Yvonne turned her back on him and strode towards the water, wondering what had possessed her to come to this deserted place with a man she barely knew, a man with nothing but disappointment to his name.

The morning sun was pale, but hot enough to bring a film of perspiration to her face. She removed her shorts and shirt and waded into the turquoise sea. Water brushed her skin like a cool caress as she strode in up to her waist. She scooped it up in cupped hands and rubbed her skin with it, like a balm. She lunged forward and swam breaststroke, pushing and kicking the water until she tired and paused to catch her breath. Only then did she think of Donovan sitting alone on the beach. She felt a surge of remorse. She stood up and turned to call out to him, but slipped on a large sea-stone and teetered backwards, and fell flat.

When she surfaced, spluttering, she saw Donovan wading towards her, fully clothed. She beat the water with flailing arms and squeezed her eyes shut to ease the sting of salt. When she opened them, Donovan was beside her, lifting her. She let her head rest against his chest, feeling thankful. She breathed in the fresh-washed smell of his shirt and the deeper, earthy smell of his skin. Back on the sand, he put her down on the mat, but she held on to him and pulled him down beside her. He drew away with a quizzical frown, but she pulled him against her and he didn't resist. She kissed his face and he kissed her back, then she was tugging at his pants and wriggling out of her bikini with no thought of the symmetry of her breasts. They lay on the straw mat, her hands roaming his skin, her legs wrapped around him, holding him deep inside as they rocked and swayed to the rhythm of the waves.

They left the cove at sundown, driven away by swarms of spiteful sandflies. Back on the road, Yvonne took the narrow uphill bends with exaggerated turns of the steering wheel, whoop-ing with glee as the beetle's tires screeched on the broken-up Tarmac, laughing at Donovan who strapped on his seat belt and urged her to take it slow. She let him out by the entrance to the lane that led to his tiny wooden house, one of a cluster of fragile-looking dwellings set back from the main road, behind a clump of trees. Less than half an hour later, he appeared at her door with a six-pack of Red Stripe. Together they foraged in Yvonne's refrigerator and found a bundle of callaloo, some onions and tomatoes which Donovan washed and chopped and set to cook in a large skillet, while Yvonne warmed a pot of rice left over from the previous day. They ate out on the verandah in the fading light, and afterwards sprawled in the two loungers, not talking much, sipping beer and tracking the moon's progress across the sky, until sun-drunk and love-weary, they fell into Yvonne's bed.

★

They had been lovers for a few weeks when Yvonne woke one morning, a dream fragment repeating in her head: Donovan striding down Seventh Avenue, smack in the middle of the road among buses, trucks and hooting cars, wearing a torn shirt, mud-smeared cut-offs, and down-at-heel, mashed-back shoes. She turned this fragment over and over. It was asking: Is there any future in this? She hadn't told him about her illness: what would he say when she did? What would he do? She sat up in bed and scanned his face on the pillow by her side. He slept on his back, one arm dangling over the bed's edge. He frowned in his sleep, and his lips twitched as though engaged in a silent debate. Yvonne threw back the sheet that covered him, exposing the soft mound of his genitals, and long, sinewy legs. Skin the colour and texture of bark, and across the shins a network of shiny, satin scars, upfront and visible, not concealed by discreet folds of skin, like hers. His skin told a story of labour and toil; hers tucked its sorrows neatly away.

So, you think you get a good bargain? Donovan was watching her through bleary eyes.

Bargain? She drew up the sheet and snuggled against his side. I pay for your labour, not your body, she said.

Yard work, bed work, it's one and the same, he said, pulling her close.

You can't mean that! She slid over him.

Well, this kind is sweeter, he acknowledged, reaching his arms around her.

And this kind is free, she added, touching her mouth to his.

When more weeks passed without even one visit from Margie, Yvonne concluded that her cousin knew Donovan was sleeping over and did not approve. She suspected that the entire community was gossiping, but she was too happy to let such narrow-mindedness worry her. How did Donovan feel? He belonged here, he knew these people, he was a married man, even though his wife had been absent for years. Did he mind his private life being public knowledge? She raised the matter with him over a Sunday morning breakfast.

People will talk, yes. What you expect? He shrugged, more concerned with piling ackees and green bananas onto his plate. Then he said: Listen, Yvonne. You remember the time we went to Kingston? You remember I went to the embassy to reapply for a visa? Well, the papers come through! I get the visa!

She reached across the table to squeeze his hand. Honey, I'm glad for you. When did you hear?

A few days ago.

And you never mentioned it?

I never said anything because... well because... He sighed and set down his fork. He put his elbows on the table and dropped his head on his hands.

Because of what?

Because I don't know if I can go.

What do you mean? I don't understand you. You have the visa, you have the money for your ticket...

The money I have is not enough, he said, raising his head. It not enough. I have it over a year now and I spend some of it. I need two hundred US more to make up the fare. His voice faded to a whisper. Can you lend it to me?

A cold mass settled on Yvonne's shoulders. She sat still in her chair.

So here it is, she said eventually. So that's what all the tea-drinking was about. And the otaheiti apples. And Strawberry Fields...

I never plan for this to happen, Yvonne, believe me! He reached across the table for her hands, which she pulled away and buried between her knees. If you can help me, if you can lend me the money, I'll pay you back.

How, Donovan? How could you pay me back on the pittance you earn? How do you even know I have the money to lend you? Yvonne was on her feet, shouting.

You come from foreign, don't you? And you've been flinging your money away on beggars... His voice trailed off. Suddenly his brows snapped together. You mean, you don't have the money...?

Yvonne stared at him across the table. His posture, slightly hunched and pleading, was a cliché, a banal picture of neediness. She felt no sympathy at all.

Donovan, she said, what happened to your pride?

She stood and turned her back on him. She strode into the bedroom, snapping the door shut behind her. She was trembling, though the morning was hot. She climbed into bed fully clothed, drew her knees up and wrapped her arms around them, but the trembling would not stop.

She fell into a shallow sleep and woke to a feeling of warmth, as if Donovan's body was stretched spoon-like against her back, his arm thrown across her waist, the way they always slept. She turned to touch him and touched instead a vacant space. She jumped out of bed, heart pumping. There was no sign of him in the living room or in the kitchen. Breakfast was still on the table, his food abandoned, her own plate empty. Her belly gripped with a pain sharper than hunger. Tears stung her eyes.

She began to search for her pocket book, almost in a panic, and found it in its usual place in a corner of the bedroom. She fumbled for her chequebook and a pen. Dropping on the bed, she wrote a cheque for two hundred dollars, then crossed out the two and replaced it with a three, breathing a loud sigh of relief as she searched for an envelope. She pulled on a pair of sandals and hurried out of the house, heading towards the lane where Donovan lived. She half-ran down the road, oblivious of the heat burning down on her head. She wasn't sure which of the small dwellings clustered along the dusty track was his and asked a boy passing her on a rusted bicycle if he knew Donovan. The boy pointed to a neat-looking house fringed with white and red hibiscus.

She knocked on the unvarnished wooden door, but there was no answer, so she bent and pushed the envelope underneath. She imagined his delight at opening the envelope and seeing the cheque. Straightening up, she felt a surge of happiness, imagining him smiling with relief. She wouldn't linger, she would hurry back home since she still had work to do on the bridesmaids' dresses for the politician's daughter's wedding. She would keep busy until Donovan came by.

He must have jumped over the garden gate while she was at the sewing machine because she didn't hear the gate creak open. He must have crept up the path to the verandah. He must have pushed the envelope hard under the verandah grille, for it lodged against a chair leg, insignificant and crumpled as a discarded tissue. She found it at sundown when she'd gone outside to sit and wait, not knowing he had come and gone.

KEVIN JARED HOSEIN

THE KING OF SETTLEMENT 4

Going to start this one off by tellin you that I was born and raise along a backroad that always seem slightly more Trinidadian than the rest of the country. Settlement 4 is that stuck-in-time, over-grown, carefree type of Trinidad you think of when you think of Trinidad.

We have it all.

We have the little boys bathin by the standpipe. We have the no-teeth man whose rock-hard gums could cut through cucumber like butter. Take a walk down this mucky stretch of asphalt and look to your right. You'll see a young, pregnant *Miss Lady* combin the lice out of the locks of she first-born. To the left, you'll see a sunburnt savannah where children fly mad bull kites next to a posse of nomad goats. Walk further down and you gon find a rusted sedan with chipped bricks for wheels, and weeds sproutin outta the glove compartment.

But then there's the features you mightn't think bout – boys like Foster and me who had plans to spend the better part of we teenage years sittin on a crate and paint bucket. Makeshift lookout points. Foster is two years older than me, and when free education wasn't cutting it for him no more, I decide it was time for me to cut my ties too.

I hope you know, I ain't no fool. I could speak proper when the time come. Not all of we could do that, you know. Put me on the board, I could solve an equation or two. Free education is a nice concept, but free paychecks is a more attractive one. When the teacher absenteeism rate start rising higher than the students', it was time for plenty of we to tip the scales. To me, it was the wisest decision. It just much quieter out here on the backroad than in a circus without the lion tamer.

Foster was out for entirely different reasons, though. To Foster, droppin outta school was just a nervous impulse, snatched right outta the Vincey weed vapours one evenin. He always seem to have it all figured out, though. I tell you, for some reason, I was always lookin up to that boy. I never coulda figure out what I was doin and always fell in line with those who did.

For me, I had to spend sleepless nights convincin myself that I was teachin the damn Ministry of Education a *lesson*.

See, I was lettin the system *know*.

I had to feel like *I* was showin *them*.

Foster never had to show nobody nothin. Never had to prove he could be a big man without a father in he life. Never had to put he chin up to nobody. Never had to answer to nobody. Except one person: The King of Settlement 4.

As did I.

And as did everybody else, when the time come.

The King is the King, after all. And when the war finally decide to get you busy, what better company to be in than amongst all the King's men? What better place to be than on the winning side?

He live at the top – four storeys up. Scattered out between there and the shadows of the fenced-off perimeter of the complexes was all the King's men. Each one placed at corners and blind spots, shifting like rooks and bishops.

It have a reason this place is filthy, you know – why the walls is always stacked the hell up with garbage bags, wood palettes and old steel pipes. It have a reason some planks seem to be loose along the dog kennels, and that the lawns is never mowed. The more pockets to hide things, the better. A lot of detail is in this painstakin scheme behind the unsightliness, the uncleanliness… the ungodliness of Settlement 4.

This is why when every Thursday morning come, and the men in grey roll up in trios, they always go back home with their hands swinging. They blare their sirens and flash their bright blue lights under the bright blue sky, like they is gods of sound and thunder.

And the entire settlement never miss a beat.

Because we all know, as determined as any man in sweet T-and-T is, the salary of a policeman just ain't paying enough to sift through a dozen piles of tetanus-laden rust and steel at seven o' clock in the mornin.

At seven o' clock in the mornin, no man jack know nothin bout no dealins or monkey business. No, sir – no mother believes their sons are bad. Drink enough of the blood of Jesus and nobody's bad. Nobody here has a gazebo or a swimming pool. So how could anybody here be bad? When it have so much worse out there. So everyone in the settlement develops – as the older folks and them say – a case of *spontaneous laryngitis*.

You ain't sorry till you sorry you get catch.

But when that time come, nobody ain't know nothin. Nobody ain't want to know nothin. Nobody dare fuck with the monarchy of Settlement 4.

So, as I was sayin – when the war decide to get busy, what better place to sit your ass on than the winnin side?

Our jobs was to do that, exactly – to sit. Sit and keep we eyes open. Crates and paint buckets. Not much change in scenery except the cars passing back and forth. I imagine the drivers shakin their heads behind their window tints. Saying to themselves, *Look at them young fellas wasting them life.* But for me, it was always the opposite. Them people behind the tints was on their way to cash registers and screens and dusty storage rooms. To tap away, lift till their backs break, and get paid in shillings.

To me, *them* was the fools.

Unfortunately, even with easy money, a lack of challenge quickly shift into boredom. Being a lookout was worse than sittin through school assembly. Foster had already predict this, so he start bringin his dog with him – small, brown, fluffy dog name, Bodie. Foster always look funny playing with this small dog, combin its fur, but he didn't care much what people say. The dog meant more to him than anybody else. So, it was the damn best-treated dog in the settlement.

The dog look like a prince among the mange-ridden, matted-tail pothounds that climb in and out of the ravines. It was probably one of the only dogs in the settlement that had a collar, and probably the only one that you would never, ever throw a stone at. Foster would kill you for that.

I tell him one day, "You spoil this dog bad, boy."

"Was Bailey spoil the dog, not me. Was Bailey dog – you remember? You remember Bailey, right?" He scratched Bodie's ears.

Bailey was his big brother. "Well, how you mean – remember? Yes, damn right, I remember."

He scrape his rubber slippers against some loose gravel. He reminded me of a little boy all of a sudden, sulkin over a schoolyard brawl. Then he say, 'Don't get me wrong, eh, Bug. The dog is the dog, and Bailey is Bailey. I don't keep the dog round to remember the man or nothin. The dog is a good dog, is all.'

At first, Foster used to chain the dog to an old fridge at the side of the road where we used to sit. But eventually, he figure that he didn't need to. The dog never roam far. All Foster used to do for the whole day was light up and pet that dog.

When the evenings set in, the other boys used to come by and rally at Foster's spot. They pull out the cards, drag up some stools, some small crates, and run *wappi* and *all fours* under the streetlights for hours. I never used to stay for long. Couldn't stand most of them.

Another corner boy one street down – used to call heself Bone – was the one I couldn't stand the most. He was in Foster's class back in school. But about two years back, he get heself kick out for sticking an icepick into another boy's leg. It was in all three major newspapers. Not front page, but it was there. But heinous acts of violence come dime a dozen. News have a short shelf-life. One week and it gone stale.

So the crime was quickly dwarfed by other blood-red head-lines. Bone's only regret was that he was too young to have he name printed in the articles.

"I coulda be a big name in these parts, boy!" The asshole went on for a *month* straight.

Bone always went on and on about meetin with the King. It was his sole badge of merit that barely keep him one step up from being vermin – the one thing he depend on for respect and honour. The way he mumbled his words, the way he twitched he nose when he stared you down– everyone coulda tell he had the morals of a lepto-infected drain rat.

"Lookin like you fellas doin some good work here," Bone said, grinnin. "Maybe I could put in a word with the King. How that sound?"

Before I could even shake my head, Foster quickly agree for both of us. Bone put his arm around my neck and jab my side with his finger. I jump. And he laugh at me and say, "Maybe not you, small man."

Foster shook his head. "Give the boy a chance, Bone."

Bone lift his chin up and say to me, "When you stop pissin the bed."

When I went home, I was greeted the same way as every evenin since I drop out of school. My mother puffing smoke at the clock, sayin that I was just as worthless as my father. "One of these days, you ain't gon come home, you know," she said to me, shakin the cigarette at my face. "You long gone, Bug. Your ship done sail!"

Boy, I hate that saying. If I live till eighty, it *still* gon make my blood crawl. For the first week that I was absent from school, I was always lookin out to see if someone from the staff would bother to come see me: The Principal. The Dean of Discipline – maybe Ms Simmons from English class. But not one soul ever reach. I figure, the energy wasn't worth it for a couple of ragamuffin boys from Settlement 4.

The Principal always drop his mantra at the beginnin of every boring assembly for each new school year. 'You ain't have to fraid the storm if you learn to sail the ship.' I used to suck my teeth every time. Sailin ships always get pull into the storm if they out there in the damn water, you know.

So, how I would put it? *You ain't have to fraid the storm if you* is *the storm.*

Make more sense! It have no place better to be than the eye. And that was where I was. No matter how big the storm get, how far it stretch, it have no better place to be than in the direct centre of it all.

A few days later, it seem that Bone actually pull through for Foster. He get him moved to the snack kiosk at the intersection near the tail of the backroad. "Movin up in life!" Bone said, pattin Foster's back.

When Foster left, I was alone. The sun used to sting a little more. The dust trails rose a little higher. The car parts strewn across the grass rusted a little faster. I had a radio, but the radio was never somethin that you actively listened to. You listen while you drive, while you cook, while you do homework, while you getting through with your girl. Not like this.

I started bringin my textbook with me. I know, I know. I know how that sound. I like science. Was just hard luck I ain't see my fuckin science teacher in two months. So, yes, I was readin about science and lookin out for police at the same time. And I was thinkin, *Aye, ain't this the perfect cover?* Who gon think a boy with a big old Physics book in he hand dealin with them other badjohns in Settlement 4?

But whenever any of the other boys used to walk past, I make sure to hide the book behind the paint bucket I was sittin on. But mostly, I ain't bother much with the other people who walk past me. In just a day, I figured out levers.

Load. Effort. Fulcrum.

Equilibrium. Balance. Advantage. The works!

That evening, I walked over to the snack kiosk. The weed smelling strong as I step up. I half-joke with Foster, "You lucky the police ain't come to buy no bananas, boy. They gon sniff you out in no time."

Foster step out of the kiosk and pat my shoulder. Bodie was good-good, wandering bout with the other dogs. Bone was standin there with Foster. Bone say to me, "Let the man blaze in peace."

I play like I ain't hear him. Foster laugh and shift aside a board from the base of the kiosk and pull out a crumpled ball of aluminium foil. He unfold it and start to roll up another spliff. I could only watch in *amazement*, yes. I chuckle nervously and ask the boy, "You sure you could take from there?"

Foster look at me serious all of a sudden. "The deal is, we just subtract it. You need to calm yourself, Bug."

"Deal with who?"

"You is the man mother now, boy?" Bone say. He grabbed the spliff from Foster and took a long drag on it. Blow the smoke in my face slow-slow. Tried my best to hold in the cough – though I'm sure it show in my eyes. He bring it towards me.

"Take the t'ing," he say to me, grittin his teeth. I just look at his hand and give him a blank stare. He push it towards me again. "You too good for it?"

I could only shake my head and walk off. I ain't no fool.

On my way home, I pass by the King's building. Even if you was from the outside, you coulda know which one it was. There was always men there, listening to the same five songs over and over again. They had cutlasses hidden in the bushes and guns stashed in hollowed planks of wood, long discarded and forgotten by Housing.

As I walk inside my house and close the door behind me, my mother say, "The Principal call for you today, boy. He want to know why you skipping school."

"What you –"

"I say, if you want that boy, mister, you come and find him." She give me a long, hard look. Then she went on, "I ain't have *time* to deal with your shit, Bug. How long I ask you to help me clean this house? Shit, man, at least help me clean. But you too big for that, ain't that so? Me, a old lady and you's a big man. Ain't that so? You can't even help me fuckin clean?"

I inhale hard and scowl. Then I made one of the worst decisions since I drop out. I mutter under my breath, "Clean out your fat ass."

She got up from her recliner and flick she cigarette at me. Sweat was pourin down she puffy cheeks. The veins in she yellow eyes throbbed. "Don't pull that shit with me, eh, boy. You want to try shit with me? *You want to fuck with me?* You done gone and drop the fuck outta school and feel you could say something to me? Boy, don't let me –"

She yank off she slipper, hoppin on one foot, and pelt me with it. As she move to take off the other one, I brace myself. I thought she was gon chase me with it. But she was suddenly calm. She grasp she nightie and rubbed the middle of she breasts slowly.

Then she sat down, facing away from me. She spoke slowly now, hoarse from the yellin. "You getting too old for me to beat your ass. Because you's the big man now. You do what you fuckin want, but not under my fuckin roof, Bug, you hear?"

I left the house and slam the door. I decide to go back to the snack kiosk. On my way back, I notice that the men outside the King's building was chatting with Bone. I kept on my way to the kiosk and saw Foster still there. Foster was sittin at the heel of the shack, scratchin the dog's chin.

"You pullin a double shift tonight, boy?" I ask him, faking a laugh.

"Just manning the front before Bone take over," he say. "He coming back now-now. I thought you went home?"

I smile at him. "Mom's being a beast."

"What you do to the poor woman?"

"I don't want to be in the house when she burn it down, is all."

Foster laugh. Then a voice spoke:

"She better be careful. The fire hydrants this side don't work so good," a man say, appearin behind us. His voice was like a cold wind. We both turn we heads to him and gasped when our eyes fell on his.

It was him. It was fuckin *him*.

The King was wearin a tattered vest and cargo pants that had rips near the waistline. His clothes look as old as he did. His elderly smile was cloaked in a scrim of cigarette smoke. He blew two snakes of smoke out of his nostrils. The slanted sinks along his cheeks tightened and sharpened like knife wounds from some Amerindian rite of passage. Straggly grey hair lined his jaw. A horseshoe pattern of hair stippled his bald head. The man radiated a cancerous heat, like I imagine the Devil always does.

We had no words. There was nothing to say. That *spontaneous laryngitis.*

"I ain't fraid fire," he say. He extend his hand to us and accept our limp handshakes with glee. "Ice is what you must fear." His voice was strong, but smooth. It didn't crinkle like brown paper, like most other men his age.

He continue, "Sadly, no way it all gonna go down except with ice. Everything preserved in its naturally ugly state. World wouldn't be destroyed, you know. Is just going to slow down to a stop. Until nothing moving. Trapped in ice."

We nodded.

He narrow his eyes. "That is how I see it. Everything becoming a mirror. Light bouncing off the ice, you know? And the frozen people in Australia would be able to see all the way over here in Trinidad, through them mirrors."

He paced around, kicking gravel as he did. He continue, "Everyone frozen in their sins. Mothers frozen with knives to their babies. Fathers frozen with their pricks in their daughters. Sons frozen with guns to angels. All for the world to see. And all reflecting through eternity."

He scrape the back of his heel with his shoe. This mother-fucker's eyes cut right through me. I didn't want to look. He turn to Foster and ask, "What sin you think you gon be frozen in?"

"I don't know." Foster tremble.

"Say sir when you address me."

"I don't know, sir."

The King furrow his brow. "You believe me to be a fair man?"

"Yes, sir."

"You know how long I's King of Settlement 4?"

"No, sir."

"I's King of Settlement 4 before it even had a Settlement 4. Before there was buildings here to speak of. I claim this place long time when it was just grass and cow shit. Since before you was in your daddy's balls. That is how long I been King." He took another drag and then ask, "What you think the other kings back in the day would do if they know you was stealin from them?"

"I don't know, sir."

The King turn to me. "What you think they would do, young boy?"

I spat out, "Chop off their hands, sir."

Foster look at me, eyes widened. The King laugh.

His eyes jump to the dog. The King look at the animal with a kinda hunger, boy, I can't describe it any other way. It was only when Foster turn to him that I realise what he was gon do.

"Sir, please." Foster's voice start crackin.

The King's calm expression suddenly contorted into intense fury – fury like I only imagine coulda be on the face of the Almighty in the Old Testament. His upper lip curl and twist as his eyes flash. He grab Bodie's leash and curl it around his fist. Foster start breathin hard. I open my mouth to say somethin, but I just couldn't.

My teeth was chattering; my muscles all jelly. Spit growing sour in my mouth fast.

The King lift Bodie from the ground. The dog start kickin and barkin, until his voice winded down to a muffled wheeze I never hear any animal make before. "Sir, sir, sir, sir, sir, come, come, please," Foster pleaded, droppin to his knees – his voice a rapid-fire stutter. Foster began to sob like mad.

The King was swingin the dog like a pendulum. The dog let out a shriek with each oscillation. Finally The King tie the leash to a nail at the top of the kiosk.

He let the dog hang there.

The dog's scruff was pushed over its mouth as its neck tilted and began to slowly fracture. We couldn't tell exactly when the dog died. It was kickin long after the life in his eyes disappeared. The King then take out his gun and shoot the dog once in the head.

It didn't take me long to figure out why he would shoot the dead dog. It was just to make a fuckin mess. Just to get blood on his clothes. Just to get brains on the road.

I look around. No one came out of their houses. There was nothin to see and nothin to say. There was nobody to call. And even if some fool decided to, there was no policeman that was gon try to hold the King on charges of animal cruelty. It coulda be the best dog in the world, the salary of a policeman didn't call for it.

Shit, I tellin you, at that moment, I realise we was all dogs here. Nobody payin any of them people enough to do anythin but drag we tails off the road, dead or alive.

Foster press his forehead against the asphalt. The King knelt beside him and rub his back gently. He ask him, "What's your name?"

"Frederick Foster," he manage to reply through the snivels.

The King then say to him, "Frederick Foster, you have to be in a fit state of mind next time I see you or it gon be your ass. That's how things work round here. Because I can do anything. You could understand that? *Anything*. That's why I'm King."

The King tip Foster's chin upwards and looked him dead in the eye. "Now, say thank you."

Foster's face was shrivelled with tears. The King repeated, "Thank me for my mercy, Frederick Foster."

The words came out slowly, subdued. "Thank you."

"For what?"

"For your… mercy…"

"You're welcome." The King grin and dust himself off. He hobble past me without even a glance. He step over my feet like I was shit. As he approach the corner, I try not to keep my eyes on him. I hope to never see that face up close again. Not even in a dream.

Foster sat in the road, still sobbin. First time in my life I ever see that boy cry. I didn't know what to say. What was there to say? Shit, man. I never had no training for this. I try hard to find the words, but they never came.

A week pass and man, I still tryin.

We ain't speak since that night.

As soon as I reach back home, I clean that fuckin house from top to bottom. Crack to crevice. I sweep every dead cockroach from under from every mat. It had so much, you coulda make a bonfire with them. I was on my knees, scrubbin every floor. My kneecaps had dents by the time I was done, I swear. I *exfoliated* that bathroom, sir. The Virgin Mary woulda be proud to come take a shit in it. Three o' clock in the mornin, I was still sandpaperin muck from the walls.

I'll tell you something – housekeepin ain't no joke.

My mother didn't thank me. She didn't apologise either. And neither did I. That's just how things is.

The next day, I didn't go back out to my point. I wasn't gon fuck with that no more. But Foster was right back at it. I walk right past him every day. We don't look at each other. That's how it is.

A mutual feelin of defeat and shame. The difference is, I could admit it. I ain't cut out for this shit. He still dealin with it.

Shame is a hell of a thing to feel in a place where there ain't much to help unshame yourself but by shooting the motherfucker who make you feel it.

That evenin, I notice that Bone was promoted. He wasn't a lowly lookout or dealer no more. Now, he held his head high as a soldier of the fortress, now with a cutlass buried in the bush and a gun hidden in a plank. He see me lookin at him. And started barkin like a dog at me, and cacklin like mad. I just keep walkin.

There was nothin nobody coulda do to him now. No revenge. No comeuppance. Not when he had all the King's men on his side. Not one thing you could do. Not one fuckin thing – if you valued your life, anyway.

You could pray for karma. You could pray for him to catch some lead. You could pray for him to choke on chicken gristle. Not much else to rely on for comfort. That boy gonna die repeatedly in my dreams, and that have to be good enough for me to carry on with my life.

Told you, I ain't no fool.

There ain't much of a conclusion to this story. That still to come, I say. There ain't much else to tell. Ain't gone back to school yet, but that ain't stoppin my studies. I guess I could end by tellin you bout what happen yesterday. It have this old broken-down playpark at the edge of the savannah. A depressin collection of pee-stained slides, wobbly swings, and a decapitated rocking horse as the centrepiece. But the seesaw was working tiptop.

Two boys was trying to use it. One was much fatter than the other, and they couldn't figure out how to balance it. The smaller boy was yellin and cussin at the fatter one. And before I know it, a fight break loose. I rush in and hold them back.

After I was finish calmin them down, I told the fatter one to sit nearer to the middle of the seesaw, and the smaller one to sit further away. Greater lengths create greater turning forces. It finally balanced and they was both able to have fun.

Load. Effort. Fulcrum.

Equilibrium. Balance. Advantage.

If you can derive some meaningful, symbolic shit in that scenario I described, then I tellin you – maybe somewhere in there, we could find a solution to all of this. But I know for sure I ain't findin a single scrap of one while sitting on a damn paint bucket.

VALDA JACKSON

AN AGE OF REASON (COMING HERE)

The Father

It's not really money you know, weh make me come here. No I didn't really come here just for that. It's the baby body buried in your granny's yard. I couldn' live there with it. And I didn't have anywhere else to take you all.

You don't remember Michael. No, you couldn't remember him. You was just baby yourself when he die. You didn't even have your second birthday yet.

I couldn't stay there. I just couldn't stay. But your mother never want to leave her mother's yard – they were real close – and if it wasn't for the baby grave, I could stay there as well, for her mother was a lovely lovely woman. And she was real real good to us.

You know, I move all over Jamaica before I end up in St. Thomas. Although is St. Ann where I born, and I live in a whole heap of other places as well, but I feel St. Thomas is my real home because nowhere else did I feel as welcome and as happy as I did there.

And it's there I meet your mother.

When I first meet her… I tell you, Julie, I couldn' believe my luck.

From the first time we meet, I know I have to marry her.

She was going to market for her mother. And another time after that she was coming back from town.

We talk for just a little while and I tell her that I really like her ways, and I would like to see her again. She tell me that if I want to see her, I have to come to her house and meet her mother and the rest of the family as well.

You know, your mother never really walk up and down.

She never go a dance, nor walk and chat. Mm mm.

She always stay at home and help her mother.
Your mother was a serious Christian. I could see that.
She was just eighteen when we meet.

She take me to her mother. And I tell you, that woman, Mistress Catherine, you couldn' find any better than she. She was so lovely. It was just few weeks after May and I meet that I talk to her mother. I say: "Mistress Catherine, I'm real serious about your daughter, and if I have your blessing, and if she will have me, I going to ask her to marry me."

It's not that I really asking permission of her you know, for I believed that she would give it. But I wanted to have her full blessing.

And also… I never want her to think that I would take advantage of her as widow-woman having no man there to protect her and her daughters. Because nuffnuff man was ready in them times to mash up young girls and then walk away. And she was a good good mother to me as well.

You know I was orphaned when I was a small boy; I never know anyone to call mother. But you see, Julie, when I meet your mother, it's not just wife I find. I find a mother as well. *Her* mother was a real mother for me.

So you see, I was happy at your granny's yard. She was good to us… but I know we couldn't live there forever. We did have a plan that when we save enough money we would buy piece a land down a Yallahs and build a little house and plant it up. But you know something? With that little grave in Mama's yard… I really couldn't stay there any longer.

I just couldn't stay.

They have advertisement all over, telling people to come to England to work.

So… I tell your mother I want to go there and work. And you know, we believed we could save even quicker to get that piece of land. I tell her it would be better if we leave you girls with Mama and go together but she say she can't leave you and your sisters them. I beg her come with me.

Even her mother pleading with her. Even Mama say we must go together and leave you all with her because she can take care of the three of you.

And I would trust her. I would trust that woman with my life.
I know that she would do her very best for unnu girls.
But May, she say no… she not leaving you all. She wouldn't
come.
She never want to leave her children.
She woul' come.
So, I leave St. Thomas on my own.
Just as I come.

I used to write your mother. And you know my writing not so
good for when my mother die I have to stop going to school. But
I write anyway for I miss her. I miss all of you.
I feel it yu si.
I really feel it.
I tell you Julie, it wasn't easy leaving you all behind… and
without your mother as well.
It was hard… them times…
I really want her with me.
Chu… them times was tuff.
Tuff tuff.

Sarah, The Eldest Sister

I don't remember having a childhood after Mummy left.
When she left, that was the end of being a child for me.
I never played. I was too busy looking out for us.
It was after Michael died.
I bet you don't remember when Michael died do you?
But I do.
It was awful.
I think I was five.
I just remember… Mummy suddenly calling out to her mother.
She shouted: "Mama. Mama. The baby dead." And Mama came
running in from the kitchen. I can still see Mama trying to hold
Mummy up… and the crying, I still hear it sometimes. You've
forgotten haven't you?
Wish *I* could forget.

It wasn't long after, that Daddy left.

And then when *she* left to join him that was it for me.

The end of freedom.

The end of play.

I mean – we weren't protected, Julia.

There was no one really looking after us.

At that time, remember, Mama still had three of her own teenage children living at home. Of course Aunty G was supposed to be helping with us, but I don't think she was even fourteen then.

Then there were other cousins living with us as well because two of Mummy's older sisters had already gone to England and Mama was looking after their children as well. So she had the three of us – you, Elaine and me – and our cousins Maureen and Collette and there was Sherrie and Millicent, and Aunty Enid's boys, and Aunty Evelyn's as well. There must have been more than eight or nine of us grand children all below the age of eight. I'm not even counting those older boys. She couldn't manage so many; no matter how much she loved us. It's not possible.

I could see that, and I was five.

Elaine was just four and you were only two. I felt I had to look after the two of you… and you. You weren't easy. They had to tear you off me every morning so I could go to school and then I'd come home and find you damp and tetchy, just rocking and banging your head against Mama's kitchen wall. It's a miracle you have any sense left… though sometimes, Julia, I do wonder.

I remember when Elaine was ill soon after Mummy left and Mama had to get her to the doctor. She had the three of us with her and I think two or three of our cousins as well.

It was a long walk and Elaine couldn't manage it. Mama had to carry her most of the way. I think that was the time she had a sore on her leg that just wouldn't heal. Of course Mama wouldn't have known, but it was probably due to the sickle cell.

No one knew it then.

To get to the clinic we had to cross the river and it was flood time.

The only way Mama could get us across was on her back.
And that's what she did.

One at a time.

She tied up her skirt – carried one over, and came back for another till we were all on the other side.

You must remember the passport, Julia.

When we came, the three of us came on one passport – and it was mine.

Bet you don't even remember what it said; do you?

It said: "Miss Sarah Andrea Jenkins aged 8 accompanied by two small children." Miss Jenkins, that was me. Accompanied by Elaine and you; the small children. Hah.

It didn't even have your names on it.

You lost your glove on the plane.

All three of us had these little white gloves when we left. Mummy sent them in a parcel from England. D'you remember? Probably the prettiest things we'd ever owned. All lacy. One of yours disappeared down the toilet on the plane and you wouldn't stop crying for it.

I didn't know what to do so I went and told the stewardess thinking she could get it back. But of course she couldn't. We had no idea then, I mean, we'd never seen a flush toilet before. And anyway, that stewardess was supposed to be looking after us. But she didn't really pay any attention to us. Nobody did. They just made sure that we got on the plane and saw to it that we got off again. Then someone else took us to Immigration where we had to wait for Mummy to pick us up.

She was really late.

You were miserable and cried all the time.

I couldn't stop worrying. I thought she wasn't going to come.

And when she did come, even *I* didn't recognise her at first. She'd put on so much weight. Elaine didn't recognise her either, and *you*... *I* had to drag you over. You wouldn't go near her. Then you refused to talk to her. Kept on saying you didn't know her, and you wanted to go back to Aunty G.

Honestly, Julia. You were so contrary. When she left us in Jamaica you wouldn't let Mama or anyone else touch you. Just hung on to me crying for your mummy. We come to her and you're still grabbing on to me and pleading to go back to aunty. Then you refused to *say* "Mummy", calling her Sister May... as if we were still back home at Mama's!

But that's what our cousins and everyone else called her.

Even her own mother, used to call her Sister May because she was a Christian. But *we* shouldn't have.

Anyone would think you really wanted her to send us back. Weren't you worried?

I was always fearful that she might. She seemed so powerful. Even when she'd left Jamaica she had power. She still managed to keep us safe. I mean, those big boys messing with our cousins, even they knew that they mustn't mess with you, me or Elaine. They knew who our mother was and that she was going to send for us. Everyone knew that *we* weren't going to be left forever like the others. And if she couldn't get us to England with her, then she would come back. I knew it because she told us. Everyone knew. Except you. *You* forgot before she even left. But *those boys knew* she'd be back; and there wasn't one of them brave enough to touch us and then face our mother.

You don't remember any of this do you?

I had to keep on telling you, "She *is* our mother, Julia, and she sent for us, and now that we're here you *have* to call her Mummy."

The Mother

You know, I was never really meant to come here.

I never wanted to leave my children. And it was never part of our plan.

I never wanted to come.

It's your daddy want to come. And we agreed that he would come and work so we could save more. I wasn't meant to come. It was never part of our plan.

And then, after the baby die... you couldn' remember him, for you were just small… your daddy say he couldn't carry on living at my mother's yard. He couldn't live there anymore with the little baby body buried there.

We did plant some Joseph's coats around it.

Yu wouldn't believe how quick they grow up and spread across the little plot.

And even before they start to show, your daddy was already gone.

But I never want to come here; for although the baby die we still have you three girls.

And I couldn't leave you. I just couldn' do that.

You must know I never want to leave you.

I really never wanted to leave you to come here.

It's not what we planned.

Those first letters that your daddy write; I know he wasn't happy.

He try to make them sound good, but I could feel how he was struggling. He write and say how he's missing us, and I must come join him because with two of us working we would manage better, and we could save more money to buy the piece of land. But I reply and say I couldn't leave my children.

I remember one letter in particular, he was almost saying his "good bye" because he couldn't see how he was going to support himself in England and send enough money back home for us as well with just one wage packet, and he begging me to come and help him.

But I didn't want to leave unnu.

It was Mama persuade me to come.

When I read the "good bye" letter, she see how upset I was and she say "You know, Sister May, perhaps you really should go."

Is she make me leave.

I tell her "No. I can't leave my children."

I wasn't going to come here. And if it weren't for Mama, I would never have come.

I ask her "How I must leave my children and go so far?"

Mama get vex and tell me that it's because I don't trust her with my children. For if I have trust in her, then I would do what my sisters did and leave the three of you there with her and join my husband in England.

But it wasn't that.

No. It wasn't that. It's just that I couldn' bear to not have you all with me.

It's really Mama make me come.

And then when I come here, I couldn't rest.

I could not rest until I had you all with me.

I couldn't rest.

And you know, the day I book your tickets, your daddy never know.

Even though he and I share a bed the night, in the morning I leave the house after he already gone to work… and I book the flight.

I tell him when he come home that evening.

When I tell him, he throw his hands up and say "Lord! Woman yu mad? Where yu goin put them?"

Yu see, is just one room we have. And by that time we already have George, and Rosie was baby… and all four of us living in one little room in Sparkbrook.

I was off shift next morning and I leave the house early and start looking. I tell you that day I walk, I walk, I walk so till.

English people not letting to me. And finding two rooms instead of one… I could find nothing. And I tell you, is when my foot swell up and I ready to drop, I walking back home I bump into Brother Wilkins on the Stratford Road.

You remember Brother Wilkins? He did have a daughter name Jacqueline. You must remember her from Sunday School. Well anyway. He say that he have two rooms in his house and it wasn't far, so I walk with him round there. I ask him how the rooms come to be empty and he say that the family that had the rooms before, had children, and their children and his daughter didn't get on. He show me around and it was really a nice house. It had three floors. The two rooms were on the first floor. Nice big rooms. My heart glad that I see him that day.

But then I meet the daughter… Oh… She was a brat.

I could see why the other family couldn't continue to live there. I couldn't bring you all up here to that house.

I just wanted a place where my children could live and not be teased.

I did see an advertisement for a house for sale on Goldney Road. But we never have money to buy house. I never really give it any mind. Remember your daddy only come to save up to buy land in Jamaica so we were not thinking of buying house in England.

I have to beg to persuade your daddy to come look at this house with me.

We had to scrimp to find the deposit.

But by the Grace of God we manage to find it.

And we have somewhere to put you.

It was almost three years yu know since I leave you girls in Jamaica with Mama.

On the Sunday night I soak up my pillow with tears and I decide I'm not going to cry any more nights for unu. I just going to have my children with me.

I book your tickets on the Monday morning and you all were coming on the Saturday. So… we didn't have much time.

Not even a full week we have.

But we found Goldney Road.

And we managed to find the deposit.

God is good.

Elaine, The Second Born

Ooh, Julia, I like this. It's like one of those tinted photos of us from the sixties.

Hang on a minute… I need my glasses for this.

Oh my life… it's… it's us. That is us. It is us; isn't it?

There we are, me, you…

How come Sarah's not there?

We were a threesome then. In those days.

Where are we though…?

Oh I know… I do know…

It's the dining room at the old house in Goldney Road.

I really loved those curtains.

And the wallpaper with the apples and the grapes. D'you remember when Daddy hung that paper? I remember that. And he had no idea how wallpaper should be hung. None of us knew that he should match up the pictures at the edges, did we? …That the fruit should be matched so you don't see the separate strips across the wall like that.

It stayed up for years that wallpaper.

Can't believe you remember all this… How much time did you spend painting this? Must have taken you ages.

Why?

Why would you want to paint this? I can't believe it.

We're wearing our judging clothes. Did anyone else call them that?

I think we must have been the only ones who called them that.

And Daddy singing and swinging the little ones on his leg.

Look how Rosie's holding on.

Wasn't she a lovely? She was a beautiful baby.

And little George waiting his turn – with his hands in his little pockets. Oaoaorh sooo cute… There are some photos somewhere of him standing just like this. So lovely.

Shame we never had any baby photos of us…

You've really captured the likeness of everyone.

He used to let them sit on his foot and hold on to his leg.

This is so… o… o funny. It's really weird… remembering all this… stuff.

Why've you painted this? It's odd. Really weird.

Why do you even think about this stuff, Julia?

I don't know why you do it.

You need to forget it! That's what I did.

I never think about those things.

I really don't.

I can't believe you even remember it.

Just look at you standing there. Looking at them.

So like you.

I don't know why it meant so much to you.

You really wanted to have a go didn't you?

You wanted to join in.

I remember… I was pulling on your skirt to make you sit back down, but you just stood there… watching.

Waiting.

Hhhuh

And then you actually asked for a go.

I wouldn't have even asked. I'd never ask them for anything.

I mean, what's the point?

I knew you wouldn't get a turn.

We never got turns at anything.

The trouble is, Julia…

You really wanted to be like them; didn't you?

You wanted to be one of the little ones.

I've always thought that. You wanted to be like them.

Even Sarah used to say that you *should* really be one of them because you were quite young when we came here and you weren't that much older than them. You were really small. Still a baby really. *She* thought you should be treated the same.

You really *did* want to be one of them, didn't you?

But you weren't born here were you?

You were one of Us.

One of the bigger ones.

Rosie, One of the Little Ones

Julia, I just peeped my head round the door of your studio. I hope you don't mind… but that painting, I had to go in and take a closer look. I was on my way upstairs to see what the kids were up to, but honestly Julia… it just drew me in.

Gave me goosebumps it did. Really made the hairs on the back of neck stand on end.

It's beautiful. All that detail. Tch, you're so clever you are.

Every thing about the old dining room at Goldney Road, you've got it all, to a tee. Even the wallpaper… That wallpaper was up forever.

All these years I never even thought about that time. Then

suddenly… Honestly, it jumped me right back to it. I mean, I found myself holding on for dear life to Daddy's leg and felt the great whoop of rising up through the air, head thrown back and looking up at him. Like staring into the eyes of God. He seemed so far away. I used to think I was flying… And the song just poured out of my mouth. Do you remember it…?

Oh my God, after all this time… and that funny little song… there it was in my head… Daddy's song – every word, just came back to me. You probably heard me singing it…

> Here on our rock-away horse we go,
> Johnny and I, to a land we know,
> Far away in the sunset gold,
> A lovelier land than can be told
>
> Where all the flowers go niddlety nod,
> Nod, nod, niddlety nod.
> Where all the flowers go niddlety nod,
> And all the birds sing by-low
> Lullaby, lullaby, by-low

One minute I was singing and then I burst out laughing as though I really was rising through the air. And swinging… Honestly… there I was, right in that room, and I was almost hysterical. I really was that tiny child again. It was utter joy. And then before I realised it, I was crying my eyes out… I mean, properly sobbing, Julia.

I had to sit down… and great idea putting the old sofa there by the way, I dropped into it; and you were right, you can't have too many cushions… So, I'm all cushioned up and just listening to Daddy's voice. Didn't he have a lovely voice, Julia? It was so soft… really gentle. Pure velvet. I could actually hear him. It's as if I was being cradled, like he was rocking me… I felt so warm… and Julia, you're not gonna believe this…

I fell asleep.

KEITH JARDIM

NEAR OPEN WATER

The world of the living contains enough marvels and mysteries as it is: marvels and mysteries acting upon our emotions and intelligence in ways so inexplicable that it would almost justify the conception of life as an enchanted state.
    – 'Author's Note' to *The Shadow-Line*, Joseph Conrad

Adam had an idea.
He and the snake would share
the loss of Eden for a profit.
So both made the New World. And it looked good.
    – "New World," Derek Walcott

I

The house was built against a cliff cut into the earth so it could be cool and shaded and out of sight from the open sea. Level with the roof there are trees, and their land slopes upward to bushes and other trees that almost hide a wire fence. The grass there crackles underfoot. The dry season should end soon. On the house's smooth white roof, half-cylindrical plastic drains line the edges to collect rainwater and direct it to the cistern under the house. It has not rained for months. The house belongs to my cousin Jason.

There are times when I feel it's impossible to just walk away, to get on with it, as they say, to look forward to a future in which our memories have been relegated to the day-to-day details on a drink-stained postcard one sends to tepid acquaintances from the lobbies of tourist hotels.
    Will we let that happen to us? Will you?
    Remember me. Imagine me.

From the balcony of Jason's house – an area sectioned off from the living room by wooden green walls of horizontal planks and varnished wooden pillars – through the trees I can see small islands on the blue sea. Apart from the northeastern tip of one, they are untouched, looking as they did, I imagine, when they adjusted to the atmosphere after being pushed up out of the sea; many of the smaller uninhabited islands in the Lesser Antilles give this impression. The touched part of that one island, the biggest one visible, Crump Island, is a scar of earth, made by idiots who ripped the green away for some resort idea they had. Thankfully, I cannot see it from Jason's house. But if I go along the driveway, past where there is a scented plum tree shadowing part of the house, to where it widens circularly and is laden with rotting plums on the dark grey gravel, toward the dull-green gate at the end, then continue through the gate and turn inland, I come to a hill whose top allows me to see the scar. There're no other signs of human habitation: no cars, no houses, no sounds, nothing, no matter where I look, whether toward the smaller islands to the northeast, where the one with the scar is, or around what I can see of the main island. There's only the dirt road I walked up the hill on (it goes no further), and another dirt road that takes you several miles away from the house to a main road into town. From up there, Jason's house is hidden mostly by the trees and land above it. The scar can appear uncanny if I watch it long enough, against the blues of sea and sky.

Jason, who is on holiday for six weeks with his wife Kim, has a dog, Ojay, a white Alsatian. She was capricious, even growling at first, but I spent time with her so now she tolerates me. When I set the alarm at night, she seems to accept me a bit more each time, meeting me at the two-car garage, even accompanying me on my rounds, as if checking to see I'm doing it properly. She's been trained not to go within ten feet of any of the seven alarms after I set the system. In the morning it's just a matter of tapping in one code, and everything goes off.

Ojay is playful, rushing blue-grey herons that feed on little crabs and fish on the shoreline. The herons break into the air when Ojay charges, and she looks after them, a front paw raised, her ears at their straightest, while she whines, as if regretting the evolutionary path her species followed.

★

Are islands cursed for people like us?

This is intriguing: "an area sectioned off"? – You mean cut off, don't you? It's what happens here, isn't it? We've been separated. Why? Islands are cut off. Removed. Is that a clue? Write something else, please, for God's sake. Write about us.

And tell me: are you going to go and take a good look at that scar again? Why even mention it if you have no intention of doing so. What is it in the blue? And are you going to mention what you found on the hill?

Is this some sort of ecological lament? And what's this: "As if regretting the evolutionary path her species followed." Really, that Ojay's some bitch.

Tied to Jason's jetty are two boats. One belongs to his brother, and is called *Miss Lisa*. It's a biggish boat, the kind used for deep-sea fishing, with a hood on top, two powerful outboard Yamaha engines, and aerials. Blue and white, it points east, as do both the boats. The next boat is Jason's – a Boston whaler called *Rumrunner*, also blue and white and smaller than *Miss Lisa*. Jason's boat has a light, sharp look as it sits on the water. Once the Boston whaler picks up speed and the bow levels off – maybe I'm going to the island near Water Heaven – the island where there are stranded llamas because of a deal some local and American businessmen attempted – the whaler skims over the water like a flying fish. Not used to the climate, the llamas have been dying. With the air becoming heavy and still, and the great heat upon the land, I think the llamas, when they die, die with relief.

What is it that prevents you from looking closely at you and me, I wonder. What is it? I'm here, there, wherever you want. The Sahara dust sticks to my skin when I run in the afternoons. Imagine it. Then the rain will come and it will rain for days on end and the sky will be washed clean. The rains are here, people will say. Rain for days. We love the rain.

The future is the future and all we can do is to leave it open to possibility. Don't you agree? Don't you see?

There are mornings when it's difficult to write. At the long table on the western side of the balcony, next to the corner of the green wall that enables me to see the sea and islands, the difficulty of finding what I want to say discourages me. At these times the colours of the land and sea, the quality of light and the massive expanse of sea (nothing between here and Africa), help to connect me to a part of myself with which I'm uneasy, that gives me little faith in my work.

That day I went up the hill I saw what might be the problem, at least a sign of it. I found an iron, one used about two hundred years ago, maybe even longer, just an old heavy, rusted iron, compact and still intact, a blunt solid thing. It seemed so weapon-like. I imagined it must have pressed many clothes, the labour of slaves who worked in those outdoor kitchens and rooms away from the main houses. I wanted to dig; maybe there was more to find, but I didn't; it felt wrong somehow – I'm not sure why, perhaps because the land belongs to Jason. He should be the one to discover what's there.

I left the iron where I found it, and walked over the crest of the hill, where the vegetation is swept like hair blown back, lashed again and again by the wind, and then began the descent to the shore, where the mangrove thickets cluster (this area is about two hundred and fifty yards northeast of Jason's jetty). There's a rough path winding down steeply through the bush. I saw footprints there last week, bare feet.

Why do you go there? You leave the hill and descend into a pit of vegetation where the close heat and loamy soil are enough to swamp the air. The curiosity is interesting, but why not go elsewhere, the other side of the hill, for example, where the dirt road runs past the old sugar mills with the slave pits? You took me there once. Why don't you go to the beach cove at the end of the road, below the stone ruins of the plantation house? It, too, would get you away from Jason's house, away from the blue, boiling eye of the sky.

Swimming occupies an hour in the late afternoons. To swim earlier is dangerous. There was a documentary my sister mentioned (when she called from London) about the high increase in skin cancer. Do the work and be careful, she said.

I try to.

Lot of good she did us... This matter of faith, and the uneasy part of yourself – you leave it abruptly. No reflection whatever; you told me that's dangerous, that's what's wrong with the world – the neglect of history, and of selves, even. And here you are, guilty of it, refusing to take your own advice. Or is it the melancholy the sea brings to most of us? It can't be just that. What are you doing? It seems an act of destruction has begun, something like the llamas, no? Or that scar on the island you seem reluctant to gaze out at again from the hill. An erasure of some kind, an attempt, rather, on your part is in progress. All I know for sure is that you're there, and I'm here. But would you put it entirely that way? Ha.

Got you there, didn't I.

Like those llamas, you're in a dangerous climate.

The occasional airplane and boat pass silently in the far distance. But once, about three weeks ago, a boat larger than *Miss Lisa* came right down past Jason's jetty. I was at the long green table on the balcony, writing, or trying to, and by the time I heard it, the boat was there, just off the jetty, cruising slowly: *Mornin' Glory*, pure luxury. I'm constantly struck by how the people on such boats seem beyond the reach of the mundane things of this world. Three men were in the stern, with a woman in a black string bikini prowling the main deck. On the upper deck a man and woman sat at the wheel. They were all stylish-looking. The women looked bought. The trees that rise above the roof of the house hide the balcony from the water but allow me to see what's beyond; yet when one of the men looked at the house with binoculars, I stayed absolutely still.

Birds, dark and brown with short arrowhead-shaped beaks, a dab of red on their chests, visit the wood-plank railing on the balcony; some alight on the long table I sit at. They have a high-pitched chirp, and sometimes I'm startled. Ojay appears then, giving a bark and glare as they fly off to the plum tree by the driveway. She patrols around the house at a brisk pace, usually in the late afternoons or at dusk and dawn. At night, when I wake, I hear her on duty.

Hummingbirds, too, are frequent visitors. I watch their tiny, sabre-like beaks, their feathers the colour of dark jade and dark emeralds that shine as if drips of glistening oil have been delicately rubbed onto their chests and heads. I hear whirring sounds from their blurred wings: it's that quiet here, now the pre-storm weather has come. When there's breeze, and the bougainvillea rustles and waves bunches of red and peach flowers to bounce against each other, I can't hear them; today, I can.

You're distracted, all right. And I know you hear my voice as sure as the sea's before you. You made a mistake by sitting before the sea in your cousin's abandoned house to write. And who were those people in the boat?

Wait a minute. Wait. I see something now of what you're doing. Do you?

One day a hummingbird meandered through the bougainvillea growing above the barbecue pit at the western side of the balcony. I was sitting at the table on the porch whose steps come up from the circular part of the driveway. The porch is an open area, the floor concrete and rectangular, and sometimes I sit there because the sea distracts me – not that I can't see it from there: I simply don't see the horizon before me, just one island and its edges of mangrove. I was sitting there one day and saw the hummingbird hovering among the bougainvillea blossoms. It lacked the dart-like movements peculiar to hummingbirds. Its movements were in slow motion, and the wings didn't whir as fast as they should have. The bird seemed barely aloft in the fragrant, soft-red air of the bougainvillea. At moments it rested with a weary look, the sabre-like beak cast down, feathers without glossiness. Then I saw the small, tired, dark eyes, the nearly imperceptible lolling of the head and, for a hummingbird, the dishevelled fold of wings. Soon, though, it was back in the air, resuming in slow motion the still precise insertion of its beak into the bougainvillea flowers.

The details' subtle insistence on the inevitability of mortality tolls a bell, but for what, *my dear? Or, who? Such focus could only signal a deeper marine melancholy. Is this why you so infrequently receive faith when you sit where you can see the open sea? The clouds piling above the blue eternity of sea and against the blue eternity of sky: gaze on that long enough… You see, it's all internal, dear, and external. You remember me in the blue; I know you do. Remember the three years we spent stealing away to hidden beaches during the week while the rest of the world laboured. On days of perfect weather we imagined we could live off the blue of sea and sky – and let's not forget the wine, cheese and crackers. We felt privileged to be alive on that long lovely beach with dense vegetation and bright beige sand when we laid our bodies out in a solitude as bounteous as a pre-Columbian landscape. We lay about nude and relaxed like natives awaiting the end of the world by cosmic forces. We had no religion. What we had were gods for our choosing. God of the blue, the sea, the air, the green mountains, the sand. Take your pick; invent another – the god of Sun and Sex, then.*

And Memory and Imagination.

I am you and you are me and we are all – *both, rather* – together *goes the old Beatles' song.* I'm crying. *Or is it dying?*

Jason's jetty begins with earth and sudden slopes of rocks on either side, then a wider piece made of concrete and lined with narrow inch-thick planks of greenheart angled upwards so anything rolling across the jetty is unlikely to go into the sea. The screws supporting the planks are rusted, and in some places the planks are brittle. I had a casual foot on a plank one morning, Kim by my side. Jason was in the house. My aunt and her husband and their son Julian were in *Rumrunner*. I was carrying a cooler down to the boat when the plank slipped and I staggered.

Kim grabbed my arm and said, "Greenheart. I thought it would have lasted longer… Trees these days, they don't grow like they used to."

I didn't think about her words then. Only now, alone on the balcony where Jason and Kim offered wine, cheese, and fruit after the return from Water Heaven and viewing the llamas – only now do I remember her words. Now, during the quiet approach of twilight, Kim's words surface more and more with meaning.

Consider your focus on the jetty, the decay of wood, greenheart no less, and your attention to the shades of twilight.

Admit it: you're lonely, you love me, and you need me: me, myself, and I.

Us. You. And I have you, all right. So come and get yourself, then.

You suggest, like some sort of Port of Spain street prophet, an ominous future for Nature and, therefore, humanity. The gentle and kind Kim should have nudged you into the sea. You would have collapsed amongst all that gnarly coral and rock and bloodied yourself into a sobriety you desperately needed then and need now.

You're trying to be romantic, claiming to be arrested by a life other than ours. It's a lie. You are permitted only the Dark Romance of my absence, whose supreme image I shall direct your gaze to – heavenward, no less.

On the sea once, twice a week, a wind-surfer's sail flaps and I look up from my book or writing to see a boy leaning beneath the oblique wing, the shapely bulge of air firm in a red, yellow, and purple sail. He moves swiftly, and I regret I never learned how to do it; there had always been time, always the certainty that the day would come when the opportunity matched my liking. The young man out there began windsurfing, I imagine, when a genuine passion was possible, one that will sustain him and his windsurfing for many years.

The windsurfer fades away as I continue my work. The hard light has gone; the late afternoon tints are more to my liking, and I wonder if it's because I am getting older. The descent of light to twilight, and the sea becoming crepuscular… The world is different. At the end of the jetty, I collapse into cool, clear-green water. This colour lasts for fifty or so feet. After that blue takes over, a warm, close blue, close because the sand particles drifting make the blue visually impenetrable beyond seven feet. But the blue remains vivid, and gives the impression I'm swimming in aquamarine.

Well, I'm glad you know that exercise is helpful for depression. And that sweet bulge of sail: the curve of my hips, my breasts, and my unforgettable ass.

Your words, not mine.

And how appropriate to pine for the opportunities of lost youth, the time for a life-affirming experience. We fell in love during the furnace of our youth, so we bound ourselves together forever. You can't undo that, can you?

Remember your mother's aquamarine and diamond ring? The aquamarine was large, cumbersome, dwarfing the diamonds on either side of it. It's the same blue colour you swim in, isn't it? You once told me she said that if you were ever engaged to marry a decent girl she would give it to you for her. And your mother liked me, eventually – especially when your sister ran off to London to be with that rugby bum.

Your Caribbean ecological lament is dishonest, yet truth escapes somehow. Isn't that just how things are? Like water, truth gets into the most unlikely of places at the oddest of times. In dreams; when you cry in your sleep and wake to hear Ojay trotting around as she waits for what will inevitably come from the sea.

Regarding your condition, that other story you abandoned, the one with the old vagrant who scares the couple driving to the lookout by running out into the road, you abandoned it, didn't you, because you couldn't imagine beyond the scare he causes. Isn't that so? So now you write these paragraphs of flat-line observation, as if steadily looking at something and lying to yourself about how it makes you feel will solve the problem.

Let me tell you something: I am the Bitch and the Bitch is not dead. You can't deny what is true. Real. You should be writing about us, for God's sake, and in a way you are. But to represent me as a windsurfer sail is the sort of priceless asininity we should leave to our banana republic politicians.

Write: She lay in the lush garden of the old plantation house and watched her daughter's birthday party, the children with fluorescent-green baby iguanas resting on their arms, the iguanas feeding off the coolness of the evening, their eyes barely moving, as if subtly registering the curiosities of the night.
Restore me.
People disappear.

On certain days the current is not strong. The blue spreads out, dipping away into depths I feel a desire to explore but don't. The nearest point is three hundred yards away. The sound of my breathing through the snorkel is as familiar as the splashes my arms make. I've been doing this every afternoon for two months, and the results are good: I sleep better and have fewer nightmares. My work has improved, at least in this journal. Being at Jason's house has made life clearer, shown me the work I have left to do. I have to finish the writing, have to make a living somehow. But seeing how the economies of the world operate, seeing how they destroy the stability of countries and peoples, of families, individuals, I fear that my labour is being done for a broken world, a world which may have no use for it, or me. It prevents enthusiasm. The menace of history, perhaps.

A blue and silver fish, its blue denser than what I'm swimming in and sweeping up from its underside to fade into the silver dominating its top, curves out of another, hidden blue. The fish circles in front, mocking my progress locked at the surface, a sheet of white light marking the edge of its world. Nearer, the thin teeth are noticeable, pointing upwards on the outside of the mouth, like a deformed grin. The fish is large and circles me several times, slowly. In two months I've seen much marine life – barracuda, stingrays, leopard-rays, parrotfish, eels, and many others – including sea-centipedes, crusty-brown, ridged, lethal-looking lengths of Chilopoda – and most ignored me.

Further on, orange starfish, settled on the vegetation below, appear about one every fifteen feet. There are pimply bumps on the top of their tentacles and their centres look like neat, tiny mountain ranges in reddish sunsets. Their undersides are a canescent yellow, and down the middle of each arm there are short feelers, with tiny suction-cup tips, lining the sides of a long thin opening, a series of mouths. The arms tighten but do not fold when I bring one to my mask. The design of their arms engages me, how they taper to a blunt point from the thick centre, the delicate, precise movements of the feelers as they sense the sunlight and then recede with a quick, tucking-in movement into a cluster. I hold the starfish halfway between surface and seabed, and let go. The creature sinks, parachuting with five extended limbs, rocking from side to side. I catch it after a couple of feet, resting its small hard protrusions in my palm. Then I deliver the starfish to where I found it.

On my right, mangrove reaches into the water in curved forks. The water is green there, clear still, and calmer. It's near the end of the path that leads down from the hill. Where I'm swimming, the wind bounces on the water, making wavelets that obstruct the passage of air through the snorkel and the rhythm of my arms. I clear the snorkel with a furious spurt of air and kick harder, concentrating on my arms too, determined to get the burning sensation in my heart and shoulders that gives my body the deep peace I've become addicted to. Later, I want to sit on Jason's balcony after a shower of cool fresh water and reflect on the day. Ojay will condescend to be stroked around her perfect ears. But I must earn it, so I sprint for a while, glancing at the shoreline for direction.

The water is as warm as my blood and tempts me down to cool depths that make me wish I had gills. An article I read a few years ago said the possibility exists for us to create humans with wings and other animal attributes. Are gills possible? A barracuda angles on my left, and I realize fins would be, if not necessary, desirable.

I'm tired, swimming slower, floppily, looking up out of the water now and then to see how far away Jason's jetty is. The water off the end of the jetty has areas of hot and cold. As I glide through them, and by the crustaceous, green growths on the jetty shafts, with openings in which fish hide, an eerie thought occurs. It's the story of an eel a fisherman in the village told me – though he also

said eels would not bother me if I left them alone – but I've seen
movies that have done considerable harm to the reputation of
eels, films showing the savagery of wildlife to man. It's all the fault
of the undisciplined years of childhood, the easy access to stupid
movies. Now trying to maintain a disciplined and focused mind
for my work helps to control my emotions concerning eels.

*And on our history together. And on imagining our future together,
if such a thing exists.*

*Are you serious about "movies that have done considerable harm to
the reputation of eels"? Sounds like some sort of radical environmental
politics. And you would like to have gills? Fins? Scales? I can't wait for
you to explain this. No doubt the sleek, canine Ojay is involved – she
who seemingly "regrets the evolutionary path her species followed".*

The ground floor of Jason's house is tiled in smooth squares
of red-brown. There is a ship's bell at the bottom of a flight
of steps. The steps go up toward the northeast then turn one
hundred and eighty degrees to the southwest. Up there is the
balcony. Downstairs are the laundry-room and guest-room.
The sliding door of the guest-room is unlocked and inside
there are a few bookshelves, a bed, a sophisticated radio (one
of Jason's hobbies), and a stack of newspapers and magazines.
The shower is all I'm interested in. The water is cool and
delights my skin as the film of salt is washed off.

Through the louvre-window near the ceiling I can see the cliff
against the house, but hear nothing. The earth smells of iron and
salt.

I walk out of the guest-room, and a dove, with streams of white
on its chest, a sleek head and wet-brown eyes, flaps violently out
of its nest above the archway leading to the jetty.

I stop. The sea is darker. Then, amid all the blues and promises
of darker blues, amid the promise of night, I have a desire to swim
once more.

*No, sit back, get comfortable, but not too comfortable, and watch
the outer dark come on and match your inner dark.*

Shall we really return to the sea? Or do you wish to lift your gaze heavenward on this lavender evening? Of course you do. There. Can you see me in the mass of clouds above the horizon, where the blue has faded to lavender, and the promise of night is as certain as day and death?

Shall we return to the sea? Shall we, as Ojay seems to wish, surrender our evolutionary outcome? Or do we go to bed, rise early tomorrow, and begin writing about us?

The path appears to have been around for a while; it has the look of regular use. Walking down, coming to the shoreline, the light sea breeze dropping off and the full force of the day's heat gripping me, in the mangrove inlet I saw something I will never forget.

First, the boat: it was small and wooden, the colour of the mangrove roots and branches, old mossy splotches of greys and browns dried by sun and sea air. When it shifted a whole section of the mangrove seemed to shift too. So I stopped. And then I saw.

A thin, naked human form took life out of the shadows of the thick mangrove. It was attempting to get into the boat, fumbling with an oar; another oar stuck out at an angle above the bow. I did not recognize the sex of the figure until it turned – reluctantly, for she wanted to get away (now, I'm not even sure she was female) – and everything stopped, even my heart, as the mangled face looked at me. A jeer of deformed, protruding lower teeth, with the mouth at an angle, like a grimace of the most tremendous pain, made me gasp and step back. The eyes had a pure stark terror, their whites dashing across her face beneath the scraggly dark hair hanging over them to her neck and shoulders. Then she, or he, snarled, or what sounded like it. I realize now as I write, as she stepped back too, that she was more afraid of me than I was of her. But in shock, I took another step back and fell onto the path. I can't remember hitting the ground; all I recall is watching from there as the woman in the boat moved away, pushing on the mangrove roots with an oar. She looked at me, confident of safety, I thought, and that brutalized mouth seemed to grin.

I got up and ran up the path, scrambling like a terrified creature. I could not remove the face from my mind: the sudden confrontation with it had to work its way through. When I got to the top of the hill, I was trembling. Then it occurred to me to try and see where she might be rowing along the mangrove. But there was nothing to see; she must have been closer to the shore.

I began to walk back to the house, and about halfway there broke into a run, in the panic that the poor deformed woman or man might be trying to break into the house. Then I remembered Ojay, and rested, trying to calm my breathing.

Funny how accurately you observe what is before you… and yet, how little you see. That tormented demon-like person in the mangrove means something terrible happened, doesn't it? Of course it does. All demons, no matter what reality they inhabit, no matter what form they take, come from something. Do you see that, at least? And if that's the case, then won't something terrible happen again? Isn't it just a matter of when? And what? And who? If the past is not dealt with, if we neglect our history, our time together, if we refuse to look at things the way they must be looked at, then the future is cursed.

Everything is about to change. Trust me. *Everything.*

II

Ojay trotted across the porch as he slept through a nightmare. She was the wolf searching for him, hungry for all of the world and for all of time. The landscape rose and plunged like a stormy sea, and he could not go in any direction for more than a few yards: he fell, grabbed branches of trees and was tossed up and down constantly (could he fly?), even somersaulting off a branch to land heavily on the writhing earth, before being thrown up again. There was no sky, just the never-ending night of a cosmos devoid of stars: the wolf had eaten them all. The wolf came on, relentless, creeping low to the ground and exempt from the physics of the dancing earth. The demon of the mangrove rose in the air above him and consulted with the wolf. They spoke in loud whispers; he couldn't understand their language, but knew they were talking about him.

He woke sweating, heart pounding just as they were coming for him. He saw sunlight in exact, corn-coloured bars on the wall opposite his bed. He could just hear the sea splashing the land by the jetty. Ojay barked: it was all right. He got out of bed, stumbled, steadying himself on the bedpost. He tapped in the code for the alarm, dropped the remote on his bed, went out to the porch and climbed the stairs to the kitchen, not looking at the sea, sky, or the islands. As he made coffee, he ate five small sweet bananas, his body cooling, the sweat drying.

He stepped out onto the balcony with the coffee and saw a sky that looked so blue it seemed alive. Where it met the sea made a horizon perfect as an edge to the world: you could fall off into the blue and drift forever. Wind came off the sea; the trees alongside the balcony rustled and creaked; sunlight dappled the wood plank floor. It had rained in the night and he could smell the earth and the rot of leaves. He was still hungry. He remembered there were boiled eggs dusted with black pepper in the fridge.

At the table where his writing materials were – laptop, with journal and dissertation; long yellow green-lined notepads; green ink pens, blue ones too; books; shells and stones he'd collected months ago along the shore – he sat and sipped his coffee and waited for her voice to begin again, waited, gazing around at the sea and sky, the islands, turning in his chair to look upon the beauty of the world. But he heard only the day: the birds, the sea picking up in the wind by the jetty, the trees, and Ojay's enquiring bark as a great blue heron rose awkwardly into the air, as if about to break apart.

Soon the wind brought the sound of an engine; but his reverie blurred it from mind, just another boat passing. Then, like scalpel-blade reflections, light came through the leaves, flickered across his manuscript, and he looked out. The boat had slowed, so the sound of its engine was minimal. It was cruising up the channel, heading toward the house, the same boat he'd seen nearly four weeks ago, *Mornin' Glory*, its upper-deck cabin-window a flame of silver light. They (he assumed the occupants would be the same group of men and women he had seen the first time) would be formed out of the flame, apparitions arriving in this world as if from another. As the boat came on, once more its voluptuous luxury made him uneasy; he saw a man with binoculars again and heard Ojay growl below the balcony, as in the nightmare with the demon in the mangrove. But she was as yet unsure, waiting, an expertly trained animal ready to act, or not: the boat was not *yet* close enough to justify an attack. Information: it was what you needed in these situations; and that cost time.

Ojay waited. The boat came on steadily, its human forms more distinct now. In a matter of minutes Ojay would be on Jason's jetty, if that was the destination of the boat's occupants.

He shifted in his chair as if to rise, thinking both of the cold eggs in the fridge and trying to distinguish whether the women were on board. It was his first mistake: the time taken to indulge the thought, to act on the desire, and consider the result. By the time he'd looked out at the boat, scanned its deck and stern, and realised the women were not there, at least not on the exterior of the boat – so where were they? – fifteen seconds had passed.

Something was happening. He knew it now. Something had been happening for months, even before he came to Jason's house to recover after the disappearance. He got up and went to the kitchen, heard Ojay's growl resume and thought of shoes and eggs, though he wasn't hungry anymore. He bounded down the stairs. In his room he grabbed his running shoes, went back up to the kitchen, put the eggs in a bag, and ran to the balcony. The laptop he tucked under cushions on a sofa opposite the table, then he put his shoes on, tying the laces without looking at the task, peering through the trees at the jetty, seeing the boat coming alongside, three men on board wearing jackets in the early morning heat, baggy knee-length pants and dark glasses. Then two men were at the side of the boat, preparing to jump onto the jetty. He heard Ojay in the shadows beneath the balcony beginning to snarl, waiting for the moment they were on her territory. He dashed to the stairs behind the bougainvillea that connected to the driveway, and leapt down four at a time, his heart beating so hard he could hear nothing else. He ran to the gate, his mouth scalded from the fire in his chest, hoping the bushes along the driveway would hide him. The gate's chain slid to the ground when he yanked it, and turning to close the gate so they would not see it open and get on his trail sooner, he saw Ojay white in the early sunlight, sprinting at them on the jetty with a locked concentration, low to the ground like a jaguar rushing its prey. She managed to leap at one of the men and both man and dog fell into the water. The other man reached into his jacket for his gun, turning and aiming down at the water between the boat and jetty.

Bent at the waist, he began running to the hill where he'd found the old iron. In the distance there were several gunshots. At the top of the hill he rummaged in the bush where he'd tossed the iron and lifted it out. Then he ran off the path into the bush and scrub, making his way down toward the cove half a mile away. He could see the sugar mill on the hill above the cove, and that was where he headed, out of breath, cutting his legs on razor grass, stumbling on rocks, and thinking about water and his life.

As he ran, keeping to where the vegetation and trees were thickest, he tried to think clearly. It wasn't him they wanted, surely they would see that, for the laptop, if they found it (and they would if they searched the house), contained nothing; it would release him; he was not responsible, or in any way connected with what they were after. What were they after? It must be Jason. But he shouldn't have hidden the laptop, for if they found it and read the journal, they might misunderstand. They'd realise he knew Jason was in Europe on holiday. So he'd been told. His phone – he'd stupidly left it in his room downstairs: it contained Jason's phone number.

He was connected to Jason, he had been in the house, Jason was his cousin, and Jason had met her, too. He didn't want to think about that; it would only confuse matters more. But he knew her and trusted her and they had no secrets – or had had no secrets: he didn't know what tense she was in, or where she was.

People disappear.

The heat increased, and the iron became heavy; he switched it to his other hand with the bag of eggs, wondering if the eggs would slow his fast-developing thirst. He usually had water after his breakfast coffee. The trees here gave scant shade, but he dared not stop. Soon they would be looking for him. They were most definitely searching the house now, and then they would come for him. He couldn't go far without going back for the car, and that was impossible. There was no one else around for miles. It could only be a matter of hours before they caught him, if that was their intention. He began to eat the eggs because he wanted strength: he was thinking of running to his aunt's house – and he needed to eat anyway. Then he thought the men would find the car keys, and while two would be in the bush tracking him, another would be moving quietly along the track in Jason's SUV. Maybe. He didn't know. He had to stop thinking. The eggs, warm now, were picking him up a bit, giving what felt like hope in the circumstances, but they didn't lessen his thirst.

He knew they would be able to see the ruins of the plantation house and the sugar mill from the hill, but it was unlikely they knew the area. Yet it seemed possible they had cruised back and forth along the coast of the island looking for Jason's house for weeks. He would chance it: get to the sugar mill and hide until night, then attempt jogging to his aunt's house.

The morning was quiet. He'd been trudging down through tall grass and past small trees, every now and then stopping for a few seconds to listen. As he came onto the shaded beach of the cove, glancing upward for a second at the branches covering him and wondering if it was possible to see this part of the cove from the hill, he saw a mongoose near the water, upright on its hind legs; it regarded him briefly, with an almost sympathetic curios-ity, then fled. He sat, facing the water, resting on the still cool mixture of sand and mud.

The remaining eggs felt hot. He leaned forward and dipped the bag with them into the water.

About fifty yards to his right along the beach, the stone ruins of the plantation house's steps descended in disarray; it seemed there'd been an earthquake a long time ago. The trees there, their green still vibrant and lush, blocked his view of the higher part of the hill and the ruins up there, beyond which were the slave pits. Along the shore a clearing tunnelled a path through an increasing cluster of bushes and small trees. He tried to listen. The blood in his head was slowing, the sounds of the world returning. He felt drained running from the house. There were four eggs left, and he ate one. The gentle slap of water, the light wind in the trees: he listened to these sounds for several minutes.

Then anger overcame him; he stood up and decided he had to go back to the house; the men were mistaken: they didn't want him, he would say, nor even Jason. Whatever they were after he would help them get it. He had nothing to do with what they were about: he was a writer, poor, with a first degree in biology, the second in literature; he had attended Boston University. He was going to be a writer and teacher. Jason had allowed him to stay here, to work. And did they know there was a mongoose nearby, behaving strangely, observing him as if he were a distant relative? Most remarkable: surely a phenomenon to be observed and noted.

But he didn't move: his run from the house, the men with their guns, Ojay's attack and death replayed in his mind, fast.

He forgot the eggs and the iron as he began to run, muttering to himself, running toward the tunnel through the clustered bushes and trees. Now he would run along the shore for a ways, then turn inland to the right, pick his way up the hill to the slave pits, and there wait until night.

The mongoose scampered across the little beach and began rummaging through the bag of eggs.

III

Two men are walking slowly, now and then glancing behind them, through a landscape of dry cedar trees. The trees are still, the coral earth dusty. The morning has lost its coolness. The men are sweating. One man, stocky, in his early thirties, has a knapsack-cooler on his back, a Magnum .38 in his right hand, a green bandeau around his head. He wears Bermuda shorts and a pale-blue cotton jersey. The other man, taller, has an Uzi slung over his right shoulder, right hand clasped around the trigger area. The weapon points straight out in front of him at hip level. He wears a khaki shirt, a grey cap with the flap tilted up, blue jeans and sneakers. Both men are unshaven.

"Like he know how to walk, the fuck," says the shorter of the two. "I not seeing if he pass here."

The taller man, a bit older than his companion, hums. He isn't looking at the grass or the earth, but ahead at the sugar mill on the hill, both coming into view.

"Look there, nuh man. He could be hiding up so."

The shorter man looks and grunts.

"The mills have pits round them. I sure he hiding there."

"Is so? How you hear about that?"

"I read it in a brochure, at the hotel."

The shorter man says nothing. He looks around, grimacing, his discomfort evident to the other man, who shakes his head.

They both stop when they hear a noise, like a cough, and then step apart from one another off the path and crouch, hiding in the low bushes sloping down to the cove. They cock their weapons and wait.

A young man, sweating, is walking with purpose and wild expectation on his face. He is coming toward them, muttering, his sneakers stirring the dust. The shorter man stands and steps out onto the path, his .38 pointing at the young man. "Stop," he says. The young man starts, halts. The gunman has both hands on his weapon, right index finger on the trigger. "Everything fuck up," he says.

The young man is confused by this comment. "A mongoose," he says. "There's a very strange one back there," he indicates with his right hand, shaking. "I have to get my notebook." He begins walking again.

The taller man steps in front of him. "Wait." The Uzi is pointed at the young man.

The young man stops. "I'm not who you looking for," he says.

"Everything fuck up," the stocky man says.

"I just stay there. I write. You have to let me get my notebook."

"Don't move," says the taller man. "You going the wrong way."

"You must be the police. Come back with me and I'll let you in the house."

"Man, everything real fuck up."

"Where's Doreen? Have you found her? Where is she?"

The taller man looks at the shorter man; they are both a bit puzzled, but only for a moment. The taller man nods to his companion, who raises his gun and shoots three times into the young man's chest. He falls backwards, landing on his left side, an incredulous look on his sweaty face. "The mongoose," he sputters. "I have to get back to the house."

Both men laugh, but the taller one turns away. In a single graceful movement, the knapsack is off the shorter man's back, and he has a machete in his right hand. He puts the knapsack on the ground, grabs the longish hair of the young man, and with two expert blows cuts off his head.

The shorter man allows the head to drain before placing it in the knapsack, which he zips securely. He wipes the blade on the headless young man's body. While they walk away, the shorter man says, "He head heavy. Must be have plenty brains. 'I write. You have to let me get my notebook! Where is Doreen?'"

BARBARA JENKINS

I NEVER HEARD PAPPY PLAY THE HAWAIIAN GUITAR

I never heard Pappy play the Hawaiian guitar, an experience they say caused big, hardback men to halt at the crunch of a hang-jack moment in an all-fours card game, jaded women to rise from the fumbling laps of drink-sotted men, and broken-nosed barmen to pause in their rinsing of glasses in basins of grey water. This was in those wrought-iron-balconied upstairs places facing the docks along South Quay where he and his Hawaiian guitar spent whole unbroken weekends after he had pocketed his tally-clerk pay envelope on Saturday mornings.

But then, there was a whole lot I didn't know about Pappy. Where he lived, whom he lived with, what he liked, or didn't, were just a few of the mysteries of my childhood, so, when I heard him eulogised at his funeral service, thirty-one years ago today, as the finest player of the Hawaiian guitar in town, I was both surprised and not at all surprised. It wasn't that I didn't know anything about Pappy, it's just that what I did know was gleaned solely through sparse but careful observation, knowledge from the tiniest seeds of clues scattered around my world. Some of the things I knew first hand. The domestic control he exercised over us even while seldom present in person didn't help me to judge him in a balanced way when I was a child, but today I'm not going to weigh and measure him. I guess the Almighty or maybe St Peter did the plusses and minuses of Pappy's life long years ago as he approached the judgement seat, brown fedora in hand, seeking the final verdict on his sixty-eight years. I'd put my money on St Peter doing the job. I don't think Pappy would've warranted a personal audience with the Almighty, with whom he had been conflated in my mind in my very early years, any more than he would have been known as an individual human being by his august employer, Mr Kennedy, of Wm. Kennedy & Co Import and Export who, I suppose, was like a god in the universe of Pappy's work.

Pappy's job at Kennedy's was to go on the docks when the ships came in and to check the company's landed cargo and also do the same for cargo going out – import and export. I never saw what came in. We girls were screened from contact with that world where, it was reported, women tossed back their heads and laughed loudly with men who whistled and called out to them – the men guiding the massive rope-wrapped pallets swinging from cranes on the ships lying alongside, down to the dockside. But I did have a first-hand knowledge of what went out since I was often at the Kennedy & Co warehouse. As the eldest, it fell to me to go to Pappy's workplace on Saturdays, to seek him out and wheedle him into sending some of the contents of his pay envelope back to Mammy, who would be waiting at home in Belmont, anxiously calculating in her head how the hoped-for fifteen dollars could be spread among her string of waiting creditors, to keep all reasonably happy and in check for the coming week.

Dressed-up in last Easter's church dress, I boarded the bus as it moved sedately through quiet, residential Belmont and disembarked on lower Charlotte Street, just where the bus sputtered to a crawl, edging its cautious way through the Central Market's overflow of vendors and their fruit and vegetables, fish and flesh – the perfume of ripe pineapple and the stench of hot animal blood mingling in a single intake of breath. I sauntered along Marine Square, so fascinated by the busyness of commercial life that I lost all sense of purpose and allowed the tide of swaying women, who balanced on their heads big, round split-bamboo baskets perched on twists of cloth, and men, who transported handcarts of boxes of goods from wholesalers to retailers, to sweep me along at their pace. I stopped to touch pavement displays of combs – family-sized, clear plastic amber ones with dark flecks trapped inside, two-sided small silver metal ones for combing out lice, small black ones for fitting in men's shirt pockets. I had to sidestep the beggars, women with cupped hands extended, squatting on the pavement, long skirts drooping in modesty between their knees, faces half-hidden by thin ohrinis draped across their noses from which hung large silver filigree nose rings, and men who were ratty-bearded and ragged, bare-footed and dirty, downcast and aggressive, subdued and loud. Everything grabbed attention – enamel cups in beige and white with blue rims, ballpoint pens that could write in three colours of ink with the slide of a knob, four-stacked metal food carriers craftily held together by rods slotted into their handles, black and white knitted alpagatas threaded with patterns of red and green wool. All this, and more, overlaid by a cacophony of sound – loud calls competing with clanging bicycle bells, the abrupt blare of car horns and the raucous shouts of donkey cart drivers.

As I passed the Cathedral of the Immaculate Conception, I made sure to make the Sign of the Cross across my chest, to invoke good fortune in my quest. I strayed and delayed my unwilling arrival at my destination. From the bright white glare of the pavement, I peered through the deep shade of the over-hanging upper-floor balcony into the even darker interior. For a long while I could make out nothing, then jute-brown crocus bags emerged in soft focus in serried ranks, wooden pillars rose to support the storey above and I could just pick out, way in the back, a platform on which was a wooden desk, a chair and a man's pale face, like a misplaced moon, floating above a khaki shirt. This man was the first of those I was dressed to impress on Saturdays. "Yuh looking for yuh fadda?" he called out, and I nodded in embarrassed agreement. He then turned his face to make a last quarter phase to shout into the darker recesses, "Jimmy still there?" At this I stopped breathing, crossed my fingers and said a silent prayer, for if I was late, late through dawdling, and if the answer came, *No, Jimmy done gone already*, indicating that Pappy had picked up his pay and left, that would be a disaster for us for the coming week, and how would I explain to Mammy why I had failed to do what she had sent me to do?

But not this time. For today, just today, I will remember Pappy still being there and him coming from that back space where he was doing whatever mysterious thing that tally-clerks do when not on the docks. He is moving slowly and fluidly towards me, wiping his hands with a white handkerchief that he is looking at intently, not pausing as he folds it first in half, then in quarters, into a neat, deliberate square, edges and corners perfectly aligned, then folding over a corner to meet the opposite one, making a fat triangle that he pats and flattens and is already placing, with a straight palm to avoid it creasing, into a back pocket, by the time he gets to me. He is bending over for me to plant an unwilling but dutiful peck on his cheek, the sickly scent of tobacco rising from his pores cancelling out, for that moment, the pervasive, unidentifiable dusty smells of that gloomy cavern. We stand facing each other, each waiting for the other to say something first.

"Mammy send me for the money." I, unschooled in tact and diplomacy, break the spell.

"And yuh wouldn't come to look for yuh fadder otherwise?" he challenges.

For years and years, I replayed that scene, just so – setting: the warehouse; characters: father and girlchild; situation: girlchild requesting child-support from father – and I wonder today whether I had been too simplistic, too judgemental in my reading of him all those many, painful Saturdays of long ago. In that scene of the past, it isn't just Pappy and me there. Standing there with us, in us, were the people we thought we were, and the people we thought we should be. I was girlchild, yes, but also convent-girl, and so I was divided between two worlds – the one that contained the expectations and standards of the chaste world of Irish nuns and their ideal students, my French-creole, plantation-owning and merchant-class schoolmates, and the less privileged underworld of my own real life. As to Pappy – at work he was tally-clerk, at home, rarely visiting father, and there was also a secret life that none of us at home was privy to. Now I see that when Pappy and I encountered each other on Saturday mornings, we were in the gladiatorial arena of malehood in the mid-twentieth century when role models were Jack Palance, Humphrey Bogart and John Wayne. So when Pappy was walking towards me, he was walking towards a camera from a long shot. He had a role to play, that while moving to a tight close-up, he was trying to show that he is Man. He is Man, to be recognized as such by a visible and invisible audience and maybe, above all, by himself.

But back then, as I stood within the warehouse of Wm H Kennedy and Sons, Marine Square, Port of Spain, I understood nothing, only that my mother had sent me to my father and I was being deflected by his challenge that I wouldn't come to see him if it were not to get money from him. It was a challenge I couldn't take up because it had a shape and size and facets and angles beyond my comprehension and I didn't know how to deal with it at any level – joking or serious, as stated or as implied. I hung my head, ashamed that it was indeed so, that I wouldn't come to look for my father unless I had been sent for money, and that he had drawn that shameful ingratitude of mine and of the whole tribe of us dependants to the attention of his watching and listening audience of fellow-men, who themselves had women and children to contend with.

Pappy throws off that pose and takes on the responsible, proud father one saying, "Come over here and say good morning to Mr. De Four." That is the moonface's name, Manuel De Four, and he is intent on spiking squares and rectangles of paper to a board of protruding nails behind his desk. I say, "Good Morning, Mr. De Four." And he, pausing in his rhythmic paper spiking, says, "So what happen, you get too big to call me Uncle Mannie now? Come and give me a kiss, chile." Chile tiptoes and leans forward to brush the roughly shaved cheek with her lips, and she can't wait to surreptitiously turn her head and with seeming casualness wipe said lips against the stiff green organdie of her puff-sleeved arm. Pappy calls out to the back darkness, "All yuh come out here and see mih daughter." Pepsi-Joe and Sonny shuffle out and one says, "But she getting big, eh Jimmy," and the other asks, "So this is the bright one?" and Mr. De Four calls over, "She must be get the good looks and the brains from the mudda," and they all laugh at this familiar joke that big people are always making on one another.

Putting his arm around my shoulders, Pappy pulls me to him. My face is against his scratchy, brown serge pants and I move closer in so as not to face the gaze of the men, because I am ashamed under scrutiny. I suspect that they are saying something else under those words and I can't guess at its hidden meaning, and I'm not sure who, if anyone, is supposed to answer. Their heh-heh-heh fades as Pepsi-Joe and Sonny disappear, back into the dim interior of the warehouse, Mr De Four resumes his paper-spiking and Pappy moves me towards the rows of sacks, his arm still around my shoulders, my two steps matching his one.

At the first row, he rolls over the loose sacking at the top of the nearest bag. At that slight disturbance, a mustiness dislodges from the sack. My hand reaches in and I take a handful of large seeds, dull, rough ovals and I close my fist and rub the contents together and as the full fragrance bursts out, I put my nose deep into my palm and inhale an intoxicating mystery, something like vanilla, but a vanilla that has journeyed through deep forests, dank leaves, slithering life, absorbing darkness, moisture, heat, decay along the way, complicating its innocent bland sweetness. I do not know where tonka beans come from, how they grow, where they are bound, what is their use. I only drink in the beans' enigmatic essence.

I drift on to another bag, to smooth, shiny-dark beans whose cloying scent I know from comforting drinks on rainy nights: the thick, oily, welcome embrace of cacao beans. These are rubbed, squeezed and inhaled too. They leave a trace that make my palms glide frictionless along each other, silky-smooth, soothing. We move to the last row – the thrill of forbidden pleasure, an adults-only pleasure – the spiky aroma of coffee beans tickling high up in my nostrils like a sneeze that won't come. Rooted there, I bury my nose into first one handful, then another, astonished at the richness and complexity of scents and sensations that have come from such undistinguished, dull, hard scraps. Are not seeds just dropped and discarded, scattered and strewn from living trees, who carry on, year after year, producing these end-products of their more attractive floral displays? Or so my child's mind runs. I squeeze, I rub, I inhale, transported in time and space, lost in my own world of the senses.

The Cathedral tower clock calls the Angelus. Everything is

suspended as the loud, metallic clang of clapper on bell rim fills the air, my head, my chest with each of its heavy strikes – bang, bang, bang, pause – four cycles of three, then a pause followed by twelve sustained strikes. The sound lingers, vibrating the air and the ear for long moments after, and as it fades, it is as if a spell has been broken and the true world has been revealed. Everything springs to life in a changed direction. The bells signal the end of the working week for Pappy and for everyone else in town and I am jolted back to Saturday in the Kennedy and Sons warehouse. Pappy is anxious to go, to meet up with the boys, to start his other life, free from duty to work and family, and I must get back home to Mammy.

We stand there together, he wanting to rush away, I wanting to detain him, for I have not yet got what I came for. But I cannot ask again. Pappy has just treated me to a little distraction for my enjoyment and I cannot bring myself to be crude and remind him of what I really came for. He gives every appearance of having forgotten why I am there. He glances at his watch. I look down on the grimy cement floor. My palms are sweating with the fear that he has indeed forgotten and I will have to say it aloud again, will have to say that I have come to visit him, my father, only to get money. Pepsi-Joe and Sonny come out of the darkness and go towards the long, stout, heavy wooden bar that slot into the iron brackets when they close the wide front doors, barricading us inside. They look towards Pappy and me, waiting. Pappy now seems to remember the purpose of my visit.

Standing an arm's length from me, he draws from a back pocket a worn leather wallet and he extracts, one by one, drawing out each note into a symphony, a five-dollar bill, pause, another five-dollar bill, longer pause, and finally, with a flourish, to the mute crash of cymbals from the soundtrack, a third five-dollar bill. He fans the three bills out, a gambler with a royal flush, and, with the faintest of nods, indicates that I should put my palm out, into which one, two, three five-dollar bills are placed flat and then folded – my hot damp fingers folded by his cool, dry ones – over the limp, many-times-used paper. I untie my handkerchief, place the notes in the middle, tie all in a double knot and loop one loose end through my waistband, knotting it securely in place. He bends his head for my parting cheek peck, I deliver, then turn and run out the doorway, leaving my father until another Saturday.

I set off along Marine Square from which life has drained, save for women, squinting in the sharp white light, spilling out the Cathedral after their Angelus devotions. As I move my palm across my face to make a Sign of the Cross in gratitude for answered prayers, the essences of the crushed seeds invade my nostrils, and I feel a strange excitement and lightness. Pappy strides off in the other direction, to the wrought-iron-balconied upstairs clubs opposite the docks on South Quay, to meet up with the boys and to play his Hawaiian guitar, to the stupefaction of hard-drinking, hard-gambling men and the adoration of soft, carefree women, reeling them in with his steel-stringed vibration, which I shall never hear.

MEILING JIN

THE TALL SHADOW

He sent his shadow to court her. He waited until the day was far advanced, then stood in the sun so that his shadow would be at its longest. Raising his arms, he whispered, "Ran-jai-pa", and sent his shadow scurrying.

Maralyn stood in the yard washing her feet, her blouse soaked through with sweat. She was tired from standing all day in the market selling roti. The fact that her basket was now empty gave her no satisfaction; she was tired and far too preoccupied. For one thing, taxi driver Winston, had asked her to the dance on Saturday night. And for another, today she had received a postcard from her cousin, Sandra. The postcard was a picture of a golden apple. It had the words, "Greetings from the Big Apple", on it. Maralyn held the image of the apple in her mind like a forbidden fruit; one day, it was going to be her turn, one day soon.

"Maralyn, girl, come and help me mix the roti for tomorrow." Her mother's voice cut through the daydreaming. Maralyn reached for the old cloth and dried her feet slowly. She would join her mother in the kitchen when she was ready. Washing her feet was a ritual she clung to, like washing away the aggravation and boredom of standing in the market. People wanted roti and more than roti when she stood there between the rum shop and the bakery. She thought about Winston again. Why had he asked her to the dance? She unhooked the mirror from the post and peered at herself: was there something different about her since she left that morning? Straight nose, flat forehead, high cheekbones stared back. That flat forehead and straight nose was the "Buck in she", Moses had remarked on more than one occasion. Well, likely Moses was right. The "Buck" in she had been the source of more than one joke at school. It was hurtful then, but now she didn't care; now her mixed ancestry had fulled out into features that were, beyond doubt, beautiful.

Maralyn smiled at the thought of Winston telling his passengers to wait in the car, while he calmly strolled over to invite her to the dance. She put the mirror back and turned to fetch water from the standpipe.

She saw the shadow when she reached the standpipe. At first she thought it was her own, but when she looked behind, she saw her own, and when she looked in front, the shadow, the other shadow, hovered as if it was waiting for her. Maralyn's heart skipped a beat. She threw the bucket on the ground and stepped backwards,

"Me na want nuttin to do with jumbie."

The shadow approached her and, even as she backed away, it reached her because it was a tall shadow. Maralyn forgot.

She followed the shadow through the gate, across the ditch and down the road. The day's heat had lost some of its relentlessness and was giving way to a slightly cooler evening. Coconut trees shimmered in the late afternoon sun, but Maralyn was not aware of it. On she walked, past Teacher Thomas' house with the red flamboyant guarding the gate, past the baker shop, past the donkey in the field, the church; on and on. She may have heard the frogs croaking in the ditch, or the kiskadee in full song, and then possibly she did not, because all she knew was the shadow.

The house stood well back from the road surrounded by trees: coconut, mango and guava. It was large and you could tell it was well kept because someone had taken the trouble to paint it recently. One hand on the bannister, Maralyn climbed the stairs to the front door. She opened the door and went in without knocking. It was already evening. The jalousies were shut, to keep the shadows in.

At first she thought the gallery was empty, then she saw him hovering, like his shadow, by the jalousie, an old man, medium height, grey hair, large ears and a hooked nose. His skin was smooth and dark brown like old leather.

As his shadow returned to him, Maralyn remembered. Her

eyes adjusted to the light and took in the gallery at a glance:
polished wooden floor, rocking chair, Berbice chair, full length
mirror, Chinese screen, long low table. Everything had an
exactness about it, like the exact amount of furniture. There was
no clutter, except perhaps the photographs, too many photographs.

Maralyn watched the old man warily, mindful of all the stories
of jumbies and die-dies.

"Maralyn?" he said.

The sound of his voice made her jump. "Who you is?" she said,
hiding her fear.

He seemed to sink a little into the shadows. "Sultan," he
replied. "My name's Sultan."

She grew bold. "How you know my name?"

He walked out of the shadows towards her. "I do because I've
watched you. You're Moses' daughter. You sell roti in the market
near the rum shop and clear fifteen dollars a day."

Maralyn frowned over the fact that he knew she cleared fifteen
dollars. She wondered if he knew she kept a dollar back when she
handed the money over to her mother. She searched her memory
to see where she could have come across this old East Indian man
before, but her mind refused her the information. She decided to
be bold, but eyed the door first, in case. It was good to be near the
door.

"Is you bring me here?"

"Yes."

"Why you bring me here?"

He spread his hands in a half-pleading, half-welcoming gesture. "I wanted to meet you. A person can get a little lonely in a
big house like this."

Maralyn felt on familiar ground. "You wanted to meet me, but
what about me? I lef me mudder and the roti just lik tha'. Me
mudder going to be vex." She turned to go.

He raised his hand. "Stay!"

Something in his voice made her pause, perhaps it was the
urgency, or the ring of power in it. She hesitated. He was an
educated man, and he had powerful magic. He crossed the room

and switched on the light. The shadows disappeared. He rang a bell. It made a tinkling sound and brought a servant at once.

"Bring some refreshment, er, some sweet drink." The servant disappeared.

"Sit down, won't you please," he said, and as if to show her how, he sat down in the high-backed armchair.

Maralyn thought of her mother waiting for her to help with the roti: Eileen was a tall, strong woman, as tall as Moses. She would beat her if she didn't go home. Maralyn considered the old man: the old man looked frail, but he had powerful magic and he had servants. She hovered, undecided. She remembered the shadow and sat down, carefully, on the edge of the rocking chair.

As she did so she looked up accidentally and stared into the old man's eyes. Young eyes locked into old: he was the first to look away. She straightened her back in triumph. She had power too: youth was her power, youth and a recklessness in the face of... of what? What was she facing?

The servant returned with the sweet drink and offered it to her. She wondered idly whether it really was lemonade, or something else.

"It's only lemonade," the old man said, apologising. Maralyn jumped, "You does read thoughts!" she accused.

"No, no not really," he lied.

She sipped the liquid carefully and, satisfied that it tasted like lemonade, drank it thirstily. She felt better afterwards and braver.

"So why you bring me here?"

Sultan clasped his hands together and leaned forward. "I brought you here because I need a companion. Someone to talk to. Share my pursuits. Spur me on to the finishing post. In short, I need a wife."

Maralyn sat back, mouth open, staring. The old man was at least eighty. Old enough to be her grandfather. Great grandfather even.

"Me. You wife! Is joke you makin!"

"No. No joke. Perhaps you think me a foolish old man and perhaps you're right. No, let me finish. I'm old it's true. And weary. When you get to my age, all you have is time on your hands and all you think about is time... running out. I need a companion, someone who will spur me on to the finishing line."

"Man, I don' even know who the damn hell you is?"

The old man smiled. "Have you ever been to the County Court House in Campbell Street?"

"No. What I would be doin there? Is only crook and tief man does go there."

"That's where you might have seen me."

Maralyn sniffed. "You never going to catch me in dey."

The old man regarded her affectionately.

Maralyn stiffened. "Any case, why me? Dey plenty other people in this damn place."

The old man gestured, eloquently. "You, because I've watched you. I like your stillness and your beauty."

Maralyn drew back. The old ones were just like the young ones, maybe a little more humble but still after the same thing in the end. She started to rock backwards and forwards nervously.

"You can live here and enjoy my wealth. Have anything you like. I have more dollars than you can spend."

"And what about the shadow. What about the shadow you send to fetch me?"

"A shadow is only a shadow."

"But dis shadow do you biddin'. How I know I ain' endin up a shadow?"

"You have my word."

"Pah! You word. You know magic and you got plenty wealth. Where from I ask meself? Tek kay you got a baccoo working for you."

The old man spread his hands wide and smiled. "No it's all my own. All belonged to my family. My father was a lawyer, a very good lawyer. My mother owned land."

He pointed to the photographs. Maralyn stared at them: they were old-fashioned pictures, framed exquisitely in gold or wood. Most of them were of East Indian people with intense expressions on their faces, as if the photographer had caught them by surprise. Maralyn shivered suddenly: the photographs made her skin creep. She looked away in the direction of the old man, keeping her eyes fixed on his chin so she would not, even by accident, look into his eyes.

The old man spread his hands in apology. "You must excuse an old man's whim. I get a little lonely so I collect photographs of people."

Maralyn shrugged. The old man shrank a little into his chair.

"Look I gotta go now, me mudder goin to kill me if I don't help she with de roti. Tanks for lettin me see de pictures. But I gotta go now."

"Stay! I will reimburse your mother and escort you safely home."

Maralyn wanted to laugh, escort her home, reimburse her mother. The old fellar was making joke.

"I could even help you get to the Big Apple."

Maralyn paused, suspiciously. The old man had strong magic, of that she was sure. Otherwise, how he could say the only thing that she ever really wanted? The Big Apple. Sandra had done it. And so could she. She could lift herself out of this grinding poverty, this small, stinking world and go abroad.

"Yes, I could help you go abroad. Tomorrow, if you like. I have plenty money."

She sat down carefully. "Wha make you tink I wan go place?"

The old man smiled and sat back, his hands resting on the arms of the chair. "I know you. I can see it in you. I know where you live. I know you share a room with your mother. Your clothes are draped over the clothes-stand because you have nowhere to hang them. The flies bother you, fetching water up and down bothers you, you bathe under the house and you can see through the floorboards because they're loose."

Suddenly, Maralyn felt naked. She could see her poverty as a stranger might see it and she felt shamed. She sat silent, looking down at her hands.

The old man continued, "The Big Apple is nothing, you know. A big city. Big buildings, too many cars, crime, poverty. People work their ass off in the shops, or worse, sell their tail on the street. You think the streets are paved with gold? No. Street paved with bodies, some dead, some alive. I could take you there, you know. They have a big hotel called the Plaza. You can ride to the top in a thing called an elevator, and see the whole of the city at your feet."

Maralyn stared at the old man; her eyelashes, long and curling, drooped over her eyes. She looked like that other Maralyn, the blond one.

"There's a place I can take you to have afternoon tea, the Savoy. We can listen to music and enjoy a civilised life."

She sat there looking at the gallery, listening to the old man talk about the Big Apple. In her mind's eye, she was there already, sipping tea from a china cup and wearing a dress made of pure silk.

"If you married me, we could travel; you would revive my interest in it all. We could see the wonders of the world, and at my age, that's all you want to see," he added.

She eyed the old man. At your age you can't live much longer. She remembered the pyramids and the Taj Mahal, from her geography book at school. Was it true that those things existed somewhere? She could see herself escorting the old man there, as a guide or something. She stopped abruptly: the old man gave her the creeps. She guided her thoughts back to something safer. Eileen. Eileen was a harsh mother, but she loved her all the same. She thought that after she went to the Big Apple she would send for Eileen. And Moses? Chia! Moses can go hang heself! He and Eileen were always quarrelling. They quarrelled like a real married couple, to hear them. She recalled that lately the quarrelling had lost its sparkle and wondered whether Moses would go back to his wife in Rose Hall. She felt sorry for Eileen. Eileen had struggled for the past twenty years to keep up the semblance of being married to Moses. As if the whole village didn't know he already had a wife. She, Maralyn, didn't care a hoot, although she herself was going to make damn sure she got a ring round her finger first.

The old man broke through her thoughts. "You're wasted here, you know. You earn fifteen dollars a day, fourteen of which you give to your mother. How long will it take you to save up enough to go to the Big Apple? Three years? Maybe four?"

Maralyn thought of Winston. Winston was not bad looking. Tall and stocky. He earned good money driving a taxi. She wondered if Winston, like Moses, already had a wife and was just foolin around asking her to the dance.

She thought not. He had too much money in his pocket to have a wife.

"And if you marry Winston, worse. He'll want you to stop working and then you'll have children. You'll be stuck."

Maralyn brought her mind round with a jolt. How did he know about Winston? Chia! This old man powerful.

She begins to be aware of the room, its stillness, the kerosene lamp, the rug brought back from his travels, the mirror, the photographs. Outside, it is dark, dark and still, except for the rustle of leaves and the crickets chirping.

She wonders how she will get home tonight and thinks of her mother again. Eileen, a powerful woman, part Indian, part African. Her mother will beat her if she doesn't return tonight, doesn't return tonight. She wonders where that thought came from.

"You could even send for your mother. There's nothing like family to make us happy," said the old man, gesturing eloquently with his hands.

Serve you right for readin me thoughts.

"Well, Sultan man, lemme tink about it. You know how things stay. I can't up and marry jus like tha'. I have to ask me mudder." A wicked thought occurs to her. Why you don't marry me mudder and I come and stay with allyou?

The old man stretches his short thin legs. "No."

She looks at him and frowns.

"I mean no need to think."

Maralyn laughs. "How you mean no need? At least I have to go home and fetch me things."

"Everything you need is here already."

Maralyn begins to feel trapped. She remembers the dragonflies she use to catch and tie with thread. She would let them fly a little and then tug them back when she felt like it. She often kept them in jars until they died. Maralyn rocks, nervously, in the armchair. It makes a creak, creaking noise. She has the feeling this is some sort of test, but has no idea what sort. Again, she remembers the string on the dragonfly: loose then tight, loose then tight and then always, always back into the jar. She looks at the old man's eyes. They look glassy. Her mind opens a little and she remembers where she has seen the old man. Why this fella used to be the old judge at the court house. Maralyn is shocked. She jumps from her chair and makes for the door; the door remains a long way away. Her legs feel like jub jub.

"Sit down, Maralyn!"

She sits down. Part of her thinks, the ole judge, fancy that. Then she panics.

"I goin home, ya hear me? I goin home." She makes a mad dash for the door again and realises that it is the mirror. "Gawd!" she squeaks. She crashes into the mirror and finds herself "inside". She knows she is "inside" because she can see him on the other side. She hammers on the glass. She recalls the people in the photographs. Her mouth forms an Ohhhh.

The old man sighs, listlessly "Why do they always try to escape?"

He thinks of the photograph he will frame that night, a beautiful photograph, a beautiful girl; she deserves the best, perhaps a velvet background and an ebony frame. He rings the bell absentmindedly. The servant appears.

The old man hangs his head. "Only one for supper tonight and then I'll work on my picture."

The servant nods.

CHERIE JONES

MY MOTHER THROUGH A WINDOW, SMILING

The fallen branches of every tree I have watched grow for the first
eighteen years of my life die at my feet as I walk my baby home.
My mother is visible through the door to the front room. She is
sitting at the kitchen table that, today being wash-day, is naked.
She has already scrubbed it with bleach and stripped the wood of
colour and texture. It is dull, pale and clean. She is hunched over,
elbows on the table, breathing fire into the telephone. Her large
legs are spread and her feet are flat on the floor. They are archless,
swollen feet – no more than usual – and the cracks of her heels
yawn when she shifts her weight from one leg to the other. Her
feet are stained by dust. They are so large and grip the ground so
firmly that it is hard to imagine her ever having been swept off
them. But then she has never claimed to have been swept off
them, never admitted to having done anything so frivolous as fall
in love.

My mother is eating the assorted left-overs of the past few
days. Black pudding stuffed into the taut tyres of pig intestines.
Fried flying fish. Breadfruit. Pickled cucumbers. She will say that
she hates breadfruit, but also that food must not waste. The heads
of the fish have been forced open to let the tails come through
their mouths like the mocking tongues of cruel children. Their
spines have been broken to facilitate the bending, and my mother
is contently crunching bone and spitting what cannot be swallowed onto a piece of newspaper in front of her – in between
saying something. "For the cat", I imagine.

Through the doorway my mother is remonstrating into the
telephone receiver, propped into the fleshy curve of her neck. She
keeps glancing at a clock ticking in the belly of Jesus above the
kitchen sink. She is wondering whether I will come back, after all,

or whether she will have to credit me with being a woman of my word. She looks outside and nods knowingly.

When she comes to the doorway she refers to the last thing I said when I called to say I was pregnant and we argued. She says, "Well, I see you are not dead."

"No, I am not dead," I say.

Against my better judgement I am decidedly alive.

She takes the baby and turns her back to say her goodbyes. I step over the threshold as he coos at her, unwary. I go in and close the door. The crook of my arm cools quickly.

"She is here," she says to the telephone before replacing it. She sets a place at the table and to my baby she says, "Come and meet your grandfather."

She goes out the back door which, when opened, lets in the whistle of a machete on greenery. It is the turn of the trees at the back of the house to die. I sit on a chair. It is hard and familiar.

"How was your flight?" he asks when he comes in. He sits behind a plate of hot pudding and cold lemonade that she sets before him. In his glass the ice melts a little and sinks lower in silence. My mother returns to her bones. The baby cries.

"It was alright," I say. "Long."

She pauses from her grinding, "Here," she says. "Or he will think he is mine."

When I take my baby he starts to wail. I try to nurse him but he rejects my breast, looking at me in bewilderment. I am already a stranger.

"He is not hungry," she says, her eyes still on her bones. "He is probably sleepy."

"He has not eaten since we left Heathrow," I dissent, but my voice is weak, plaintive. "He *must* be hungry – he slept all through the flight."

I am rubbing my nipple across his lips. He is turning his head and screaming. My father averts his eyes.

My mother chews her last fish-head thoughtfully and the eyes disappear with two wet slurps of her lips and a sigh. Even with evidence of my womanhood she fears she cannot attribute to me certain womanly talents. She takes the newspaper to the back door and spreads it at her feet. She calls the cat, who waits for her retreat before he approaches his dinner. She washes her hands slowly. She dries them and returns to me on her solid feet. She does everything noisily and between her and the baby I am almost beside myself. When she takes him I am relieved.

"Come to mama," she says to my son, "you poor, sleepy baby…"

She starts to sing a nonsense song.

> "Big rat had a spree
> L'il rat went to see
> Big rat take up l'il rat
> And throw him in the sea…"

My mother says Big Rat like it is someone that she knows. It could be a neighbour. A friend. It could be she herself. But no image presents itself for L'il Rat. My son's eyes start to close and his writhing stills with her patting. It is her manner more than her method that he responds to. She is the woman of this house. When I became as infantile as he is he did not know me.

"You are looking like your Aunty Sissy," she says to me in the new silence. "Dads, don't she favour Sissy?"

My father scrutinizes my face like he would a picture of a remote relative.

"A little," he says.

My mother smirks.

"But Sissy run to fat. She don't work as hard as I do. All she do is have babies for foolish men."

She looks hard at me.

"What is it you were studying again, before this…?"

"Voice, I was training my voice to be a singer."

It had been a bone of contention in its day – before it became negligible in the face of an illegitimate baby. Who in their right mind travelled thousands of miles and borrowed money to learn how to sing? Singing was not something that people needed. You could not eat it, wear it or use it to live. Who studies something that you either can or cannot do? Only someone idiot enough to turn around spoil it all by having a baby without the security of a husband.

"Your song is probably too sweet," says my mother.

"Some girls cannot tell the difference between a man who wants to help her sing a song and a man who just wants to hear it," says my father.

"Finish your food," says my mother.

My father gulps the last of his lemonade, the ice so small he swallows it all with one quiet motion. It makes no sound on its way into his throat. He returns to the murder of the garden.

My mother tells me that he started to axe the trees since I called and told them I was taking a year off college to come home with the baby. It has been three days and they are almost all gone. The mammy-apple, the breadfruit, the cherry will henceforth be referred to in the past tense. She starts to sing a hymn. A requiem for the departed.

She is removing my father's setting with one hand and holding my baby with the other. She has rendered me useless and I take as long as I can to replace my breast.

"Your old friend Mellie has gone to Cuba," she informs. "On scholarship to study Doctor-work."

Loosely translated it would read something like, "Mellie is making something of her life and learning something people can use."

We are momentarily lost in our private thoughts. But we speak at the same time.

"She will probably come back home soon with a Cuban baby."

"That's good. Mellie's very bright."

"What?" she asks, with her eyes flashing.

My father's pyrex bowl has fallen but is not shattered. The noise starts the baby crying again.

"About the scholarship," I say.

I take my baby from her arms and put him over my shoulder. She eyes my hold on him with doubt. I pat him and he burps and then he settles down again. When he does she sucks her teeth as if she has already forgotten about Mellie. She is singing her hymn again. It may be for herself.

"Come," she says to us, quietly, "let me show you where to put him down."

She goes up the stairs on her solid feet, the cracks of her ankles yawn with each step.

I am home.

HELEN KLONARIS

WEEDS

It was hard not to notice them. They lined the path leading to your front door – giant amaranths you called callaloo, a leaf of which you broke off and handed to me. It's something like wild spinach, you said, amused by my hesitation. Go ahead, taste, it won't poison you. You had names for the weeds that grew up in the limestone soil of your front yard, and round the back where grass swayed knee high, and you knew what they were good for: cerasee toned the blood, blue flower for fevers, and for an upset stomach, shepherd's needle – tiny yellow and white flowers I had seen and ignored all my life – staples in the unkempt corners of yards, the edges of streets that bordered onto bush, vacant lots, and poor soil that seemed not to want to grow anything else. You left them to flower and seed. You let them be.

That night, I smelled limestone soil in the crease of your belly, tasted it where my tongue found the back of your right knee, the hollow of your left armpit. I surrendered to something impossible, or to an unfamiliar sense of possibility and felt the shadow of callaloo darkening my skin, like a tattoo. I had the sensation I had been a shadow, till this moment. I was afraid to leave your bed, the weighty tangle of your arms and legs round mine, in case I forgot what it felt like to be flesh. I lay awake listening to the syncopated thrumming of our hearts. I watched your eyes flutter side to side under closed lids. I heard myself sigh.

In the days that came after, it was me and you, and you and me. You drawing the curtains in daytime, against the watchful eyes of neighbours. Me drawing you back from the front door to kiss you before leaving the house. In the car I threw a grey sweatshirt across the space between us where our fingers might mingle. Together, we were vigilant in parking lots, in grocery stores and pharmacies, in front of Mrs. Taylor's fruit stand. At a red light I felt something shimmer between us, evaporating on the stretch of road ahead. But when night came, in the sanctuary of your bed, we hung onto each other desperate for fingers and shoulder bones, the soft skin between toes and an ankle and heel, the certainty of a broad shin gleaming in the dark, the generous solidity of thighs, and finally, gratefully, that place between them where inside and outside came together.

It must have been what was between us that watered the shepherd's needle, the blue flower, the cerasee, the callaloo, and caused them all to flourish outside in the dirt, and then inside, on the white walls of your house. Behind drawn curtains, at dawn you rose, made us tea from something you'd gathered the day before, and I'd watch you carve giant woodcuts of each plant. Evenings, I helped you brush green vegetable dye you'd made from callaloo onto the wood, and press the panels onto your walls; every few days a new plant appeared. Leaf of life hands, rooster comb, hurricane weed. They seemed to take on a life of their own, turning this way and that, depending on the position of the sun. You said these were the plants your ancestors used to heal whatever ailed them, and it felt as if we were amongst them, even at night with the lights out.

Selfish, you called me in the beginning, months ago, when I told you I preferred living alone. I liked my solitude, I'd insisted, inside my homemade church, watching you pick up a rock and rub its smooth grey surface between your long brown fingers. You smelled of sweat and coconut oil, and I had wanted to reach over, take those fingers and pull them to my mouth. I didn't. Instead, I said you could keep the rock, that it was a present to remember me by. You looked up mischievously, as if you wanted to laugh, but stopped yourself, and I knew my cherished solitude was in danger.

I let you go that night, leaving with the women who had come for the meeting; we were protesting the new hotel development, the potential damage to the coastline. You were fresh back from university, teaching biology to high school seniors; you wanted to be involved. I stole glances at you in between questions about government policy and environmental impact reports. When we were done, I watched you leave, your long purple skirt brushing the ground, your right hand holding the rock I gave you.

Then, against my will, I dreamed you. You appeared to me the way spirits do, your face as close to me as my breath. I dreamed you a presence, woke with your breath on mine, breathless, awake, pressing myself into the sheets, the pillow.

That Sunday you invited me to your father's church. He was a minister, from a long line of ministers. He was outspoken, too, on radio talk shows every week, making sure people knew God wanted them to live well on earth, not just in heaven. You loved him for that.

I met you in the parking lot of New Bethlehem Baptist. The morning sun made the lemon silk of your dress shimmer. Your cheeks flushed as you peered over at my white patent-leather shoes, my starched and ironed white linen slacks, my pink polo shirt, items I had picked up in the men's section of the Island Shoppe. I looked away from you to the front door of the church, at the men in brown and black suits standing on either side, shaking the hands of the people streaming in. I wondered if I had made a mistake, if I should have worn a skirt instead. We hugged awkwardly. I followed you inside. The pews were crowded. Women in white dresses and white hats filled the front section. Behind them families with small children were on their feet singing, swaying and clapping, the organ and drums and tambourine leading their voices in a celebration I was not familiar with. We squeezed into a row of people towards the back. Women turned to look at us, put their arms around your neck, pulled you to them, kissed your cheeks. They eyed me and said welcome.

I could feel my heart thrumming against my ribs, out of time with the organ and the drums and the tambourine. My hands were clammy. My breath came and went in shallow draughts. Churches made me nervous. I remembered the last time I had been to the church I grew up in. We did not sing or sway or clap in time with tambourines or drums. We did not sing at all, unless it was Easter and we were burying Jesus, and then it was a song of lamentation.

That Sunday, I had come to church on my own. I had not been there for months, nor spoken to my family. But it was the Feast Day of the Virgin and I was missing the candles and the frankincense and the thick church walls that reminded me of the stories my grandmother told me of her village in Crete. She said the women had once gathered in caves, in secret, to make offerings of honey, sleeping there overnight to receive visions of Her, the one who could protect women from danger – a hard labour, a mean husband, or no husband at all. I remembered how she would whisper these things behind the back of my grandfather. She told me how blue and white stone churches had been built on top of the caves so that women would come instead to church, forgetting the honey at home, coming empty handed, the dark caves fading into dreams and myth.

I had decided that morning I would not wear a dress. My mother and I had fought about this the last time I saw her. I came wearing pants. I came with a jar of honey in my hands. I stood at the back of the church until it was time for Holy Communion. I planned to walk to the front of the church and place the honey at the foot of the large icon of the Virgin. I was nearly at the altar when I heard the commotion behind me. I saw the priest's eyes glance over my head, the golden spoon in his hand poised between the chalice and the open mouth of the woman awaiting communion. I felt hands grip me, my arms dragged apart so that the jar of honey fell, shattering against the black and white tiles of the church floor. Then I was walked backwards, out through the front door, as the congregation, women on the left, men on the right, stared, shook their heads, whispered behind their hands. Shame, what a shame.

The music inside New Bethlehem Baptist had lifted all who had not been standing to their feet. A deacon was intoning hallelujahs into the microphone. I stood there clapping and watching you sing; your eyes were closed, your face glowing, tilted to the ceiling. I thought you looked so at home in your body, but then, too, as though at any moment you could fly up out of yourself, into a place that was not here.

We left without seeing your father. We walked back out into the sunlight. Shading your eyes from the glare, you said, Can I see you again? I nodded, yes.

A week later, on the red couch in my apartment, you kissed me. You had never kissed a woman before, but you leaned over while I was talking about wetlands and how they were disappearing, and kissed me. At first you tasted like Bermuda cherries. Then, behind the sweet, like Shiraz, red and smoky, so that I gasped and said, Oh, God. You had slipped your hand under my favourite t-shirt, the black one with the spiralling white snake, palm open and warm against my naked breast. I had circled your wrist with my hand, wanting to pull you back and pull you to me at the same time.
    You sure?
    You talk too much.
    Thick warm fingers of your hair grazed my cheeks, my neck; the current between us hummed.
    That had been April, when woman-tongue and silk cotton trees flowered and their downy blossoms drifted in the breeze, when the weeds on your living-room walls grew thick and wild. By June the weather had changed. You became quiet, introspective and didn't want to be touched. You said you were hot. You needed space. To breathe. You said it wasn't me; it was the heat. The smallness of the island. There was too much noise, in your head. There was tension in the air, something that had not been here before. You didn't know what. You said it would pass. You said God was trying to tell you something. You had looked at me accusingly. A Nina Simone CD I was playing skipped, got stuck like a record and played the same stuttering note till I went to the stereo and stopped it. By then, you were up and walking to the door. You paused in the room I called my church, and said, Don't you ever think, maybe it's wrong?
    I looked around at the rocks lining the windowsills, at crooked branches I'd hung from the walls, at long streams of osprey and heron and sea gull feathers that waved in the breeze from the windows. I looked at the blue and yellow and red scarves draped

over a narrow table that was my altar: mounds of shells circling blue bottles crusted with coloured wax, white candles rising tall from their mouths; a long black and red snake carved from driftwood winding its way between clay figures of Cretan goddesses, their arms stretching to the sky. In the centre was a statue of a woman's torso carved from lignum vitae wood. And watching over the entire room from behind the altar was the painted face of a woman on a square of canvas, red and black and brown brush strokes strong and broad. I thought of her as the Ancient One, as the Goddess of the Mountain. We had refused her entry to the altars of our churches, buried and forgotten except as the obedient virgin. I thought of her as tiptoeing outside our houses in the streets at dawn, and again just after the sun set, crossing over into our dreams at night. A spirit fugitive, a spirit outlaw. I thought of her every time you and I touched, or made love, had a new idea. Or had questions about old ones.

No, I said. I don't.

The weeds on your walls began to wilt and so did we.

On my way to the grocery store next morning I heard two men tell the radio talk show host they were gay. The host said, You know that's not how God made you, but you sound proud of it anyway…

One of them cleared his throat and said, You know Steve, every morning I drive down Shirley Street. I see this guy in the same spot every time. He's sitting on that mustard-coloured wall outside Mrs. Mortimer's Tuck Shop. Half his face is a mess of skin and scar tissue, the other half looks like you and me. I heard a couple of guys found out he was gay and decided to punish him by assaulting him with a bucket of lye.

That's rough.

Every time you tell us 'That's not how God made you', you're giving guys like them permission to turn us into monsters.

I didn't call you that night. I lit candles in my homemade church. I burned frankincense and watched the smoke rise. I sang old Greek songs my grandmother used to sing when I was a child, the pieces I could still remember. I waited for a vision to tell me we weren't wrong.

In the weeks that followed it was you and me and some other thing that wouldn't leave us be. It was you turning your back to me in bed; it was me storming out of bed and slamming the front door shut; me revving my engine on the road outside, alone. It was us yelling at each other across the table in your kitchen and a half hour later making up. It was me saying I should never have let a straight girl kiss me. It was you saying why don't you get a job? It was me saying just because it doesn't look like a job, doesn't mean I'm not working; I freelance. I sell words. The space between us had become hard to cross.

Outside our four walls a storm was brewing.

I passed Rawson Square as I drove over to your place on Saturday evening. Already hundreds had gathered in front of a makeshift stage to protest homosexuality and the abduction, rape and murder of five boys. Across the square a large white banner stretched: *Save Our Nation*. We had heard a group of ministers had spearheaded the rally; your father was one of them. We had heard a small group of gay rights activists had set up camp across from the rally. We stayed home. I fried yellowtail and plantains and mixed boiled potatoes with olive oil, onions, and parsley, but we barely ate. Then the phone rang and you answered, hoarse. I heard you say yes Ma, and no Ma, and I'll talk to you soon. When you came back to the table you pushed the plate away from you.

My mother is asking questions. Wants to know who my 'new friend' is. What my friend's name is, and who her people are. You tried to laugh it off, but your laughter was tinny, the corners of your mouth strained. Then you began the litany.

We've been careless. People have seen us together. How else would she know I have a 'new friend'? You were up and pacing the living room floor. Remember that day in the video store I introduced you to my cousin and she mistook you for a man? And the time in the car when we kissed and held hands at the red light and my mother's sister, Auntie Joan, was in the car next to us? What about the time you were leaving my house and Dante drove up at the exact moment we kissed goodbye – did we have the door open, or was it still closed? I don't remember. Damn it, I don't remember.

I wanted to make you feel safe. I wanted to feel safe too: But he was still in his car; it was so fast, and the door had to be closed.

It didn't matter what I said; it was as if the voices of the preachers downtown had floated all the way into Shirlea, down Yellow Elder Road, through the white gate, under the door and windows and into the air we were breathing. I felt it too. My throat constricted. You coughed, blew your nose, worried your lower lip.

Come, sit with me.

You shook your head.

You said, I feel transparent, pulling the curtains to. You said, I feel as if the walls of this house are made of Perspex, and drew your orange terry-cloth robe closer around your shoulders. I offered you a hiding place between my two arms, but you slapped them away: Everyone can see us.

Then you said: You should never have come to church wearing men's clothes. What were you thinking?

Jesus, Addie.

It's my father's church. You think you can just go anywhere and be however you want?

If you want me to leave, just say so.

No, no. I don't want you to leave.

We slept burrowed into each other like snails.

The next morning I woke early, made us a breakfast of mango slices and sour-leaf tea. You traced the arch of my left eyebrow with your fingers. I said, Don't go to church. Stay here with me. I tugged at your T-shirt. You smiled, uncertain. You let me kiss your chin, the corner of your mouth, your right ear.

We heard a knocking at the front door. You pulled away.

Adeline, you home?

It's my mother. Shit. Stay here. You lurched out of bed, threw on your robe and hurried to let your mother in. I considered climbing out the window, but the windows were obstructed by white wrought iron, crafted to look like birds in flight instead of burglar bars. Your voices sank dully in the humid air as winged shadows played across our tangled bedclothes.

Your father wants to know what's keeping you from praising the Lord.

I can praise Him anywhere, Mama; I don't have to come to church to do it.

I'm worried about you.

I'm a grown woman.

That's what I'm worried about. What a grown woman like you doing with that mannish woman who I hear don't even have a job?

She's an activist, she freelances. And anyhow, I can have friends.

What you have in common with her, your friend?

Mummy, she's not anyone… You don't have to worry.

I could hear crows rustling in the bougainvillea outside the bedroom window, their big voices croaking a warning under the eaves.

And what's all this? You don't have enough plants outside, you have to bring them inside too? Looks strange to me. Like some kind of voodoo. Get these off your walls, hear me? And I want to see you in church.

I know. I'll come.

After I heard the door open and shut, you didn't return to the bedroom. I didn't know whether to wait in there or come out. I fingered my keys. I sat on the edge of the bed, making patterns in the carpet with my white high tops. I thought, if it had been my mother visiting, and you half naked in my bed just feet away, would I have said anything different?

I sighed and got up. I crossed the hallway into the living room. You glanced at me, our eyes met, and for seconds I imagined this could be our home, our paintings on the walls, our books on shelves arranged in the order of our most beloved authors. I imagined my guitar leaning against the white wicker armchair, photographs of my nieces next to the ones of your nephews on the round table by the sliding door that looked out on weeds we knew by name. But we couldn't hold our gaze; I looked away first. When I looked back, so had you.

I'll call, I said.

★

I did call, but for two weeks your phone rang and rang, unanswered. I imagined you ignoring the ring as you brushed your teeth, poured yourself a glass of water, set it by the bed, turned down the sheets, turned out the lights, lay down frowning at the too warm air and the sliver of persistent yellow light reaching its way in through the crack in the curtains from the street outside. I imagined hearing you suck your teeth as you rolled onto your right side, away from the street light, pulling your knees up to your breasts and hugging them, childlike. I imagined the weeds on the walls limp, leaves turning brown along their edges, their roots snaking deep into the walls in search of wetness and dirt. I imagined how it was only when the phone stopped ringing that you allowed yourself the luxury of stretching your legs out to the full length of the bed.

I gave up calling and drove over to see you instead. I parked my car alongside the white gate out front and slipped through it into your yard. The moon was full, and under its light I could see something was different. At first I did not see what that difference was. Then I saw the soil on either side of the walkway had been freshly turned and was bare; the callaloo had been uprooted and cleared, the grass had been weeded and cut, cerassee vines stripped away from the garden fence, blue flower and shepherd's needle had disappeared.

Addie? I tapped the door three times. I heard stillness, then movement and clatter. When the door opened, your face was softly round, your brown eyes bright as sandstone washed clean after a rainsquall. You didn't speak as I followed you inside. You padded towards the kitchen, to stir the pot boiling on the gas stove.

I've been calling.

I've been busy, you said, stirring.

The walls of your room, which had been home to weeds that could cure diabetes and asthma and whooping cough had paled, the plants covered over with a fresh layer of white paint. Shelves once arranged neatly with books like *Bush Medicine of the Bahamas*, *Mangrove Ecology, Sisters in the Wilderness* had been emptied of their contents, which now sat in orderly columns beside photographs, and a small oil portrait of your father benignly looking on.

What happened? Why have you painted over the walls?

I'm renting the house.

I sucked in my breath and concentrated on the only object left on the wall facing the door: a large acrylic painting of an old woman smoking a tobacco pipe. She sat barefoot on the steps of a blue wooden porch, her eyes, like a crow's, staring back at me, her legs wide, her skirt an orange valley between them. Behind her an open door led into a darkened room. I wanted to disappear into that room, to sit with the old woman, rest my head in her lap.

I watched you holding a wooden spoon and stirring. You staring at your own hand holding the spoon. You breathing in deep, and then turning to face me.

I'm moving back to Canada, you said.

What's in Canada? I felt my hands and legs drift away from my body.

I wanted to talk about love, but the word seemed made of airy stuff, seemed to come from a long way off, from a foreign place where other people lived. Maybe Canada.

But this is your home. I waved an arm in the direction of the whitewashed walls, emptied bookshelves, the stripped backyard.

You turned back to the stove and the pot. Your figure was weary and small under your robe. I watched your shoulders rise, then fall. I watched you bow your head, concentrating on the spoon and the stirring. Under the terry-cloth I imagined your breasts were tender and full; I had listened to the ocean moving beneath them, sometimes so swollen it spilled out over your skin, wetting my cheeks, stinging my eyes. My heart was full and aching, my hands empty and aching. I was about to go to you when you said, There's nothing for me here.

It had been four months and two weeks and four days and everything I had been yearning to touch and smell and hear was in this room.

How I feel about you isn't nothing.

This is not about how you feel.

We've been having a hard time. But we can't give up, Addie. Not now. Not yet. At least talk to me. At least give me that.

I should have seen it coming. It was his birthday. I went to please him. You had turned to face me now. Your face flushed. He brought me up to the front of the church. I didn't understand what was going on. Why everyone was staring at me when it was his day. He stepped down from the pulpit. He stood next to me, had his arm around me. His arm tightened. I didn't know what was coming but I wanted to run. Then he started praying. He said he wasn't going to let the devil take his youngest. He made me say it out loud, in front of everyone. He made me say I wasn't what people were saying.

I'm so sorry. I reached for your hand but you pushed me from you.

He had the whole congregation praying for me. He said a spirit of abomination had taken over the country, and he wanted the church to be a congregation of warriors, a congregation of soldiers, to fight for the souls of the ones who were lost. I started to weep. I started to feel lost.

Baby… I tried again to hold your hand, to touch you, but you wouldn't let me.

You folded your arms against your breasts. You looked down at the tiled floor, then back at me.

God wants me to change my life.

Your father isn't God.

What do you know about God? You don't even believe in him.

I felt the ghost of weeds pressing in on us. Dogs barked in the street. A child began to cry.

Look at me, I said.

You shook your head and traced the square tile with a slippered foot.

In the silence I heard a clock ticking, the gurgle of okra soup simmering on the stove.

You should go.

There is no place else to go.

Okra soup simmered and its scent crept along the walls.

This isn't something that's … you unfolded and folded your arms, possible.

I was about to leave, but something about the okra soup, its scent creeping along the walls, the old woman sucking on her pipe and eyeing me, wouldn't let me go.

I sat down on a bucket of paint. I was a sophomore in college. It was mid-semester and my parents came to pay me a visit – at least that's what they said. They had found letters, mine, to a woman I'd been seeing. So, they came up there and took me out of school. Just like that. They took me to a motel, forbade me from seeing her, or contacting any of my friends, made me leave behind all my clothes, my books, everything. We were holed up in a motel room outside a New England college town, the two of them in one bed, me in another. In the middle of the night I woke up to a yelling, my father pitching up from a nightmare that he was battling the devil. The next thing I heard was my mother reading from the Bible. *Yea though I walk through the valley of the shadow of death I shall fear no evil*... She said, Maybe she's possessed. I eased the pillow over my head and pretended to be asleep. I pressed my face down so hard against the white sheets I couldn't breathe. All I could do was pray I wasn't crazy. The next day they drove me through Connecticut suburbs looking for a Greek Church. They wanted to find a priest who could perform an exorcism. You know, run the devil out of me. Thankfully, the priest wasn't in.

They took you out of university?

Yes.

What did you do?

Dropped out. Came back here. Became an activist. You know, a troublemaker...

You smiled, your brown eyes sad. You are a troublemaker. You turned the stove off. You stirred the pot of soup then put the wooden spoon down. You said, Take me to your church.

Right now? It's probably closed.

Take me anyway.

We drove through town, past the library that had once been a jail, past the harbour where cruise ships floated like small cities, past office buildings and nightclubs and hotels to the other side of town, an in-between place that was not west or east, where the Greeks had lived in small blue and white and pink wooden houses with concrete porches before they moved out to neighbourhoods where houses had gardens and pools. As we drove, me in the driver's seat of your car, I thought about the two times I had ever seen brown people enter our church, and how nobody had turned to say welcome.

We parked your car on the street outside. An old man and a dog were sitting on the curb. They watched us cross the street to the black gate. The church walls and domed roof glowed white and blue. I unlatched the gate and walked up to the double wooden doors, rattled the handle, but the doors wouldn't budge. I knocked and the sound reverberated off the walls, the concrete courtyard, the warm stillness of the air around us.

No one's home, I whispered to you.

Show me anyway.

I found a window at the back of the church, nearly at knee level. It was loose. I shook it gently, back and forth, till it shifted, opening just enough to wedge a stick under it and lever it up. I lowered myself into the passage. I turned and looked up at you. I held out my hands.

You took my hands and you let me lift you through the opening and into a bathroom inside the basement of the Church of the Annunciation. I took out my flashlight from my backpack. We walked through a narrow hallway and up some stairs that led into the altar. Women were not allowed here.

Hanging bowls of oil lit the corners at the front of the altar, their flames darting tongues of light. We walked out into the nave. Moonlight filtered through the stained glass windows so that we could see each other's faces. We stood in the centre of the church listening.

You reached for my hand. It feels so ancient.

I know.

I grew up in the church. It was everything. I used to listen to my father practising his sermons and then I would make up my own. While he was at the front of the church, preaching, I would be at the back preaching inside my head. When the people shouted their amens and halleluiahs, I imagined they were hearing me, saying amen to my words.

I had a best friend, Angie. One summer she got pregnant. She was only fourteen. They made her leave the church. I asked my father why. He said she was a bad example for other girls. There was a rumour that one of the deacons had been messing with her. But nothing ever came of it. My sermons dried up. My words got lost.

I squeezed your hand. I shone the flashlight up at the altar. There were paintings of the saints – John Chrysostom, Gregory of Nyssa, John the Baptist, St. George spearing the dragon – all of them old and white and male.

I said, They're happy when our words get lost. It makes it easier for them to keep talking.

I thought of the white statue of Christopher Columbus a few blocks over on Government House hill, presiding over the town, his sword in the sand, something like St. George's spear in the belly of the dragon; I thought of the pink walls of Government House, how you always said pink was a colour the English used to lull slaves into obedience.

I said, Any chance there's a bucket of callaloo paint in the trunk of your car?

You said, Yes… What for?

I said, Wait for me.

I came back with a bucket and a brush. I peeled the lid open with a key. I stirred the dye with a stick.

Take off your clothes.

Here?

Yes.

You did. You took off your T-shirt, your bra, your pants. I took off my T-shirt, my bra, my pants. We were standing naked on the black and white square tiles of the church I grew up in. Your breath on my lips. Our eyes liquid. The air electric. Your fingers grazed my breasts. I looked over at the bearded faces of pallid saints. We laughed.

Then I was dipping a brush into the thick green dye, and stroking it on in great swathes across your breasts. Frankincense and callaloo and the muskiness of our bodies filled the air. You pressed yourself against me, our bodies painting each other, then, without speaking, we walked towards an empty white wall. You first, then me, hand in hand, we leaned into the wall, as if it were a third lover. The soft flesh of our breasts, your right cheek and my left, made sucking sounds against the wall; the wall like skin, lips, a forehead. I whispered into the wall, Can you feel us? When we stepped away from the wall we had left ourselves there.

You took up the brush and stroked my breasts, then my belly, my pelvis and thighs; you were anointing me, the palms of my hands – there were no nails here, and no crosses – we were not dying… We embraced the wall, again and again, leaving ourselves everywhere, in between wooden pews, in between mourning faces of old men, in between golden wings of angels, arched around the body of the Virgin, our fingers reaching for each others' fingers, bellies, lips… our bodies intertwining, insistent, against the wall. We did this as if our lives depended on it, as if it were high mass, as if it were a forgotten ceremony erupting out of a fissure in our memories, a waking dream. What was lost is remembered.

As the light of morning began to stream in red and purple and orange through stained-glass pictures of Jesus and his cross, Joseph of Arimathea bearing up the cross for him, Mary weeping for her son, nighttime shadows on the walls became callaloo green silhouettes of two women standing, holding hands, embracing, arms raised high, their legs and breasts and fingers as visible as if they had always been there.

The callaloo had dried on the walls and on our skin. We helped each other put on bras, shirts, pants, socks, shoes. I gave you a leg up to the window and when you disappeared, I gripped the ledge and pulled myself out too.

Outside, we felt thick and solid and large, as if our bodies had become giants and our hands, if we wanted to, could reach over and across town and caress the surface of ocean waves. We chased each other hooting all the way down the hill to the strip of beach at the island's edge. We took off our clothes again; we waded into the water. We used handfuls of sand to scrub each other's breasts and arms. The water turned deep green all around us.

SHARON LEACH

MORTALS

The baby's cancer has come back.

Lisa watches the doctor's mouth forming words, which she doesn't hear, although she knows them all too well. It's like watching TV with the volume down, only there is sound, a blur of noise around him, the normal sounds of the ward. Lisa continues watching him, dazed, her mouth slack, as if she's in a dream. But it is no dream. After six months of cautious optimism and finally beginning to breathe again, Lisa feels a familiar weight settle in the pit of her stomach.

Then the volume seems to be turned up again and she can again distinguish his words, though not clearly, as if they are coming from some distant place.

"I'm sorry, Mrs Stanton. I know this is the last thing you wanted to hear. I mean, we knew the risks with AML. But, I guess one never is fully prepared for a relapse. Of course, we'll do everything to fight back – we'll use a new combination of drugs. And there's the clinical trial for that new chemo regimen I spoke to you and your husband about. The hope is for remission, so an allogeneic stem cell transplant can be performed. The outlook, as we've discussed before, is not the best. Whatever happens, though, you should know we're in for the long haul."

That's it, then. He is sorry. It's over? Lisa feels confused. What is he saying? She feels like a child, unable to comprehend, though she thinks she should, and decides not to ask him to explain. She feels exhausted. She wants to lie down somewhere, curl up and go to sleep.

Lisa is nearly always exhausted. She walks with a plodding gait and regularly emits weary sighs. Though she is still good-looking, thank God, when she looks at herself in the mirror, she says to her reflection, "Who will love me again?", staring into eyes that are often bloodshot and have dark smudges beneath them. She keeps a tube of concealer in her medicine chest to cover the circles; it's the only make-up she ever uses now. Peering some more at the face, she made other unpleasant discoveries: her cheekbones seem too exaggerated, too pronounced for her now gaunt face, as though they belonged to someone else – perfect for some ano-rexic runway model but for her, they're too severe, making her look like a fierce-eyed savage. Worse was her discovery that her post-pregnancy body with its luscious, womanly curves – the full boobs, the accentuated hips – with which she'd fallen in love, and with which Steven had been enthralled, had all but disappeared. She's actually quite skinny now – emaciated even; she'd stopped eating again, and lost weight rapidly since the baby has taken a turn for the worse. For her visit to the hospital, she has brushed her hair back severely into a neat bun, from which not one loose strand can escape. She is prophylactically dressed in a high-necked, ruffled pink Victorian blouse, a knee-length dun-col-oured pleated skirt whose waist is now too loose, and sensible tan pumps. She looks like a believer (which she isn't) in a particularly strict Christian sect, or perhaps an old-fashioned woman dressed for work at some government office. But Lisa no longer works; she quit her job after the baby's sickness reappeared.

She stands looking at the child almost serenely, and brushes her hand against the baby's feeble arm and offers it a small, placating smile before turning away from what she sees as a look of simultaneous hope and dismay clouding its eyes.

It's a setback, of course, the doctor continues, staring at the baby's chart – and avoiding looking at her, Lisa realises. Her mind wanders listlessly. His words sound almost like an admission – though of what, she is uncertain. It can't be of guilt. She's the guilty one, she's the one responsible for passing on this sickness from her womb.

The doctor is a slightly built, light-skinned man with a slight stoop, sloping shoulders and a smattering of freckles across his nose and cheeks. Lisa thinks it is funny for a black person, regardless of lightness of hue, to have freckles. Staring at his thinning widow's peak, she has a sudden urge to giggle. We're all going to die, she thinks, and the thought makes her queasy. Beads of sweat erupt on her forehead.

A fat nurse waddles by in her too-tight uniform, her pudgy, white-stockinged legs rubbing together noisily with a hissing sound. Lisa wonders if she plans to start a fire. Overweight, Lisa mentally corrects herself, that's the politically correct term. The nurse gives Lisa a tight, sympathetic smile, her chins wobbling, and Lisa, who is unable to look away from her, feels somehow exposed, diminished by this fat woman who perhaps has perfect – normal – children of her own.

To take her mind off these spiteful feelings brewing within her, Lisa focuses her attention on the doctor. He is reputedly one of the best paediatric oncologists in the Caribbean. She looks at his nameplate through a sudden blur of tears. Dr J Paul Mountbatten. Mountbatten. A regal name. Isn't the Queen a descendant of some Mountbattens or other? And what about his Christian name? Is the J for John? No, it wasn't something that common. She'd heard a doctor colleague of his, a well-preserved woman, maybe in her late-forties, greet him by his first name. Something Spanish? What was it? *I ought to know my child's doctor's first name*, she thinks angrily.

The doctor is still flipping through the baby's charts, as if for the answer to some unknown question. Lisa feels offended by this action. The tears that had been gathering in her eyes and in the back of her throat a moment ago have evaporated. *Look at me!* she wants to scream at him. *Why are you telling me this?*

In a corner of the ward, which is painted a soothing, neutral light yellow, a bald baby begins to wail. There is a movement towards the cot by the overweight nurse. Lisa looks at her with contempt.

Lisa's knees feel like rubber. She turns back to face the doctor and is struck by a wave of nausea. Hug me, she thinks wildly. Squeeze the loneliness out of me. She imagines herself collapsing helplessly in a sobbing ball at his feet. She would indeed launch herself at his feet, if that would help, if that would save her child's life.

His beeper goes off. He retrieves it from his waist and frowningly examines it before replacing it. He does not excuse himself, which is a relief for Lisa, who just now feels the need to be near him. As she watches him go over the chart she wants to throw herself at him, peel off his skin and burrow inside. But she will not embarrass herself; she will not embarrass him. Her own embarrassment is secondary, unimportant. She knows about other people's embarrassment; it is something she has become intimately acquainted with during the past few years. She is accustomed to the nervous titters of preschoolers, the shifty looks in their parents' eyes when they are out in public, in the waiting room at the doctor's, for example, when the baby is seized with nausea and starts projectile vomiting. "It's the chemo," Lisa would explain, compelled to apologise in her *forgive-me-for-all-this* tone of voice, the voice she had often used on her husband before he left. The parents would huddle their children close to them, nod uncomfortably, avoiding eye contact. As if they, too, thought it was all her fault that her child was sick and dying.

Outside the hospital it's a gloriously brilliant March day that makes the eyes hurt. After eleven successive days of rain the sky is clear and blue; everything is lush and green, cruelly alive; as if the greyness and death inside the building does not exist. Lisa breathes in deeply, looking up at the sun. Nobody tells you how hard it is being a single parent of a sick child. She even wishes that she had been raised with some faith so that she could pray. It feels like there's a conspiracy of silence about the difficulty, even among other parents of chronically and terminally-ill children. It was how it was with women who'd had children and were reluctant to tell the truth about the real pain of childbirth or that pregnancy often made a woman horny, endlessly dreaming of penises, penises and more penises.

She tries to throw up in a corner of the recently mown front lawn and when she is unable to do so, goes to sit on a concrete bench beneath an ancient lignum vitae tree; under it, mounds of raked leaves mixed in with mown grass and general trash and debris stand waiting to be bagged and tossed out. She stares at a bug marching up the side of the tree trunk, the dappled mid-morning sun's rays warm against her face. There are many benches like this one, scattered across the grounds. To help family members compose their thoughts about what faces their loved ones, she imagines. She notices a man and woman seated on a nearby bench beneath another tree. The man has his hand around the slender slumped shoulders of the woman who is staring blankly into space.

Lisa averts her eyes. She can hear the muffled sound of traffic in the distance, the world going on without a care for her problems. She thinks about her mother, who died in the first year she and Steven were married. Thinking about this is not a good idea. Never has she felt so much like an orphan. She has never been in touch with her father, who'd never taken an active role in her life. A divinity student from a prominent Westmoreland family, he'd had an affair with Lisa's mother for almost two years, then dumped her when Lisa was born. Her mother was the secretary at the Bible College where he'd been studying. His family's lawyers had discreetly arranged for a generous maintenance package for the child, with the stipulation that there would be no public identification of their bastard grandchild's father. Who was there to tell? Lisa's mother had no other living relatives. She found another secretarial job after she had the baby, and devoted herself to Lisa's welfare and happiness. She'd raised her more like a sister than a daughter. They'd even double-dated a few times in Lisa's teenage years. Lisa's friends had all been amazed at the openness of their relationship, how they spoke honestly about sex, for instance. Because of her own bad experience, Lisa's mother urged her daughter to give her virginity only to a man who was worthy of her. Lisa *had* waited until she'd finished high school to engage in her first sexual encounter, though the man had undoubtedly not been worthy – his name had long escaped her – simply a man who'd offered her a lift one rainy day as she stood waiting at a bus stop. Lisa, at eighteen, felt as though she hadn't completely disappointed her mother because she'd waited, and that had to count for something.

Now, Lisa feels the familiar dull ache in her breasts. She remembers how sharp the pain had been, the burning pain in both nipples, when she'd been nursing. How that electric suck of the baby's lips on the swollen tips, the lightning rod sensation zigzagging straight to her womb and oh, the delicious but illicit thrill of the pain, had made her feel more of a woman than at any other time in her life. How desperately she wishes she could still speak to her mother – the former festival queen who drew swarms of men buzzing like bees around flowers. She had been so young looking, and in seemingly good health, when a stroke felled her one morning and she'd died a week later. In retrospect, Lisa remembered the lingering flu that had developed into a bronchial infection. Lisa had been crippled by a sense of abandonment that whole first year of her marriage, leaning heavily on Steven for emotional support. For two weeks after the funeral she had stayed home in bed, too depressed to face the world, beseeching Steven to take time off work to stay at home with her. She had imagined her mother being around to enjoy the arrival of the grandchildren she'd anxiously anticipated from the day she'd walked Lisa down the aisle.

What comes after? Lisa asks herself now. "Let go, and let God," is the reply inside her head, which is really nothing but the echo of a non-sequitur she'd heard her father using to his well-heeled congregation, several times during one of his sermons. Lisa had kept close tabs on him and knew when he'd moved to Kingston to take up an appointment there. He'd become a respected and charismatic figure within ecumenical circles. Despite her bitterness at his treatment of her, she would sometimes creep into the back of the church to watch him. She was always struck by his handsomeness, his articulateness. He'd gone grey at the temples and some of his muscle tone had begun to go soft, but she could still divine the lover in him. She could understand how her mother had been seduced by him, by his silver tongue that she imagined had called on the name of Jesus even as he'd thrust, swollen and insistent, into her mother's yielding flesh. The truth was, as she glanced round at the adoring faces of his female congregants, who hung on to his every word, throwing their amens and hallelujahs wantonly at him as though they were undergarments, she was secretly a little proud of him. That day, as the organ swelled mournfully in the background, Lisa had watched him in his sober suit and formal tie, his secret life locked within his breast. "When nothing's left," he had intoned – a flash of a bracelet appearing from beneath his cuff when he held up a forefinger in admonition – "Friends, God is there."

But he isn't really, she thinks now. Faith was what people leaned on to get them through difficult times, but she can't bring herself to start believing in a god she despises, one of whose representatives was a hypocrite like her father. Still, where did it leave her as far as her understanding of the end of life? It's an issue she's been thinking about more and more. You go through all that shit, that pain and suffering in life and then, at the end, what is there? More pain and suffering? There was no guarantee of heaven, especially for someone who did not believe there was such a place. But, if not heaven, what?

She closes her eyes and tries to summon the presence of this god of whom her father spoke. But she can't. That god doesn't exist. The baby will return to the dust, that's all. So will she, when it's her turn to go. Nothing comes after. All that she can believe in is what's real, what came before, what is here and now. But wallowing in the morbid does no good, so she forces herself to think about other matters. Eyes still closed, she tries to reconstruct images of what her life had been before the baby. She'd been reasonably happy despite the less-than-perfect circumstances of her childhood. She'd grown up and had friends and she'd even known love. When she'd gotten pregnant, she'd felt her life was complete, especially because she'd believed that having children would be impossible. The baby. What joy she'd felt on her safe arrival. This perfect creature. Ten fingers, ten toes. All functioning parts. She was in love, again. There had been no thought, in those early days and nights when she cradled her to her bosom and gazed lovingly into her eyes, that she was one of those defective models that ought to be returned to the manufacturer. It hadn't occurred to her that there could be a problem.

Then, as the days turned into weeks, irritability, melancholy and restlessness had crept in. She felt guilty, as though she'd fallen out of love with the baby. Postpartum depression, the doctor had diagnosed. She didn't exactly ignore the baby, but she was no longer as fascinated with her every move. It was during this time that she also began to sense that things with Steven had hit some kind of snag. Her doctor encouraged her to return to work, and she did. Now, she cannot really remember what her days were like when she had a computer on her desk and wore daring high heels with professional cotton-blend suits that her boss and co-workers admired.

She will have to dismantle the baby's room, the room she'd spent so much time preparing. The furniture will have to be put in storage. Then there are all the cute little clothes to sort: she'll give some to Joan from the office, who recently had a baby; the others she'll give to goodwill –

Horrified, she realises that she's already begun to think about the baby as dead; she forces herself to stop.

She pulls out her cellphone and dials her husband. He left her and their child because he couldn't "stand the smell of sickness" and the way it made her so "damn needy".

"Yes, Lisa," Steven answers wearily, on the fourth ring, just before voice-mail chips in.

"Steven," she says without preamble. She pictures him, slight and effete, fragile as a baby bird. Neat, well-groomed. Dressed in a pin-striped suit, the jacket close-fitting, double-buttoned. People called his look metrosexual, he'd once told her, and she'd had to stifle the snigger that wanted to burst from her throat. "It's back." She thinks of their days at Lamaze classes, and pictures Steven holding her hand in the delivery room. They were once best friends. When had they become enemies? She listens to him breathing noisily through his mouth on the other end of the line. Adenoids.

"What? What's back?

"It's the baby," Lisa explains. "It's back."

There is silence. Then: "Jesus Christ." He expels a long frustrated sigh, and she can imagine him rubbing the elegant high bridge of his nose. "Where are you? Well, look, I'm in the middle of something here," he says. "I have to call you back. This evening, OK?"

She hangs up before he does, knowing what he's thinking.

He's thinking she is using the baby's sickness as leverage to get him to come back home. There is a hurricane of emotions swirling around inside her, feelings she is unable to express. She doesn't want him back, and yet she does; she can't go through this alone. Mostly, though, she's confused; the idea that *he* would ever have left had never occurred to her.

She gets up and wanders back towards the building, but at the sliding glass door, changes her mind. The thought of going back inside there with the sickening hospital smell of antiseptic makes her want to retch again, and so urgent does the need to pee become, that she hurries around the side of the building instead.

The hospital's grounds are huge. She remembers seeing them first on a brochure someone from her workplace had handed her. She remembers thinking that surely the baby would be cured at such an impressive structure as this. The hospital itself is a magnificent ivory-coloured edifice with sloping green-shingled roofs. It had been built in the economic boom of the mid-1980s, by the government with assistance from the Jewish business-men's league. Lisa's footfalls are soundless in the high grass around the side of the building.

Lisa vomits, then squats to pee when she finds a suitable spot, near a pile of leaves under a tree. A sound somewhere makes her pause, mid-flow, a Kegel contraction that makes her pubis throb with pleasure. She looks up and sees that she is being observed by the grounds-keeper, a stocky deaf-mute she's seen around the institution. He also works as a cleaner on the wards; Lisa remem-bers seeing him with his mops and other accoutrements. They had on occasion exchanged looks; there was one time Lisa noticed something in his eyes. Steven had noticed it too. They had been on the ward one night, when he'd come up the hall, noisily dragging his roller bucket with the squeaky wheels, dirty water sloshing out over the sides. The baby had just been diagnosed; they'd been keeping vigil beside her cot.

Lisa had looked up and had seen him in the hallway, staring at her, his mouth half-open in his deaf-mute gape. She could tell then, simply by looking at him, that something was wrong with him. Lisa knew it was impolite to stare but she was unable to drag her eyes away. Perhaps because of what had befallen them, she couldn't help finding something morbidly compelling in sickness and disability. Their eyes held for a few seconds before Steven put a protective arm around her. "Is it safe to have that guy here, on the ward with the children?" he had whispered when the cleaner had moved down the hall. "He's kind of creepy."

Lisa looks at the deaf-mute now and realises that she cannot estimate his age – it could be anywhere between late teens and thirties. He is dressed in khaki and water boots and carries a coiled-up garden hose. His fleshy lips are hanging open, the way they had been when she'd first seen him on the ward. She wonders if he remembers her. Probably not. Possibly he's retarded as well. No sooner is the thought out than she feels ashamed for thinking it. Her mind runs back to the nurse she'd judged as fat. When did she become so mean?

She is frightened by a sound he makes in his throat.

"Oh," Lisa says, and, filled with a reckless daring, empties the rest of her bladder.

He mutters something unintelligible and backs away.

Lisa knows what an incongruous picture she must have made with her serious hairstyle and dignified clothes, the sensible pleated skirt hiked up above her knees, squatting down above the high, vomit-sprayed grass like a Vietnamese peasant, the gusset of her pants pulled aside by her finger, pee splashing against the sides of her tan shoes. But in that instant, she doesn't care. Her pants have gotten wet, too, so she pulls them down, wads them up and stuffs them into her handbag. He probably hasn't taken in any of it, she tells herself. She takes out a square of Kleenex from the mini pack she keeps handy in her purse, and dabs at herself before reaching down to dab at the leather of her shoes splashed by urine. "God," she says aloud. She tosses away the tissue, looks around. "God," she says again.

When she finds him he is attaching the hose to a standpipe. From where she stands she can smell the rank odour of sweat in his clothes.

She approaches, her heart beating erratically. She feels awkward, as if she is just learning to walk; it has been a while since she seduced anyone. She must tread carefully, she cannot spook him. Above, a bird alights from a tree, wings flapping, startling her.

She stops.

He stops dead, too, looks up, slack-jawed. She smiles at him. She has not been with a man in more than a year; her smile is meant to inspire desire, despite the awkward circumstances. She hopes it does. Unable to stop herself now, she hikes up her skirt – what *is* she doing? – revealing her crotch with its untamed bush.

She hears the same strangled sound come from him, and her eyes travel boldly to the front of his pants, which she sees has formed an appreciative tent. She is glad he is unable to speak. Glad that in spite of this, he can nevertheless be made to understand.

She is down on all fours – her dun-coloured pleated skirt bunched up around her waist. He kneels behind her. Nothing matters now – not her dead mother, the infant lying inside the sick children's ward, the goddamned husband who puked the first time he smelt the baby's puke, and then moved out, not the fact that she has no money left for this go-round of hospital fees and medication and whatnot – nothing matters except that there is a strange man inside her, and all she can feel inside her is him.

But this isn't quite enough. She pulls away from him, and pushes him down on his back and straddles him, impaling herself on his rigid cock. His shirt is ringed with the sweat stains of one who labours for many hours beneath the sun; she peels it off and flings it as far away from them as she can. He is young, she decides – twenties, maybe – solid. She can see now that what she thought flab is actually muscle. His eyes are glazed with excitement and fear; his slack mouth reveals crooked yellowed teeth.

Her face feels flushed, a vein pulsed in her forehead; her nostrils flared. She feels good, in charge of her circumstances, for once. The feeling of power is almost more than she can bear. It's better than thinking of the unfairness of it, belonging to a god she can't see or believe in. As if from a distance, she can hear the sound of their laboured breathing – grunts and groans – and a voice urging, *Faster, faster, faster, faster* that she does not recognise.

After, she vomits again. Then she adjusts her hair, and examines her knees where the earth has bruised them. She looks at him, the deaf-mute, dazed, his pants bundled around his ankles, and sees it had been a new and not unpleasant experience for him. She imagines him thinking about her later that night in his bed, and knows she will absolutely not want him again. This episode will remain a secret.

Secrets.

Lisa knows all about secrets, and how to keep them. She has never told a soul – except, of course, Steven – who her father is. It would be a colossal embarrassment to him, his family – perhaps cost him his church if she were to decide to come forward now. She remembers once fantasising about it and telling Steven, "Maybe I should just stand up one day and tell everybody that he's my father." They'd been lying on their big comfortable leather sofa one Sunday evening while they watched TV.

She'd returned earlier that afternoon from one of her visits to his church, which had been more frequent after her mother died. As usual, Steven had prepared dinner, Italian fare, and they'd eaten and gone to the living room to watch a movie. She was still in her stockings and frowned when Steven took one of her feet gently into his lap and started massaging it with his soft, pampered hands. Lisa told him how her father had bragged to his congregants that his son, his "firstborn", had been accepted into a foreign Bible school and would soon join him in the ministry. "I should have just stood up, made a scene. Told everybody that I'm his firstborn," Lisa said, quite taken aback by the venom she was feeling.

"Are you crazy?" Steven had asked sharply.

Lisa had assured him it was only a joke; she had no interest in ruining the man's life. But Steven had stopped rubbing her feet and turned his attention to the TV. Secrets were important to him, too, particularly the sanctity of keeping them. He himself had a secret: a big one. When they'd agreed to marry, it entailed acceptance of the regular late-night sounds of male laughter seeping through his adjacent bedroom wall, for example. For her, it was a small price to pay to allay the fear of becoming a lonely, childless old maid. He'd entrusted her with custodianship of his secret, depending on her to guard it with her life.

To this day, she had.

She re-emerges from under the tree into the brilliance of the day, the pulse in her throat throbbing like an explosive device on the brink of detonation. The day has begun to heat up, she notes, glancing down at her blouse moist with perspiration. Beneath the fabric of her skirt, her nakedness feels exquisite. It reminds her of the days when she was desirable, when she had lovers – married ones, and single ones. She would call them, teasing that she was naked beneath her clothes and she was touching herself, thinking about them. She pauses to steady herself, her secret furled deep within her like a prayer. Yes, she knows how to keep secrets.

At the sliding glass door entrance, she bumps into the baby's doctor.

"Mrs Stanton," he says, a concerned frown creasing his brow. "We were wondering where you'd got to. Are you all right?"

"Yes. I'm fine, Doctor. I just needed, I needed some fresh air."

"Oh. Well, let's go up to see your daughter." He touches her arm lightly, propels her through the lobby, which is bright with crystal sunshine, oversized potted plants and a shiny marble floor, to the elevator that will take them up to the children's ward.

As they stand side by side, quietly staring up at the lighted buttons that signal which floor the lift has reached, Lisa suddenly remembers what the J stands for, and this recollection of the elusive Christian name brings her more satisfaction than any-thing else that has happened to her in a long while. She repeats the name in her head like a mantra. For a moment she is invincible. She closes her eyes and sighs deeply, breathing the name softly on her lips. She can feel the doctor standing there beside her. All around her, she is aware of people rushing about, the sick and the un-sick – mortals – their murmured words rising up like some strange and wonderful force field.

BREANNE MC IVOR

THE COURSE

He's always had thirsty skin. Sitting in the rain, washing off the dirt from last night's exploits, he lets his pores drink.

The air is streaked with thunder.

He's spent the earliest part of the morning retching up a chunky concoction brindled with blood. Tendrils of wispy hair have wrapped themselves around his fingers. There is no way hair like that could have belonged to an adult.

A child he thinks, feeling sicker. He doesn't know for sure, though – he can never remember.

Looking through the rain, he sees Coraline's face behind the window. Her terracotta curls swirl around her head in an early-morning mess.

When the clouds have bled themselves dry, Coraline picks her way through the puddles.

"It happened again last night," she tells him.

"I know it happened."

'It'. It is the thing neither of them knows. They tried to medicate 'it' with doctors' visits, sleeping pills and hypnosis. But it still leaves their doors hanging off hinges, scratched as if a giant wolf were trying to get out. It leaves Coraline to wake up to his torn clothes and an empty house. There is a local word for men who turn into monsters – lagahoo – but they have come to an unspoken agreement to never say the word aloud – after all, neither he nor she has ever witnessed it.

"You remember it?" she asks.

He hates the high, hopeful sound of her voice, almost making him wish he could remember.

"No. But I've been throwing up all morning."

The first filaments of sunlight find their way through the clouds.

"Mrs. Cooper called this morning," Coraline says. "She asked if we saw her daughter."

He barely has time to lean forward before the sludge bursts from his lips. His throat convulses with wave after wave, and even when his stomach is empty, he keeps heaving.

Coraline has somehow sidestepped the vomit.

"Cora, you must know that I–I would never…"

"I know," she says gently. She stoops down and runs her fingers through his hair. "Still. I've been researching what we could do about it."

"Researching?"

"Of course," she says. "I think there are alternative channels we can use. Maybe visit a non-traditional doctor."

"Non-traditional doctor? You mean Obeah?"

She brings her teeth to her lower lip and chews–as if tasting the word. "Yes, Obeah," she says eventually.

Where would he – or she – find a practitioner? The thought of Coraline asking around for someone who dabbles in the occult is ridiculous.

"I Googled it," she says, as if he'd spoken aloud. And, seeing his face, she continues, "They're businesspeople like anyone else. They need to advertise their services."

He isn't sure he can trust an Obeah man who advertises online. What would an obeah man do? Pay for a Facebook ad?

He wants to say that this sounds absurd – but isn't his whole life an absurdity? Why not? Now that they've discussed it, he's amazed that they haven't tried it sooner.

She holds a slim arm out and helps him to his feet. He wipes the last of the bile from around his mouth. "I suppose we could give it a shot," he says.

★

The road to the Northern Range was chiselled into the edge of the mountain long ago. Their car winds through its curves. To their right the precipice gapes green; trees have clawed their way up the steep rock face and are growing where he would not have thought anything could grow.

"So you really found this man on Google?"

"It's a woman," Coraline says.

In the car, a string quartet is playing Michael Jackson's 'Human Nature'. Coraline is the only person he knows who listens to this kind of music. He doesn't know enough about music to be able to hear the instruments speak to each other like she does. When they first started dating, she would say things like, "Listen to the first violin" but she'd stopped that – maybe because she didn't want him to feel as if she were lording her upbringing over him. She'd been born to parents who played classical music at dinner and who discussed, in dead seriousness, whether Shakespeare was more of a comic or tragic genius.

"Do you know what I'm thinking?" Coraline asks.

He imagines that she's thinking that if she were in love with another man she wouldn't have to go through this.

"No," he says.

"I was thinking that if this works – if you get better – maybe we can talk about having a baby."

A flock of parrots rises from the canopy in a fury of flapping.

He can't believe it. A baby? How could she even put such a thought into words?

More than that, Coraline has never been the type to want traditional things. Wasn't that part of the reason she'd asked him out? Wasn't that the reason that, after years of dating, she'd told him that she didn't believe in marriage?

Suddenly, he is aware that the car is very small and cold and, even if he wanted to get out, there is nothing but trees around them. There seem to be no words to capture the monstrosity of his aversion. Coraline turned thirty last month – is this some sort of feminine thing, where she's worried that her woman's clock is ticking her baby-making years away?

"Cora..." he says, trusting that she will hear the meaning in his voice like she does with the violins.

"I mean, we wouldn't do it until we're sure that you're better," she says. Only her hands betray her – the knuckles squeezing the steering wheel are bright red.

"Is this something you really want?" he asks.

"Yes. Look, I know why you're worried. But you would never hurt our baby. I know it."

How can she know it? When they started living together, she'd thought he sometimes went to the bar down the road at night. He'd told her the truth – he couldn't really remember those nights. But he'd never told her about the disfigured shreds of human bodies that he woke up with. Skin under his fingernails. A mangled earlobe clutched in his palm. Hair wrapped around his fingers. Somehow, she'd connected clues he wasn't aware of leaving. And even then, she hadn't left. Was it because she loved him? But why would someone like her love someone like him at all, let alone enough to stay?

He thinks of Mrs. Cooper's daughter. A few months after she was born, Mrs. Cooper pushed her around in a pink pram showing her off to the neighbourhood. He remembers the awful smallness of the baby's hands. How could hands that feeble do anything? He'd taken the baby's foot in his own large hand and marvelled that a whole human foot could nestle so snugly in his palm.

No. No. Best not to think about it.

The deepest string instrument is groaning. Is it the viola or the cello? He's not sure.

Coraline turns up a steep road – the car is almost vertical and he wonders whether they can manage this ascent. Her lips are mashed into one another as if she can drag the car up by willpower alone. All around them is green. The car keeps climbing until they've reached what is, apparently, the end of the road. Coraline reverses into a miniscule space between a mora tree and a yellow poui. If she is afraid, she doesn't show it.

"There's nothing here," he says, and he's surprised to feel relief.

"This is the place," Coraline insists. She gets out of the car and looks around.

He gets out too. "What are we looking for?"

Coraline doesn't answer, she just keeps combing through the trees with her eyes. "There!" She is pointing to a thin track of dirt that leads further into the forest. She walks over and loops her arm through his. He leans into the warmth of her and almost tells her that they should go back but she is already pulling him onto the path.

The walk through the trees is long and slow. To him, it feels as if they are going nowhere. Coraline lifts his hand to her lips and kisses the tips of his fingers. "Don't worry about what I said in the car – about the baby."

He'd forgotten about the baby until she brought it up.

Abruptly, their eyes are assaulted by the relentless turquoise of the Caribbean Sea. The earth falls away and, miles below, they see the white froth of the waves rolling into the shore. "It's beautiful," Coraline breathes.

Beautiful isn't the word he would use – it's too sudden, this absence of land. He would like a hill that slopes sweetly to a white sand shore, not the viciousness of this drop or the barbaric yellow of the beach below.

"Are you two enjoying the view?"

He jumps.

Coraline presses her hand into the small of his back. "We are, thank you very much."

If he can avoid turning around, maybe he can ignore that there is another person here with them. Maybe he can just pretend that they're taking a Sunday drive through the Northern Range and they've stopped to sightsee. Coraline pivots and he is forced to face the speaker. There is nothing terrible about the woman in front of them; in fact, her face seems to be a composite of many women he's met before.

"I'm Coraline." Coraline holds out her hand as if this is a business meeting.

The woman shakes Coraline's hand. "Edith," she says.

Edith. It's the name of an old lady who should be baking cookies for grandchildren.

"Thank you for agreeing to see us," Coraline says. "It's hard to explain. But he…"

"Oh yes," Edith says, "It's screaming out of his skin."

She walks up to him and takes his head in her hands. Her eyes drill into his – her pupils are horribly dilated, a mass of blackness almost the size of a coin. His scalp starts to burn under her fingers.

She lets him go. "Only ever at night?" she asks.

"Yes."

Edith nods. "That's when the shadow is strongest."

"You know what it is? What is it?" Coraline asks.

Edith turns to look at her. "There are some things you do not name."

He can see that Coraline wants to ask why.

"To name something is to give it more power," Edith says. "And if you call a name, you never know what might answer."

Edith spreads her arms wide. Only then does he notice that the parrots are not shrieking. Even the waves seem subdued. He has the awful feeling that they are listening.

"It won't be easy to overcome," Edith says. "And you won't be the same afterwards – it will be like tearing yourself apart."

"We'll do whatever it takes!" Coraline says.

"Will you do whatever it takes?" Edith asks him.

He thinks of Coraline who poured six years of her life into him. She's given up so much. "I will," he says. It feels like a wedding vow.

Edith nods. "For the next three nights, don't sleep. Not even a wink. You need to starve this thing before you can start the course."

"Course?" Coraline asks. "Like a course of antibiotics?"

"A lot like that," Edith says. She reaches out and grabs his hands. "If you stop the course," she says, "it would be better never to have started at all."

"I understand."

"And you can pay," Edith says.

★

"You can sleep," he tells Coraline when they are home.

Naturally, she has decided to stay up with him.

She shakes her head. "Who will keep you up if you start nodding off?"

"But you have work tomorrow."

"Daddy can write me a sick note," she says. He tries not to think of her doctor father, who always looks at him as if he is a disease to be treated.

Coraline crawls across the bed until she is sitting opposite him. In the darkness, she leans forward and presses her forehead to his.

"Imagine," she says, "Everything can be totally normal. We won't have to move any more. We can pick a place we like; buy a house."

He hopes that she will not mention a baby again. Maybe to prevent her doing that, he kisses her. Coraline always sighs when his lips part hers. She threads her fingers together behind his neck and pulls herself on top of him. She says, "I suppose this is one way to stay awake."

★

On the third night, he feels the weight of sleeplessness behind his eyelids. Although he's been drinking water, his lips are cracked and dry.

He insists that she sleeps. "How will you drive back there if you're exhausted?" he asks.

Coraline is unsure. "What if you nod off?"

"I won't."

This isn't good enough for her. He can see Coraline thinking. "I know! Why don't you stand in the shower?"

"For the whole night?"

"You can take a chair and sit in there," she suggests.

Why not? He gets one of the cheap plastic chairs that they use to sit in the garden and lets the cold water sluice off him. "Don't close your eyes," Coraline warns. "Not even for a second."

"I promise."

Alone, he thinks of Mrs. Cooper's daughter. There are electronic signs scattered throughout the country to help the Anti-Kidnapping Squad locate missing people. Large letters read HELP FIND ME; below there's a picture of the person who can't be found and numbers that those with tips can call. He's always found these pictures to be tragic—the person in the picture is often smiling. To think that person used to be so happy and now they're kidnapped. Or worse.

Pictures of Mrs. Cooper's daughter have started to appear on the signs. HELP FIND ME. He can't bear to look at the girl's chubby cheeks and wide-mouthed smile.

He isn't just doing this for Coraline. He's doing this for Mrs. Cooper's daughter and for anyone else who may have come before.

He realises that he is relaxed in the shower – his skin is happy to be bathed so generously.

Time passes.

He dreams he's sitting in an enormous shadow. Or is it his shadow, swollen to monstrous proportions?

The water spatters into his open mouth.

How could he be dreaming if he were never asleep?

He looks around as if expecting to see the shadow pooling around him but there is only his own, a blob beneath his feet.

★

There is no violin music for their drive back into the Northern Range. Coraline is worried that it may put him to sleep. Instead they're listening to music where cymbals clash and something that sounds like cannon fire thunders at regular intervals.

"Maybe we could ask my mother to help us find a house," Coraline says.

He wishes she weren't so hopeful. He wonders how disappointed she will be if it doesn't work.

The car groans as Coraline forces it up that near-vertical inclination. The headache that has been banging around in his skull intensifies. But he knows that he can't suggest going back.

As they walk the path through the trees, he notices that it seems darker than before. Did the trees always shield the sunlight like this?

He reaches for Coraline's hand and is reassured by the feel of her fingers interwoven with his.

"Did you sleep?"

Goose pimples rise on his skin.

He swivels to see Edith waiting for them. Her head is wrapped in a brilliantly white cloth. It is the only speck of brightness in this place.

"Did you sleep?" she asks again.

"No."

She stares. And he almost tells her that he isn't sure. But he thinks of Coraline, who needs him to be better.

"I didn't," he says.

Coraline squeezes his hand.

Edith picks a wooden box off the floor. It's filled with glass bottles, each a different colour and shape. Surely the colours can't matter. He's forced to confront the possibility that this is nothing more than showmanship and after all this money and effort, nothing will have changed.

"This is your last chance to tell me anything you need to," Edith says.

He remains silent.

She nods. "Drink one a day after the moon comes up. Start with the shortest bottle and end with the tallest."

Edith squares her shoulders and looks from Coraline to him. "You cannot stop the course. No matter the side effects."

"Side effects?" Coraline asks.

"Of course. Something like this – you think it's going to go quietly?" Edith asks.

Coraline lets his hand go and stands between him and Edith. "What can we expect?"

"I'm not asked to do this kind of thing a lot," Edith says. "Let's just say that he may feel unwell."

He can see the possibilities bouncing around in Coraline's head. "How often have you done this before?" she asks.

"Once."

He looks at Coraline's face and he loves the determined line of her mouth, as if she can make this happen by wanting it enough.

"Am I allowed to sleep?" he asks Edith.

"If you can manage it."

He feels so exhausted he doubts that there is any potion that can stop him from sleeping.

"Begin tonight," Edith tells them.

Coraline draws a fat envelope from her purse and hands it over.

★

That night, he pours Coraline a glass of wine. They've stored the wooden box in the coolest, driest corner of their kitchen. He runs his fingers along the glossy glass of the bottles. He finds the shortest bottle and he uncorks it. It is a brilliant orange.

"Do you think the colour matters?" he asks Coraline.

"I doubt it."

They clink the glasses together and drink. His throat is rigid, waiting for the worst but there is no flavour. The liquid is syrupy and thick.

Coraline's fingers are locked around the stem of the wine glass. He worries that she'll snap it if she keeps clutching it like that.

"How do you feel?" she asks.

"Fine."

He doesn't want to admit that he's doubting whether anything will change. Instead, he slips the glass from her fingers, wraps his arms around her narrow shoulders and rests his head on hers.

She squeezes him ferociously. He hasn't ever felt this iron embrace from her before. How has he missed her desperation? Has he become so wrapped up in himself that he's only thought of her as someone who cares for him? Someone better connected, who always makes a call when they need to get out of a neighbourhood quickly.

Coraline loosens her grip and looks at him. "Nothing?" she asks.

"I feel a bit queasy." This is a lie but he says it because he wants her to think it's working.

She nods. "Let me know if it gets any worse."

★

On the third day, he still hasn't felt any differently. There are seven vials and he suspects that the whole thing is a hoax. Coraline constantly feels his forehead for a fever. She's even brought a bowl to the bedside in case he throws up. He hasn't had the courage to tell her that he feels exactly as he always has so he's invented a series of minor aches and pains.

On this night, Coraline pours herself more wine than usual. He pulls the third vial out of the box. It's an aggressive azure, like the sky on a blistering day.

"To us," Coraline says as she touches her glass to his.

He drinks it all.

She is looking at him with her head tilted to one side.

"What's wrong?" he asks.

She blinks and her mouth moves. Is she speaking?

Did he hear himself when he spoke just now?

"Cora?"

He knows he said her name but he hears nothing.

He claws at his ears. What the hell?

"Cora?" He wonders whether he's screaming.

Her lips are moving but there is silence. The total absence of sound is a horror. Surely this will end? Edith would have told him if the potions were going to make him live in a soundless world.

Coraline's hands are on his cheeks. He sees them but he feels nothing.

He grabs her arms but there is no texture to her skin.

He looks at her – focusing on the thing that first made him love her, her wide eyes. He sees her emerald irises stretching bigger than he's known them; he sees the whites of her eyes streaked with red.

"Cora?"

Sweat bursts from his pores in a paroxysm of feeling. He is convulsed with tremors. He doubles over, digging his fingers into Coraline's hips. He feels as if a fist has grabbed his oesophagus. Even as he drops to his knees, he welcomes the unforgiving hardness of their kitchen tiles.

"... hear me now?" Coraline's voice touches him like a kiss.

"Yes." His teeth are chattering so violently that he can barely say the word.

Even the air seems to be stinging his eyes. The tears burn as they roll down his face; his skin screeches.

He doesn't know how long he kneels there savouring the return to sensation. He feels her fingers soft on his arm. She clutches his hand and pulls him to his feet. He staggers, lumbering into her so that they crash into the fridge. He wants to ask if he's hurt her but there is no way he can speak.

She forces his arm over her shoulder and guides him to the bedroom.

He collapses onto the bed. She steps away and he reaches out to her. He tries to talk but spit dribbles out of his mouth and all he can taste is salt.

He must tell her – he never meant to push her. He wants to see if she's been bruised from being shoved against the fridge.

BREANNE MC IVOR . THE COURSE

She covers her mouth with a hand but although she drops her chin, she never turns away. Even after one of his nights, when he'd awoken with no memory of what he'd done, she'd never been afraid to meet his gaze.

Is she afraid now? Is he frothing at the mouth? Is that what this spit is?

He grunts – the closest he can come to words. Her eyes meet his and it's not fear he sees. It's pity.

★

"You have to drink it."

He will sooner die than drink the fourth bottle. He reaches out to push Coraline away.

His sweat has soaked through the sheet and is beginning to saturate the mattress.

No. He wants to go back. Nothing can be worth this.

"Please!"

His neck groans with pain as he turns his head to look at Coraline.

"Please!"

She presses her palm to his chest. Even her touch is torture. He jerks away.

"Please. We're doing this for our future. For the baby. You don't know this but I stay up at night and think about names." Coraline's voice cracks. "I know you'd be the best daddy."

Daddy?

"Please."

She pushes two fingers between his teeth and forces his lips apart. He imagines biting her – anything to prevent this. She raises the glass to his mouth and pours the liquid in. It sears his tongue and it takes every shred of willpower to release the muscles in his throat so that he can swallow.

He doesn't know what he can do to get relief. He hadn't imagined that a person could hurt like this.

★

He dreams. Coraline appears to him in a myriad of incarnations. A ribbon around his ribs. A hand up under his heart. A bow pulled across a violin.

"What do you want most?" Coraline asks him.

He wants her. He wants love. He tries to tell her but his throat burns and the words rise and drift away like steam.

★

The whole world is agony. Had he ever missed hearing? Each noise now is a nail in his eardrum. Had he ever wanted to feel? He's torn his shirt off because the fabric was fire on his skin.

Coraline appears with another bottle. He drinks the pain.

Another bottle. How much time has passed? He can't track it. He can't track anything.

Let me die.

Anything would be better. Anything at all.

He realises that he is swallowed by the shadow. It devours everything he touches – everything he's touched. It wraps Coraline in its darkness. It pours into the many-coloured bottles they've stored in the kitchen.

When he wakes up, the sweat on his skin is cold. The pain is a rawness in his throat. A hollowness in his stomach. But the bone-shattering shaking has stopped.

"Cora?" He can't believe his mouth had found the word.

The door bursts open and she flies inside. They look at each other. He has no idea what she is seeing.

He realises that the thing sticking his thighs together is urine. He tries to sit up but is too weak.

"Are you hungry?" she asks.

"Starved."

After eating almost everything they have in the house, he showers. Coraline strips the sheets from the mattress and soaks it with shampoo.

He slips coming out of the shower and bangs his elbow against the wall.

In the mirror, he sees his ribs push out against his stomach like inverted wings. How long has he gone without eating? Is the course over?

Coraline is standing in the doorway with fresh boxers and a T-shirt. Her eyes rove over his body, pausing on the protruding ribs and his jutting thighbones. He wants her to look away. He gestures for the boxers and she stoops and helps him step into them as if he were a child.

He bends forward and they put on the T-shirt together.

"Today is the seventh day," Coraline says. She squeezes his hand. He winces and her hold relaxes.

Her eyes are lustrous. Now that the pain has subsided so that he can think, he allows himself to imagine – for the first time – a baby with her corkscrew curls and his copper skin.

"Do you think you can make it to the kitchen?" Coraline asks.

"Of course."

But he has to lean on her to get there.

She pops a bottle of champagne and it hisses as she fills her flute.

He opens the wooden box and is confronted with the last ruby bottle.

It is surprisingly light. He uncorks it and peers inside. Is there anything in there?

It couldn't be empty.

"To endings," Coraline chirps, clinking her glass on his.

He tips the bottle upside down. A single droplet falls onto his tongue. It sizzles before slipping down his throat.

Is that it? Was there supposed to be more?

"What's wrong?" Coraline asks.

"There was only one drop."

She frowns. "But you drank it?"

"Yes."

Coraline's lips are compressed as she contemplates it. "No one could have interfered with those bottles," she declares. "That's probably how it's supposed to be."

He wishes he could feel so sure.

"Don't worry so much," Coraline says. But her voice is saturated with doubt.

He remembers, as if seeing it through a haze, Coraline's confidence when she'd insisted that they visit an Obeah woman. Where is the confidence now that the deed's been done?

"Is the bed dry?" he asks.

"I don't think so," Coraline says. "I've been sleeping on the couch."

They pad to the living room and fit themselves awkwardly on the couch. He is sandwiched between her and the oppressive softness of the cushions.

Their curtains cut the moonlight out of the room.

Coraline shifts against him and then turns so that her face is buried in his chest.

She presses her lips just above his nipple. It's over," she says. "We just need time to realise that we can start a normal life."

He buries his nose in her hair and breathes the hibiscus scent of her shampoo. Although it makes his wrists hurt, he runs his hands in gentle lines across her back.

He feels her shoulders relax as she nuzzles into his chest.

"I love you."

★

He wakes up naked. Blades of grass are piercing the back of his neck. He lifts his eyelids to see the impenetrable greyness of the sky. His eyes adjust and he sees the myriad of mahogany trees that surround their backyard.

Something sloshes inside his stomach.

The vomit shoots out of his mouth and splatters on his face. He rolls onto his hip and his throat expels brown lumps slicked in blood.

What is that? It looks like an earlobe.

He retches again.

Lightning explodes across the sky and he waits for the thunder. It feels as if the rumble starts in the marrow of his bones.

He pushes himself to his knees and his eyes turn to the windows but Coraline isn't standing behind them.

He walks to the back of their house. The door is wide open. It isn't like Coraline to leave it unlocked. He steps in, listening for any sounds from inside.

The kitchen is a tangle of steel, wood and glass. The husk of the microwave seems to have been hurled against the wall. The fridge door is torn off and the hinges hang uselessly off its edge.

Who could have done this?

He looks down at his hands. Red curls are knotted around his fingers.

Chills. He would never.

"Coraline!" His voice ricochets off the walls and bounces back into him. "Cora!" His feet fly out of the kitchen and into the living room. The couch has been turned over and ripped to shreds. Tiles are cracked. Nails appear to have scraped the paint off the walls. Splotches of something violet stain the floor.

He shakes his head.

No.

He races to the bedroom. The mattress lies uncovered. Coraline's phone is lying on the nightstand. He tries to turn it on but it's dead.

He plugs it in and then plunges in and out of each room.

What time is it? What day is it? Maybe she went to work?

All around him is emptiness and watery light streaming through the windows.

He returns to the bedroom and turns the phone on. The date and time stare at him.

Impossible. All that time couldn't have passed.

The phone vibrates. 59 missed calls. 10 Voicemail messages. 66 text messages.

No.

He closes his eyes and presses Coraline's phone to him.

Not this. Let anything have happened but this.

He has never. Never in the six years they have been together.

"I wouldn't," he says.

He remembers the day they started the course, Coraline had asked Edith if she'd done this before.

"Once," Edith said.

They'd never asked her if it had worked.

ALECIA MCKENZIE

PLANES IN THE DISTANCE

I saw my mother, father, brother and sister fully for the first time when I was eleven years old, thanks to Mr. Fitzpatrick, my art teacher. He told my mother the whole story and she blamed herself bitterly for the gap in my earlier life, especially as she imagined the danger I'd been in.

When Mr. Fitzpatrick raised the alarm, he also managed to save his dwindling self-respect as an artist. There were twenty-two of us in his class and I always sat at the back. Mr. Fitzpatrick, who'd come over from Grenada to find this teaching job, would arrange some objects on his desk and tell us to draw them. While everyone else struggled to render faithfully the bowl of oranges and bananas, the neatly arranged mugs and jug, or the vase of hibiscus flowers, I always drew something quite different.

Mr. Fitzpatrick's eyes would flicker strangely, with something like envy, when he saw my drawings. He would hold my paper up to the class as a model of originality, saying that I was someone with a great future as an artist, but that first I had to learn to draw what I saw.

He watched me carefully during each class; I could feel his drill-like gaze even when he was at the front of the class and my head was bowed over my paper at the back. Sometimes he came to stand right over my desk, and I would look up and see the angry brown eyes, the untidy mass of curly black hair, the round weak-chinned face. As we stared at each other, I would smile uncertainly, feeling vague guilt, and Mr. Fitzpatrick would shake his head and slowly move away, becoming a blur.

"He doesn't like you," my best friend Elsa whispered from the next row. I loved Elsa. Whenever I dropped something on the floor, she always picked it up for me. When we had tests, she passed me the answers.

Somehow we knew, without being able to put it into words, that Mr. Fitzpatrick hated teaching – and us. We knew he held exhibitions to which very few people went. And the one time he'd been written up in *The Gleaner*, the reviewer had thrashed him, saying his paintings looked like badly taken photographs. We also knew that Mr. Fitzpatrick was married to a famous artist, a Trinidadian woman named Rampair. She daubed canvases blue, splashed a black spot in the middle and called the things "Plane in the distance, Number one", "Plane in the distance, Number two", "Plane in the distance, Number three". Our headmistress, Sister Ursula, had bought a couple of her paintings for the school office; they went quite well with the carpet.

At the end of each semester, our school held an exhibition of all the students' artwork, and we covered the walls of the big Mckay Assembly Hall with our charcoal drawings and watercolour paintings, waiting for our parents' praise. My mother and father stared at my semester's work, tilting their heads from side to side.

"Mmm, nice. Very nice," Daddy said.

"And what is it, Elaine?" my mother asked gently.

Before I could answer, Mr. Fitzpatrick strode over.

"That's a real little genius you have there," he said, with a half-mocking smile. His left eye blinked rapidly, out of control.

"Oh yes?" my mother said, beaming.

"Yes," Mr. Fitzpatrick declared. "I've never seen such original drawings before." He put his left hand on my shoulder and squeezed so hard that I barely managed to hold back the "aoww". Meanwhile, my father shook Mr. Fitzpatrick's right hand without saying a word. I squirmed away and went to search for Elsa.

Later Sister Ursula, the headmistress, announced the prizes for best work: fifteen dollars for first prize, ten dollars for second, five dollars for third. Elsa held my hand and we walked together to the platform – she to get her five dollars and me to get ten from Sister Ursula. A bug-eyed teacher's pet, name Claudene, got the first prize. On the way back to our chairs, we passed Mr. Fitzpatrick, who whispered, "You should have won, Elaine." I glanced in his direction and gave what I hoped looked like a smile.

The next semester, I moved up a grade and found that Mr. Fitzpatrick was now our form master as well as our art teacher; we would be seeing him quite often as he had to mark the attendance register each morning. I hoped I would get through the term with the minimum of attention, but my luck was soon to end.

On the first Wednesday of the new semester, I got lost. St. Ignatius High School for Girls was only a fifteen-minute walk from my house and I had memorized all the turnings I had to make. The school was set between two different neighbourhoods: to the north were modest three- and four-bedroom houses where people competed to grow mango trees, croton, bougainvillea and red ginger plants, while to the south were small fading houses with dry-earth yards where whole families occupied one room. Elsa came from that neighbourhood. She never invited me home.

That Wednesday, too busy thinking about the probing stare of Mr. Fitzpatrick, I missed one of my regular turnings and found myself in strange streets of potholes and garbage. A few children sat on walls, calling out to me. I smiled timidly. I wandered around for what seemed an hour, afraid to talk to anyone. At one intersection, I went over to peer up at the street sign and found myself among a group of boys who wore their shirts hanging outside their pants in the fashion forbidden to my brother.

"What you doing here, little girl? You no should be in school?" one of them said.

"I can't find my school," I croaked, trying to stop my lips from trembling.

"What, you lost?" He looked at my uniform. "Is St. Ignatius you go to?"

I nodded.

"I soon come back. I goin' take this little girl to her school," he told the others. He scowled at me, "Come. Walk fast."

I walked beside him, noticing that he was only slightly taller than me. He had a thin, serious face with thick eyebrows and a wide mouth. He wore a black cap, light blue shirt and black pants. I couldn't make out what kind of shoes he had on. He noticed me inspecting him, narrow-eyed.

"What's your name?"

"Elaine. What is yours?"

"Mickey Dread."

"Thanks for helping me."

"No problem. But next time, watch out where you going. This is not a nice place, you hear?"

I nodded. He took me all the way to the school gates, where the watchman refused to let him pass. I waved goodbye to him and made my way to class where everyone was in the last stages of drawing what looked like a bowl of pomegranates and guineps. I had to explain to Mr. Fitzpatrick why I was late and he muttered something about my being lucky before telling me to go to my seat. I didn't draw anything that day.

At the next class, Mr. Fitzpatrick marched in with an air of determination. Although I couldn't see his face well from where I sat, his mellow voice sounded happy, and the scent of Old Spice aftershave wafted over the class. Two days before, *The Gleaner* had blasted his wife's new show, saying Jamaicans were getting tired of seeing planes in the distance, they wanted to hop on the blessed aircraft and be taken to interesting destinations. A plane in the distance was a painfully boring sight when you saw it every day, *The Gleaner* said, and suggested that Rampair go on a long BWIA (Better Wish It Arrives) flight back to Trinidad if she was so fond of planes. My father had read the review aloud to my mother.

"Okay, let's get to work," Mr. Fitzpatrick instructed. He put a large bluish-looking object on his desk, telling us to try to capture it as exactly as possible. He described how the light coming through the window hit the object and how the other side was in shadow. The contrasting brightness and shadow gave it the three-dimensional aspect, he said.

As he spoke, in his rhythmic Grenadian accent, seeming always to be on the verge of telling a joke, I filled my paper with triangles. As I drew languidly, without bothering any more to look at the object on the desk, Mr. Fitzpatrick strolled by my desk. He stopped for about a minute, and the aftershave made my stomach heave.

"Mmmm, ha. Brilliant," he said and moved on.

When he was back at the front of the class, he boomed my name. "ELAINE!"

I looked up, taking a few seconds to locate him.

"ELAINE, how many fingers am I holding up?"

I stared, I squinted. I refused to answer. The class laughed. Mr. Fitzpatrick summoned my mother that day, and she was in a terrible nervous state as she took me home, bombarding me with questions. In the evening she had a long talk with my father, while my sister and brother whispered to each other and treated me with deference for the first time in my life. My sister Jennifer gave me some Icy Mints, which she always hoarded, and my brother Keith gave me a piece of his chicken leg at dinner, saying he wasn't hungry. Later I heard the words "nearly blind" as they whispered together.

I loved the eye examination at the doctor the next day. The light he shone in my eyes sent a tingly beam of pleasure down my spine. Then came the different lenses to look through and the letters to read. I enjoyed it all and was sorry when it was over. I was sorrier, though, when I saw the glasses. Black-framed and pointed at the sides, they looked like something Catwoman would wear. When I tried them on, the world became a crowded place with too-sharp lines and overwhelming colours. And I saw my mother's face – she had warts. Lots of little warts under her eyes and on her cheeks.

Back home, I studied my brother and sister; the lenses didn't make them look any more interesting. But they, with typical jealously, clamoured to have glasses too. When my father told them not to be stupid, they got their revenge by calling me "four-eyes".

At school, Mr. Fitzpatrick was pleased at what he'd accomplished. The first time I drew something with my glasses on, he rushed to stand beside my desk. He looked at the pretty bowl of oranges and grapefruits on my paper.

"Nice," he said, "quite quite nice." He sauntered away, whistling.

MARK MCWATT

THE BATS OF LOVE

by H. A. L. Seaforth★

At the graveside at Lloyd Cadogan's funeral I had hoped to remain on the fringe of the mourners, since I felt awkward about my own role in his life and death; but in the cemetery it quickly became clear that there were two distinct groups in attendance: the small party of Lloyd's family and family friends and a large gathering of the curious, who were attracted by the scandal of the dead man's suicide and rumours of the derangement that led to it. This latter group kept back from the grave in a wide circle. Under the circumstances I felt I had no choice but to attach myself to the smaller group immediately around the grave. Mama, Lloyd's mother, acknowledged me with a nod, her face streaked with tears. It was an especially gloomy occasion, as we were all mourning not so much the death, as the events stretching far into the past that ensured the sad waste of a very promising life.

After the interment no one chose to linger at the graveside and while we were walking back to the cars, Mama came over to me and leant on my arm.

"Ah David," she said, "I'm glad you came – glad that you were here at the end, when this happened, since you were so close to him at the beginning… " I said nothing but patted the arm that held onto mine. "Listen," she continued, "you have to come home with us – we're all going there now – just for an hour or so. I know you're busy packing…" and a sob shook her large frame. We stopped and she turned and looked into my eyes: I nodded and we went quickly to the cars.

The house seemed strange, as though the absence of Lloyd was something palpable, something that clung to my skin as soon as I entered. Everything in the living room was as it had always been,

since my earliest childhood when I used to come running in with
Lloyd from the veranda or off the street, headed for the kitchen
or for Lloyd's bedroom, for we weren't allowed to play in the neat
and polished living room. The piano stood in its corner, where
Mama taught music to generations of students; the walls were
hung with photographs, many of Lloyd at various stages of his
life: in school uniforms, primary and secondary; in his Sunday-
best after church; he and I standing in our scout uniforms on the
stelling in front of the M.V. Powis, about to embark on one of our
scouting jaunts to the interior; a shot of him as a student on a
railway platform in England (self-consciously aware of the en-
cumbrance of a dark, heavy coat); and a studio photo of him in his
graduation gown, (a photo which I had insisted he have taken and
which came out with him looking much darker than he was in
reality – as though it was the policy of the photo-studio in Leeds
to avoid offending their black customers by ensuring that they
appeared as black as possible). Also on the wall were the framed
certificates of O-level and A-level results, of his degree, and the
yellowed clipping, from the local newspaper, of the photograph
and story that appeared when he won the Guyana scholarship.

But I felt strangely out of place among all these familiar
reminders of his life and mine. This was the first time that I'd
been in the house without him, and I kept half-expecting him to
emerge from his room. Mama and her nieces had prepared lots to
eat and drink – black-eyes and rice and stewed chicken and black
pudding and souse and heavy coconut bread – but no one seemed
to be in a mood to eat much. We nibbled quietly and sipped our
ginger beer and talked in hushed tones about the things we
remembered in the life of the dead man – the good life, that is,
before the first breakdown – the life of incredible brilliance and
promise. Mama came over to me and quietly took my hand and
said, "Come." I followed her down the corridor to the first door
to the right, which she opened – Lloyd's room. I saw the neatly-
made bed, the shaded light hanging from the roof, the bookshelf,
the wardrobe, the desk in front of the window.

"This is where I found him," Mama was saying, composed and
dry-eyed by this time. "I knew his light had been on all night, which

was not unusual, as you would know: he frequently read or worked at his desk until foreday morning, so although I was worried about him, I didn't look in on him when I got up – it was quiet and I thought I would let him sleep. It wasn't till nine-thirty that I tapped on the door and opened it, and then I saw him hanging there… " – she indicated the stout wooden beam that ran across the room beneath the slanting roof – "and there was like smoke in the room, or maybe not smoke but the smell of burnt paper, and when I look in the waste bin I see ashes and burnt scraps of pages: some of his old essays, I think. One scrap was saying something about love poetry." On the desk was a large brown envelope which I picked up. "May I?" She said, "Of course," so I reached in and pulled out a dozen or so pages of typescript that had become discoloured with age and handling. I knew what it was before I looked down at the title page: "*The Bats of Love: Poems* by Elena Gutierrez Ramirez. Translated from the Spanish by Jeremiah Lloyd George Cadogan". This, I thought, he could not bring himself to burn.

"I know that that is something from you all days at university in Leeds," Mama said. "I often saw him reading and reading those pages and I knew his mind was back there in those happier times… Would you like to keep that – to remember Lloyd?"

It was clear that she thought I would be happy to have this memento of her son and of our joint past as students in England, so I said, "Thank you very much, Mama," and gave her a hug. She could not know how painful a reminder this particular typescript would be for me. On the little notice-board on the wall next to the window was a reminder of more recent pain: the little flyer put out by the University of Guyana announcing the two-week Summer Workshop on "Critical Writing about Literature and the Arts, conducted by Professor David Adams of the University of the West Indies, Cave Hill", and giving details about dates, cost and registration. That was all over now, I reflected gratefully, but it had turned out to be the final push that had propelled my dear friend over the edge. I hesitated in front of it for an instant, wishing I could tear it down, but I turned instead and followed Mama out of that painful room. When I got back to my hotel room it was dark and I began to pack my suitcase, determined to focus my thoughts on my departure the following day.

The LIAT flight to Barbados departed on time shortly before noon. I had slept badly the night before, staving off the inevitable self-confrontation that Lloyd Cadogan's death made necessary and urgent. As the plane took off and climbed above the brown rivers, I decided that the two-hour flight would be given over to a review of the life and death of Lloyd Cadogan, and my part in these. By the time we landed in Barbados I hoped to have laid some ghosts to rest.

★   ★   ★

I don't remember a time when I didn't know Lloyd Cadogan. From the infant class at Main Street I remember him, tall and silent, his large eyes looking on apprehensively as Sister Brian lashed me on the legs with a tamarind whip. Nothing like that ever happened to him: he was, even from then, a perfect student. Lloyd wrote out his letters and numbers neatly on his slate, recited his Hail Marys and other prayers flawlessly and did not talk in class. I was the unruly one, always in fights, my slate cracked and my slate-pencil lost, my letters and numbers indecipherable, my shirt-tail out of my pants. I remember Lloyd telling me once with genuine concern, when we were in second standard: "Miss Gill only beats the bad boys, you know; it's not hard to be good – just stay quiet, don't say anything, and do your work," and I remember really wanting to do as he said, but I could not. I suppose he felt protective of me because I was so hopeless – and because my uncle took us both home in his car after school. He would pick us up outside the gate and drop us both off at the top of our street and we would walk down. Lloyd's house came first and I would invariably go in with him, hoping to play till night-time, but Mama would always send me packing after a few minutes because "your poor mother must be frantic with worry – it's nearly quarter to five!" And I would walk down the street for what seemed to me like ages, cut across a pasture and arrive home through the side-gate – frequently without my cap or book-bag or some other item, forgotten "over at Lloyd".

It must have dawned on me at some point that life would be

more peaceful if I managed to do at least the minimum amount of class-work and homework necessary to get by, because I did keep up with Lloyd, moving steadily up the school, even skipping third standard, until we both ended up in the scholarship class. It was in the scholarship class that I first got Lloyd into trouble. We were walking home one afternoon after extra lessons and had finished too late for us to catch my uncle. We came upon a laden mango tree in somebody's yard on Lamaha Street. Before Lloyd realized what I was doing, I had picked up a stone and flung it at a bunch of mangoes. Miraculously, and entirely contrary to my expectations, I hit the bunch and about five mangoes fell. Ignoring Lloyd's advice to leave them alone and walk on, I was over the gate in a flash and picking up the mangoes when this lady came up behind me and grabbed my collar. Apparently Lloyd had been shouting, "Look out, you idiot! Run! Run!" But I hadn't even heard him. The lady carried on for several minutes about how shocked she was to see boys in Main Street uniforms stealing her mangoes, and she ended up by demanding to know my name. Sensing that she might let me go, I told her, but she continued to hold onto my collar and asked for the name of "your accomplice at the gate, the boy shouting at you to run when he saw me coming." I had no choice but to give her Lloyd's name as well.

The upshot the next day was that we were hauled before Sister Joseph, the Headmistress, and given six lashes each in front of the whole school. It was a shocking occasion – not because of me: people were surprised that it was the first time I'd been flogged by the Headmistress – but Lloyd Cadogan! Lloyd Cadogan who had *never* been beaten by a teacher since he'd entered the school; that was shocking indeed. Everyone, without having to hear the story, knew immediately that it was "that wretched David Adams" who was to blame, and even Sister Joseph said as much, going on, as she administered his lashes, about bad company leading him astray! As usual, I was weeping even before the first lash; but what I and everyone else found amazing was the fact that Lloyd did not shed a single tear: his face remained serious and composed throughout. The only thing he said to me about the incident was: "Next time I'll know better than to hang around and get blamed for your wickedness." I was relieved to discover that he was still talking to me.

Lloyd won a big Government scholarship and I scraped enough marks to get a lesser award and we ended up at college together. At college it dawned on me that Lloyd was an exceptional student – he immediately found his way to the top of the class in most subjects and quickly attracted the delighted attention of the teachers. I, of course, was at first far too busy enjoying myself with new friends and participating in sports and clubs to pay any serious attention to school work. I was content to drift along somewhere around the middle of the class. In second form I joined the scouts and one afternoon, when I turned up at Lloyd's house in my scout uniform, Mama asked Lloyd if he wanted to be a scout. He said he didn't know, he'd have to think about it, but the following Friday he turned up at scout meeting, and in a couple of weeks, he too was in uniform. Lloyd took scouting very seriously, of course, and in a short time he'd accumulated many badges and was made a patrol leader, and a very good one, too.

A couple of years later, at one camp at some mission in the interior, Roy Sankies and I became aware that several of the younger scouts had a lot of money that their parents had given them for the trip, but there was nowhere to spend it where we were, so one rainy afternoon we cooked up a deal with Bertha, the barefoot teenage girl from the village who swept the school in which we slept. We would charge the young scouts a dollar a time to view and touch Bertha's bubbies. Bertha would get half the takings and Roy and I the other half. We rigged up a groundsheet across one corner of a classroom and Bertha did her thing behind there and the boys lined up and paid their dollars and disappeared one by one behind the sheet – while Roy and I collected the money. God knows how Colin Bishop ("the archbishop", as we called him), our sanctimonious troop leader, got wind of what was going on, but he stormed in and shut down the show, vowing that he would report us to the scoutmaster and have us kicked out of scouts and probably out of college as well. He added for good measure that we would also certainly end up in hell at the end of our days. A couple of the youngsters were in tears. Shortly

afterwards Lloyd came looking for me, having heard about the
fiasco, and that was the first of several occasions when he had to
lecture me about my behaviour. It's funny because he was only
two months older than me and we were in the same class, but my
respect for him was so great that I listened in silence. In fact I was
very impressed by what he said about responsibility and about
whether I ever thought about my parents and the good name of
my family when I got involved in these hair-brained schemes. He
sounded like an adult and he seemed so genuinely disappointed
in me that I remember being thoroughly ashamed and fully
repentant. Then he spoke to the youngsters about scout rules and
about respect for women and he calmed their fears about ending
up in hell. Then he looked at me and said quietly: "Never let me
hear anything like this again; I will have a word with the archbishop." And that was the last any of us heard of the incident.

In the sixth form it was a foregone conclusion that Lloyd
Cadogan would win a Guyana scholarship. We were both in the
Arts sixth, Lloyd taking Modern Languages and Literature and I
doing English Literature, Latin and Ancient History. By this time
I was capable of short, but intense bursts of concentration on my
work, and I was actually doing quite well, much to my own – and
everyone else's – surprise. Over at my house one day Lloyd pointed
out to me where my problem lay. He'd been looking over some of
my recent essays (at my mother's behest) and he said: "You see,
none of these teachers questions your ability and understanding,
only your steadfastness and your will to finish the job properly,"
and he pointed out the frequency of such marginal comments as:
"good point, but it needs amplification" and "interesting argument,
but you need to support it with textual quotes and references… "
He turned to my mother: "Everyone's clear the ability is there,
Aunt Mavis, he just needs to spend a lot more time on his work and
take more care." So that became my mother's mantra for the next
year: "What do you mean you're finished? Go and read it over and
make sure that there is nothing more that you can say… " I was
resentful, but I kept getting better marks.

When the exams came Lloyd was a nervous wreck, uncharac-
teristically unsure of himself and sick to his stomach before each

paper. For me, not nearly as much was at stake – I was not going to win a scholarship so, although I studied hard, I took the exams in my stride. When the results came out, Lloyd got his four As and I actually got an A in English Literature, with a B in History and a C in Latin. I was euphoric. We had both applied, long before the exams, to several British universities, and I begged Lloyd to choose one of the three that had accepted me (he was accepted by all). Lloyd, with his scholarship, chose to go to Leeds, and my father said he would pay for me to go there as well, so that Lloyd could keep an eye on me! So in 1970 we both ended up in Leeds, living on different floors of the Henry Price, a brand new hall of residence for foreign students.

★   ★   ★

I suppose it was inevitable that we would not be as close at university as we had been in school. For me the university, Leeds, England was a whole new world, full of wonderful distractions; for Lloyd it was simply a change of scenery in which he continued to live the one life he knew – that of intense study and scholarly reading and writing. He was like a hermit in his room – when he was not in class or in the library – and emerged only to prepare his meals. Very rarely would I see him in the TV lounge, and when I did he was only there to look at a specific programme, disappearing as soon as it was over: not like many of us who were there not to watch specific programmes, but to watch TV, period – whatever was on. In my case, since there had been no TV in Guyana, I was making up for all those lost years.

Then I met Linda, a Welsh girl, and was amazed to discover that she was interested in me. Before university I'd never sat in the same classroom with a girl and the result was that girls now became a major distraction from my studies. I'd always considered that it was a kind of "duty" for boys my age to pursue girls in the hope of some kind of sexual favour (in my mind this was unlikely to be sex itself – which couldn't be that easy – but some kind of physical proximity or contact that would fuel my fantasies and longings until I managed to advance a step further, perhaps with another girl), but it never crossed my mind that a girl could/

would pursue a boy for the same reason – and it wasn't really the same reason either. Linda's ideas about what we might do together were not along the lines of coy explorations and small advances over time. She was typical of a modern culture that had long decided to short-circuit such time-wasting preliminaries and home in on the big event. But although she kept repeating it as plainly as she could, it took a while for me to realize that she *wanted* to sleep with me. I knew there were men in the residence who had girls in their rooms overnight, but from what I could see, apart from the mature students, these were mostly hot-blooded Turks and Persians, whose oriental aura, I presumed (this was long before I'd heard of "political correctness"), attracted women the way the musk of gaudy, exotic blooms attracts insects. When the enormity of Linda's suggestion finally came home to me I was in a fever of excitement and apprehension. I consulted a few of my English friends in class as well as some of the other West Indians in the residence, particularly the four Trinidadians who lived on my floor. None of them thought it was any big thing and advised me to go for it. One Trinidadian, whenever we met in the corridor or the kitchen, would sing out: "Ay-yai-ai, Dave-o, you fix the date yet? Look na, man: any night of the week is a good night for losing your virginity." I was mortified when others nearby would look at me and laugh. It's strange, but it seemed I needed someone to tell me "Don't do it, you'll regret it", so I went to see Lloyd in his room and, in his wisdom, he did advise against it. I should think about my parents, he said, and didn't I already have sufficient distractions from my studies… ?" It was exactly what I wanted to hear, so I went ahead and happily made the arrangements with Linda and I lost my virginity one overheated Saturday night in my room. It was a very unsatisfactory thing really, but there were other nights and it got better. I was devastated when Linda decided she'd had enough of me and moved on to somebody else, but I quickly got over it…

There were other distractions: I had a couple of cousins down in London and I was frequently down there for weekends, going to the pub or playing dominoes all night in their council flat. I visited all the landmarks I'd heard and read about from childhood, just to say that I'd seen them. Then I became a football fan, going to most of the Leeds United home matches at Elland Road – and the occasional away match if it wasn't too far – and that was in the days when Leeds was a top team, with Billy Bremner and Jackie Charlton and Eddie Grey and Peter Lorrimer... And when the cricket season came around I would spend lots of time down the road at Headingley and travel to Nottingham and Old Trafford for test matches, even if it wasn't the West Indies playing. I persuaded myself that all of this was a very important part of my education.

But of course my university studies paid the price. When the final year began (so suddenly, it seemed to me), after a wonderful summer of bumming around London, Paris and the south of France with a girl called Abby and a bunch of other happy vaga-bonds, I realized that I was not ready to take final exams in a matter of months: far better, I thought, to take the year off and travel some more, get the wanderlust out of my system and give myself time to get tired of chasing women and sports teams and then come back the following year and complete my degree... I wrote my parents what I considered a reasoned and reasonable letter outlining all this. They phoned me the night they got the letter. My father was horrified and wanted to know if he had been paying all that money just to have me abandon my studies so close to the end. What, he wanted to know, did I propose to live on during my year of idleness and self-indulgent travel? My mother, on the other hand, couldn't say anything, she only wept into the phone until my father took it from her and hung up. The next day I found out they had phoned Lloyd as well; he came to my room to see what was going on. This became another of the occasions on which he had to lecture me and save me from myself, as he put it.

"What you're running from is the work," he said, "the hours of study and reading that will interfere drastically with your wom-anizing and pub-crawling and running down to London; but, whether you do it now, or come back next year or resume your studies years from now, you will still confront the necessity of having to do the work – there is no other way. What I should say to you is: "Do what the hell you want, you're an adult, aren't you?" But your mother phoned me in tears and begged me to speak to you and urge you not to give up your studies at this stage. So I'm doing this for Aunt Mavis, not so much for you, though I will tell you this: I'm convinced you could do it if you wanted – you have a sharp mind and there's enough time. All you lack is the will and determination and the necessary sense of responsibility… "

I found I had no choice and decided that since I was going to do my finals in eight months, I'd better do them properly: I threw myself into my work for the first time and discovered that I enjoyed the reading and studying in the library. I did many assignments, including a long research paper, for which I got an A – fuel for increased effort. Lloyd was not surprised at my effort and apparent success and I was a little put out at how infallibly he had read me. I wondered how many people knew that I was lazy and irresponsible and needed a kick in the ass to accomplish anything worthwhile. "Ay-yai-ai, Dave-o," my Trinidadian flat-mate now said, "you give up the women and you beating book – you ent no Caribbean man for true… " This from someone who was doing brilliantly in his "AccA" courses at Leeds Polytechnic. I made a point of seeing Lloyd more regularly than before, seeking encouragement and support – or sometimes just information: we would have long discussions about specific authors and literary periods. He always knew so damn much.

The week before finals I was feeling confident: I was thinking that I could, perhaps, scrape second-class honours, but I dared not hope for too much. One night I decided to go to Lloyd's room for a last chat about modern poetry, his speciality. When I knocked on the door there was no answer, so I went back to my room, puzzled that he was out at this time of night a few days before finals. I went to my window and checked for light in his room. I could not see into the room, but the light was on so I went back up and knocked again. I thought I heard movement inside the room and I called his name. "It's me, David," I said and waited; after a while I heard the door being unlocked and I turned the handle and went in. I was shocked: Lloyd's room was a disaster, there were books and papers flung everywhere, on floor and bed and dresser – even in the sink. Many of the papers were torn or crumpled, and the desk, bathed in bright light from the desk lamp, was strewn with bunches of pages ripped from books. I looked sharply at Lloyd and received a further shock: he was in tears, his face distorted and his mouth trembling and drooping at the corners.

"What's wrong with you?" I asked in horror.

"The exams!" he shouted, "I *hate* exams!"

I was astonished by his vehemence and very worried. I wished I had the strength – the words – to help and console this scholarly giant, but every phrase that formed in my mind sounded hollow, I thought, coming from me. Eventually all I could think of to say was: "Lloyd, don't do this… you're behaving like me." But this only made things worse, because he began to laugh and cry at the same time and I wondered if he'd gone mad.

"You're right," he said, throwing himself back onto the bed, "our roles are reversed," and he laughed loudly. Then he began to cry again, more quietly. "I can't face the exams, David; it's tying my stomach in knots; you remember my A-levels – if it weren't for Mama constantly consoling and encouraging me, I could never have taken them. Everybody thought – even I – that because I had done so well in them, I would never suffer these exam doubts again, but they were wrong."

"But Lloyd, you know everything," I pleaded; "the exams will be a breeze."

"It's not the exams themselves," he said, after a moment's silence. "Once I turn over the question paper I'll be OK; it's the days and the hours leading up to that, when I can't eat, I can't sleep, I can't stop trembling, I can't shit… "

This was a revelation to me, discovering this chink in the armour of my hero. I felt as though someone had knocked away one of the main pillars supporting my world. My whole life (I now realized) was predicated on the certainty that there was an invincible, infallible champion who would swoop to my aid or rescue whenever required. It didn't make any sense to me. If I knew as much as he did about the subjects, I would relish the exams; in the period before they began I would luxuriate in the delicious sense of mastery and the confident expectation of success. Yet here was this most able and upright of students reduced to tears and destructive rage, shredding his notes and text books in despair.

"You know David," he said suddenly, "you're lucky; you enjoy yourself, you indulge yourself – and I'm not being sarcastic here – and yet you always end up doing what is expected of you…"

"Only because of you, Lloyd," I said. "I hope you don't think I'm ungrateful."

He began to sob again: "It's not that – can't you see – at some point soon you will have a university degree *and* a full and varied and rich experience of life. I will have a university degree, but will scarcely have lived; I may *die* before I experience half of what you have enjoyed over the past three years."

"Once your studies are over," I said, "you will enjoy all that and much more. You will enjoy everything much more than I do because you will be much better prepared."

"No," he said, "I think you're wrong. Marvell was right."

"Who?"

"Andrew Marvell, the poet: we *don't* have "world enough and time", only the briefest opportunity for pleasure and happiness, and then… nothing: "yonder all before us lie deserts of vast eternity". I will enter those deserts without ever having tasted life – except vicariously: the little bit I've sniffed in books and from knowing you – your activities and experiences… "

"Oh, Lloyd," I said, "don't get me scared with that kind of talk, please. No one could be further from being a role-model than me. I beg you, don't destroy your books, your notes. My "wonderful" experience of life is nothing, compared to your brilliance – you *have to* write your exams, for Mama, for yourself – for me. Just tell me what I can do to help; you've always helped me when I've been in trouble."

He got up, took his face towel and wiped his eyes. Then, without turning to look at me, he said: "Just stay with me in the room for a while; I just need a human presence," and he sobbed again, "to support me in this dark time… "

So I ended up spending the night sitting in his room; we hardly spoke. Near morning he began to clear up the mess and I helped him. At dawn he lay back on the bed and fell asleep. I left quietly. When I checked at midday he was still sleeping. He sat in my room for most of the next night, rereading a long Spanish novel, while I studied. Nothing was more important to me in those few days than Lloyd's health and his peace of mind. I reasoned it was the least I could do for one who had helped me so much in the past. We arrived at the day of the first exam and Lloyd vomited before we left for university, though the only things he had eaten over the preceding twenty-four hours were four nectarines, which he called "curious peaches". When he saw the exam paper he was OK – he wrote fluently for three hours and felt good afterwards. The next day he vomited again, but that was the last time. He seemed to be coping, and after the fourth paper, he seemed to be himself again. After the final exam he hugged me and thanked me profusely. The following day I went to a West Indian shop and bought ground vegetables and salt-fish and coconut and cooked an enormous pot of *metagee* and Lloyd and I feasted on it for the next few days. He left for home soon after, but I remained in London for the summer, awaiting results.

* * *

In late September both Lloyd and I were back in residence at Leeds. He had achieved a first, as expected, and his scholarship had been extended. He was registered as an M.Phil student, writing a thesis on contemporary love poetry and hoping to be upgraded to a Ph.D. candidate. I had got an upper second, which was enough to get me into a one-year coursework M.A. programme. I had decided in the summer (a very tame summer for me: I had no money, so there was lots of reading in libraries and visiting museums and galleries and even writing a bit) that I wanted to do a Ph.D. myself, but I would get there via this M.A. Lloyd brought me a big parcel of goodies from my mother and told me that he had decided to adjust his lifestyle: he planned to go out more, to spend more time with friends in the pub, see something of the rest of the country... "How about finding yourself a girl?" I asked him, but he said that he wasn't sure that he was quite ready for that yet.

It happened, however, that a girl became interested in him. Towards the end of the first term I became aware of Elena

Gutierrez, a graduate student from Peru. She was quite attractive
with a smooth brown skin and long black waves of hair lapping
against her shoulders. She spoke English with an accent, but quite
well, although she would lapse into loud and rapid Spanish when
she got excited. I had tried nibbling around the edges to see if she
might be interested in me, but although she was friendly, she didn't
take my advances seriously at that time. Fair enough, I thought, and
went down to London for Christmas. Early in the second term
Lloyd gave a seminar paper on two or three Spanish Caribbean
poets. It was a polished performance: of course the quotations were
read in fluent American Spanish, and he knew so damned much
about his subjects. Everyone thought it was a great paper, most of
all Elena, who asked several questions in Spanish and Lloyd had
responded in Spanish, before translating both question and answer
for the rest of us. A few days later Elena came looking for me:
"Lloyd is from your country, isn't he?" she asked, and that was the
prelude to so many other questions about him and my relationship
to him, that I grew tired of whispering (we were in my carrel in the
Brotherton library) and suggested we go to the cafeteria. It was clear
that she had a crush on Lloyd, but had the impression that he didn't
take her seriously, because he never seemed to have time to chat
with her. I explained that he was shy and consumed by his studies,
that he was an only child, had attended boys only schools and had
no experience with girls. I offered to have a word with him on her
behalf, but she immediately said no.

"No, please, David, do not talk to him about me, that would
spoil everything because he will think that I am after him."

"But I thought you were."

"No – yes, yes of course I am, but it's not good for him to know
this from somebody else, believe me."

"So what are you going to do," I asked, looking at her across the
cafeteria table.

"I don't know yet – nothing – he will like somebody whom he
can admire for some achievement, I think… " And we chatted on
for some time, ending up talking about her and about Peru and
Guyana.

There were many such conversations in the following weeks

and I grew quite fond of Elena, and comfortable in her presence. Sometimes we hardly mentioned Lloyd and she sometimes permitted me to indulge in idle flirtations. Then one night she came to the hall with me and I cooked her a meal. As we were sitting to eat in the kitchen, Lloyd passed through, going back to his room from watching the news in the TV lounge – perhaps he'd passed through the flat because he had checked my room to see if I was in – at any rate he stopped and chatted with us for a while, but he declined my invitation to join us for dinner.

After he had left, Elena said, "You know, he adores all that poetry he reads: he talks about it with such passion. If only I were a poet."

"Well, aren't you?" I asked.

"What you mean, David? No, no, I'm not a poet, I have never written a poem."

"Well maybe you should try; it's not that difficult. Write a few poems in Spanish – I'm sure Lloyd would be interested in seeing them."

"No," she said with a sigh, "I can translate literature, but I can't write it."

"Well," I said with a mischievous grin, "you could always settle for second-best."

"What is second-best?"

"Me."

And she laughed and said: "Oh, David, you know I like you: you are the only person who talks to me – no, I mean you are the only person who lets me talk and talk… "

"I'll tell you what," I said, "together we can write some love-poems, you can translate them into Spanish and we can present them to Lloyd as yours… "

It was, I see now, another of my "hair-brained schemes", as Lloyd would have called it, and to tell the truth I didn't really think that she would agree to it. In fact nothing was agreed but that very night we went to my room and fooled around with a few lines from something I had written in the summer.

Without definitely agreeing on anything, we kept meeting in my room and fashioning lines of love poetry – in English first, then she would translate them into Spanish. Before we realized it two things had happened: first, we found ourselves in the middle of this writing project to which we seemed to have become committed; and second, we had drifted, just as inadvertently, into physical intimacy. The two things fed on each other: composing and translating images and poems of love fuelled in us a surprising passion for each other – and vice versa. Our intimacy proceeded in measured steps like a slow dance. She seemed to delight in our mutual exploration of each other's body with our hands (perhaps this is a Latin thing), and by the time we actually went to bed together (weeks later) we were already thoroughly familiar with all the bumps and hollows, the flats and narrows, and knew how to summon into shrill conversation all our eager blood…

It seemed at one time as though we were going to abandon the project of the poems: it had become, after all, just an excuse for us to be together. But such things tend to develop a life and momentum of their own. We grew very fond of our concocted poems and it became necessary to show them off, and who better to judge them than Lloyd? So they were duly typed up: twelve poems on fourteen pages, and Elena had fun doing the title page: "*Los murciélagos del amor: poemas. Por Elena Gutierrez Ramirez* – and, near the bottom of the page, the year: 1974. She took the typescript to Lloyd's carrel in the library and told him she had typed up some poems she'd been working on and would be grateful if he would look at them and tell her what he thought. She was not pressing him, but if he had the time she wondered if he might care to translate one or two of them into English, so that her friends in Leeds could read them – she had tried herself, but had found it impossible.

Apparently Lloyd's first comment was: "*The Bats of Love*, what a wonderful title!" And, after flipping a few pages, "I'd certainly like to read them, and I will let you know what I think. I'm not sure about translating them, though, I might not be able to spare the time; but let me see how things go – and thanks for letting me read them."

Actually the title had been something of an "in" joke between

Elena and I. The poems had lots of bat imagery, particularly tactile imagery about the skin of bats, because it had emerged in our mutual sexual explorations that Elena considered the scrotum was like a bat – a warm sack of wrinkled skin – and the erect shaft of the penis, like the taut membrane on a bat's open wing. So she would say: "Oh David, your bat of love is in full flight tonight," and I would probably reply: "Well it's dark, and there is ripe fruit in your low branches… "

As it turned out, far from not having the time to translate the poems, Lloyd allowed the little typescript to take over his life entirely. He became obsessed with the poems. He told Elena that he was very excited with her collection: the imagery was startling and original and as love poetry her work was powerful and disturbing. The moment I heard this from Elena, I became apprehensive and wished that we had abandoned the whole idea. Elena was not too worried – in fact she was rather pleased at Lloyd's enthusiastic response and she felt certain he would want to translate them.

"But Elena," I said, "they are *already* translations – and while it may be mildly interesting to see how his translations compare with the originals – I don't think it's fair to let him go through all that; he will be taking precious time from his research. The whole thing is a deception, a lie, and we have to let him know before it's too late."

But she would not hear of it: "Oh but he has not *said* anything about translating it yet; let him have some fun with the poems, he's obviously very excited by them – we can tell him later that it was all a trick – I mean a joke."

"Trick or joke, it's very cruel," I said. "Lloyd is a formidable scholar, but I've discovered that he's quite frail in certain respects – emotionally – and I don't think we should put him through this."

"I will take the responsibility; just let him have them for a little while more, please… "

What could I say?

The Sunday morning after this conversation Lloyd came into my room, clutching a sheaf of papers; his eyes were bright with

excitement: "Listen to this image, David," he said, "It's from one
of Elena's love-poems – give me your honest opinion about it; I
think it's fantastic; I will read the passage in Spanish first and then
the translation I made. This is from the title poem:

> *Cuando el sol se pone*
> *el corazón va de caza*
> *como murciélago liberado por la oscuridad*
> *a comer las frutas en tus ramas mojadas…*

And in English:
> The heart goes hunting at dusk
> like a bat liberated by darkness
> to feast in your damp branches… "

Before I could say anything, he flipped over a page and went
on: "Here's another one, tell me if you can't actually feel the
sensation of a bat and the thrill of fear it inspires:

> *La superficie del amor es suave*
> *al tacto, como una ala desplegada*
> *en la noche, rozando tu mejilla*
> *y llenando tu corazón de miedo y felicidad.*

And my translation:
> The skin of love is soft
> to the touch, like a stretched wing
> that brushes your cheek and fills the night
> with fear and wonder… "

"Well, I don't think…"

"You see," he said, not letting me speak; "it's wonderful stuff,
and so fresh, so full of real feeling. She *has* to get this published…
I will do the English translations… Perhaps *London Magazine* or
some other journal."

"Look, Lloyd," I said, raising my hand, "take it easy – it sounds
like fairly ordinary love poetry to me."

"Ah, but you're not an expert, you're not writing a thesis on
precisely this kind of imagery and its cultural provenance and the
way it encodes a repressed emotional life… This has to do with

a whole world of experience and sensation in a particular geographical and spiritual context – oh, never mind! You will appreciate it when you see it in print. I must get back to work." And he left as abruptly as he had burst in.

I was devastated. I didn't know whether to laugh or cry. I cursed my short-sightedness in creating yet another monster – and of the very person who had been strong and compassionate enough to slay all my monsters in the past. I wanted to rush up to Lloyd's room with all our drafts and discarded efforts and *make* him see that the poems were a hoax. It had to be done sometime, and it would be more painful the later we left it. But I could not do it; perhaps I lacked the courage. I told myself I needed the guilty support of Elena at that time. I telephoned her, but she could not be located.

Two tense days drifted by and I could not find Elena; a friend thought she might have decided at the last minute to attend a conference on Culture and Translation in Birmingham, and had left on Sunday – if so, she should be back by Wednesday… Late Wednesday night Elena knocked on my door. She was coming from Lloyd's room where he had summoned her "to help him with the translations".

"Elena, are you mad!" I shouted. "Do you know what you're doing?"

"*Yo sé*, I know, David, I know – is problem," and tears came to her eyes. "All night I am telling him – I *try* to tell him that I did not write those poems, *pero* he would not listen. He said, "Of course you did not write them, you are the mouthpiece of a whole culture, a way of apprehending and feeling… " David, he does not believe me, he talks and talks about translating and publication, he is *como loco, no?* And I can no longer talk to him… "

We decided to go back up to his room at once and show him the folder of drafts, but he would not open the door. He kept shouting: "Go away, I don't believe your lies. You, David, have put Elena up to this to cheat me of my first chance of pleasure and prominence in this world. You think I don't know that you two are lovers… I must translate these poems, for her sake and mine."

We went back to my room and I typed a long letter explaining how the whole deception had come about and apologizing for his pain and wasted time, and put it in the folder. I would make sure he saw it the following day. Elena said she was scared and wanted to spend the night with me, but I called a taxi and sent her home.

Early next morning I went up again to Lloyd's door. "I'm not speaking to you," he said from behind the locked door. His voice sounded weary.

"I don't want to speak," I replied. "I have something for you."

He opened the door; I looked past him, afraid the room might be disordered, as on that night before his finals, but everything seemed OK. I pushed past him and flung the folder on the bed: "Read that, for God's sake," I said, and walked out of the room shutting the door behind me.

I don't know when he actually read it, because he did not speak to me for ages after that morning. For days I never saw him and then when I did, he made a point of ignoring me. I blamed myself, I considered I deserved his contempt, but my heart grieved for the loss of his friendship. My exams were approaching, however, and I used the fact that I had to prepare for them as a way of hiding from the hurt I felt about Lloyd. Once or twice I would see his sad and drooping figure in the distance and I wondered if he was grieving like me. I consoled myself with the thought that at least this exam time would hold no terrors for him as he did not have to write exams, just work away at his thesis. I tried not to, but I think I blamed Elena for what had happened. I used the excuse of exams to see very little of her and I suppose it was inevitable that we should drift apart.

In the middle of the exams I got a message that Lloyd's supervisor wanted to see me and I turned up at his office just after my penultimate paper.

"Ah, Mr. Adams, isn't it? So good of you to come. This is about your friend Jeremiah."

"Who? Oh yes, sorry, you mean Lloyd."

"Mr. Cadogan – isn't his name Jeremiah?"

"Well, he is Jeremiah Lloyd George, but his family and friends call him Lloyd."

"Good heavens, why would anyone permit himself to be called

Lloyd when he has such a wonderful first name as Jeremiah?" He smiled and shook his head. "I'm just a little disturbed by the fact that I haven't heard from Jeremiah – ah, Lloyd – for quite some time, and I have not been able to get hold of him. I have some work of his that I need to give back and it's about time for him to hand in some more of his draft so that I can recommend his upgrading. He did, though, send me a note, some weeks ago to say that he'd found an exciting new collection of poems – by a Peruvian woman, I think – and he was excited at the prospect of translating it… "

"Well, I'm fairly certain that he has abandoned the translation project, Professor, but I didn't realize that he's not been around. I don't think he's gone away anywhere. I will try to find him and let him know that you're looking for him."

"Would you? Excellent. I know you live in the same residence, he's spoken often of you… That's fine, then. As soon as you find out anything, just let me know."

The next few days I spent looking for Lloyd and worrying about him: he had apparently been seen on his floor up to a few days before I spoke to his professor, but no one had seen him since then. His room, duly opened by the warden of the hall, contained no clue about where he might have gone, but he didn't appear to have taken much with him and his passport was in a desk drawer. The warden informed the police that he was missing. It was the day before my final exam so I had to resume my revision and I spent a troubled day in my library carrel. The exam went quite well and that evening, just as I was rehearsing what I would say to Mama on the phone (for it was time that she were told), word came that Lloyd had been found.

He was discovered, all bearded and dishevelled and his clothes filthy, doing a black-Lear-on-the-heath thing at the ruins of Fountains Abbey, north of Leeds, near Ripon. Apparently for some days tourists at the Abbey had been puzzled and amused by this unkempt black man who was pacing up and down the site reciting poetry in a strange language and gesturing wildly. At times he would laugh loudly; at others, tears ran down his face. He walked off down the road in the evenings and would reappear the following day – God knows where he had been sleeping and eating all this time. The story made the local newspaper and Lloyd was sectioned and taken to the psychiatric ward of St. James's hospital in Leeds for observation. Within weeks he was back home in Guyana. Elena Gutierrez and I had a long, guilt-ridden conversation in a corner of the cafeteria. We deeply regretted what we had done to Lloyd and also, perhaps understandably, what we had done together in those feverish nights of sexual dalliance and poetic composition. We saw very little of each other after that, and when she left Leeds that summer, I never heard from her again.

★ ★ ★

When I returned to Guyana in August of that year, I was very apprehensive about meeting Lloyd. While he was in hospital and preparing to return home, I'd spoken several times to his parents, but I had not told them the whole story. I feared that Lloyd would have told them by now, and that I might no longer be welcome in their home. I was also fearful that the sight of me might upset him, particularly since he'd had to withdraw from his studies. As a consequence I did not go to visit them as soon as I arrived. When I ran into Mama a few days after in Fogarty's, however, she gave me a huge hug and a kiss and seemed hurt that I'd been in the country four days and had not gone to see them. She brushed aside my fear of upsetting Lloyd.

"He isn't in the same state as when he left England, you know; he's recovering very well. He can never complete another degree, but he's back to his old self and he frequently talks about you, though I have the feeling, David, that he's afraid he may have lost you as a friend, since he has not heard from you. I keep asking him if you all had a quarrel, but he wouldn't tell me anything."

This news brought tears to my eyes and I promised Mama I would visit that very afternoon.

When I arrived at the house, Lloyd certainly seemed to be his old self – in fact I wondered at first whether he remembered what had happened to trigger his breakdown; but later on, when he and I were sitting on the veranda at dusk, he told me that he hoped I didn't think that the business of Elena and the poems was what caused his illness, as it was only one of several factors. I was not sure how he worked this out, but I was grateful for the reprieve, though I told him that I would always feel responsible and apologized (as on so many occasions in the past) for my behaviour.

"Perhaps it's true," he said with a smile, "that the behaviour of you two was the last thing I needed at that specific time, but I've learned that mine is a clinical condition that can occur at any time of great stress or anxiety. It's an illness that cannot be cured, though it can be kept in check by carefully avoiding stressful situations and I have medication to help keep me calm. I'm grateful that I understand it much better now, but the doctors tell me that I will never be completely safe from further episodes. It means that my life has to be simple. I have my room and my books, and – from next month – I will have a job: I will be teaching French and Spanish at college... "

All this was wonderful news and I saw a lot of Lloyd for the next month or so, and even gave a talk to his sixth form literature class when he started teaching. After I left to embark on my Doctoral studies – this time at Canterbury instead of Leeds – we corresponded regularly and I was able to send him, from time to time, books and teaching materials from England. Not long after I went to Canterbury, my family migrated to Toronto, and that became the "home" I visited during the vacations. My contact with Lloyd dwindled to birthday and Christmas cards and the occasional long letter – from him; I was always too busy to write more than a few lines. When I got a job in the English department at Cave Hill in Barbados, I wrote and invited Lloyd over for a holiday, but he never came, and I got married and started a family...

When I first visited Guyana after a long absence and took my family around to meet Lloyd and Mama (his father had died a few years previously, as had mine), it was like old times: Lloyd and Mama were very happy to see me and to meet my family, and I returned at least once a year thereafter, sometimes on holiday, sometimes for conferences or to do something or other at the University of Guyana. It was one such "working trip" that had culminated with Lloyd's funeral. I was always looking for excuses to get back "home" (as I still referred to Guyana in my mind), and when Al Creighton asked if I'd like to conduct a summer workshop at UG, I jumped at the chance. This one was a workshop on "critical writing", as described in the flyer I had seen in Lloyd's room, and would last two weeks, with three-hour morning sessions on Mondays, Wednesdays and Fridays.

When I went around to see Lloyd the evening I arrived, he greeted me with a copy of the flyer announcing the workshop in his hand, and declared that he was going to register. My heart sank at the news: I was concerned about him returning to *any* kind of "studies", and the course was going to be a fairly intensive one. When I mentioned this to him, he said he wanted to give it a try as it might help him to do reviews and other writing for one of the local newspapers. "I'm not sure that I can spend the rest of my life in a classroom at college," he said. "Besides, I'm not sure that I will attend all of your sessions: I'll just sit in on one or two and see how it goes." I felt I could hardly deny him that, but I told him not to register and pay for the course – just to come and audit a few sessions when he felt like it: I would have a word with the people at UG.

At first Lloyd was wonderful: he stood out in the group and his contributions to the discussions were excellent. By the Friday session, however (and he had skipped none of them), I detected in what he said the rasp of some powerful emotion – a desperate nostalgia, perhaps, for the days when his intellectual acuity and scholarship were recognized and celebrated. When he did not show up in class the following Monday I was happy, because I thought that he had probably recognized that he was pushing himself too hard. Lloyd phoned me on Monday night, however, and as soon as I heard his voice I realized that something was wrong – his tone was the same as on that Sunday morning, years ago, when he had burst into my room in hall to read and comment on the poems that Elena and I had concocted. There was a kind of driven, manic quality to the flow of sentences and the (now rather outdated) scholarly jargon that came tumbling out of him in that telephone conversation. I tried to suggest that he should take it easy and perhaps give the Wednesday session a miss, but he was most indignant, informing me that he had not felt that good in years and he'd stayed home only to work on his "assignment" so that he could read it on Wednesday… With sinking heart I put down the phone when he'd finished and immediately called Al Creighton and explained the situation as delicately as I could.

"Well… OK… Do you want me to have him barred from attending the class? We can do that, I think… if you feel he will be disruptive … I mean… OK…. it's not as if he were a registered participant in the workshop… "

"Oh, I don't know," I said. "I'm reluctant to go that far simply because of an impression I received over the phone. How about if we just make arrangements to have you – or security or somebody – intervene if necessary during the session?"

"We could… OK… we could do that… yes… if that's what you prefer. I'll have a word with Agnes Duncan, one of the workshop students – I think you know her – and if there's any trouble… Well… just signal to her and she will leave the class and come and inform me."

On Wednesday morning things started off badly. It was still a few minutes before the class started when Lloyd came to the front and announced that he was going to read his assignment and he hoped it would inspire a lively discussion and provide him with valuable feedback. I had to interrupt him and point out that it was not yet time, people were still arriving and settling down, and besides, I wanted to say a few words before any assignments were read. He seemed surprised at this, but returned to his seat. In my preamble I reminded the class that I'd asked them to read *a page or two* from either something they had written in the past about a work of art (poetry, play, painting, sculpture, music), or something that they'd written specifically for the exercise. The idea was to provoke discussion about the aesthetic values or critical perspective evident in the passage read and the appropriateness of the language for conveying these…

"I need to go first," Lloyd said, "because I'm not sure I can stay for the whole session."

I held out my hands in enquiry to the class and they shrugged, so Lloyd came up to the front.

"I'm talking here," he began, "about a small collection of poems which I once translated from Spanish. It is called *The Bats of Love*."

"I'm sorry, Mr. Cadogan," I interrupted, "but I don't think that's appropriate here."

"Please," he said, in an awful whining voice, "you *must* let me have my say – I've waited a lifetime…"

I sighed and he continued, but he was not really making sense, except when he read, in impassioned tones, quotations from the Spanish version. Many of the others were squirming uncomfortably in their chairs as he turned over the third page. I reminded him of the page limit but he ignored me and read more quickly and loudly. He got so fast that what he read was incomprehensible, and there was spit flying from his mouth. A feeling of utter desolation, mingled with an ancient guilt swept over me and I looked around for Agnes Duncan – but she was nowhere to be seen. I didn't know what to do. But as it happened Agnes Duncan had already slipped out of the room on her own initiative and now returned with Mr. Creighton and a couple of security officers. It was announced that the fifteen-minute break would be taken immediately and that the class would reconvene in a different room.

Lloyd was quiet by now, his body limp and there were tears in his eyes. I asked Al if he could hold on for me for an hour, as I wanted to take Lloyd home. Lloyd said not a word in the car, he just clutched his papers and sobbed. When we got to the house I went in and explained to Mama what had happened and she immediately phoned for Lloyd's cousin to come and take him to the doctor, whom she also phoned. While we waited for Bernice to arrive, Mama said she thought she had noticed one or two warning signs in Lloyd over the last couple days.

"Oh Mama," I said, "I know this has something to do with me. This always happens when I'm around."

"Nonsense, David. Don't talk like that. You're the person he admires and respects most, when he's himself: he says you are his best friend."

Then Bernice and her son Victor arrived and took Lloyd to the doctor. I told Mama that I had to get back to my class.

"Don't feel bad, David," she said. "I haven't told you yet – in fact I haven't told anybody, not even Lloyd – but the headmaster from college came to see me and he said he was sorry, but he couldn't have Lloyd back as a master in September: he had become rambling and incoherent at times in class; he no longer followed the syllabus and he shouted at the students and upset them… " And Mama started to cry for the son she loved so much. She said she had not yet told him, but I immediately thought that he knew, or at least suspected. Perhaps that's why he had talked of leaving the college and writing for a newspaper…

The class was in no mood, apparently, to continue the workshop after their early break that day, and Al had taken the decision to announce an extra session the following Monday instead. This was OK, as I was not booked to leave until the Wednesday. The Friday class went well, and I was beginning to feel quite buoyant again that evening in the hotel, when the phone rang and it was Mama.

"I didn't want to call you while you were up at university this morning," she said, choking back tears, "but I have very bad news. Lloyd is dead. He took his own life this morning…" and she wailed inconsolably into the phone.

All this about our intertwined lives I went over in my mind on that little aeroplane to Barbados. I feel I cannot escape my own culpability for what happened to Lloyd Cadogan's life. He may have had a mental illness, but my own thoughtless and selfish behaviour as his friend had been an unnecessary burden he'd had to bear – and he'd borne it so well out of a sense of loyalty and duty, out of compassion, out of love… It was his misfortune and mine that I had failed to match him in these qualities, as indeed I'd failed to match him in almost everything else. As the plane touched down in Barbados, I prayed for forgiveness…

★H.A.L. Seaforth is one of the contributors to the anthology of stories written by a group of Guyanese sixth-formers who were last together on the day Guyana gained its independence in 1966. Many years later, Mark McWatt undertakes to gather a story from each member of the group. None of them now lives in Guyana.

SHARON MILLAR

THE HAT

Somewhere in San Rafael, in the centre of the island, Chale sits in the front seat of the small black car waiting to kidnap a woman. The woman's name is Maria Estella and that is all he knows. He takes his instructions from Dougla who is sitting in the back of the sedan. While they wait, Chale drums a tune on the steering wheel to pass the time. He's only just turned seventeen but last year Dougla paid for the licence tucked in the back pocket of his jeans. The car is parked off the main road, under the teak trees that run to the clearing of razor grass. The house sits at the end of a winding bridle path and the woman's car is parked so that it is not visible from the main road. In the ashy dusk, the fruit bats swoop under the mango trees before fanning out into the forest.

While he waits for the signal from Dougla, Chale idly un-packs the glove compartment: three lipsticks melted and ruined by the daytime heat in the car, an insurance certificate, and a wedding invitation. The sedan belongs to a woman they held up in Curepe last night. Moving up the ranks, Dougla told him. Now Chale opens the door of the car and steps out into the chill evening air. Carefully and slowly he makes his way down the hill and around the back of the house. He must knock on the door at precisely 6.45 pm. June evenings run long and he must pick the moment when it is neither day nor night.

Through a Demerara window at the back of the house Chale can see Maria Estella soundlessly counting as she places the cash in tidy packets, each secured with a pink rubber-band. She places each packet neatly in a suitcase lying open on the wooden floor in front of her. The room is bare except for two chairs and a long dining-room table. Above the table, a chandelier sways gently in the evening breeze and moth shadows grow with the dusk. One side of the room is already in darkness.

"Come boy, time to move." Chale says to himself.

Maria Estella comes to the door with the first knock. He smiles at her through the window, raising his hand to his mouth as if he wants to ask her a question. He has deliberately made his face slack and pleasant. In the moment it takes for her to look away, her face frowning with worry, her hand reaching to slide another lock, he has gotten through the door. When he pushes her hard, she goes down quickly. With his hands on her shoulders, he straddles her. His jeans slip and slide on her shirt as he bounces on her chest. Between his thighs, she is solid and he comes down hard on her, squeezing until he feels the outline of rib under the flesh. With each bounce she exhales little puffs of air, blowing into his face a woman smell that must come from deep inside. Keep calm, he tells himself. You can do this.

When he raises his hand to push her she misunderstands the gesture, thinking there is something behind her that he wants to hit, perhaps a moth or a bat. When he pushes her, she is surprised to find herself down, weak from fright and anger, the back of her head slamming into the wooden floor. There are three locks on the door. She thinks how angry the man will be that they were not all latched. Within seconds, the boy has straddled her, climbing onto her as if she is a bicycle. Her heart thuds until she can't catch her breath and she sucks desperately for air, her ribs straining against the weight of his thighs, her shirt sliding under his jeans. Behind his head she can see another man coming through the door. It's happened so fast, she's caught somewhere between detachment and panic; the keening takes a few seconds to come. She hears it as if from a distance; a sound unrelated to her voice. It stops when the boy spreads five fingers across her mouth, starfishing the centre of her face.

"Cool yourself," says the other man to the boy, cool and calm. "You don't need to fuck up now."

She turns on her stomach, panicked and wailing, kicking back hard, her mouth spilling an odd bird cry.

In the car she tells herself, Calm down, calm down. Pay attention to where they are driving. In pulling her down the stairs, they hurt her back and now it pulses in little angry spasms. The man drives and the boy sits in the back with her, his hand resting lightly on her head, keeping her under the blanket they have used to conceal her. She worries that she will suffocate so she lies quietly and paces her breathing. They drive for a long time, turning sharp corners until she is dizzy and carsick. When the car stops, there is the smell of night forest and the hum and chirrup of tree frogs.

It is only when they make her walk through the forest that Maria Estella cries for the first time, her childhood terror of snakes rushing back. She thinks they are somewhere in the Guayaguayare forest, heading east. She remembers all the stories she's heard of hunting dogs dying from the bite of the mapepires that hide under rotting logs. Soon she is sweating, breathing heavily, trying to map where they are going. The boy who walks in front of her is young. His hair is long and she can tell it has been a few days since he has washed it. It is oily but combed and straight, parting randomly and exposing the yellow skin on his skull and the tender lines of his ear cartilage, delicate as an agouti. He keeps looking back at her. As her eyes grow accustomed to the underwater light of the moon, she sees the dougla man has his gun trained on the boy as well. She walks on a leash between the two men, the older, heavier man bringing up the rear. By the time they stop, her feet are stinging and bleeding, her toes stumped and sore. They tie her to a pole in a pit latrine and bring a bottle of water and a tin bucket. She grew up in a house with a pit latrine and the smell takes her back to the little hut above the river. This latrine is a cocktail of different shit. There is the frothy smell of diarrhoea and she hopes she does not get sick. They leave her blindfolded, her hands tied behind her back.

That night Maria Estella thinks about her mother's house above the scattering of board houses on the Arima-Blanchisseuse road, surrounded by forest trees with names that she likes to roll on her tongue, imagining the texture of a bark: the pain d'epice and the cajuca; the bois canot and the balata. They grew up near the river, away from the spiny brush of the coast. She remembers the sound of the river after rain in its hurry to get to the sea. She senses there is a river nearby and when it rains sometime after midnight, she can hear the water rushing, adding to the sound of the surf, which cannot be far. From underneath the old piece of galvanize that is the door, a sea breeze mixes with a rain breeze and makes her think of her mother.

"Don't mind, auntie," Chale had said. "We'll take off the blindfold in the morning. Kick the bucket when you want to pee. You hear? Don't make a mistake and pee on the floor."

As if the floor is not already stinking and rank.

As an afterthought he leant in and whispered, a soussous sound hardly audible above the sound of the trees, "Or call me, call my name soft. It's Chale."

When her bladder stretches hard and tight, she feels with her foot for the bucket and kicks it until the Chale comes. He pulls her jeans and panties down and tells her to squat. She puts her hand on his shoulder to balance and smells the oil in his hair as the warm urine runs down the side of her leg, splattering into the tin bucket that the boy then pours into the latrine hole. After two days of peeing, the hole fills and stinks. By Sunday she can smell herself. The dougla man comes to visit, smelling of expensive cologne and cigar smoke. She can't imagine where he's made camp to be looking so clean. Perhaps Mayaro with its coconut trees and fancy beach houses is nearby.

"Just a little water, please," she tells him. "I'll tell him you treated me well. The man. I'll make sure he knows you treated me kindly. It will matter."

The dougla man looks at her for a long time before flicking ash into the bucket.

"You bathing for me, sweet thing?"

It is then that she is sure this is not a test. The dougla man has kidnapped her because he thinks he can outsmart the man, mistaking discretion for weakness. If they'd been real professionals they would have taken her north into the hilly northern range. It was the geographical move that made her think at first she was being tested. But now she realises it is merely stupidity and greed on the dougla man's part. By now, the man will have missed the money. He'll be looking for her. Looking for his suitcase.

For a moment, Maria Estella thinks the dougla man will rape her and for the first time she is truly frightened. Before this she has been angry, bent on retribution. But now, the dougla man's dumb, blunt features make it clear that he has no idea that there will be consequences for stealing both her and the suitcase. She knows that amateurs are the most dangerous. But there is no interest in the dougla's eyes. He could be someone she'd meet at a fete, looking just like thousands of Trinidadian men, no defining edge. He is brown skinned with a smooth, high forehead and the beginnings of a receding hairline. He doesn't look dangerous. A true true mix-up dougla. His mother might be Indian, his father black; maybe some Chinee in him. The kind of saga-boy her mother always liked and she bets there's a woman somewhere in the background. Men like this dougla man don't move without a woman for long. While he talks, Maria Estella lowers herself to sit with her back against the raw bricks of the latrine, her feet filthy and swollen.

She notices that the boy, Chale, does not take his eyes off the dougla man. The boy, thin and young, positions himself between her and the man.

"The man is going to pay the ransom." The man stands away from the latrine, throwing his voice like a stone. "You understand how these things work don't you?"

She does. But does he?

★

Sometimes, before the twins were born, rich people from Port of Spain would call for Maria Estella's mother to cook in their weekend homes on the Blanchisseuse coast. Maria Estella looked nothing like her mother. Her mother said she looked nothing like her father either. Maria Estella did not know whether this was so, because her father died as she was beginning her descent into the world. A hunting accident. His friend had mistaken him for a deer. When next her mother had grown big and round, the houses on the coast stopped sending for her.

Maria Estella had cut the birth cords on both her sisters, taking each placenta out into the yard in a Breeze laundry detergent bucket and burying them deep under the silk cotton tree in the backyard. She'd buried the little navel strings, stringy and twisted, on the other side of the tree. They must never forget where they've come from, her mother said, her legs still spread and bleeding, the twins huddling under their mother's arm like naked birds. The iron smell of blood stayed on Maria Estella's hands for days, mixed with the smell of baby shit and breast milk. She was ten and afraid that her mother would die and leave her with the mewling babies.

Maria Estella was a panyol bred on a cocoa estate high in the northern range. Like any sport grown in the rain forest, she emerged with talents exceeding either parent. Born with the caul over her face, she had a peculiar sallowness that radiated off her skin as a tender green that eventually settled in the corners of her mouth and around her eyes. When she showed her gift, it was an unusual one for a young girl: an uncanny ability to understand how the business worked. With little effort, she mapped in her head the routes between Peru, Bolivia, and Colombia, how they funnelled into ever smaller channels via ship or light plane until destination zero was reached – the metropolis where rich white people were willing to pay big money for altered states. The man taught her about the Golden Crescent, the heroin routes that ran out of Iran, Afghanistan, and Pakistan through Amsterdam to New York. She understood that real money could no longer be made in sugar, cocoa or coffee. It lay in oil, cocaine or women.

At thirteen she'd gone to the man to ask for work. He'd never been charged with shooting her father. Her father had been a big man, her mother said. Maria Estella found it hard to see how he could look like a deer even on the darkest night. By the time Maria Estella went to see him, the man owned a fleet of light airplanes and managed a small island in the Orinoco Delta that specialised in hiding fugitives and processing high-grade cocaine. Soon she was travelling with him, listening, her chameleon-colouring making the men in the rooms doubt her presence in the shadows. She learned to trade and distribute cocaine. She learned to sell the guns that arrived with each shipment, part protection and part cargo. She learned to kill.

But when they kidnapped Maria Estella, Dougla told Chale nothing of this because Micheline, Dougla's woman, had told him nothing of it.

★

When Chale turns up at the beach-house at the end of the second day, Dougla is sitting at the kitchen table reading the papers, eating a plate of stewed chicken and rice. In front of him is another plate of neatly sliced avocado. Chale is hungry but Micheline doesn't offer him food. Chale has been guarding the woman all day, sitting outside the latrine and listening to her shift around inside. They've paid one of the villagers to watch her through the night so he can sleep. The village is not far from here.

Dougla's house leads onto the beach. Just that morning, the villagers had pulled seine in front of the house, the net coming in slowly, spilling the dying fish onto the sand. Most of the villagers know that a woman is being kept in a backyard latrine. She's hidden across the road, up a track past wild guava and fat-pork trees, but it's not far. Dougla supports all the church bazaars and pays for the school's sport supplies. The papers say every village has a Robin Hood and he supposes that's what he is to them. Whenever there's a job, they cook food and lend their latrines.

"Let the woman bathe," Chale tells Dougla when he is leaving. "I'll fill a bucket and take it for her."

He is shame to say he is sorry for the woman, but the place is so damn hot and the latrine so stink, he wouldn't leave a dog there for long. It has been a long day. Good thing this job isn't supposed to last long because he's begun to wonder if he has the stomach for it. To shoot someone and walk away is one thing – you can tell yourself all kind of thing to justify it. But to sit and watch someone suffer, that took real stones. She looked like a nice lady and he's still vexed with himself that he pushed the gun in her mouth. She'd been so frightened when he'd pulled down her pants for her to pee. But he wasn't interested in raping no big woman. When he'd had to help her, he was sad for her, thinking of his mother's panties hanging on the clothesline in their backyard. He wouldn't want his mother in some latrine. He knows his mother is proud of his pretty brown colour and that he has his Bajan granny's eyes, a funny kind of grey that makes big hardback women give him talk when they pass him downtown. His home is nice too. A decent house in Belmont. But people still have it in their head that bandit could only come in one colour, and they have to be poor and downtrodden. It's that kind of mentality that made room for him to climb up. His father works hard as a clerk at Hi Lo Food Stores, but Chale's too smart for that life; he wants to be rich with a pretty wife on his arm and a garage full of fancy cars.

"Wait for me outside," says Dougla between mouthfuls.

Chale has to pass Micheline to leave the room. She doesn't move aside to let him by so he has to press his back against the sideboard and sidle past her. Talk on the town is that she's the real boss, bad like crab, the only girl-child of a rich, high-brown family. Chale has heard her talking to her mother on the phone: Hello, Mumm-ya. Chale is trying to listen to Micheline and Dougla who are talking softly in the other room. He will learn if he keeps his ears open. This is like school and he thinks he is learning from the best. There has been just one phone call.

"Forty-eight hours tops," Dougla is saying. "Her man can cover the ransom. He will pay if he has to."

"I think you should let her go," says Micheline.

Chale cannot see that she has stopped counting the money in the suitcase. He cannot see that she is suddenly very frightened at the possibilities of what they have done.

"Dougla, there's a lot of money here. This is not a small operation."

Dougla sucks his teeth, a long leisurely steupse.

"You think I could make money if I walked away just so? You think that is how I make money, Micheline?"

Chale hears the newspapers give an irritated shuffle.

"It supposed to come tomorrow night; we'll wait it out."

Chale cannot see that Micheline is standing over the suitcase, her hand to her mouth, thinking, thinking, thinking.

Maria Estella needs to pee badly. She's been holding it all night because she's afraid of the man guarding her. In the middle of the night, he came in and peed a long donkey-stream pee in the bucket, right in front of her. She's listening for Chale. She'd heard him say that he'd be back on Monday morning and she'll call him when he comes. Until then, she'll hold it. She may have slept for an hour or two but it can't have been longer than that. She is trying to imagine the man's next move.

By late Monday night, Dougla sends a message to Chale that the ransom has been dropped. Chale is to pick up the retrieval team in a stolen Cortina Ghia with new plates. It is just four young boys he's given some small change. Thirty years on will be a different story. Thirty years on there will be smart phones and GPS tracking. But in the 1980s, on that night, it was all new territory. And somehow they'd pulled it off. When they pulled up at the Valsayn traffic lights, the highway was empty, the backseat of little boys silent.

Chale is the boss that night, but he is nervous about the pickup. The money is supposed to be in the market by the Croisee, the Sunday night market, packed with vendors. No one notices the boys as they spread out among the lettuce and tomatoes, the dasheen and the eddoes. The ransom is packed in a jute sack, the kind used to pack cocoa for market, hidden behind the decapitated head of a slaughtered cow. The ransom sack says **Attention Mr. Ali** in big black letters. The whole operation takes less than six minutes and they are back in the car. The boy counter wears surgical gloves as he checks the money for counterfeit, counting the packets quickly. An hour later they are outside Dougla's beach house, just beyond the periphery of Mafeking village.

Take her to town, carry her on the Lady Young Road, just past the lookout and throw her down the hill. That is the instruction Dougla gives Chale in front of Maria Estella, who stands shivering outside the latrine, a dog chain tied loosely around her ankle.

"Lady Young?" Chale repeats, looking from Dougla to Maria Estella and back again. "Lady Young? Why we don't just drop her close to the man. That was the plan."

Dougla looks at Chale for a long time before spitting on the ground and walking away. Chale cannot know that the instruction has come from Micheline who'd pondered the problem like a math sum all Sunday night. If they let Maria Estella live, she'd lead the man to them. It had to be Lady Young and it had to be done by Chale.

"Come auntie," Chale clicks his fingers at her as if she's a dog. "Come and bathe."

At first she will not come and she holds stubbornly to the side of the flimsy galvanise structure, cutting her hand on the sharp edges of the metal framework. As he pulls her, she grunts with exertion and he can hear the tightness in her throat. Lady Young. The bodies pile up there, hidden in the long grass and overgrown steps of the carved mountain. They both know what Lady Young means. Dougla has changed the rules on Chale. The woman is pulling hard now, grunting and cursing, but he pries her hands away from the wall and leads her to the makeshift bath.

The threadbare towel smells of mildew and the garish nightie is meant for rosy bedroom light. The word *Sexy* is emblazoned in black on the frilly short skirt.

"Do I have to come in with you?" His voice is kind because she is crying.

When she does not answer, he lets her in, unspooling more of the dog chain that keeps her tied to him.

"Is okay, Auntie. We will talk. Is okay."

Maria Estella strips behind the few planks of wood and galvanized sheeting that make a makeshift bath out of a lone tap. It's been years since she's smelt herself, that funky odour that belongs to her alone. Sometimes she's caught a whiff of it on the man, but now it is concentrated, pungent. Even though she is alone she turns her back to slip her panties off as if the boy can still see and smell her. She squats by the tap and scrubs with a bar of green Palmolive soap that has a crown cork stuck in the bottom to stop it from sticking to the concrete. The bottom of the soap is slimy and leaves long trails of green scum on her fingers when she puts it back on the mildewed concrete plinth under the tap.

★

The house where Maria Estella lived with her mother had two

bedrooms. A tiny kitchen looked out over the road and the small living room was lined with raw planks of pine that bled tiny beads of oil from its knots. Her mother grew begonias and ferns on the front balcony and each morning she squatted over a bucket and peed her morning stream before diluting it with water and dousing the plants. When her mother was pregnant the begonias grew wide fat silver leaves and the baby's-breath ferns jumped their pots to catch in the damp soil under the stairs.

Maria Estella slept with the twin girls in the back bedroom that bunched up between the mountain and the cannonball tree that sent long branches through the window over the sleeping girls. Maria Estella slept between the toddlers, their little bodies following the lines of her body. The tree grew round red and yellow flowers off its bark – wide impossible things with frilly edges. High in the trees' canopy, mosquito larvae bred in spiky bromeliad nurseries, which released them, fully winged and hungry, into the bedrooms of the small house.

Maria Estella remembered how she and her mother chewed green pawpaw and kissed the pulp into the mouths of the toddlers. They brought buckets of cold river water to the house, bathing and sapping infant skin so hot that she could remember the drops evaporating. The littlest one held out her arms to Maria Estella, mewling and reaching up, her tiny fists opening and closing. Water. Water. Two days later the doctor arrived wheezing from his climb up the hill, his car hissing gently on the road below. Dengue, he said. Empty your barrels and turn over your buckets. Cut your trees. There is an epidemic in town. It seemed that this was all he could say over the tiny, lifeless bodies, gently laid head to toe like dolls. Her mother wanted to bury them where they could see them and talk to them. The village priest buried them in the Catholic cemetery that lay on the edge of the cliff. Everyone knew that, sooner or later, the unanchored bones would slip into the ocean.

After this, Maria Estella slept in her mother's bed, windows open to the night breezes. In the other room, her mother lay naked on the floor, her arms and legs spread on a black sheet, the mosquitoes hovering, grey and gauzy.

The villagers said Maria Estella showed signs of the pawpaw cure when her skin grew mossy and tender, beautiful and verdant. Her mother lay in the other room until her skin turned ochre and cold. When the village policeman and the doctor came, the policeman remembered the night her father had been dropped by a single bullet. It was he who gave her the man's number. Call him, he said, his voice, flutish and high, and tell him your mother is dead and your father was not a deer.

★

"When you finish, throw the clothes out and put on the ones I gave you."

The boy's voice is hushed and she realises they are moving her without the village knowing. The night air is cold and her teeth chatter as she dries with the damp towel. The boy slips a pillow-case over her head. The boy is still gentle, no shoving and pushing. They walk for a long time before coming out into a clearing where the small sedan sits dwarfed by the forest trees. There is no one to hold Maria Estella down in the back seat and it is here on this lonely back road on the edge of the forest that they must begin their compromise, each bargaining for their life.

When the sedan drives off, Maria Estella is in the front seat next to Chale. He is bareback and she wears his shirt over the nighty, still shivering.

★

"Are you absolutely sure you can trust him?" Micheline asks.

"One hundred percent," Dougla says. "That boy love me like a father. The man will kill him before he has a chance to make it off that Lady Young road."

"So we good, Dougla? You sure?"

"We real good. Better than good."

"We'll lie low for a while. Hide the money in the forest."

★

By time he's made it back into town with Maria Estella sitting bold-faced in the front seat of the stolen Cortina, Chale knows he doesn't have what it takes to be a professional kidnapper. He'll have to tap some other lucrative stream. There are little tributaries breaking away from the river of enterprise that followed the wave of cocaine in the 80s. The possibilities are endless for a young boy with ambition.

She tells him on the back road in Guayaguayare who paid the ransom. The name that comes out of her mouth makes his stomach drop. If this was the man who'd paid the ransom, that makes Maria Estella the man's woman. The Spanish woman. Even he has heard of the Spanish woman. Does Dougla know? His tongue sticks to the roof of his mouth.

"Was there a woman?" she asks.

"Only Micheline."

"Micheline?" Maria Estella now knows who is behind it all. Micheline. Micheline. She'd been the man's woman before her.

Chale avoids the Lady Young road on the way back into town, coming, instead, down the Beetham highway, past the shanties on the right, the landfill on the left, all the garbage and rubbish from the island heaped in stinking piles for the corbeaux to plunder and loot. All the while Maria Estella sits planning, her green skin pulsing, the plan unfolding in her mind like the unpacking of nesting boxes.

Chale doesn't hear what she says to the man when he smuggles her into his parents' home after three a.m. and directs her to the telephone in the kitchen. He wonders if she can smell his mother's breath on the phone because he knows his mother will have been on the phone all night calling every one of his friends. Chale had told his parents he was going to Mayaro for a week with friends, but he'd expected to be back by last night. He knows his mother will be worried.

Even though it is three in the morning, Belmont is still playing Road March 1985, "Soucouyant" by Crazy, unfurling through the fretwork jalousies and from under doors, even though it is already Lent.

"Hide me for three days," she says, whispering as she comes out into black night to find him. "That's what he says to do. Can you do that?"

It is difficult to read her face in the night but he imagines the soft ochre freckles forming along the bridge of her nose, spreading in a mask, while she thinks. As if she has known all along that this is how it would end up.

"Will my family be safe?"

"Yes, I can promise you that. He knows you were played by them."

She hides in the outside room at his parent's Belmont home, the one his grandmother lived in before she died. She eats smuggled food from his mother's pot for three days, raising her head from the pillow on the small cot in the backroom to take small bites of choice pieces that Chale has handpicked from the pot. He brings titbits of tannia and plantain fritters, tender pieces of stewed chicken with white rice, soft macaroni pie, tempting her as if she were a difficult child. And all along he apologises. I'm sorry, he says. I'm sorry. Tell me what to do.

★

Thirty years on, the mountains still grow their emerald pelts for the rain. Chale is proud of the quiet hum of his Porsche Cayenne when he turns into a quiet street in Woodbrook. The house is one of the last of its kind on the street – the kind of house he'd been raised to think was his ambition. With their delicate fretwork, it seemed as if the ground itself had grown these houses out of the Taino bones-mangrove sludge that made everything in the ground bloom obscenely. Maria Estella would be happy to see him. It has been months since his last visit.

"Maria Estella? Maria Estellaaa?" With his shouting, the pack of pot hounds start barking in the back.

"Chale? Is that you?" She comes to the door wearing an old print housedress. She is wiping her face with a towel and pulling a brush through her hair, walking forward to unlatch the gate. In the time since he's last seen her, she's aged that bit more. Not anything that you can put your finger on, just a subtle desiccation of the body – the marrow calling the flesh home. She puts her cheek forward to be kissed. The skin under his lips is warm and soft with the lightest of amber fuzz running along her jawline.

"Come, Chale. It's been too long. Come and tell me." She is already walking back into the drawing room with its familiar floral-printed Morris chairs. Above the door leading into the kitchen is a new statue of the Sacred Heart of Jesus, the heart overgrown and blowsy, disturbing and garish. Has she gone religious? He's never seen any sign of it before. Maybe once. All those years ago when they'd first met. He'd heard her pray that night.

"How your tomatoes going, boy?" She comes out through the door with a glass of lime juice covered with a small-netted doily, its gay beads holding the thin net on the surface of the glass. She's gone to the trouble of adding a dash of angostura bitters, the darker, heavier liquid swirling through the lighter coloured juice. Always been a good hostess. He listens for Micheline's voice. There'd been a kidnapping that morning and with the sun just going down, people will be getting into position to work through the night. That's how it works now. Tonight, the operation will be all over the city. While they sleep, the negotiators will be up with the family and the Anti-Kidnapping Squad. Impossible to imagine they'd been able to do anything at all in 1985. Thirty years on no decent kidnapping occurs without a counter and a driver, one on the phone to the boss, constantly changing SIM cards to foil the trace and the last man there as the runner to pick up the package. They are always young and smart. Chale recently heard that a team used a boy from the International School. Another one was supposed to be a contender for an island scholarship at CIC. Those priests would spin if they knew what these Catholic schoolboys were getting up to on a Sunday night in 2015.

Micheline is one of the best negotiators on the island, working out of a back room in Maria Estella's house. In the early days, before there were professional negotiators hashing it out like overpriced lawyers, Micheline had dealt with the families directly, her convent accent creating a trust that persuaded the families to part with their money easily. Now it is different; now she deals with the negotiator from the Anti-Kidnapping-Squad and he is never swayed by her uppity accent. But still Maria Estella keeps her, under the weight of a key, in the back room.

"So tell me, how those tomatoes going?"

★

In times of heavy rain, the Orinoco Delta floods and any number of things can make their way on floating clumps of water hyacinths with their gay violet flowers. The water turns brackish and sweet, brown streaks filtering out and turning the water a deep muddy green. On that moonlit night so long ago, someone had made a smart hat, a type of bowler hat not often seen in these islands, papering it with counterfeit money. Dougla had come out to return the ransom money. The man had sent a message to meet near Quinam, but by the time Chale and Maria Estella arrived there was no sign of him or Dougla.

"How do you know he'll come?" Chale had asked Maria Estella on the long drive out.

"He will come," she'd said. "He wants to live and he thinks it is as easy as returning money."

As he'd walked towards the beach, Chale had seen the hat at the tideline. From where they stood it looked as if it dressed a rogue coconut – perhaps a swanky coconut, picked for its bravado from all the other coconuts on the tree. The ransom money was still in its jute bag, under a pile of copra and discarded coconut shells. Maria Estella sat on a beached log on the silver beach and began counting.

"Bury the head," she said, counting, her mouth silently sounding the numbers.

Chale had looked back at her, sick to his stomach.

"Bury it deep behind the trees so the dogs can't get it."

He'd had to go back to the car to get a shovel; it took him over an hour to bury the head, hat and all. They never spoke of it again, but after that everyone knew he belonged to the Spanish woman, knew that his loyalty was only to her. She'd taught him everything he knew. Things might have turned out differently if Micheline had offered him a plate of food that night.

For many months, Chale dreamed of Dougla, his mind working hard to attach Dougla's head to his body. When a body was buried without a head, would it return to look for it? He'd heard his mother say her own mother had come back to look for shoes, enraged that her only daughter had buried her with bare feet. Would that also apply to a head? But for the rest of his life, when he dreamed Dougla back, the stocky, bulky body would be instantly familiar, the jolt of fear only coming from the confused, disembodied head that opened and closed its mouth like a fish out of water.

It would be years before he met Maria Estella's man, deep in
the Orinoco Delta. But the man had let him live and Chale had
been put on the payroll, his loyalty to Maria Estella never ques-
tioned. Chale had picked up Micheline in a grocery not long after.
They'd come upon each other so quickly that the air was suddenly
turbulent. They hurried past the bottles of ketchup and the jars
of salsa, Micheline carrying her new self like a fragile package,
Chale pushing her quietly into the car, the gun a mere formality.

★

Sometimes Micheline writes poetry when she is bored. She slips
these under the door for Maria Estella and asks her to keep them
safe. They are two old ladies now. What harm could come of it?

> The lilies in the pond drown like loons
> Outstretched white necks
> Drinking rain on water stippled as a moon
> Stretched thin as any Saturday

Maria Estella keeps them all in a binder.
"Who knows?" she tells Chale. "We may have a real poet on our
hands. Everyone has a different side."

ANTON NIMBLETT

SECTIONS OF AN ORANGE

When police and store security responded to a 7:25 a.m. alarm, they found a hole in a street display window at the shop at 744 Fifth Ave., near 58th St.

The train bursts out of the subway tunnel onto elevated tracks that climb up to the Smith Street Station. The gritty view – stark contrasts of shadow and light, Brooklyn tenements against Manhattan skyscrapers – launches me into the world, reminds me that I haven't been out of my apartment in well over a week. The days glided by with slick ease and I'm glad to be doing something other than sitting in front of my computer, playing Free Cell and trying to break my last record in Minesweeper.

The theft at the 63-year-old store was captured on videotape, though the police said the footage was of poor quality.

As I step off the F-train, I feel the rickety platform vibrate under me, and a moment of uncertainty flashes through my mind. I remember my encounter with Brian last month. Truth be told, if he hadn't spotted me, I'd have walked right past him. But he came walking towards me with body language that seemed to say, from half a block away, that we'd planned to meet right there, he and I; and if not at that time, then five minutes earlier. On Fulton Street that day, he looked different – he'd cut his locks off, he'd gained a couple pounds, and aged a couple years – but he still looked good, especially when he smiled. When he smiled, he looked like a ten year old who'd just stoned down a juicy yellow mango and caught it before it hit the ground.

Getting past "Damn, it's been a long time" and "Oh man, I almost didn't recognize you," we'd talked outside South Portland Antiques, in a bright February light that masqueraded for spring. "Every last barber in Brooklyn jealous me," he explained as to why he wasn't working. "But that's a'ight 'cause I still have my photography, yuh know, my vision." I thought back to the last I'd heard about him, before this encounter: "Brian's off his rocker, yo," my regular barber had said. "I don't know if it's drugs, or what, but that cat was acting strange; they had to get rid of him." Not the response that my offhand question had been seeking, I'd discounted it at the time – "Nah, you're exaggerating again, Karly" – and then I'd changed the subject. I'd always had a thing for Brian and I hadn't been ready to give up on him so easily.

On Fulton that February afternoon, Brian was wearing a furry headband. He stooped down to tuck his jeans into black combat boots, talking all the while, bouncing through a stream of unconnected ideas – thoughts separate from the moment. But at intervals he returned to the sidewalk radiating charm.

"I can see that life's treating yuh well… yuh looking good."

I was flattered that he'd remembered me. "Yeah, it's good to see you man." At the end, he'd left with my phone number and a promise that I'd let him cut my hair.

> *A hit-and-run driver sparked mayhem on midtown Manhattan streets early yesterday – mowing down pedestrians in a wild, zigzag ride, police said.*

Now before doubt turns me around, I walk the short blocks from the station to the address he'd given me. Brian answers the door.

"Yuh early," he says, in a black T-shirt, that looks too small, and grey sweatpants that look too big. "I thought we Trini people don' show up on time for nothing." I walk in as he pulls the door wide and steps back.

"First time for everything though," I say, glancing at my watch. "This place was easy to find." 'This place' is a small private house. He locks the front door saying that his sister and her husband are out at work. He's been staying here for a while – they let him use the basement.

I follow Brian down the hallway. Going down the stairs, our feet hit alternate steps, drumming an impromptu tribal rhythm. I sit down in a chair next to a battered dresser. Rough wood frames an abandoned space where a mirror once was, and bare spots show through cloudy lacquer like a telltale birth certificate. A large aluminium lamp, clamped to the top, cuts a sharp arc of light into the dim room, drawing a curve that a geometry class could convert to an equation in two variables.

Brian drapes a cloth around my shoulders, clipping it at the base of my neck.

"Damn, man, so when was the last time this head saw a pair of scissors?" he asks, laughing. His fingers wiggle through the long, tight curls of my hair, moving close to my scalp.

"Well it's not my fault man," I say laughing too. "I lost my barber – Karly, got married and moved down to Atlanta," I remind him.

"Hmm, huh," he mumbles. He reaches over to the dresser, opens a drawer that protests with a squeak of wood against wood, and pulls out a pair of scissors.

Standing behind me, he starts clip-snip, snip-clip passes in the air – a silver hummingbird flitting around my head. This is the start of the rite, and though I can't see him because there is no mirror, I know he's sizing up the hair – his canvas – snipping those blades together with practised flourishes. American barbers don't give me this sense of ceremony. No, this is a Trini-style thing that always takes me right back to my childhood. Here, with only the sound to create the image, it takes me back to my first haircuts in San Fernando. Gawd, I used to hate haircuts – I got in trouble with my father on many a Saturday over a trip to the barber. It started with Mr. Thorpe, an old friend of my dad's. They'd been in the same football club as teenagers, and played bridge together as adults. 'Torpers' did the clip-snip thing too, but back then it sounded menacing. Torpers had an extra digit on each hand – useless little joints next to each pinkie. One nub bounced in and out of focus under the scary blades on my right, and on the left, the other hung limp on the hand that held my squirming head in place.

As an adult, I'm still uneasy in the testosterone-laced world of the barbershop, uneasy with discussions of last night's game, and last week's conquest. As Brian's scissors go to work, I find myself thinking, "I could get used to this special, private haircut arrangement."

> The driver struck several people ending in Chelsea, where he plowed into a group of high-school students while zooming the wrong way down a side street. None of the injuries was life threatening.

"Yo, I dig your mini soul-'fro, though," Brian says, early in the rite. And once he's renamed what I'd just been thinking of as my *unemployed-black-man-who-don't-care-look*, making it somehow legit, we agree on a trim – just shaping up the edges, making it a more definite statement. Snip-clip, clip-snip as cut hair falls quiet past my eyes. Before long there's a dark, irregular areola of hair sprinkled on the floor around me, and Brian's snip-clipping air again. In this final flourish, maybe only one or two strands of hair will be cut, maybe none – it's all about style and the perception of precision.

Next, the presentation of the mirror, normally matched with the slow spin of the barber chair to give a three-sixty view for inspection in the wall-mounted mirror. But today we have no swivelling barber chair and only a hand mirror, so I move it wide from left to right, angling my head and cutting my eyes to see the top and sides – settling for just a bit more than one hundred and eighty degrees. I nod my head once for the left angle, again for the top and finally a double nod on the right while saying my line, "Cool, cool." I pass the mirror back to him, he puts it down, undoes the clip at my nape and whips the cloth away from my body with a brisk matador's sweep.

Now, nearing the end of the ceremony, I stand so that he can brush off any wayward hair, my final movement in the *pas de deux*.

"Ah don' have a clothes brush, so don' mind this, okay," he says grinning. Once again we improvise: he grabs a little cloth and flicks it at my chest and shoulders, moving all around me, brushing my white T-shirt clean.

"Oh, gawd man," I say. "Yuh beatin' me like yuh is a obeah man trying to drive out a spirit." This time I have him laughing. Standing directly in front of me, he takes the joke to the next step, placing the palm of his right hand flat against my forehead, pushing my head back hard, and in the same movement his left arm comes around my back to steady me as I rock backwards.

"Be clean my son," he says in the priest's role. "Be cuh-lee-een." We're both laughing like kids now.

> *The driver scattered pedestrians like bowling pins. "He started hitting people and they kept falling and falling," said witness Gerald Cromwell, 31, of the Bronx.*

As we settle down, Brian says, "So, you want a drink – I think we need to offer a libation." Before I answer he's bouncing up the stairs, saying, "Lemme go and raid my brother-in-law's liquor stash."

I follow, trying to catch him. "Nah man, skip that." Not sure of what the living arrangement is here, I don't want to contribute to any domestic trouble. "You know what, I'm no big drinker anyway," I say, at the top of the stairs. It's brighter up here. "Let's just go to that bodega I passed on the way here. Get some beer, you know."

Brian agrees without too much discussion, he throws on a 'hoody', I grab my jacket, and soon we're walking down the street.

"Yuh know yuh ain' going to get no Carib in this 'hood," he says.

"Yeah, I know we not on Church Avenue, but I don't only drink Trini beer…"

He cuts me off with, "*Mira,* I hope you up for a Corona then."

"You wrong for that man," I say. "Just wrong." And as if to prove my point, the corner store is stocked. "See, your ass was way off!" I say. "We got selection."

"True, true," he nods. "A'ight, you in charge, I drinks anything, so you can pick," he says wandering off. I reach for a six-pack of my favourite dark ale, but then I mix in a couple Heinekens to be safe.

I find Brian near the door. When he sees me coming over, he starts to juggle some oranges. He does a throw-catch thing with a couple of them and ends up dropping one back on the heap. The greying man behind the counter is looking at us evilly.

"Okay, I got the beer – something new for you to try," I say. "Let's roll."

"Ahm, okay if I get some of these oranges too?" Brian asks. I shrug agreement, surprised when he fills up a plastic bag with about ten of them.

At the counter, Brian grabs one of the oranges from the bag, tossing it high and then snatching it out of the air. The deli man jumps when Brian telegraphs a fake throw straight towards him. "Think fast," he says, catching it in his left hand as his right comes within a foot of the man's face. Brian laughs and the deli man's face registers fear, quickly followed by a braver annoyance. I pay and we walk outside. Feeling that I've just glimpsed the Brian of Karly's story, I remind myself that up to now he's been real cool. As we walk back up to his sister's house, though the sky is bright, I'm drawn to a striking new formation of metallic-gray clouds coming over the hill.

> *"I don't know what is happening in this city," said account-ant Roselyn George, who suffered a broken ankle in yester-day's crash. "I got knocked down and one of my legs folded under me."*

Back in the basement, Brian puts on a cd, bragging that his boy brought it back from Carnival this year. "It's hot, you'll like it."

I open two bottles of Dos Equis, telling him, "You'll like this … it's cold." He groans at my bad joke, but grabs the beer that I hold out to him. Minutes later we're sitting on a futon mattress against the wall, drinking. He pulls out a pack of Bambu, a nickel bag from his pocket and starts rolling a joint. I'm thinking, "Damn, what the hell am I doing?" I've never hung out with this cat before, he didn't ask me if I smoke, or if I mind if he smokes, and I don't even know what the deal is with him. But I just sit back, secretly glad that he didn't ask. I haven't smoked weed in years, and right now I just feel like saying yes. If I'm not lying to myself, I know that I'm enjoying being here with him. I don't want to leave. Back when he'd started working at Nappy Image, I'd deliberately gone into the shop on a day when I knew Karly was off, just so I'd have an excuse to sit in Brian's chair. I'd wanted to be close while his grin lit up his face and his loud jokes brightened the whole shop.

By the time he's done rolling, the first two bottles are empty. He hands me the sleek joint, gets up to get two more bottles from near the dresser and adjusts the aluminium lamp so that it's now angled up, casting the light towards the ceiling. There's no more or less light in the room, but the glow is easier now, no longer a sharply defined area on the floor. He sits again, pulls a book of matches out of his pocket, strikes one and holds it out toward me. Again, no questions asked. I put the joint to my lips and puff until it's lit. Then I take a nice drag, and pass it over to Brian.

We sit in the long narrow room, beneath an artificial sky of smoke-clouds and aluminium sun, and the talk comes easy. A haze captures the low ceiling tiles, dancing around the exposed pipes and revelling in the upturned lamplight. I'm on a plane of calm that I haven't known in a long time; and I see that Brian's made the same journey too; and even more, I feel that we needed each other to get here. I pass the joint to him, warm from my lips on one end, glowing fire at the other. His fingers brush against mine. On his dark hands, the tendons and veins form a pattern like exposed roots. Energy transfers along an unseen path between us.

When I release the last herbal mist from my lungs, Brian takes a drag at what is now a roach, looking at me through tiny eyes.

"I want to take your picture," he says, unguarded in this found space. I don't react right away, the question bobbing up and down on the river of my thoughts. "With the oranges. When I saw the oranges I decided that I wanted to take your picture with them." In the silence that follows, he exhales, puts the roach out and looks back towards me, his eyes brushing my neck, my jaw, and my mouth with a soft force, and then resting deep inside my eyes.

"Where's the camera?" I reply.

After hitting George, the car lurched into the intersection and swerved; barely slowing it turned left onto Seventh Ave., mounting the curb and scattering commuters.

Soon, he comes balancing the oranges – piled on a shallow, wooden bowl – in one hand, a professional-looking camera in the other, and a plain white sheet folded over his arm. I remain on the futon, watching the preparation: he drapes the sheet over the seat of the chair, letting it fall in a pool on the floor; he sets the bowl on the seat; he swings the light down to frame the chair again; and then, he peels an orange, a knife orbiting the golden fruit, disrobing it, and leaving bright strands of rich natural fibre that fall on the chair and floor. Slicing the orange, he looks over to me, for the first time since he's started creating this scene. "Want some?" he asks, holding out half.

I take it and sit on the floor with my left arm resting on the chair, bent at the elbow, I lean, my face close to the bowl, half an orange in my right hand. I look up at Brian, about to ask him "What now?" and he just picks the camera up and starts taking pictures. I stare at him for a while, hearing the click of the shutter, the advance of the film, watching him move. But I have the munchies, and I bite into the orange, feeling the flesh give against the pressure of my lips, mashing pulp against the roof of my mouth. Each individual bead gives up its tiny treasure, until sharp-sweet juice flows past my teeth. I slurp and eat – conscious on one level of the camera, yet enjoying being as messy as an unsupervised kid.

When the juice starts running down my chin and spilling unto my hands, I stop to push my shirtsleeves up over my elbows. But before I've picked the next half of the orange up, Brian is kneeling next to me. He rests the camera down on the floor, and his face is close to mine, staring. Holding the stare, he grabs the hem of my shirt, and pulls it over my head.

"I don' want yuh to dirty your clothes." Before I respond, he's standing again, camera back in hand. "A'ight, go ahead." Bare-chested now, I let the juice bead and run where it will, as Brian continues to snap.

Before long, I'm cutting the oranges in quarters and not just drinking the juice, but tearing pulp from pith, absorbed in the act. Brian comes over again. This time he grabs a section of orange, holds it six inches in front of my face, and steadying himself with one hand right next to me, he squeezes with the other hand. Juice falls through the air, hitting my chest, pooling at the centre and trickling down my belly. He waves his hand around, still squeezing, so that juice hits my face and shoulders, collecting in the hollow at my collarbone and forming a liquid necklace at my throat. His eyes follow the movement of his hand, a hand that seems to swallow the orange, tracing some deliberate pattern that only he knows. His fingers, smooth dark peninsulas that end in crowns of perfect pink nail, are wet now, and I want him to touch me. I want to bridge the scant inches between him and me, to follow the trail of his ring finger with my tongue until I reach the centre of his palm.

After the crash, the man pulled his car over to the curb and waited as a traffic cop walked toward him. But then he sped away.

But Brian doesn't touch me. Instead he grabs the camera and starts shooting again. He's talking all the while now: "I had to do this … since you first sat in the chair today … when I reached in to cut your hair, you smelled like chocolate … and I knew then, when I smelled the back of your neck, like chocolate … like I was a pregnant woman, I had a craving, man, a craving … I wanted some chocolate … then I saw the oranges … I saw you covered in juice… I had to see you… and drink man… just drink… smell you, chocolate and orange… tell me it don' feel good, eh … cause damn, it looks so good … you have lil shiny beads of juice on your neck… nice, nice … like plenty, plenty little diamonds, man… on your beautiful skin… and that juice baby, yeah… so good."

At 18th St., the driver turned right as Pablo Vargas walked to work at a nearby bistro. Vargas jumped back but couldn't get out of the way as the car again bounced onto the curb. "I thought the guy had a heart attack and lost control," said Vargas, 36.

Then the camera's down for the third time. Now when he nears me, he doesn't stop all those inches away. His lips are soft on my neck and his fingers trace thick lines of electric current over my arms and chest.

Then, his mouth sticky and hot right next to my ear, he says, "I want you to be naked, man ...naked." And when I close my eyes, and sigh deep, he knows that the answer is yes. While he loads new film into the camera, I drape the sheet in a wide, loose sash over my shoulder and between my legs. I feel cool cotton cloth gather around me, and he matches my thoughts, telling me how good the white looks next to my skin. He snaps slower now and we take our time, changing positions, exploring poses: sitting on the chair with the sheet on my lap, holding the bowl in outstretched arms; standing with the white cloth shirred at my waist, knotted in front and falling to my knees; the sheet wrapped around my back, crossed at my collar and knotted at my nape, the bowl resting between my wide spread legs. I remember playing "fashion show" with my cousin Gail when we were young, excited but afraid that I'd get caught "acting like a little girl". But when the fabric is girding my middle and slung over my shoulder, Brian tells me that I look like an African prince. I feel like a man, like all that is a man, aware of each taut, strong curve of muscle that I wear – raw and real – with the orange's sugar and my salt about me. I'm strong through the lens of his wanting, male through his eyes. Chocolate and orange, muscle and cotton, a camera's lens and Brian's vision, fit together like sections of an orange, making me feel whole and natural now.

★

Later, I walk to the train station with a newfound posture that lifts my step and props me as I surf the urban waves of the subway. I fight an uneasiness that's vague and wispy in the grey moments before sleep, but becomes so specific, as I rise, that I can almost smell it. Brian calls later that day. "Just wanted to let you know I had a great time yesterday Chocolate Man... Can't wait to see you again... I have a great idea for us... Just wait, gonna make you shine, baby." I don't know Brian well enough to plot his next step and I wonder if I'll spend the next days and weeks avoiding strange calls or enjoying the vision of an eccentric artist. I'm worried, but thinking all the while of accessories for our next encounter – silk and mangoes, raffia and honey, body paint and flowers.

Days later, in this web of afterglow and anxiety and desire, I'm stopped in my tracks as I walk past a newsstand. Brian's face, black and white, beneath a tabloid headline: **SWIPE-AND-RUN RAM-PAGE.**

> *After a jewelry heist yesterday, the thief sparked mayhem on Manhattan streets, plowing a stolen car into crowds in a ride of terror. Almost $200,000 worth of jewelry was stolen from the Van Cleef & Arpels store on Fifth Avenue early yesterday after someone smashed a small front window, grabbed the jewelry and fled, the police said. "No one made any penetration into the store," said a spokeswoman for the jewelry store. She declined to say what was stolen, but police identified the items as a $98,000 necklace, a $72,000 bracelet and a $25,000 ring. The theft at the toney jeweler was captured on videotape, and the items were found later in the green Buick Regal driven by a hit-and-run driver who was cornered by cops in Chelsea.*

GEOFFREY PHILP

MY BROTHER'S KEEPER

When Papa dead, I cry till I almost vomit. I never know I would miss him that much because I used to never see him plenty, even when him was alive. I used to see him during Christmas when him would come back from Belle Glade in Florida. I can't even remember him face. I remember that him was a tall, bowlegged man who used to make some chaka-chaka sound when him eat. So when Ma tell me that Papa dead in a car accident in Miami with some woman, and that me have a little brother name David, I couldn't believe it. But when Ma tell me that the boy was going live with me and share my bed. I know I was going hate the boy even before I meet him.

I don't like hating people, but when him step in through the door with him new bag, new shoes, new shirt, and new pants, and me sit down there in the living room, barefoot and tear-up, tear-up, I hate him even more. Worse, him was wearing the watch that Papa did promise to give me the last time him leave at Christmas.

Papa did say as soon as him get back to America, him would send the watch to me in the mail. Him say him would wrap it up tight tight so them thiefing people at the post office wouldn't take it out and keep it for themself.

Now it wasn't a fancy watch with gold or anything like that. It was just a regular Timex, but it had a calculator and timer and a whole heap a thing me would never use. But nobody else on the block, not even Richard Chin Sang, who used to get me in trouble with Ma, and who used to think that him was better than everybody else, including me, had one. I ask the boy for the watch, and explain to him that Papa did promise the watch to me, and that him should just hand it over there and then. You know what that little idiot have the nerve to say? **No.** I did feel like to just box

354 PEEPAL TREE . CONTEMPORARY CARIBBEAN SHORT STORIES

him over him head, and take it way, but I never want to get into
any more trouble with Ma, so I just let it be. It was then I decide,
fly high, fly low, I was going to get that watch.

So the boy start to unpack and everybody start to make a fuss
over him like him was Marcus Garvey son. I couldn't believe the
fuss that them was making over that little red 'kin boy. It was like
Ma never realise that the only way that him could be my brother
was that Papa was sleeping with another woman, probably the
woman who him dead with. And from the look of that boy, it was
probably a white woman. I guess it never sink in, for if anybody did
do that to me, orphan or no orphan, him would be out in the street.

But that is Ma problem and where me an she different. She
always take up these hardluck stories and trying to save people and
change the world. That is why her brother, Uncle George, living
with us. Him used to own a bar down in Papine till him drink off
all the profit. Now, everyday him getting drunk. So when the boy
take out a present for him and it was a bottle of Johnny Walker
from the States that him aunt, who couldn't take care of him any
more, send with him, eye water start to run down the man face
and him say, "This is a good boy, Doreen. A good boy. David, I
want you to stay out of trouble and don't follow that little
hooligan over there. I love you boy. I love you."

Uncle George would love anybody who give him a drink. That
old rumhead fool will say anything for a Appleton and when thing
get bad, bay rum. But the boy take him serious and start to hug the
old rum head. And Uncle George hugging him back and bawling.
Everybody forget that is me always have to fetch Uncle George,
sometime in the worse bar in Kingston, clean him up, and take
him home.

Then the boy start to take out all the trophy him win in school
in Miami. Basketball trophy, baseball trophy, football trophy, and
Uncle George, who start the bottle already, rubbing the boy head
and saying, "Doreen, this boy is a athlete!" And Ma put all the
trophy on the dresser. My dresser. Then Ma begin to cry and say
how strong him was and that Papa was strong too. She hug the boy
and leave me in the room with the trophy. I feel like break every
single trophy on the dresser, but I know if I did ever do that it

wouldn't be Ma who would beat me, it would be Uncle George and him beat hard. Since the last time him beat me, I never want him to beat me again. Especially when him drunk, which is all of the time. Ma you can fool with a little scream, but with Uncle George you could bawl and scream as loud as you want – *"Lord, Lord, Lord God! Stop! I not going do it again. I not going do it again. I promise. I promise. I promise you. I promise you I won't do it again. I going dead now, I going dead. Lord, Lord, Lord God, Lord God!"* – and him wasn't going stop until him was done. And then dog eat you supper.

So I just look at the trophy them and pass aside. All them trophy. Me never get a trophy in my life for nothing. The one thing that me know me can do good is bird shooting, and you don't get trophy for bird shooting. Plus Ma make me stop because one time I kill a mockingbird. Now I was only trying to help because every morning, before she had to go to school, she would wake up and say how this mockingbird was waking her up at five o'clock in the morning and that she couldn't get a good night sleep. So I wake up early one morning and as the bird open him mouth, baps, him dead. So I walk into the kitchen big and broad with the dead bird, but Ma start to cry and give me this long speech how I was wicked to shoot a bird during mating season and that God was going to punish me and I was going to hell. She made me feel so bad. But that is just how Ma is, you can never understand her.

Even my father could never understand her and that is why him leave the last time. I know she did really love him, but I know that they was married because of me. How I know is one time Papa and Ma get into a big fight and Papa lick Ma.

Well, she phone Uncle George and him come to the house with him gun. Them have a few words and Papa say something and then Uncle George say something.

Then Papa say him would never marry Ma if it wasn't for me. And then Uncle George slam the door and I think him pull the gun. That is how I find out that I was a bastard.

Anyway, *that* bastard was back here in my room, and Ma was running her hand through him hair and saying how straight it was and how him was so light skin. Uncle George was patting him on the shoulder and looking at him teeth.

Uncle George don't have a teeth in him head. Him lose all of them by fighting and the rest of them rotten out and him have to pull them. But this boy did have all him teeth, and some with gold fillings too. That impress Uncle George. Me, I lose two in a fight, but I never been to a dentist. I don't think I ever going to one.

Ma hug him again and say she was going to fix dinner and if him did like chicken. Him say yes and Ma just wrap him up in her bosom and give him that smile that you couldn't help but smile. But I never smile. I just show him where him could put the rest of him things. Uncle George say I was jealous, but what did that old rumhead know?

One thing I can say about the boy though, him was hard to fool. Him wasn't like me cousin, Owen, from the country who me did lock in the closet. I tell Owen it was a elevator and him believe me. As him step inside, I just lock the door and keep him in there for about a hour until Uncle George hear the knocking and run come inside the room. I let out Owen right away. When I see Uncle George, I tell him we was just playing, and I guess him never feel like beat me that day, and him believe me. But this one you couldn't fool. I try, but it never work. Him was smart. Him was dangerous.

So I leave him in the room and run down the street to meet my friend over by the park. As I jump over the fence, I hear these footstep behind me. I chase the boy back to the yard. I tell him that him couldn't come because him was wearing him new shoes. Him say the shoes wasn't new, them was six months old. Real American. I tell him that him couldn't come and play and wear the watch, for it could break. Him say it was shock proof. I tell him that him would have ask Ma first before him leave, and it was then him have the gall to call my mother, my own mother, "Ma," to my face. I tell him there and then that she was my mother. She wasn't him mother. Him did have a mother of him own, and that whoever she was and wherever she was, him should go find her. I tell him if him ever call her Ma in front of me again, I don't care what Uncle George would do to me, I was going to beat the shit out of him.

Him walk off and start to bawl, but I never care, for him wouldn't be trailing me all around the place, so that all my friend would laugh after me.

When I get back home that night though, it was bangarang. Ma start to give me a long speech about how I must think about my little brother feelings and after what I learned in Sabbath school about Cain and Abel. She go on for about a hour about the Sabbath school business. Sabbath school. I only used to go there to please her because she always talking about how she going to dead and how she want me to grow up to be a good man. Good man, good woman. Them things dead from the start. She is a good woman and look where it get her. A little elementary schoolteacher in Back O' Wall or whatever they call it now. Good woman. The only thing that worth is a whole heap a pain and a little boy following you around the place and asking, "What's this?" and "Why do they call it that?" while all you friend laughing after you. Which is what I have to put up with because Ma say so. What nearly kill me, though, is that she say him could call her Ma if he wanted to. She say it. I hear it from her own mouth. But I take one look at him and him never do it in front of me.

So the next day me and him was walking down the street and him start telling me story about how Papa take him to Disney World, how Papa this and how Papa that, and I never want to hear it. And then him tell me how Papa dead and how him cry and cry, and him glad that I was him brother. And that was why him want to keep the watch because it remind him of Papa. It was then I know how much I hate him, for nobody could love Papa like me.

When we get to the park, I tell him to keep him mouth shut. I never want my friend to find out that him was me brother. But as we step through the gate, Richard Chin Sang say, "Who that with you, Umpire?" Umpire is my nickname, but that is another whole long story. Before Richard could finish the question, the little idiot shout out, "I'm his brother."

Well, everybody start to laugh because him never look anything like anybody in my family and Richard say him must be a *jacket*. Richard did want to change my name from Umpire to 'Three Piece Suit and Thing'. 'And Thing' would be David.

But Richard wouldn't have him way. Me and him did fall out from the time him try to tell a lie on me and it backfire. Richard used to thief for nothing. One day me and him was in the staff room at school and him thief ten dollars from a teacher purse. Them find out that it was only me and him who was in the room that morning, so it must be one of us. Richard say him don't need the money for him bring at least thirty dollar to school every week. And him pull out the thirty dollar.

So everybody say it must be me. I nearly end up with a caning because everybody know I used to get into a whole heap of fight and they say I was a troublemaker. Now I couldn't get a caning, for if you get a caning they call your house. Then I have to go home to face Uncle George and get another whipping. So I take everybody to the other end of the school where I know Richard used to hide all the things him used to steal. When they open the locker, comb, toothbrush, chewing gum, even somebody slide rule fall out. He never need them, but him thief them. So they suspend him from school, and when him get home, him father beat him so hard him never come out for three week. It was from then me and him never get along. So the truth come out, but it never set me free. Even my friend Peter from up the road did try to call me, 'Three Piece Suit' because him did know I couldn't get into any more fight. But I tell him if he ever called me that, I would tell Laura Spenser father what them was doing at the Christmas fair behind the Ferris wheel. I had to threaten all of them like this, for I know everything about all of them, but they don't know a thing about me. I always make sure people owe me, not me owe them or them have anything on me. Just because I can't fight anymore, don't mean that anybody can take steps with me. I keep everything to myself, but this little idiot was going to mash up everything. I never like that.

But him did have some use. In time we teach him how to play cricket and football. Him call it soccer. Teaching him to play cricket was a joke. The boy lick four runs, drop the bat and start to run like him hear news. We just tell him to pick up the bat, and tell him that it wasn't baseball him was playing. We teach him how to hold the bat, to dip and score runs. It did take time, but him learn.

But the best thing was all them trophy that him did get from basketball. Him never play football good, so we put him in the goal. Papa, now that was a goalkeeper. From the ball land in him hand, that done. Him catch it. From that day on, Richard Chin Sang and him friend never score a goal on we. We beat them team ten games straight. That never happen before. Every Saturday them used to just win all the games and send we home with a bus ass. But when we start to win, them did want stop play with we, but them soon realise that if them did really want a good game of football, even though them never like we, them would have to play against we. Now, don't get me wrong, is not that I did start to like the boy, but we was winning, and that make a difference.

So when we start win all the game, everybody else start to like him. Sometime I wish them did call we 'Three Piece Suit and Thing'. But all of them forget. People have short memory, especially when them is your friend. Peter even wanted to call David, 'Little Umps' but I put an end to that too. I wasn't sharing my name with him.

But everything broke loose one evening after a football game. I had to go help Uncle George get home. Him was drunk again. And it was a bar way down in Hermitage. So I had to get him and clean him up. When I finally find him, it was about seven o' clock and by the time we get home it was eight-thirty. Just as I finish clean him up and put him in the bed, Peter little sister run inside the house and tell me that David in a fight with Richard. I just take me time, for I know David couldn't take on Richard and win. Him was finally going get the bus ass that him should get from the first day him step inside my house.

By the time I get to the park, Richard was holding the boy like a piece of stick and licking the boy in him face. Well, sooner or later the boy would have to learn, and I wasn't going to get into any fight for him. If I was going to get in a fight, it would be my fight. And whoever I fight would have to be worth the beating I would get when I go home. This boy wasn't worth it.

When Richard see me, him stop and pretend like nothing was going on. But when him see that I wasn't going help the boy, him lick the boy so hard I feel it down to me shoes. Is then I find out what the fighting was about. Richard hold him and say, "See, I tell you, him afraid of me. Him not going fight for you. Him don't even like you."

"I still say," David was shouting, "he can beat you up any day."

The little idiot. Him was fighting to defend me name. Some people never learn. You shouldn't say things, even if they true, if you can't back them up with your fist. Richard throw him down on the ground and kick him in him side. Now that wasn't right. Beating up somebody is one thing, but when you kick them on the ground is another. But it wasn't my fight.

Then Richard tear off the watch off David hand and was going crush the face with the heel of him shoes, and David bawl out, "I'll give you the watch, Paul. But don't let him break Papa's watch."

And as Richard foot come down, the boy dive underneath it and take the heel in him chest. Him really did love Papa.

Well, before Richard know what happen, I sucker punch that Chinee boy so hard, him was seeing Chop Suey. Him stagger for about two yard and then I lick him cross him face with my fist. Him get a good blow to my face and bloodup me nose. But I kick him in him seed and him fall down and then start to run to him yard, bawling like a dog and saying him was going call me house and tell them what I do to him.

Is then I know I dead. Uncle George was going beat me this time. I was dead. I couldn't hide my nose with the blood; it was all over my shirt. Even if I could bribe David not to tell – although I never know with what, I never have anything on him – Richard was going to tell him father. Then him father would call my mother and embarrass her with, "What kind of wild animal you have there in your house that you calling your son? If you see what he do to my son and bla, bla, bla, bla, bla." I might as well run away from home.

I pick him up off the ground and clean him up. I help him wash him face with the hose near the badminton court. It was the first time I see him face. Him look at me and say, "I hope Ma doesn't beat you too hard when we get home,"

I almost forgive him for calling her Ma that time.

"Here, take this," him say and try to give me the watch. I

couldn't take it. The boy earn it. I push him hand away and tell him to keep it. As we was walking home though, I ask him if I could borrow the watch every now and then. Maybe I could borrow it for the Christmas fair, if I was still alive. Him say yes and as we turn the corner, I look on the verandah and I see Uncle George, drunk and holding onto one of the column with one hand and the belt in the other. I know I was dead.

I couldn't run away, I never have anywhere else to go. And if I run away, I would have to come back, and the beating would still be waiting on me. I would probably get it worse then. I couldn't do a thing. I could only hope that him was too drunk to stand up and that him would fall asleep or throw up before him finish. But what if him remember that him never finish tonight and start on me tomorrow morning?

David see the look on me face, and run straight up to the verandah. Him start to cry and say how if it wasn't for me how them was going to mash up Papa watch. And him tell some lie about what them was calling Ma, all kind of bad word me never know the boy know. Then him say that Richard and him friend was running joke about Uncle George, that him is a rum head and how me rescue him from Richard and three of him friend. Three of him friend! The boy was good. It did sound so real. Me was there and even me did start believe it. The boy put on one show. Uncle George drop the belt, hug me and say, "For the first time, you do good, boy. You do good." Ma kiss me, rub me head, then take him inside. And all the while him smiling and winking with me. I couldn't believe it. It end up that me owe him. The little idiot save me.

VELMA POLLARD

RUTHLESS AT NOON

If you were walking along the main road you would hear it. But you wouldn't be able to see who was singing

> We plough the fields and scatter
> The good seed on the land
> But it is fed and watered
> By God's almighty hand
>
> All good things around us
> are sent...

And you would hear the deep melodious bass stop and you wouldn't know why.

But if you were hiding your slight eight-year-old body behind the cabbage palm tree and looking down beyond the trench to the neat yam hills so recently weeded you would see a young woman, barefooted, wearing a faded shirtwaister dress, stretch her hand out to offer a package – a clean calico cloth tied over two enamel plates one on top of the other – through a break in the fence to the singer, Deacon, choir master, foundation of the church, upstanding citizen. You would see him take the proffered package with his left hand and with the other stronger right, pull the young woman over. You would notice him pay scant attention to the package after he has rested it on the pile of grass he had so recently weeded from among the yam hills.

You would see Deacon take a quick look around and apparently see nobody. Indeed why would he see anybody, least of all you, on top of the hill behind the cabbage palm trunk. He quickly unbuttons his fly with one hand. (Is he about to urinate in front of her?) You watch the young woman turn as if to run but the strong right hand pulls her and shoves her on to the ground, the bare ground, and begins to struggle with her underwear. She is kicking and his left hand is over her mouth. You feel a scream begin in your throat, then you think better of it. From where you are you can see that the hem of her dress is soon almost up to her neck. Then you don't see her any more only Deacon going up and down as if he is pumping the church organ with his whole body. Is he never going to stop, you wonder.

Beyond them is a pile of cassava sticks waiting to be planted. You could imagine leaves barely sprouting from some of the joints. Slight green on the brown, almost maroon.

Eventually Deacon does stop, gets up and strips pieces from a dry banana leaf, wipes the legs of the young woman who is standing now and not trying to run away any more but keeps her head down. She is gazing at the cassava pile. She pulls some more banana leaves and wipes herself again, roughly. She is sure to scrape her skin. He wipes himself, buttons his pants and sits down to undo the cloth wrapping the plates and to put the top plate on the ground beside him.

The young woman leaves him and walks along the pass. You recognize Missis, the maid in Deacon's house.

Deacon drinks water from a long bamboo joint and starts to work again. And to sing:

All good things around us
Are sent from heaven above
Then thank the Lord, oh thank the Lord
For aaaaahl his love

One rainy Friday when few children are in school and the teachers are having a meeting and middle division is allowed to do what it wants, Biddy (who they used to call, ambiguously you thought years later, Big Puss), the biggest and oldest girl in the class, who protected you from aggressors in exchange for your doing her sums under the desk when teacher wasn't looking, produces pencil and a dirty piece of paper and says she wants to draw something to show you. You don't know, she says, and you better get to know, how people get children. The disconnected lines soon become a man on top of a woman. You only recognize the woman because of her hair. But you are sure of the man because she draws his you-know-what on the outside of his pants almost as if it is falling off the picture. Then she writes in a terrible scrawl "Soon put it in" and shows you and giggles.

The next cut. On another piece of paper the woman alone. Same woman. Same hair style. But with a very big belly. Scrawl again "Six monts afta".

Final cut the woman with a baby. One breast is hanging loose and the baby is sucking it. "Nine monts afta".

For a split second you contemplate correcting the spelling but think better of it. You spend most of the time looking at the first cut and ask her if you can keep it. NOO she insists and smiles in a conspiratorial fashion. Her tongue squeezes itself through the space where she is missing a tooth. You always find it funny when she does that.

"You might go get me in trouble."

Your mind goes to Deacon but you don't say a thing.

Myra is deacon's daughter and she is your friend. Sometimes. Something had told you that you shouldn't let her know what you saw although you used to share most of your secrets with her.

One day Myra tells you that Missis not working with her family any more. Say her mother cuss her off and throw her things out of the room. You ask why. Myra say nobody tell her anything but her mother call all kind of words like "slack" and "lie" and "slut" and Myra gone with her belly swell up big big.

The last thing she do was chop up a set of cassava stick that was in the kitchen. They was waiting for Deacon to plant.

Years after you thought about it and wondered how many lunch times, after that time that you saw, did Deacon do it to Missis? What could she have done if she didn't like it? Could she have told the wife of the Deacon of the church that she couldn't take the holy man's lunch to the field because she was afraid of what he would do? Could she have simply refused to go and lose her job because she was disobedient? What if she had grown later to like what he did and didn't mind going. Does it really matter which was the case?

She must have told her employer eventually when there could be no further hiding the belly. So she became either a slut, for having tempted him, or a liar for having suggested he would do such a thing or both, in some convoluted sort of way.

And how would Missis feel towards the child she would bring? The child who caused her to lose her job; the child who, ironically, would be dependent on her for the very things only a job can buy?

But at the time all you did was wonder what would happen to Missis and why she chop up the cassava stick.

JENNIFER RAHIM

STRANGER

"Yvonne!" Auntie Jemma shouted.

Next thing I knew, she had grabbed hold of my arms and that was how we both did a jump and wave as my mother ascended the narrow steps to the plane. She struggled with the two bags that were stuffed to capacity with things for Uncle Boysie, things that Grandma swore he must have so he would not forget where he was born. There was her coconut sweet-bread and cassava pone that people from all over Trinidad placed orders for; a biscuit tin packed with sugar cakes and fat tulums; the pepper-sauce that had stood on the veranda where it could catch the sunlight for one whole month; the bottle of mango kuchela and dhalpourie skins ordered special from Miss Ruby.

Grandma and Mr. Roger had nothing to do with all the commotion as people flocked to the railings of the waving gallery to see their people for the last time. In fact, Grandma never bothered to move from the bench where she had taken up residence from early o'clock. The huge handbag in which she stored everything under the sun sat like a weapon on her lap. Mr. Roger, who was Auntie Jemma's newest *friend*, stood apart from the crowd, stroking his chin and generally behaving like a stranger to all that was happening; but I had a feeling that behind the Miami Vice darkers, his eyes were fixed on me and Auntie Jemma. We were squashed among the other wavers trying to get a last glimpse of Mammy, who looked to me like a fuzzy orange ball that disappeared into the black hole at the top of the stairs.

There was even more waving and shouting of good-byes when the plane started screaming down the runway, the big stub-nose pointed forward, and the huge wings spread wide like when mongoose frightened Grandma's layers. To me, it was all foolishness – people dressed up like Sunday evening and bunched up in circles talking and looking like something important was about to happen to them. I wondered how getting left behind could be such a fête.

Auntie Jemma tried her best to assure me that everything was going to be fine.

"Before you know it, sweets, you will be a big-time Yankee living up in New York, playing in snow, riding the subway and shopping in K-Mart and Target. Just wait!"

She only stopped her chattering to adjust her spandex top that kept riding up above the waistline of her jeans, the thousand and one bracelets on her wrists quarrelling with each other as she fussed with her clothes.

"Think about it, sweets, all the fun you will have when you living up there with your mother in NEW YORK CITY where all the action is. Coney Island, Broadway and the movies! McDonald's! Labour Day jam on the Parkway!"

Right away her waist started wiggling and her shoulders pumping like she was really chipping down the road behind a sweet steelband on Carnival Tuesday.

Nothing she said could console me. My mother was gone. Grandma had to hug me close to her side all the way back to the car park. Even Mr. Roger felt sorry for me; he asked if I wanted to stop by KFC, although he was running late for some appointment that I guessed didn't include Auntie Jemma, because she let go one wicked suck-teeth at his offer. That meant he was to take us straight home.

I must have fallen into a deep sleep. I never knew when Mr. Roger turned his car into McInroy Trace and started the slow, zig-zag climb up the hill, careful to avoid every pothole in his way. Outside was pitch-black as not one streetlight was working. Mr. Roger tried to make a joke that McInroy people can't see the light because they voted for the wrong party. Nobody paid him any notice. I looked out at the darkness thinking that this was going to be my everyday home until my mother saved up enough American dollars to send for me. Grandma said that would happen in no time because my mother was a born workhorse set on getting what she wanted. At that Auntie Jemma let go a heavy sigh that meant *BORING* and shifted in her seat. But even tomorrow seemed a long time away and the invisible hand that was squeezing my heart wouldn't let go. I was only happy that I didn't have to go to school because it was the beginning of the long August holidays.

Everything about him was strange. That was how he first struck me the morning he turned up in Grandma's yard. It was the end of the second week after my mother had left for New York. I was on the veranda dressed in her favourite blue duster-coat, busy untangling rows of the too-tight plaits that Auntie Jemma had arranged the day before. There was no one to disturb me. From the gallery I could see the steady flame of the candle in the middle of the kitchen table. Grandma was saying her prayers. Auntie Jemma was sound asleep. She had stayed out late with her other *friend*, Mr. Wayne. That meant she wasn't going to show her face before eleven o'clock. Grandma was sure to be mad vex because she could not understand how a body could be sleeping when the sun was high in the sky and things were waiting to get done.

The stranger announced himself with a round of noisy bang-ing on the rusty galvanize sheets that made up the front gate. Brownie and Rambo immediately began their watchdog racket, yelping and barking as they paraded up and down the front of the house. At first, I could not see who was approaching because the pathway up was steep and lined on both sides with all kinds of trees, including the sprawling *bois canoe* that Grandma refused to cut.

I continued undoing my plaits as I waited to see who the visitor might be. The business of combing my hair had turned out to be a big mêlée as Grandma would say. No one could comb it the way I liked now that my mother was gone. Grandma's plaits were too loose and reminded me of her swollen dough waiting to be put into the hot oven. Auntie Jemma insisted on making me look fit for a circus with her fancy styles and tight cane-row creations.

"You don't expect to go around in two plaits all the time so, child. A woman can't afford to get stale. You have to keep them surprised."

The *them,* I knew, were men like Mr. Roger and Mr. Wayne who came to visit with Auntie Jemma on Grandma's veranda. On Sundays, they took her for long drives in their amazingly clean cars, or to the sea when the weather was good. Last Sunday, Mr. Roger even invited me to go for a dip with them to cheer me up, but Grandma said I had no place in big people business.

I missed my mother.

The dogs finally abandoned their stations and ran in search of the visitor. It was not long after that I saw the owner of the voice. He was the poorest looking whiteman I had ever seen. The shirt-jack he wore was a dingy shade of cream, and his khaki pants were splattered with what looked like stains from coconut milk. The bottoms were rolled up to the knees to expose a very flat pair of rubber slippers on very dirty feet. When he got closer, I saw that a big safety pin held one of the rubber straps in place.

By this time, the barking had changed to an excited whining, and Rambo, who was the younger of the two, rushed forward and started prancing around the man's legs. He was obviously no stranger. Brownie didn't bother to join in the welcome. Once it was clear that the visitor was no threat, he slipped away to his favourite resting spot under the back steps.

The man spoke kindly to Rambo as he inched forward.

"So you are glad to see me, my boy. It has been a long time. Take it easy, my friend. We can't risk an accident."

He spoke better English than the Principal, Mr. Fraser, who went on during morning assembly like he was giving a speech on TV, boring us all to death. Rambo, like a crazy fool, made leap after leap trying to lick the man's hands, which he kept lifted to shoulder level in an attempt to keep them and the dirty-looking market bag out of reach. In the end, Rambo got fed-up with the game and disappeared to somewhere in the backyard.

The man never saw me sitting on the veranda, or so it seemed, because he simply made himself comfortable on the bottom of the steps, fished out his glasses and a newspaper that didn't appear at all new. He began reading in the strangest way. His left hand held the paper at arm's length from his face, while his right hand clasped the frame of his glasses as though they could not stay in place without his help.

I was busy watching him as he read when it appeared, slithering over his left leg. The creature, a brown whip-like thing, eased itself up from somewhere between his legs and paused, its head extended in midair as if trying to decide in which direction to go. Then, to my alarm, it began to make its way up the left side of his back. That was it.

"Snake on you, mister!" I shouted.

The man swung around so violently that the thick lens he was holding in place dislodged and went clattering down the steps and into the grass.

We both froze. He stared at me draped in my mother's duster-coat, my disarrayed hair striking the air. My eyes were locked on the creature that was now nestled at his neck. An eternity passed before his hand reached up and gently removed the snake, which promptly coiled around his wrist.

"Oh, you mean Pilate? He's my guest, my friend," he said and proceeded to stroke the flat head with his index finger.

"He's harmless, really. Here, see for yourself. He loves to be petted. Go on, he wouldn't bite."

He extended his arm, inviting me to touch. The pair of glasses that had lost its right lens was still on his face and the watery, grey-blue left eye seemed so large behind the remaining lens, I felt I would be swallowed if I moved one step closer.

"Come on, he's harmless," he coaxed.

Just then, the sound of Grandma's voice asking who was in her yard so early came as my salvation. The stranger-man quickly tucked Pilate into his pants pocket and placed his finger on his lips, indicating that the snake was our secret. When Grandma appeared on the veranda, saw my condition and the man she called Mr. Espinoza sitting at the bottom of the steps, she immediately shooed me inside with the order to put some clothes on my body.

Mr. Espinoza was long gone when I came out again, but I was in time to help Grandma with her morning rounds of scattering corn for the chickens, and checking the break-down coop and special hiding places, like under the house, for eggs. After that we cut water-grass that grew behind the old latrine and fed the big rabbit called

Crazy-Horse that Grandma was always promising to stew because he was so disagreeable and ungrateful. The last stop was the mother goose who we found sitting at attention on her eggs.

Grandma stroked her long neck and said comfortingly, "Not long again, madam. Not long."

Auntie Jemma was stationed at the kitchen table sipping from a mug of steaming coffee when we returned to the house. Between sips, she was busy filing her nails. I sat next to her partly to watch and partly to take in the smell of ground coffee that I loved, but was not the right age to drink.

"You up early," Grandma said.

"Roger coming for me just now. His office having a fête-match down on the Base," she offered in a kind of absent-minded way.

Mr. Roger was a technician with the telephone company. It was he who had pulled a few strings to get Grandma's application for a phone fixed-up in two-twos. Though she was grateful, Grandma never really took to Mr. Roger. So when Auntie Jemma mentioned the fête-match, she grunted and started to sing *Just a closer walk with Thee* as she measured out flour for the golden fried bakes that she always made on Saturday morning.

Auntie Jemma never bothered with Grandma. She even painted my little finger with her red nail-polish called *Flamingo* and winked at me mischievously.

Bakes were fussing in hot oil when a car's horn sounded from down the hill. I ran to the gallery to see who it was. The gate scraped open and from under the house the dogs turned on their racket, but never bothered to come out. Mr. Roger strolled up the path.

"Is for Auntie," I shouted back to the kitchen.

I could hear the mad scramble for the bedroom.

Mr. Roger was dressed all in white, except for his brown leather shoes that Auntie Jemma called *loafers*. She knew because she had picked them out for him. Sweet smelling cologne wafted up to the veranda when he got to the base of the stairs looking like one of those smooth, clean men Auntie Jemma called *sexy* on *The Young and the Restless*. He propped up his sunglasses on his forehead and sank his hands into his pockets.

"So how the girl, this morning?"

I didn't answer.

"What happen? You vex with me? Still crying for your Mammy?"

Again I wasn't going to answer. I could tell he wasn't really interested in talking to me. He was busy looking up at the house to see if Auntie Jemma was coming, but it was Grandma who emerged asking, "Is who in my yard, child?" pretending she didn't know.

Mr. Roger suddenly became very cheerful. He adjusted his stance to face her square on in a show of confidence, his feet planted widely apart. Grandma looked down at him hard, as if waiting for him to ready himself for whatever she might ask. Mr. Roger was now swaying from side to side and smiling broadly.

"Morning, Moms. Everything good?"

"After God I good," Grandma answered. Her frame filled the little entrance to the veranda.

"And how you do?"

"Good, good. Everything good. No complaints. I there with them."

"And how work going?"

"Good."

"And the family? How the . . ."

Grandma was never allowed to finish her question because Auntie Jemma swooped down from nowhere and hustled Mr. Roger down the path.

"We gone!" she sang over her shoulder. "I coming back late so don't put the lock on the gate."

They left the yard in a flash.

Grandma gave one of her disapproving *who can't hear will feel* grunts and disappeared into the house complaining that she was tired running her blood to water over Auntie Jemma's stupidness.

About a week later, the same week of heavy rains and the miracle the mother goose performed by hatching six very yellow ducklings, my mother's first letter arrived. Grandma huddled over the kitchen table to read it. She read aloud and very carefully, as though she didn't want to miss a word. My mother wrote that she was doing fine up in Brooklyn and was holding on by Uncle Boysie until she could find some steady work. She also said that his Yankee wife was an okay lady. The only thing was that she smoked cigarettes like a chimney; but she was getting to learn the place and to ride the trains, which she didn't like because the subway smelt frowsy and people looked straight through you.

After the last part that said Grandma should give me a big hug and that there was a special surprise for me in the barrel she was sending down, Grandma folded the letter and put it between the pages of her Bible.

I didn't get the hug my mother sent, but Grandma prepared her special hot chocolate with nutmeg grated on top and talked in a hushed voice about the sacrifice my mother was making for me by trying to get through in America.

Mr. Espinoza turned up again the following week. He came up to the steps and stationed himself there. This time the man was nursing a bad cold. From my spot on the veranda where I was again undoing Auntie Jemma's handiwork, I looked down at his mud-stained feet, clad in the thin rubber slippers. It had rained heavily all week.

"Is because you not wearing the right shoes, Mr."

I had startled him again. Maybe this was because of my unruly hair, plus the fact that he didn't have on his glasses, which he hastily fished from his shirt pocket and settled on his face.

"You shouldn't wear slippers in the rain. Granny say so."

He examined his feet.

"Your grandmother is a very wise woman," he said in a serious tone. "Is she at home?"

"She gone out, but she coming back just now."

"Well, in that case, I shall wait right here until Madam Williams returns."

He began rummaging in his bag again and brought out a copybook and a pencil. After adjusting his glasses and opening the book to a clean page, he began to write very slowly, looking up every now and again to stare into the distance and to suck the tip of his pencil. I watched him labouring in this way with the book balanced on his knees.

"What you doing, Mr.?"

"I'm writing down my thoughts," he answered, without lifting his head.

"Why?"

He stopped writing and turned around to face me apparently surprised that I should ask such a question.

"Well, young miss, one's thoughts are one's life. The only difference between man and the beasts is that he can think. It is all we have – the thoughts that tell us who we are and where we have been. That is why I write – to know who I am in this world."

It all sounded very solemn and important. I was not at all clear what he meant. Mr. Espinoza continued his writing.

"What you writing now?"

"I am writing about my encounter with the Medusa."

His eyes were large watery wells behind the thick lenses.

"The what . . . dusa?"

"Me-du-sa," he said, deliberately prolonging all the syllables. "I suppose you never heard of her."

I shook my head.

"Well, the Medusa is a gorgon, meaning that her hair is a nest of poisonous, snapping vipers or, if you prefer, snakes. Her cold stare can turn men into solid stone."

I looked at him in amazement. It was the weirdest story I had ever heard – a woman with snakes in her hair. I reached for my own untangled plaits and wondered where Mr. Espinoza had gotten that story.

"Why would the 'dusa lady want to turn men into stone?"

Before he could answer, the gate grated open. Brownie and Rambo yelped excitedly and hightailed it down the hill. It could only be Grandma. The man quickly replaced the copybook.

Grandma returned with a cardboard box that made the sweetest commotion. That was why Mr. Espinoza was there that morning. He was going to build a new coop to house the twelve baby chicks Grandma had bought from the market.

"Just now," she said, "we going to have eggs to sell."

Mr. Espinoza set about his task with great ceremony. Grandma told me to stay out of his way, so I sat on the back steps and watched. He measured everything carefully, once then twice. He walked around the spot Grandma had picked out next to the plum tree. It was not too far from the house so she could throw her eye on the coop from time to time. Various things were written down on a piece of paper he carried in his shirt pocket.

Next, he examined the roll of chicken wire, counted the nails, extracted and straightened more nails from the pile of wood he had retrieved on Grandma's instructions from under the house. Laths were sorted, the pieces lined up by size, and it seemed by age. Those that were of no use he threw aside.

"What he think, is a palace he building?" Grandma grumbled from the kitchen, then shouted, "Is only a coop, man. Build the thing!"

By lunchtime, I was free to explore the building-site. Mr. Espinoza had settled himself in the shade of the starch mango tree that grew near the abandoned latrine – the reason why, according to Grandma, her mangoes had no match anywhere for their sweetness. He sat propped up against the trunk and was busy writing in his copybook, in between taking quick bites on something wrapped in a brown paper bag.

The coop was a very neat wooden frame that was tall enough for me to walk right through the doorway without bending, and long enough inside for me to make five whole giant steps with a little extra. Grandma wanted a proper coop with laying boxes hung on the walls and feed trays on the ground. She had had enough of the little break-down thing that Pappy had constructed *since Adam was a little boy, rest his soul*.

Then Grandma called me inside for my own lunch of split peas soup that had my favourite little dumplings hidden in the thick, steaming liquid. Auntie Jemma was nowhere to be seen, but Grandma still covered down her bowl and put it on the table. She had left early that morning with Mr. Wayne for Port-of-Spain.

When I had cornered and fished out my last dumpling, the front gate made its usual protest and a car tooted its horn twice. Auntie Jemma came in loaded with fussy plastic bags, happily exhausted from her morning in town.

"Wayne, say hello Mammy."

Grandma grunted in response.

I guessed that Auntie Jemma liked Mr. Roger more than Mr. Wayne because she was never in her rain-cloud moods when Mr.

Wayne dropped her home. I wondered if real love was something that let you down, the way Mr. Roger could make Auntie so sad she would listen for the whole of Sunday evening to the radio station that promised to *soothe you with hits from yesteryear* while she filed her nails.

I thought of my mother all the way up in New York, and that invisible hand reached in and grabbed hold of my heart again. A heavy cloud was about to burst when Auntie Jemma waved an airmail envelope before my face.

"Guess what Mr. Johnson put in the box this morning?"

My mother had sent another letter. Grandma immediately dried her hands and came to the table. Auntie Jemma made a big fuss of handing over the letter that caused even Grandma to chuckle and complain in her *I not really vex* voice about her foolishness.

10th August

Dear Mammy,

I hope things going good with you and everybody back home. I still OK though is one whole month gone already and I not working. The good news is that I went Long Island (a real rich people place) to see about a job taking care of a baby girl that just three months old. Poor thing. The mother is a Jamaican woman who hook up with a whiteman that tell me flat he have no problem with blackpeople. Make me wonder why he say so in the first place. Anyway, imagine is fifteen years since that woman last see home – fifteen years! She want to upgrade herself so she starting school in September. That is why she looking for a live-in helper. People up here don't make joke with education. I hope Lydia not forgetting her books even though school on holidays. All in all, the lady seem alright, only a little prim. I have to wait and see if I get through. But I put that in God hand.

Boysie wife take me down 14th street last Thursday. That is her day off. Mammy, I see all kind of things I want to buy and send home for Lydia. Imagine you could get a good school shoe for $7.99 US dollars! Summer sales

going on like CRAZY all over the place! I want to buy a
few things and send them down. Tell Jemma I sending
some jeans and tops for her to sell. We could make some
good bucks that way.

I can't write more now. But I have you in mind
everyday. Take care of yourself and not to worry about
me. Kiss Lydia for me and tell her to be a good kid.

Until next time. Love you all.

Yvonne

The sound of hammering came from the backyard. Grandma
folded the letter carefully and put it with the other one in her
Bible, while Auntie Jemma went on about selling the things that
were coming in the barrel. She said that tights and handbags
would make good sales for Christmas. Then they had Carnival to
think about. Grandma was also excited, but mostly about the job
my mother might get.

"That will settle her," she said. "It not easy sitting down in
people house and you not working. Not that Boysie mind but he
have that foreign wife, and Yankee ways not like ours."

She filled a plastic bottle with mauby and told me to take it out
to Mr. Espinoza, but to come right back to the house.

"I don't want you hanging around out there," she said. "Let the
man do his work."

Mr. Espinoza was busy nailing the planks in place. When I
handed him the bottle, he smiled and said in a soft, sad kind of
voice, "Ah, relief for the sufferer. Thank you, my lady Veronica."

"My name is Lydia," I said.

He proceeded to make a dramatic apology by bowing very low
and asking many pardons.

"Accept my humble apologies, my lady," he said. "My error. I
should have recognized that brand of frank hospitality as enterprising Lydia's."

He performed such a ridiculous bow – with one leg sticking
out and his face almost touching his knee – that I burst out
laughing. I wanted to ask him about the women he had mentioned, but I didn't because he had spoken as though everyone
knew about them and I would be the odd person out.

After he had taken a long drink from the bottle, he let me help him build the coop by handing him nails while he hammered, grumbling every now and then about the condition of the wood. Some of the laths had holes and other signs of rot.

"Sometimes one is forced to compromise one's standards. Sometimes, my dear Lydia, life asks you to become less than you are. You see what I mean?"

Again, I didn't understand what he meant and wasn't sure if it would be rude to ask. I wondered if it had to do with him being a whiteman and building a chicken coop for Grandma. I watched him hammer in a few more nails before Grandma called loudly from the kitchen. I remembered what she had said about hanging around and disturbing Mr. Espinoza.

No one had noticed when he left the yard. Maybe it was the quietness that made Grandma venture out to see what was going on with the coop. Mr. Espinoza was nowhere to be found. He had packed up his tools and left without even saying good-bye. Grandma didn't seem too surprised. Four ducklings had also disappeared. Grandma said she had her suspicions, but kept them to herself.

"Some people don't know how to thank God for the talent and blessings he give them for free" was all she had said on that business and never mentioned the ducklings again.

I found out later that Mr. Espinoza was a man with plenty education, but things had gone wrong and he ended up drifting around doing odds and ends for people and basically catching his tail. Maybe Grandma knew his whole story, but she didn't say what it was that had gone wrong with him. I thought it must have been bad because Grandma said that his wife had packed her bags and went to Canada with their son.

Mr. Roger passed by that afternoon about three o'clock. Auntie Jemma was not at home. She had gone to braid her hair. I was in the backyard playing with the wood shavings that had collected around the base of Mr. Espinoza's workbench. Brownie and Rambo had been missing all day and I didn't even hear the gate open. Mr. Roger seemed very surprised that Auntie Jemma was not there and as usual didn't take much notice of me. He was too caught up scanning the house, hoping, I supposed, that she would appear.

"How long your Auntie Jemma gone?"

"Long time and she coming back late."

"And where your Granny?"

"Resting," I said. "Headache."

Mr. Roger was behaving like there was a question he didn't want to ask. He hung there glancing from the house to me. I continued framing the face I had scratched into the ground with the shavings. I had decided it looked like my mother's when Mr. Roger's big hand slipped a chocolate bar into my pocket.

"Well, your Auntie Jemma miss out on this."

His breath was a puff of Colgate hotness behind my neck.

Two days had passed and there was still no sign of Mr. Espinoza. The unfinished coop drew sporadic bursts of disapproval from Grandma every time her eyes happened to fall on it. She swore that she would never give him an end since he was bent on dragging himself all over the place. We kept the chicks in a corner of the kitchen where they would be safe. I didn't mind because I got to open the box whenever I wanted and let them pick away at my hands. My favourite was a very yellow one I called Butters.

Then, one morning, we woke to the sound of hammering. Grandma flung open the back door and sized up the situation. Mr. Espinoza paused briefly from his work and they both looked at each other. When she was sure he had read what her body had to say, she turned abruptly and went about her business.

Mr. Espinoza looked like he had been *to hell and back* as Grandma used to say when Grandpappy picked up his guitar and went on one of his drinking rounds that could last for days. Again, he had a bad cold. I thought that explained why he had stayed away.

Grandma's vexation must have been really serious because she didn't send any mauby for Mr. Espinoza at lunchtime. Maybe it didn't matter because he never stopped for lunch. He worked and worked on the coop. Grandma said that was because he had the devil in his backside.

During Grandma's after-lunch rest, I slipped out to see how far he had gotten. The three sides were already walled up and the chicken wire was nailed across the front. He was preparing the boxes that he would nail to the walls for when the hens wanted to lay their eggs.

"Why you have to nail them so high?" I asked.

There was the usual pause before he answered that made me think he had to replay the question in his mind in order to catch up with it. He was always so far away.

"Snakes, mongoose – that kind of thing. They love to eat eggs."

His mention of snakes made me think of Pilate. I had not seen the creature since the day it had crawled up his back.

"So why you like Pilate if snakes bad?"

Mr. Espinoza seemed surprised.

"No, not my Pilate. He wouldn't trouble eggs. He's a good boy. Not so Pilate?"

He patted his right thigh and a great bulge coiled deep in his pocket. "He's my inspiration."

My mouth dropped in disbelief and I ran back to the house.

By evening, Mr. Espinoza was finished. In spite of everything, Grandma was pleased with the job he had done, and in her excitement got the chicks from the kitchen and let them go on the floor of the coop. They seemed lost in all the space and huddled together in one corner chirping weakly. I took the little pan of water from the cardboard box and put it in the middle of the floor. They were not at all interested.

"Not to worry. They going to get accustom just now," Grandma said.

I was not convinced.

"Well, Espinoza, we break even now that the coop finish," she said.

Mr. Espinoza looked from the coop to Grandma, who held his gaze like a challenge. His face got very red. We left him tidying up the yard.

He was gone when I came out again. The coop looked very lonely in the growing dark. I thought of the chicks and ran to check on them. They had not become any braver and were still packed up in one corner, pressed close for warmth. Only Butters was off by herself. She perched on a brown paper bag that was tucked away in the far right side. I thought that Mr. Espinoza had forgotten his lunch. I put Butters with the other chicks then turned my attention to the bag.

To my surprise, my name was written in bold pencil marks across the front. Inside was a copybook and an orange pencil with *God is* © written in deep blue. The first page of the book had the word WRITE printed in the middle. I could tell it was not a new book because some pages had been torn out. Mr. Espinoza had written his thoughts there and now it was my turn.

I wrote the date and my name before I hid the book and pencil in one of the laying boxes, which I could reach only if I stood on a turned over bucket.

In the morning Butters was dead. Grandma said she had caught a cold. I decided to bury her under the starch mango tree.

The holidays slipped quickly by. I never saw Mr. Espinoza again. Grandma said that shame had kept him away for stealing the ducklings. I couldn't believe he would do such a thing. But Grandma said that was what to expect when a man loved rum and God knows what else more than himself, so she didn't want him around the place any more.

No more letters came from my mother. Then one night she called to say that she had gotten the job and would be moving to Long Island soon. She had also shipped the barrel that included something special for me. Auntie Jemma said she would organize with Mr. Roger. He would borrow a van from a partner to transport it from the docks when the notification came.

I spent most of my time in the coop playing with the chicks. They had grown and were losing their soft yellow feathers to firm white ones. Sometimes I hid there to undo my plaits or to write things in my book like *I miss my mother . . . I hate New York . . . Rain fell whole day . . . Auntie Jemma smells like flowers . . . Mr. Rogers is the sweets man, big hands in my pocket make my nipples feel funny . . . don't tell anybody . . . Dear Jesus, this is Lydia. I want you to know I am a good girl and my mother loves me plenty more than the little girl she taking care of in that Long Island place.*

Sometimes I recited for the chicks the psalm Grandma said I should learn by heart because it was for protection. She said hers every morning with the lit candle standing on the table. *The Lord is my light and my help; whom shall I fear.* I had mastered the first eight verses.

The barrel came a whole month after I had started my Standard Five class. The postman, Mr. Johnson, and Mr. Roger lugged the huge, brown container up the path. Every step of the way, Mr. Johnson repeated like a stuck record, "I get catch this morning!" Auntie Jemma's face shone with excitement as she directed them from the front when she wasn't shooing Brownie and Rambo out of the way. Grandma opened both sides of the living-room door and pushed the centre table into a corner so they could get the barrel inside. It stood like a trophy in the middle of the polished floor. Written in large black letters that slanted downhill was: TO MRS. SYLVIA WILLIAMS LP 12 MCINROY TRACE, SANTA CRUZ, TRINIDAD, W.I.

Mr. Johnson left in a storm of thank-yous, with Auntie Jemma promising to put aside something for him from *foreign*. She and Mr. Roger worked to get the lid off, while Grandma looked on with a very stern face.

When the cover was finally removed, the smell of newness and plastic filled the room. Mr. Roger immediately retired to the kitchen from where he leaned over the counter observing all the confusion. Auntie Jemma started behaving like it was Christmas morning, tearing open wrappings and exclaiming at the various items that were mostly things to sell like clothes for big people, sheets, towels and kitchen stuff. There was a whole set of things in bags and tins with green and red tags marked 10% discount stuck on them – shampoo, soap, toothpaste, bags of Snickers, almond nuts, preserved prunes, peaches, body lotion, Tang orange juice.

Many more things came out including a gadget for zapping flies, a cake mixer, a set of plastic bowls of assorted sizes, and a tinned ham that Grandma laughed at saying it could never taste like *her* Christmas ham that she cured for herself every year, so she didn't know why Yvonne had wasted her good money. Nothing

for me emerged except a bag of about a hundred plastic hair clips
of all shapes and colours that Grandma quickly confiscated, a set
of copy books for school and a pair of track shoes that lit up red
when they hit the ground. The trick the shoes did with the light
fascinated me, but Grandma said I could not try them on until I
had cleaned up myself good and proper.

I became even more anxious to see what my mother had sent
for me when Auntie Jemma fished a set of cake-icing accessories
with a label marked *for Mammy*. Grandma immediately sat in her
chair with the box on her lap, too pleased to say anything more
than, "A-A Miss Yvonne." I kept asking Auntie Jemma if there
was anything in the barrel for me, and I must have been getting
in the way because Grandma finally chased me outside to play. I
knew better than to protest and spoil my chances of getting the
special gift my mother had sent.

The chicks were glad to see me. I placed the one I had named
Hero on my shoulder and he made me laugh by pecking at my ear.
Grandma had shown me how to recognize the cocks from the
hens by looking for the red comb. Hero was going to be a big
brown rooster. We were great friends. When I told him things
about my mother and how she was far away, or about Auntie
Jemma and her boyfriends, he set his head to one side and listened
attentively. Already I was determined never to let him end up in
Grandma's pot or anybody else's.

I was thinking about getting out my copybook to write something about Hero when the spring door squeaked open and Mr.
Roger squatted at the entrance.

"So this is where you hiding, young lady? You have space in
there for me?"

I could hear Auntie Jemma exclaiming about something that
had probably come from the barrel. Mr. Roger entered the coop
and took a seat on the overturned bucket I sat on when I wrote in
my copybook.

"This is a nice place to hide," he said, looking around at the
boarded-up walls, with only the chicken wire to the front and the
door to one side.

I stooped at the other end and cuddled Hero, whose neck was
stiff with alarm at the stranger in his house.

"Guess what I have here?" he patted his shirt pocket with his big hand. "Come and see. Take it out."

He stretched forward and drew me into the space between his legs.

"Go on, take it out. Is for you."

I reached in and found a Mars chocolate bar. My favourite.

"Go ahead, eat it before your Granny take it away from you."

The hot breath between us clashed with chicken crap. I pulled away and returned to my end of the coop. Hero's red eyes were blinking, blinking at me.

Auntie Jemma squealed again over something, making the dogs bark and howl.

"What you get from New York? Like your Mammy forget you or what?"

"Plenty things," I said. "Grandma keeping them for me."

His laugh thundered and made the chicks jump.

"Is true," I blurted out. "She send everything I want!"

I could hear Rambo and Brownie yelping somewhere down the hill. Maybe someone had come into the yard, or Auntie Jemma's excitement had sent them wild. I was thinking that I liked Mr. Wayne more than Mr. Roger even though he never gave me sweets.

"I have something else for you. Something you will like better than any foolishness that come in that barrel."

He glanced towards the house. I followed his eyes, wondering what he might mean, and was in time to see Auntie Jemma appear in the top half of the kitchen door wildly waving a skinny, half-naked dolly in a pair of blue shorts and matching halter top.

"You see what you get, Lyds. Look, what your mother send special for you. Is a Barbie!"

Mr. Roger chuckled behind me. I pressed my face into the chicken wire for a closer look, but Auntie Jemma had already disappeared into the house. When I turned around another Pilate was pointing at me and Mr. Roger had his finger pressed to his lips.

Suddenly, there was nowhere to run and I had forgotten how to say my psalm.

RAYMOND RAMCHARITAR

THE ABDUCTION OF SITA

"Master, what's this I hear? Who can they be,
These people so distraught with grief?" I said.

And he replied: "The dismal company
Of wretched spirits thus find their guerdon due
Whose lives knew neither praise nor infamy."
(Dante, Inferno)

"Hey, Dara Singh…"

I recognized the words as his lips formed them rather than heard them. The rain was thundering onto the awning I was trapped under, its jarring staccato adding a martial dimension to my imprisonment. My back was pressed up against a store window, a backdrop of cut-rate faux-silks and curtain taffetas, and my feet were turned inward, toes curled inside the shoes, away from the relentless rain. I don't know how long he'd been there. It was getting late, and darker than usual, and I'd broken off from staring at the discoloured sky to look down. My shoes were drenched and, if it continued like this, they and my trousers would be ruined. And that was when I saw him through the rolled-up window of his car. He met my eyes, nodded, and leaned across from the driver's side to the passenger's door. It cracked open and I ran to it. My mincing rush over the slippery concrete, the awkward hop over the shallow gutter and slide into the car had exposed me to the rain's full force for only a few seconds, but I was soaked.

"Shit," I muttered loudly as I slid into the seat. "Shit, shit. Fuckin' rain."

"Here." A white towel with *Port of Spain General Hospital* stencilled on the bottom in thick blue letters dropped into my lap.

"Hospital." I fingered it tentatively.

"What?"

"Hospital?"

"That's what it says." He spoke as if to a precocious child. His eyes were already on the road, steering the car into the traffic. I took in his profile as I unfolded the towel, saw, along the curve of his forehead and through the dark, straight hair that dropped across his brow, the fine-boned, almost elfin boy I'd sat next to all those years ago. He was still handsome in a weak sort of way, but heavier; the brown skin around his cheek was bloated, and faint striations of excess flesh were visible along the line of his jaw.

"Well," I said, in between patting my face dry and carefully pressing the towel into my hair, "this is a coincidence. Twice in a week, after not seeing you for years. You're literally the last person in the world I would've expected to pick me up."

He half-smiled, still staring intently through the rain.

I'd met him the week before at a Hindu thing in Chaguanas. Thinking back on it, that was it – the *going back*, I suppose, that was the one random act that had set in motion the series of events that took my life off the road I'd chosen, to the place I'd spent years trying to convince myself did not exist. But perhaps the circumstances were inconsequential, and it would've happened anyway in another form, but the essence would have been the same. For months before, I'd been caught in the grip of an unmistakable weariness. I would lie in bed in the morning, looking around at the room with a vague dissatisfaction, and go through my days robotically, coming to life only in the afternoons to go to the bar, knowing I'd provoke an argument with Val and not really caring.

I was jaundiced, bored and tired. Nothing about love and stability had remained the way I'd thought it would remain. There was no easy movement through the happiness; that had to be worked for, harder and harder, and I began to romanticize what I'd left behind. I had been allowed to roam, and now a cord I did not know I was bound by was being pulled tight, inexorably bringing me back. I felt like a man who has accidentally averted a terrible misfortune and returns to the spot to mourn his salvation.

★

I saw the god from way off, surveying the landscape, looking for me, towering a hundred feet over his vassals. The sight awakened the stirrings of a faint dread, but it was all so long ago I deceived myself by considering the artistry of the creation. A hundred feet tall, of papier-mache and depicting Rama, the hero of the *Ramayana*, who had killed Ravana, usurper of heavenly harmony. The god's face was fleshy and powerful, and even in the obvious plainness of his construction, the cruelty in the curve of the moustache and in the painted eyes was evident. The display was out in the open, on a plot of land cleared amidst a sea of canefields.

Walking down the hillside from St Ann's, I'd looked out towards the central plain of the island and been struck by the verdure, like a sea, with the little patches of brown in relief. Closer to the god, I felt the peculiar familiarity pervading it all; the engine of a battered carnival ride – the kind that lifted the rider aloft and spun him in a circle for several minutes – bleated loud and continuously; tents and booths huddled together displaying religious effigies, books and food; and people in Indian costumes walked around self-consciously, handing out leaflets and gazing reverently at everything.

The ground had been hastily pitched so it was lumpy and uneven, and the display booths were of gnarled wood, quickly put together, and decorated with perfunctory strips of crepe paper. The textures of the wood and paper, the meanness of the construction, the scent of the food, the colours of the clothes, the hum of voices and the washes of high-intensity light from pillars sprouting out of the pitch, tingeing it all to a hyperreal pallor, took me back to my childhood: to a relative's house where I'd be trapped for a day, or a weekend; stultifying heat, blaring Indian music, raucous voices, odious children, crushes of people I feared, oily food that made me sick. It was terrifying.

I held on to one of the light-posts, savouring the feel of the cold metal and brought myself back to the present. Nothing had changed: old, bovine grandmothers were being led by children in cheap, colourful clothes; there were giggling teenage girls in Hindu costumes, and boys with their dark-eyed beauty, even in early adolescence, already infused with the germ of the dissolution I knew and abhorred. As I drew back from them, they formed set-piece images from my memory, images that accompanied the silent rages, the suffocation, the longings for escape.

I'd forgotten the power of those images. My other life had become more real to me in the years I'd been away, but now the soft curve of Val's jaw I saw in the mornings over the sheets, the black and white faces of the painting that Oudwen had given us for our housewarming which hung over our bed, the spare white walls, Coltrane in the evenings – all of it seemed far away and ludicrous.

The feeling of distance, as of watching a plane lift off, stayed with me as I walked. People thronged on all sides, but I was unaware of them. I felt only the strange silence of childhood. I walked to stand at the flower-festooned feet of the god and looked up at his face, and the lines of cruelty were unmistakable. Unmistakable, familiar.

I backed away from him into a tent, and found myself looking at photographs of the oldest man and woman I had ever seen. They were the only living survivors of the journey across the black water by the last batch of indentured workers in the early part of the last century. The legend "Revere The Past, It Will Guide You To The Future" was written in flourishing script below the heavy, gilt-edged frames, and facsimiles of the original indentureship agreements which bound them here were spread out below.

The objects of reverence looked to me just painfully old. The man was wrapped in a striped blanket and stood in front of a door constructed of splintered boards. Behind his brittle shoulder, with its collarbone protruding from beneath the tight skin, the door, its hinge rusted and held by a single nail, hung at an angle. They had probably only been able to get him as far as the door. The photograph of the woman was indoors. She sat in an old chair. Her image occupied most of the photograph; no details of the room were visible, but I could guess them. Her face was the saddest thing I have ever seen – no sign of femininity remained, nothing that had ever made her beautiful beneath the gray fabric that shielded her from the world.

I looked away, suddenly angry that I had come here. I fumbled in my pocket for my keys, the keys to our house. This was not real, and I wanted to return to my reality. As my fingers closed around the keys, I caught sight of another photo, of their family, a wretched group of souls, young-old, ground-down men, blighted children, worn-out, emaciated daughters, huddled in the same verandah as the survivors.

I walked toward the exit. I had neither spoken to nor looked directly at anyone since I'd arrived.

"Hey, Dara Singh."

And the images stopped. My name hadn't been used like that, both in rapid succession, as if they were one word, in years.

I turned. He was much bigger than he used to be, but there was no mistaking.

"Sunil." I smiled broadly and took his hand. "Sunil, how the hell are you?"

I had not seen him for years and had not, during that time, thought of him once. But at that moment, another flood of memories rushed in: carefully tended lawns, cool white shirts and the white robes of the priests in the College of the Sacred Virgin, an extraordinary oasis of Catholicism in the flatlands in the centre of the island whose inhabitants practised a religion that was older than the Church, and who held it in as much contempt as those men of God held their heathenism.

Sunil and I had been the first in our families to go to the college. Even then, he'd wanted to be a doctor, but I don't think he ever shared my longing for escape. Looking at him smile that shy smile of his, I wondered briefly if I had done the right thing, but only briefly.

He was heavier, too, than his years. His shoulders were broad and he extended beyond me in all directions now. But the old weakness hovered in his face.

"I'm alright."

"Or is it Dr Varana?"

"Last year of internship," he said, diffidently. "I read you all the time in the paper."

"Oh?" I was relieved to fall into a comfortable script. "So you're the one."

"What?"

"Nothing. Bad joke."

"You remember my sister, Veela?"

I noticed for the first time a fair, fine-featured young woman standing next to him in an expensive looking shalwar kameez, worn with a colourful scarf (as paraded by the giggling girls who flitted about the uneven ground). I'd seen that outfit many times, worn by the heroines in the Indian films my father used to cart us off to see in the drive-inn on Thursday nights.

"Hello."

I smiled vaguely, remembering the small pigtails in yellow ribbons with red polka dots that bounced around inside the car that came to pick him up from school. "How are you?"

"Well, right now I'm looking for my husband."

"Mm..."

"...He's one of those who don't like what you write."

"...Hmm," I said. "Do convey my apologies."

"Look, Sunil," she tossed a sheet of black hair impatiently, "I'm going to look for him, you stay here."

He nodded docilely as she walked off purposefully.

"So," I said, "what about you? Married yet? Found God?"

"About to, in a few months, we're not sure about the date."

"Where is she?"

"She...?"

"The wife to be?"

"Oh, not here."

"Ah. So..." I gestured at the stalls behind him, "you're involved in all this..."

"Well, I suppose..." he said, uncertainly.

"...the devout Hindu, pillar of the community..."

"Oh," he smiled faintly. "You don't think much about this kind of thing."

"Well, you've got to admit..." I vacillated a moment, looking at him and chose the placatory route. "I might not know enough about it to know better."

The withdrawal pacified him. "My father became quite involved in it, you know," he continued, "the religious thing, before he died. He got quite close to Baba Ji..."

"The Baba Ji that writes a column in the *Standard*?"

"Yes," he said, brightening. "You know him?"

"Do you know him?" I asked, cautiously. What I knew of Baba Ji did not accord with the image Sunil seemed to have of him.

"Yes, he helped me through the time after my father died. We were never close you know..." He drifted off uncomfortably.

"Hey." There'd been a disturbing tremor in his voice. "Hey, were any of us? I was glad when the bastard died... but now... I suppose it wasn't all their fault. That's what this kind of life," I nodded around, "this obsession with dead things does to you. That's why I never come back."

I'd spoken in a rush, said things I'd wanted to say for years and which were not what he wanted or needed to hear, and I instantly regretted it. I waited anxiously for him to answer, to laugh it off.

"Sunil." The voice came from behind me and jolted us.

"I couldn't find him. Baba Ji is looking for you." Veela placed herself directly between us.

"Ah. We," he said, turning to me, "are going over there."

I understood, but out of perversity I said: "Well, look at that, so was I." And I followed them. The place they were going to was a small stage where a portion of the *Ramayana* was being enacted. It was being done with music and dance, but no words that I could hear. The scene was of a man, wearing a crown, but dressed in a peasant's dhoti, apparently chastising a woman, who was looking down to the ground, as if in distress.

"So what's happening here?" I asked. "Do you know the story?"

"Rama has just rescued Sita from Ravana," he said. "He's telling her how unworthy she is."

"But why?" I asked, intrigued despite myself. "It's not her fault. And why bother to rescue her if he's going to cuss her out?"

"It was his duty to recover his wife. But she's become unclean because she was around Ravana, and Ram can't have anything to do with her any more."

"You mean he can't... uhm, make any little Hindus?"

"That's one way to put it," he said, unsmilingly.

"If you have no respect for our religion..." his sister said, looking sharply at me.

"Well, did it occur to you that Ram might be gay? And he's not sleeping with her because he had a thing with, you know, one of the generals or something? Or maybe Ravana isn't such a bad guy, and just did what he did to get to Ram?" I knew I shouldn't have said this. They both looked ahead and adjusted their faces so I was out of their range of vision. I shook my head and walked away, and in another minute he had evaporated from my mind. I suppose if I'd thought about it, it might have seemed strange that he was getting married in a few weeks and the woman he was getting married to was nowhere in sight, but I did not give it a second thought. I walked out to the street and got into the first taxi that came by and went home.

"So, where are you going?" His voice barely registered above the rain beating down on the car.

"Good question. Where are you going?"

"Nowhere. Home."

"Home?"

He shrugged.

"Well," I considered. Val wouldn't be home yet. "Why not come to my place, let me get changed and we'll go where I was going."

"Where's that?

"*Wendy's.*" I wanted to impress him, for some reason, so I let it drop with more casualness than I felt.

"Wendy's? Who's Wendy? Friend of yours?"

I turned across to him in amazement. "Are you serious?"

"Not a friend?"

I laughed. "Yes. No. You'll see."

Two hours later, the black looks that shot at us as we slipped past the hundred or so people in the line bothered him initially.

"Are you sure this is alright?" he shouted in my ear over the music that blasted out of the dark tinted doors, pushing against us with physical force. I thrust my press badge into the face of the huge, bald black man who stood with his arms folded, surveying the throng of men and women pressed into a tight circle around the velvet rope that secured the club's entrance.

He studied the pass for a moment then leaned down and raised the rope.

"Power to the press," I shouted as we walked in, separating ourselves from the throbbing mass of pouting lips and taut arms perched on hips.

Inside, past the music and the strobe lights and smoke and crush of people in the dance club, were stairs which led to a lounge. I nodded to the second guard, almost identical to the one outside, as I led Sunil up behind a ragged stream of men in jackets and open-necked silk shirts and women in short black dresses with deadly serious faces. The lounge was darkly lit, with a long, polished bar and crowded tables. There were booths off to the side. The mood here was less frenetic. The music was jazzy and cool, and a few prints by artists of the moment hung on the walls.

I led him to the back past the bar and waved to the bartender. A few minutes later, as the waiter left, I sank back into the seat, resting my back comfortably against the wall. I felt my shoulders sag and I took a long drink.

"So tell me..." I started to say.

"Dara, darling," a body dropped into my lap and kissed me on the lips. I pushed it away.

"Jesus, Sey, I told you if you're going to do that, shave, dammit."

"You never minded before." Sey batted his lashes at me, breaking off to admire himself in the mirror that ran along the wall above my head. He was a hairdresser in his early twenties, with long, curly hair, sensuous lips and an intensity many young women found irresistible – an attraction which, they discovered after five minutes, was quite misplaced – but his appointment books were always full.

"Stop that fag stuff, you damned invert, you're scaring my friend."

But Sunil seemed remarkably composed.

"Hello." Sey offered his best business voice and a limp hand, which Sunil, seemingly dazzled by the thumb ring and the rubies and silver bands that adorned the fingers, cautiously inched his hand toward.

"You don't have to shake his hand, Sunil, you don't know where it's been. Or actually you might know better than he does where it's been."

Sunil smiled weakly and shook Sey's hand.

"Nice to meet you."

"Now, it is nice to meet a gentleman with breeding." Sey deposited himself next to Sunil. "You could learn something from him, Dara."

"So could you," I said. "He's a doctor. Free testing. Just how much a rectum can stretch. The scientific view." My words came fluidly now, and a sharp joy flowed beneath them.

Sey tossed his mane and cut back at me out of slitted eyes. "Now that is being too bitchy, you bitch."

"What's the matter, Sey? That time of the month? His wife giving him a hard time? I warned you about married men."

Sey got up, produced a pink card and said to Sunil, "With my compliments, sir." Then he turned to me; "Fuck you, Dara. And you'd better look at your own marriage."

"Fuck you too, Sey."

The waiter knew me well enough that I didn't have to signal, and by that time I'd finished off the first drink, I was nursing a second.

I shook my head sympathetically at Sunil as Sey left. He was contemplating his drink, fastidiously ignoring my eyes.

In the instant before I opened my mouth to speak, I caught a glimpse of myself in the mirror, the slight tremble of the hair as if fell over my cheek. I brushed it over my ear and said, "Hey, sailor..." but my voice was slurred, so I let it trail off.

I felt the warmth brought by the liquor spread to my face, and the familiar routine of entering the larger life began. Everything around me suddenly revealed itself to me: I was aware of the textures of the seat, the table, the coolness of the water that had condensed and was rolling off the glass, the red light that fell onto the table. Each note of the music expanded, everything began to envelope me in a comforting, safe embrace.

"...Uh huh, you," I laughed as he looked slowly up at me. Our eyes met, and I saw nothing there I could penetrate. I was reminded of the god in the middle of that little world I'd returned to. "Oh, for god's sake, you're safe, I won't have my toes up your pants' leg anytime tonight, I promise. We're harmless. Didn't they teach you that in medical school? Or do they still tell you it's a disease you can cure?"

He remained silent.

"Yep, everyone in school was right. Hey, Maryse..."

She'd already seen me and was on her way over. She slid into the seat and sat carefully next to me, smiling. Maryse did everything with a delightful languor. Even the way her body passed through the air was careful and elegant.

"Hello Dara. Only two?" She pointed a red-painted nail at the glasses on the table. "Rain slow you up?"

"Now now, my dear, let us not be catty, let us, rather, be otherwise." I reached over and gently took a handful of her brown, lustrous hair and pulled her over to me, and as her face came close to mine and her lips parted, I looked just below her eyes to her ebony skin, thinking that the red of her lips looked like the pulp of an exotic fruit, and slowly bit the lower one and pulled back. Her eyes were faintly amused.

"Display for your fri...?"

I kissed her suddenly, harshly, and I held the kiss until she started to kiss back. Then I broke off.

"It's magic. He can convince everyone." I caressed her hair and brushed a strand over a perfect ear.

He looked over at me, and then her, and I recognized in his eyes a calmness I was too far gone to be afraid of. She removed my hand from her hair and said, "I'm not in the mood tonight, Dara."

"Wait." He reached over the table and put a hand on hers. "Please, don't leave, stay a while."

"Yes, stay, Maryse," I said. A strange cruelty welled. "Let me introduce you. This is my friend, Sunil. He is a doctor. Sunil, this is Maryse, who... well, what can I say that is not evident to any man worth the name within three miles?"

"Cut it out, Dara."

She smiled at Sunil. It reminded me of Sita, watching her beauty fade as the years passed, waiting for Rama to rescue her, only to find out he would never touch her again. "And I really have to go. I'm with... a friend."

"Hmmm," I said. "Progress."

"What I came over to tell you, Dara," she said as she slid out of the seat, "is that I saw Val here earlier. He was with someone."

And she was gone.

"Was she...?" Sunil let the words trail off.

"Was she what?"

I looked him straight in the eye.

He looked away.

"Did your father ever know?"

"My father," I took the glass from the waiter and signalled him to bring another, "is fucking dead."

That was the last thing I remembered saying that night.

In the three months between the time I last saw Sunil and first day of June, the only things I remember are Val's moving out a month later and the invitation arriving. I had a moment of sobriety and I begged him to stay. But things had been happening for too long. I knew someone was waiting, but Val wouldn't let him come round to help get his things out of the house. He was always sweet like that.

The rest of the time coagulated into a formless mass. I saw no one, but I did try without success to call Maryse to apologize. To occupy myself I stayed at work far longer than I needed to. My taste for liquor evaporated. The unhappiness I had felt, I realized, was purely my own, and our life had just been a mirror, showing me what I feared most about myself. Now, with the mirror gone, there was nothing; no reflection, no sound, no sensation. How long I might have continued like that I don't know, but on the first day of June something flicked on inside me. I got up, got the blue suit out, shaved, and made my way to the Hilton. The invitation was a gold embossed affair, with a picture of a slender Hindu goddess showering flowers which fell over the text of the announcement of Sunil's marriage to Vidia. The reception would be in the Water Room of the Hilton.

II

It's my fault, I suppose. I could have said no at any time. I could have told him to go away, to not come back, to fuck off. But I didn't. I didn't say anything. I kept answering the phone, and I waited for him, and I went where he said, and I did what he asked. Damn Dara. Damn him. Damn him for being weak. Damn him for everything.

He'd come to me as I was leaving. Dara was sick, he said, he didn't know where to take him, would I come with him. Dara was as bad as I'd ever seen him, so drunk he didn't even struggle when we each took a hand and limped with him to the car. His head drooped onto his chest and the fingers of the arm round my shoulder were loose and limp, almost caressing me as we struggled through the night. As he fell into the back seat his head lolled to the side, and for an instant I saw his face in the moment of confusion and pain as the mask lifted, and I felt a shudder. I sat in the back seat with Dara's head on my breast till we got him home. Val wasn't there, and we put him to bed, and he took me home. He said nothing to me, and I had nothing to say to him.

He called me the next day.

"I want to see you."

"Look," I said, "if this is about Dara, I'm not..."

"No. Not about Dara."

And I agreed. I don't know why. I think I'd meant to say no, but the surprise, the unexpectedness of it – and there was his tone. He hadn't asked me. He'd told me he wanted to see me. And I found myself waiting with a little expectation. I didn't even remember what he looked like. But he was, well, boyish; the voice, the shyness and although I didn't know what he wanted, I couldn't stop thinking about Dara, his weakness, his sickness, and his absence, most of all.

After all that time. I remember the last time Dara and I walked up Chancellor Hill, right up at the very top where you can look out to the sea over the city. It was late evening and he'd just told me and the tears were swelling in my eyes and my nails were beginning to dig through his T-shirt into his shoulders as he stopped me.

"Wait."

He took my hand off his shoulder and kissed it and said: "Look at the sea."

The bay was dull grey, and there were no ships, not a cloud, not a bird, just the sun, reaching for the water, to rest, to hide.

"Just look at it for a while. Look at the sun. It's warping itself to reach the water. It's not a perfect circle when it touches; the end is stretched out, yearning so strong it doesn't care about being perfect. But the deformity lasts only a short time, and then even the sun has to go back to being what it was made to be. For a short, precious moment, a second in endless time, it seems to defy its own nature, but it's just an illusion. What we see and feel are meaningless to the world, to the god that made us the way we are. What we feel is like the sun reaching for the sea. But the moment of illusion is still beautiful. Still precious. The sun in its dreams probably remembers the sea it can never touch."

That was the one moment in my life that I've ever felt more than the sum of my flesh. That someone could feel that way for me, could spread himself so wide for me, to encompass the sun and the sea and time, changed the dimensions of my world, destroyed them, and me along with them.

Outside of that, I've done nothing out of the ordinary, accomplished nothing. This beauty I wear came with its own rules, it steers my life without me, makes it... easier. Sometimes even the way I move surprises me. The way I talk, laugh, how I stretch my arms along the contour of my stomach and spread the fingers slightly as they curve along my thigh, how my hips curve in an arch, like a bow stretched to its limit, when I'm fucking. I don't control it, this body; most times I think I only observe it. Dara recognized me inside the body and, in that instant, showed me something outside it. But even before, there was something else. There was a lightness about him, surrounded by a semidarkness; a wonder about life inside a vague revulsion for living with the sweat of the world. Everything we did, even the mundane things, had a careful privacy about it.

We did what people do, we walked together, we held hands, we spoke of inconsequential things: the blueness of the sky on that particular day, the pleasantness of the wind at a particular moment. And he couldn't satisfy a woman if his life depended on it. But even then, there was always the sense of the separate existence of the world apart from us. We belonged together, the way two pieces of a branch broken by a violent storm can be fitted together, but can never be joined as before. I suppose if it had been different, we would have married and lived as close to happiness as anyone gets, but it didn't happen that way.

That's why I agreed to see him. Despite everything, I still needed to know Dara was safe.

I wasn't ready when he came to my house. I don't remember what he wore, except that his trousers were black and he wore a belt, and I don't even remember what I said, what I planned to say. He seemed tired. Not a tiredness of exhaustion, more of frustration, constraint.

"I'll be just a minute," I said, and pointed him to a chair and turned to go inside.

"No."

That was the first word he said.

"What? No?"

He hadn't raised his voice, but alongside the tiredness, there was an arresting force.

He took my hand, and that is what I remember most clearly: his hand closing around mine, the bigness of his hand around my wrist, and the feeling of weakness, of inevitability. He took me on the bed, face down. He didn't take his pants off. He unbuckled them, that's how I remember the belt.

When he was finished, he said "I'll call you when I want you." And he left.

I could say that somehow I saw him as if he was Dara, but that would be untrue. I knew all the time who and what he was, and the deep, cancerous hatred behind it all. And I shared in it. Hatred for the body that bound me to the world and all the pain I could not control. Here was pain of my own choosing, and I revelled in it.

He never wanted me to come to him, meet him anywhere, show me off. He came to me, in the night, always. He never called my name. He would look me in the eye and I'd know what he wanted. Some nights he just told me to take my clothes off and sit on the floor. He would sit on a chair and talk to me. He'd tell me what an ugly nigger bitch I was and that someone like me deserved to have a faggot fuck them. Sometimes he grabbed me between the legs as he came in and once or twice he hit me. The bruises never showed. I think the reason he didn't hit me more often was that hitting was an effort for him. The exertion was too much for his small darkness. (Yes, and I suppose that made my life and Dara's all the more pitiable. His darkness was a small, insignificant one, thriving only on our weakness and desolation. Even the slightest resistance would have been enough to defeat it. Yet it overpowered me, the both of us, so completely. Strange.)

This went on for three months. During that time, Dara would also try to call me, but I never took his calls. Each time I heard the voice on the answering machine, I became more repulsed with Dara and with myself.

And then, one night he told me he was getting married and I was to come to the wedding. I was to be beautiful and then I was to disappear. I was never to be seen again. And on that final day, as I prepared for invisibility, I saw Dara at the wedding.

III

"Maryse... oh Maryse." I was overjoyed to see her. I'd walked in to the Water Room, not quite sure of myself, or sure of anything. The geography of the place seemed immense and unnavigable. The light was soft and a low roar of voices came ominously from all directions, and then I saw her, like an island in a raging sea and the heaviness fell off me.

She stood in profile, her eyes fixed intently on something I couldn't see. She was breathtaking, a soft white dress that bent along the curves of her magical body, and in profile her face seemed as perfect as an image on a Grecian vase, or a cameo set in onyx: the straight nose, the lips, the air of regality that surrounded her. She did not see me approach, and I followed her eyes to Sunil. He stood in the middle of a group of older men who looked like versions of himself, heavy-set, jowly and for the first time, I realised, evil.

"Maryse."

She turned to me, and I found myself staring into the face of someone I did not know.

"Hello, Dara."

Her voice was listless and sad.

"What's wrong, Maryse? Why are you here? What happened?"

She laughed quietly and for an instant, I saw a flash of the easy, satin elegance she kept about her like a shawl.

"I'm preparing for invisibility."

"What are you talking about, Maryse?" I reached over to touch her face, and stopped short as she pulled back.

"Invisibility?"

"Invisibility." Sunil had come up to us. "She is going to disappear."

He smiled as he spoke. He could have been discussing the decor of the room.

"What the fuck is going on, Sunil?" I tried to drop my voice, to muster some menace, and was astonished at the emptiness I found inside me.

He looked at me and laughed. That was the first time I'd heard him laugh. It was a full, booming laugh; the laugh of a man who was sure of everything.

"You don't know, do you?" He shook his head in amazement. "That day I picked you up in the rain, did you think it was an accident? I'd looked for you for three days. You know why? But when I saw what a sorry bastard you were I changed my mind. And decided to fuck her instead."

He leaned over and kissed me on the cheek and whispered in my ear: "You think you're the only bastard whose father ever fucked him up the ass, Dara? You're such a weak shit." Then he was gone.

I stumbled out a door on to a terrace and sat staring out at the sea. She came out after me, as I knew she would. I took her hand, and put my arm around her, suddenly enraged that I could not protect her, that I could not save her from him, and now that it was over, I could never protect her from it. She put her head on my shoulder, and there, just as the sun began its painful descent to the sea, just for that little interval, it was perfect, or so it looked.

JACOB ROSS

RUM AN COKE

Norma Browne got up early, cried a bit, stared at her hand and muttered to herself with bitter conviction. "What a waste. A waste!"

Nobody heard her except perhaps the boy, but even if he had, he would not remember much, come daylight.

Come daylight, he would lurch out of the house, hungry, ill and angry, his body starved of something that neither she nor any food on earth could satisfy. He would be away a couple of hours or maybe the whole day, and then he would return to lie below the house, the turbulence gone except in the working of his eyes. He would not be able to look at her, not until the shivering started again, very late in the evening, and he began, once more, to hit her.

She got up early because a thought had nudged her out of sleep, an idea which, with the coming daylight, became a resolve.

She waited until he left, then put on the light blue dress that she'd bought for his christening and which, ten years later, she also wore to take him to that scholarship school in St. George's.

He was a beautiful boy then, clear-eyed and quick, his little body full of purpose. "Remarkably intelligent" was what the teachers said; and to prove they were not lying, they'd written it on a pretty piece of parchment paper, framed it and handed it to her.

Not like now. Not like now at all. What she used to feel then went way past pride. If, in those days, she felt embarrassed or even terrified, it was only because she could hardly believe that some-one like her could be so blessed.

With awkward haste, she knelt and reached beneath the iron bed. She dragged out a pillow and emptied its contents on the floor. Several objects rolled out, things she would never use, but

kept "just in case": a couple of heavy silver bracelets, a ring of pure
Guyana gold, an old passport with a photo of a man who looked
exactly like her son and a small blue book on which "The Co-
operative Bank" was printed in large letters.

She took the little book, stuffed it down her bosom and went
to the main road to wait for the only bus that travelled the twenty
miles, twice a day, to and from St. George's.

It was evening when she returned. The migrating birds that
spent the November and December months in the swamp half a
mile away were already dropping like black rain out of an in-
flamed sky and settling on the mangroves.

She went to the bedroom to replace the book and leave a small
but heavy parcel beneath the bed. Then she began to look for
things to do. She would have gone to the garden at the top of the
hill above the village, but she'd already sown more corn and peas
than she had ever sown before; she'd weeded the sweet potatoes,
reinforced the mud rows with wattle and bamboo, trimmed the
bananas and cleared the stones which, every year, appeared
miraculously in the soil. She'd put new campeche pillars under
the house, added a kitchen and re-laid the yard with stones that
she'd gathered from the roadside – anything that hard work could
possibly achieve to ease her days. If she could have undone it all
and started again, she would have. Hard work saved her from
remembering – though that was not the same as forgetting. Not
remembering was holding back the shame, or redirecting it – the
way the drains she dug during the rainy season turned excess
water away from her garden.

She saw him coming and studied his face, his walk, the set of
his mouth. Such clues determined how her day went, although
when he first returned he was never violent. He would have gone
over to Teestone's house next door, or to some friend of his, and
pumped his veins with a needleful of that milky stuff that did such
dreadful things to him.

The milky stuff, she did not understand. She thought she had
already seen or imagined every awful thing there was, but nothing
had prepared her for what they called *de niceness* – niceness,
because of the way it made them feel, they said; niceness that had

sucked the life out of her child and replaced it with a deadness that had reduced her to nothing in his eyes.

Before the deadness was the hunger. He was hungry all the time, but the more she fed him the thinner he seemed to grow. He'd become secretive and had lost the even temper he was born with. When the shivering started and there was nothing she could do for him, he would scream and hit her.

She wondered which was worse: his torment or her own shame before the village. Once she caught him doing it to himself, panic-ridden and slobbering, until he'd fed the beast inside his veins.

For this – for this especially – she did not blame him because he was her child and she had known him as a different person. True, she'd seen him do things that did violence to her sense of decency – like the time she caught him with his cousin, younger than him by two years, on her bed. She'd almost killed him – but Daniel was still her boy.

She would never know how it started, or what she had done or had not done that made him need "de niceness". But now she knew who gave it to her boy and that was partly why she went to town. Nobody had told her; they'd only confirmed the truth for her.

It was that gold chain she'd bought him as a present that made her know. He'd asked for it before he did the exams, told her that if he got an "A" for all of them, she should buy him a gold chain with his name written on it. And of course she'd sent her macmere, Grace, to St. George's to get it straight away. Then she hid it in her pillowcase and waited. When he came home one day and told her that he'd got all his "A"s, she went straight to the bedroom and brought it out. That amazed him, not the chain but the fact that she believed he would get the "A"s, just because he said so.

So when she saw that gold chain around Teestone's neck, it suddenly made sense. Everything made sense: the house Teestone was improving, the way the children flocked to him, the girls warring amongst themselves for his attention.

Over the months she'd studied him. Teddy Stonewall – that boy! That boy who'd never seen a classroom in his life, who'd never lifted a finger for his mother, who'd grown up by the roadside near the rumshop watching the world slip past; that boy who, having worked for nothing, wanted everything. Now it was all coming to him: the pretty clothes, the new, red Suzuki bike, other people's children. Then the large cars with darkened windows began to arrive from St. George's.

She would watch them come and go till well past midnight, or till the beast awakened in Daniel's veins and she had to attend to him.

At first her interest in Teestone was no more than curiosity about the goings-on of the young. That was in the early days when she knew nothing of the powder. She had seen Daniel suck it up his nostrils a couple of times and believed him when he told her it was no different from a sweet, a new something to tantalise the young; and she thought that it would pass like those little obsessions her boy had developed from time to time, and then relinquished for his books. It didn't seem to make him ill, and he hadn't begun to hit her.

Why she hadn't thought of going to see Teestone sooner amazed her. Now, she couldn't wait to meet the young man whom a powder had made so powerful.

The rest of the day burnt itself out rapidly. When her boy began to stir in sleep, she straightened her dress, left her house and crossed over to Teestone's yard.

He came out when she called, his body blocking the doorway. She had to look up to examine his face against the darkness of the door mouth. This she did quickly before bringing her head back down. Now she watched him with her eyes upturned.

"What you want, Miss Lady."

"I want to come in," she said.

"Come in where!" He glared down at her. "Come inside o my house! What you want in my house?"

"Is someting," she lowered her voice and her eyes, afraid that he would not let her in. "Is someting I want to buy. I kin pay," she added hastily.

"I tell you I sellin anyting? What you waan to buy!" He was still fuming, but his voice, like hers, was lowered.

"I waan some niceness," she said flatly, and lifted her eyes at him. He paused a moment, shifted his body and she slipped under his arm. Teestone pulled the door behind him.

Now that the door was closed, he was transformed, almost another person. Relaxed, smiling, he drew a wooden stool from under the mahogany table in the middle of the room and placed it before her. Carefully, she lowered herself.

Teestone grinned. "Miss Norma, what you say you want?"

"I jus waan some, some of dat ting dat make my son, make my son so happy." She halted on the last word, made it sound like the most frightful thing on earth. But she managed a smile and that put Teestone at ease. He seated himself a few feet in front of her. He smiled wider and she noticed the gold tooth. She did not remember him having a gold tooth. He'd had bad teeth, the sort that prised his lips apart.

His shirt, she also noticed, was of a soft material that hung on him as if it were liquid, made, no doubt, from one of those fabulous materials she had seen in pictures in Grace's magazines, and in the large stores through whose wide glass windows you feasted your eyes but never entered.

"What you offerin?" he whispered. For a moment she did not understand him. "What you have?" he repeated.

She allowed her eyes to wander around the room before easing her fingers down her bosom and pulling out an old handkerchief. It was rolled into a knot. The curl of her fingers holding it accentuated their frailty. There was a scar at the back of her left hand, as if she had been burnt there. She unknotted the bit of cloth to reveal a ball of crumpled notes.

"A thousand dollars," she said, and dropped it on the table. It was all she had. The gesture said so, that and her trembling hands. She was never likely to have that much again, for it had taken a lot to get it. One thousand dollars that would have gone to her boy, along with the house and the piece of land that had been in the family for as long as anyone could remember.

Teestone did not reach for the money. He looked at her with a sudden probing suspicion, as if he were seeing her for the first time. She was an old woman, in trouble and confused because her

JACOB ROSS . RUM AN COKE

son was in trouble and confused. The stupid kind. The kind he despised most: those women who would do anything to please their sons, who never saw the sky because all their lives they were too busy looking down, digging and scratching the earth. It always puzzled him how people like that ever came by money. A thousand dollars? It had always been his! If she had not given it to him herself, her son would have, bit by bit. They were all coming now, these old women. When their children could no longer get to him on their own, they were the ones who came and begged for them. Norma Browne was not the first, and she would not be the last. These days he did not have to do a thing. These days, money made its way to him.

"Hold on," he told her, opening the door behind him and disappearing into his bedroom.

Slowly, her eyes travelled around the room.

In the centre of a tiny table in the corner there was a framed picture of Teestone, his mother, and the man his mother had lived with, but who, she knew without a doubt, wasn't his father – although she'd made the man believe he was. To the right of that there was another photo of a child.

She examined the picture of the baby sitting on a straw mat, staring out at the camera with a wide-eyed, open-mouthed, bewilderment. He hadn't grown out of that wide, wet mouth, nor indeed those eyes that seemed smaller than they really were, because of the heaviness of the lids. She replaced the picture, cautiously.

He was rebuilding the house his mother had left him, or rather he was replacing the wood with concrete, which meant erecting blocks against the board walls outside. When they were set in cement he would knock the planks out one by one from inside. Now, even before he'd done that, the wet concrete was seeping through the boards, leaving a pale sediment that left an ugly trace of powder and tiny bits of wood on her fingers. Electrical wires ran everywhere – along the floorboards, the ceiling and the walls. The rumours she'd heard were true. Teestone was bringing electricity to his house. Or he was having that man who came in the long, black car on Fridays – the man they called The Blade –

make the government do it for him. A couple of large, soft chairs lay upturned in a corner, completely covered with transparent plastic, and to the left of her there was a gaping hole through which she could see the earth below the house. Perhaps they had opened it up to replace the wooden pillars too. The smell of concrete was everywhere.

She was still contemplating this scene of devastation when Teestone came out with a small brown bag, the type the shop sold sugar by the half pound in. He did not place it in her hand but on the mahogany table in front of them. She took it up, and for a moment she felt confident, self-possessed.

She opened the bag carefully and dragged out the small plastic sac that was folded inside it.

"S'not a lot," she said, shocked. "Not a lot for all my money."

Teestone laughed till the fat vein at the side of his neck stood out. She watched it throb and pulse. "S'what you expect? Dis, dis worth more dan it weight in gold, y'know dat? More-dan-it-weight-in-gold." He spoke the last few words as though he'd rehearsed them till they sounded rhythmic and convincing. "Ask anybody."

"Didn know," she apologised, and then she brought it to her nose. She froze, fixing very dark, very steady eyes on him. "It s'pose to smell like dat? Like, uh, baby powder?"

Her question had taken him by surprise. The slight narrowing of his eyes and the way he tried to close his mouth without really managing it, confirmed her suspicion.

"It not s'pose to smell o baby powder," she told him quietly, a new hardness in her voice.

Is so it smell, he was about to tell her, and ask her what de hell she know 'bout niceness anyway, but her directness stopped him. He snatched the packet off the table and went back inside the bedroom. This time he returned sooner, dropped a different packet on the table and sat back heavily.

Norma took it up and passed it under her nose. She could see by his expression that he wanted her to leave. He was tired, or perhaps, now that his business with her was over, he just wanted to be rid of her. But she was not finished with him yet.

She wanted to know how she should prepare the stuff and he showed her. Her hands shook when she took the needle to examine the thin, evil thread of metal that slipped so easily into flesh. The first time she saw her boy use it, it had made her sick. He had taken it standing and had fallen straight back against the floorboards, his body rigid, like a tree deprived of its roots, doing nothing to break the fall. He'd cut his head badly and did not even know it, just laid there with that smile, that awful inner peace, while she turned him over and tended to his wound.

In her hand, the metal shone like an amber thread of light against the lamp.

"All of it is for de boy?" asked Teestone, showing her his tooth.

Some was for her son, she answered, and well, she was goin to use de rest. Was de niceness nicer if she used all of it in one go?

No, he told her, and the gold tooth glimmered in the light. If she used more than he just showed her – at that he pulled out a pack of razor blades, extracted one, opened the packet he'd handed her and separated a small portion, working it with the same care that she used to mix medicine for her boy's illness when he was a child. If she ever used more than *that* – he pointed at the tiny heap he'd separated – it would kill her.

"Too much niceness does kill. Y'unnerstan?" He laughed at his joke, lit a cigarette and leaned back against the chair. That too was new, the long cigarettes with the bit of silver at the end. In fact everything about Teestone seemed new. There was not the redness in the eyes, the dreadful tiredness that went deeper than age, the loosening of something precious and essential in the face, the damp surrender of the skin – once smooth and dark and beautiful with youth – to that terrible hunger that made her son strike out at her. Teestone looked fresh and happy and as alert as a cat. Money had made him handsome.

"Could be a nice house," she said, looking around the room, smiling the smallest of smiles, happier now than she had been for the past twelve months.

It was perhaps out of that odd sense of abeyance that she reached out suddenly and fixed Teestone's collar – or she might have been prodded by a desire to get an idea of what that shiny material really felt like. Her fingers brushed the side of his neck, touching the laughing vein. The young man recoiled with a violence she thought entirely undue.

She pretended not to notice his outrage, got up slowly and shuffled towards the door. There, she stopped and turned back.

"He lef school last year," she told him with a quiet, neutral look. "My Dan jus come an tell me dat he leavin school, and I say, "You can't. You can't, because you always tell me dat you want to see de world, dat you'll make me proud and build a nicer house for us when you become someting. You say you know how hard it is for me. How much I does do for you and how much I'll always do for you." An he laugh, like he was laughing at someting he know inside he head. He say he don't need to go nowhere no more to see de world, because he could see it from right dere where he lie down whole day on his back below my house. He tell me what he see sometimes and I can't make no sense of it. Cos I can't see inside mih boy head. I can't make no sense o people walkin over precipice an dem not dyin, o animal dat talk an laugh with you inside your head. I can't. But he say he see them and it make im happy.

"But is when de niceness get bad," she added softly, apologetically, "and I can't do nothing and I just hear im bawl an bawl an bawl, an he start hittin me, dat I does – well I does jus tek it.

"Y'know sometimes he hit me – my son? Hit me like he father used to?" Her voice had dropped to a whisper, thick and dark and gentle. "I let him. I let him till he get tired an fall asleep. He don' sleep no more like he used ter. Is like someting in he sleep, in he dreamin, beatin him up same like he do with me. All de time. Dat's why – dat's why I does…"

Teestone got up. "You get what you want, Miss Lady. Go!"

He'd already pushed open the door for her.

She walked out into a close, choked night. There were some girls outside, one or two not more than fourteen years old. Their precocious eyes fell on her incredulously, before turning back to the doorway with that still and hungry gaze she'd seen so often in her son during the quiet times when the shivering stopped and she'd force-fed him, or tried to. She knew all of them. Some she'd even delivered before her hand went funny. As children, she'd kept them for their mothers when they went off to St. George's for medicine or some necessary thing that their hillside gardens or the sea could not provide.

At their age, life was supposed to be kinder than it would ever be again – a time of an enormous promise that never lasted long, but was part of growing up. It belonged to that age. Was part of what kept you going for the rest of your life.

She decided not to go home. Her boy would be there now beneath the house, laid out on his back. He would remain there until she came and brought him in. If she did not feel like it, she would leave him there until some time close to morning when he would beat on her door until she let him in. Tonight he would not touch her because she had what it took to quiet him.

And that was another thing: he would not beg anymore, or offer Teestone anything for the relief of a needle. Once she saw him beg and it had shamed her. Saw him do it yesterday and it had shamed her even more because Teestone's refusal had brought him raging to her yard.

She took the track that ran off from the main road, which used to take him to the school in St. George's.

It was a long, hard walk because the rains from the weeks before had made a drain of the mud track and she was forced to steady her progress by grabbing at the bushes at the side. Ordinarily, she would have taken a torch, but she had not planned this visit; tonight, it had suddenly seemed like common sense that she should visit Grace. It was Grace who first told her about how, when he left for school, Daniel got off the bus a mile away, and doubled back to feed his veins on Teestone's powder. It was Grace who, without moving from her house, had found out where it came from and the nickname of the government man who visited Teestone every Friday night.

Grace was the only one to whom she spoke these days. Grace who'd had the gentlest of husbands; whose five daughters had all gone away and sent her money every month, from England, America and Canada; who'd offered to buy her son's uniform as a little present for winning the scholarship.

The back of her hand was itching – a deep, insistent itch that she could not reach because it was beneath the skin. It was the white scar where the skin had been cut away and then healed very badly. Many people thought she had been born that way, but she hadn't.

Grace's place was neat and small and full of colour. There were large blood-red hibiscus on her curtains and the enamelled bowls, cups, and the glasses in the cabinet had bouquets of flowers patterned all over them. Even her dress was a flower garden. God had given her eyes that shone like bits of coloured glass which, in some moods, were exactly like a cat's. Three kerosene lamps burned in her room. Their combined brightness gave a stark, shadowless quality to the room.

Grace settled her down and retreated to the kitchen. She returned with a bowl of soup and handed it to Norma.

"Eat!" she grunted.

"I done eat already."

"Then eat again. When trouble eating people, people have to eat back! So take de food an eat!"

The sweet smell of stewed peas and provision and salt meat almost made her faint. She hadn't eaten and Grace knew that she was lying. She'd lost her appetite for everything.

She placed the packet on the table and took up the bowl. Grace looked at the brown bag frankly, a question in her eyes.

"How's de boy?" she mumbled, still staring at the paper bag.

"Cost me everything. All that was left – a thousand dollars."

"What cost what?" asked Grace.

"That." Norma nudged the bag with the handle of the spoon.

Grace reached for it and opened it. The powder was on her fingers when she withdrew her hand. It could have been the effect of the candlelight on her silver bracelets, but her hand seemed to tremble. Her face went dead. "A thousand dollars! Fo' that?"

"What money I had left, I draw it out today."

"Jeezas Christ, you buy dat poison for your boy! You mad!"

"You think so?" The unconcern in her voice left a chill in Grace's stomach.

"Where he is?" Grace asked.

"Below the house. Sleepin. He tired."

"Still – erm hittin you?"

Norma stopped short, the bit of meat held between her thumb and index finger. She nodded.

"First the father and den the son. God bless me I don't have no boychild. But I wish, I wish I had a boy to raise his hand and touch me! Jeezan bread, I wish that if…" she stopped breathless, eyes flaming in the lamplight. "God forgive me, but I'd make dat sonuvabitch wish he never born."

Norma smiled, "Dat's de problem. You don't see? If he's a sonuvabitch, dat mean I'z the bitch dat make dis son. I don't wish he never born, but sometimes, sometimes I wish he don't live no more. To ease him up a bit." She looked up apologetically.

Grace grunted irritably. "You – you not goin to let him continue!"

"Nuh." Norma licked her fingers. "Nuh, I goin stop him. Tonight."

The certitude in her voice made Grace lean closer. "You goin ter… Jeezas, girl. Jeezas!"

"I not goin to, y'know… But like I say, I think of it sometimes – sometimes, all the time – I think of it. If y'all hear im bawlin, not to bother. Tell everybody not to bother." Something in her tone turned Grace's eyes to Norma's hand, the one that lay curled up like a bird's claw in her lap.

That hand alone was reason enough for everyone to bother. What kind of woman would place her hand between the cogs of a machine so that she could get the insurance to send her boy off to a high-class school in St. George's? Inside a canemill, besides! And if she could do that to herself for him, what on God's earth wouldn't she do to make her sacrifice worthwhile?

"Go easy," muttered Grace, taking up the bowl of unfinished food and heading for the kitchen. It was both a warning and a farewell and sensing this, Norma got up.

"If you hear him," she started.

"Uh-huh," Grace answered without turning round. "Rum-an-coke is what they call it – mix with something else." She called out from the kitchen. "They take dat ting and drink down rum right after. Dat's what make dem mad an beat up deir own flesh-an-blood so bad."

"Ah know." Norma curled her hand around the packet. All of a sudden the room felt too bright. She lifted her bad hand above her eyes as if to shade them from the sun. She paused briefly at the doorway, made as if to say something, then changed her mind before slipping out into the night.

Back home, she helped the boy from under the house and led him to the bedroom. He was quiet and aware of her but she knew that soon he would be shivering. She lit the lamp, undressed him and bathed him, like she used to. The way she thought she'd forgotten. And then she went back to the kitchen.

There, she carved out a portion of the stuff exactly as she'd seen Teestone do. She knew where he kept his needle, knew what she had to do.

She went in. Laid the small bag down beside the door. He'd already begun to shiver.

"C'mon Bumpsy, take this for Mammy," she said, and he seemed, from somewhere deep inside, to recognise that tone; began curling his shirt ends between his fingers like he used to when he was a child, while he looked at her with a tired, helpless uncertainty.

"Is for you. Tek it from Mammy," she urged, her voice soft and angry at the same time.

He took the needle and she watched him unflinching, while he served himself, so hungry for the ease it offered he was almost sobbing. Then, while he recovered and began floating away from her, she reached below the bed, opened the bag and took out the length of chain and the padlocks she had bought in St. George's. Still cooing her mummy-talk, she fastened her son against the bed.

If you hear him bawlin, she'd told Grace – who would, come morning, pass the message on to everyone – if you hear him bawlin, tell everybody not to bother. She knew the bawling would begin soon, or some time in the morning, or perhaps the next day, and it would go on for a long, long time.

Back in the kitchen she mixed most of what remained of the

powder in the paper bag. Finished, she leaned out of her window and observed the precocious girls, the motorbikes, the occupants of the occasional car sneaking back and forth between the road and Teestone's house.

Soon the traffic would subside, the lamps go out and the whole world come to a pause while Teestone slept.

It is a warm, tense night and the great, starless emptiness above her makes her think of futile distances, of the vastness of the world, her own smallness, and the place she feels she no longer has in it. Because a time does come, she thinks, when a woman can only hope for what comes after her – her children and the children that will come from them, that would pass on and on, if not her name, then her blood and perhaps a memory of her – an acknowledgment that they were alive only because she once existed, and that was what does mek life worth someting.

Her hand is itching again. Perhaps it will rain. Her hand always itches before rain. A low wind stirs the air, shakes the trees above the houses and leaves a smell of cinnamon, swamp and charcoal over the village. As if this is a signal, she straightens up, steps out into the night. Full height, she is much taller than most people have seen her, and she has lost her shuffle as she walks across the yard.

She remembers the hole in Teestone's living room and avoids it. In her head, she carries a very clear picture of the house and everything in it.

The lamp is lit in his bedroom and he is asleep, rolled over on one side and snoring softly. He is naked. One of the girls lies curled up in front of him, also naked, the young hips turned inwards, giving her a curious air of innocence. Sleep has stripped away what remains of the womanishness she wears by day and made of her a child again.

She kneels beside Teestone and he stirs, perhaps sensing her presence.

The jab wakes him. He erupts out of sleep, his hand clutching that laughing vein at the side of his neck, but she is strong and she keeps him and the needle there until she empties it of her thousand dollars worth of niceness. Eyes wide, Teestone stares at her. His fist closes on her wrist. It is the bad hand that he is crushing and it hurts. But she offers him a smile – beautiful and alluring – something wonderful to take with him.

He eases back on the pillow, releasing her, and sighs the longest, most restful of all sighs, his face still incredulous, still profoundly outraged.

The girl has not stirred from sleep, and for that Norma Browne is grateful.

She walks out of the house, turns and spits carelessly at the dark before crossing to her yard.

Before she goes in, she pauses, turns her face up at the sky and sniffs. She could smell the morning. But it is still dark. And the world and the birds down there are very, very quiet.

LEONE ROSS

PRESIDENT DAISY

Mary sat on the train and worried about it going bang-a-lang underneath her. Her cousin Toby said that when the train started up it would make bang-a-lang noises because it was full of devils trying to get out. "Them going to fly out an' eeeeat you!" he sang, as soon as he heard she was going.

Mary sat. The train hadn't started going bang-a-lang yet, but it *was* making a *sshhhh-caaah* sound, like the devils were getting ready to wake up. She tried to calm herself by looking out of the window. People were moving busily back and forth, talking and lifting things: baskets and hampers and what her Auntie Greenie called scandal bags – because you could see through them – full of fruit and vegetables. A man rushed past, lugging a small goat under one arm. Mary giggled nervously.

"Tee-kets." A man walked through the carriage, a little iron machine around his neck. His teeth were big white lumps in his mouth. He could hardly close it because it was so full.

Mary gave him her ticket like Auntie Greenie had said, and tried to smile when he smiled at her.

"You 'lone by you'self, girl?" said the ticket master.

"Yes, sir."

Auntie Greenie told her she should call everybody "sir", and that she should mind her peas and queues, which confused her a little. There had been queues at the train when Auntie Greenie came to see her away, but there had been no peas and she didn't like peas. Maybe the ticket master would try to give her peas? She watched his back meander down the train as her fist closed around the money pinned into her pocket. Thirty dollars in case of a 'mergency, and a piece of paper with her uncle's name and address in Aunty Greenie's fancy writing. Auntie Greenie had gone to a big school with lots of tall-haired people like herself.

Mary didn't look like them, so maybe she looked like her daddy, but she'd never met him so she didn't know. Mary knew about the stoosh school because Auntie Greenie showed her old photographs. Rows of pretty light-brown girls standing with her aunt and Mary's mother, who was called Vi before she went away to America and left Mary with Auntie Greenie. Now she wrote letters and always signed her name Violet, not even Mamma. Auntie Greenie scolded Mary when she cried over the first letter.

"You mother have a nice white husband now," she said. "You must be happy for her."

Auntie Greenie hadn't packed her any lunch and they'd forgotten breakfast because her aunt got up late, even though she had twice knocked politely on her bedroom door. Mary thought she would give her lunch money instead, but it seemed she'd forgotten that too. It was the helper's day off; *she* would have remembered. She was a nice fat lady.

She couldn't use the 'mergency money for food. She wasn't sure she knew what a 'mergency was. Her stomach hurt. Was that a 'mergency? Auntie Greenie was mean not to remember. After all, she *was* going away – *Forever More* – as Toby kept saying all month, in a big, scary voice. Toby was twelve, and he knew things. *Forever More* sounded like something for grownups, not what happened to a little girl. All morning she'd been trying to stop herself thinking about where she was going.

Montego Bay. To live with Uncle Barney. It didn't sound nice.

Toby had an opinion on this as well.

"*Country* Uncle Barney? You goin' turn into a ugly country gyal."

"No I'm *not*!" she'd answered him back, but she didn't feel brave.

"Nobody don't like Uncle Barney. Him so ugly him have to run go country to find a wife." Toby smacked his lips. "Country fulla duppy too, and di whole ah dem stink like saltfish. When dem come at nighttime, dem suck out you spleen and you marrow, down to you bone-part."

So, if she survived the train devils, there would be more to deal with. She would eventually get off the train, but who would save her at night? Uncle Barney would laugh if she got to country and talked about duppies, and his wife – who was probably an angry person because Uncle Barney was ugly – would be angry with *her*.

She had to remember what the helper said: that Toby told lies to get attention because nobody liked him. Which made her feel sad. And Auntie Greenie would never send her anywhere bad. Her aunt had a sharp tongue, but she let her make tamarind balls in the kitchen every Sunday, picking the tart, dark flesh off the fruit, sucking the sticky seeds until the top of her mouth burned. Then her aunt's friends came over and she was sent away with the top of a condensed milk can to soothe the mouth, because it was time to talk big people business.

She hoped Uncle Barney would have a nice house and that his angry wife wouldn't take her to church for *too* long.

The train hissed and she sat upright, fingers gripping the seat. She could see men and boys running up and down outside, banging the sides of the carriage. They were leaving. Mary squinched up her eyes and held her breath.

"Everybody come 'pon dis train now!" the ticket master yelled down the platform. Mary watched people scuttle into their seats with handfuls of chickens and green bananas and ackee and everybody talking at a great rate. Most of them were women.

"Lawd, my dear! Me never know waffi do when Berylou come to me yard lookin' fe her man…"

"Everybody come pon dis train *now*!"

"You want busta? Icy-mint? Suck-suck? Weh you want?"

"Anybody who nuh deh pon dis train *now* get lef ah Kingston!"

"Likkle girl, I goin' sit down right here. You mind?"

Mary stared. The man standing above her, smiling, reminded her of an antelope from one of her schoolbooks. His legs were stretchy and thin and he wore a brown pinstripe suit. Best of all, he was wearing a tall red hat, an American daisy sticking out of the side. She couldn't speak. He was the most interesting-looking man she had ever seen. She could see that the women around them thought so too, as they were rolling their eyes and using their lips to point.

The interesting man stretched out his hand for her to shake.

He had very long fingernails, like the bus conductors grew on their little fingers and then painted red. But these nails were silver, and they'd been shaped into wicked looking points, and there were little daisies painted on them.

"You don't mind?" asked the man. He was looking at her very seriously now, but it wasn't the glare of other grownups, hush you mouth and don't come inna big people business. He looked like he might just listen to what she said.

"Anybody can sit down here, sir," she said. It was strange that an adult was asking her permission to do anything. It made her feel very grown up.

"Good!" The man sat down and continued to regard her, folding his legs underneath himself. He was smiling a smile of such beatific good will that Mary's chest felt fizzy, like when she drank too much ice cream soda.

"So you alright?"

"Yes, sir."

"You is a *likkle* gyal."

She wasn't sure what to say to that. People always said things that you could see in front of your face, and sometimes they said it twice. A fat man was *fat-fat*; a tall man was called Sky; the one-armed man was Oney; Auntie Greenie had a friend called Pot Cover, because of the shape of his forehead.

"Yes, sir."

"So what you name?"

She was proud of her name.

"Mary Anne Bathsheba Clientele Switzie Pearl and Ezmereleena."

The man smiled even wider.

"Brown," she added.

The man seemed suitably impressed.

"Mary Anne Bathsheba Clientele Switzie Pearl *and* Ezmereleena Brown. Dat is one *rahtid* name."

She liked him even more now. Auntie Greenie would have had him straight out of her house for the bad word, but Mary thought he was quite exciting.

"So what I must call you?" he asked.

Mary considered this. No one had ever asked her to choose. Only adults got to change Vi to Violet. She curled the baby hair at her temples, pretending to think. But she knew.

"Ezmereleena." Mary was a boring church girl. But Ezmereleena would not be afraid of duppies or devils.

"Good!" The man clicked one silver finger against the other. "And you can call me President Daisy."

She stared at him. "Um… dat is you name for true?"

He leaned forward. "You see how you choose Ezmereleena? Well, me did choose President Daisy."

She was confused. Everybody said never to question an adult, but this man wasn't like any adult she had ever met. "What you is President over?"

President Daisy laughed. "How you mean?"

"President have tings dem rule over. Like… like a country. Or a city."

"But you smart! Well, I used to be President over Cockpit Country, but now I live in Montego Bay." Something about that seemed to amuse him a great deal.

Mary realised that the train had already puffed out of the station, and it was going bang-a-lang, but she really couldn't believe that devils would dare hurt her while President Daisy was sitting nearby.

"You live inna Montego Bay?"

"Nearby there."

He began to tell her about the countryside, but she found it difficult to concentrate on his stories as he swept his long arms around in circles. He had more dimples than she had ever seen on a person: two in one cheek, three in the other. Even his nose seemed to have a pleasant dip in its tip. His nails flashed in the sun as he spoke.

"When I was just your size, I used to go to river in de morning time, wash clothes wid mi madda. All I could see as I look over de place is green hills and people ah tell you *morning*. Dem forget how fe do dat inna de big city dem. Nuff-nuff pickney deh bout, play cricket, climb all big tree, ketch fish and croakin' lizard, and in de evening man and man play domino, roast fish an' breadfruit, eat till belly full. You ever stand under a waterfall, Ezmereleena?"

She shook her head.

"Auntie Greenie say I musn't put mi head under water."

"Well, that is a shame. What else she said?"

Mary folded her hands and recited obediently.

"Remember to cream your skin a morning. Don't sit with your leg spread; that is not a lady. Don't eat and laugh, nor eat and drink at the same time. Chicken merry, hawk is near. You go to school to learn, not put on a fashion show. Don't talk too loud – we are not up in heaven straining to hear you. Badder dog than you bark, and flea kill 'im. Go to Sunday school and mind when preacher talk. Time is longer than rope. What sweet nanny goat, bound to run him belly –"

"Lord have mercy!" President Daisy interrupted. "What a whole *load* of things for one girl-child, and what a good memory you have!"

Mary beamed and then exhaled in one big puff. She wished Toby could see her, travelling into *Forever More*, like a big girl. President Daisy was looking out of the window, humming to himself. She looked, too. They were running out of city, the last pieces of Kingston stretched out around them, tenement shacks topped with zinc sheets, like foil glinting in the sun. Up and down the carriage women continued loud discussions, mothers cuffed bawling children, mounds of produce threatened to burst and overflow into the corridors.

Mary's stomach, no longer distracted by fear, began to grumble again. A woman to her right sat with a tray of sweets between her knees. Mary craned her neck. Sticky Bustamantes, black with Demerara sugar; her beloved tamarind balls; coconut grater cakes all lumpy and pink on the top; gizzada tarts – her mother used to call them "pinch-me-round"; Chinese sweeties in salt and sweet flavours – all scattered on a bed of humble blue icy-mints. Mary's mouth watered. Even one little icy mint would be so good. Her hand played with the money and instructions in her pocket. Auntie Green had written it down: "If you uncle not there, take the 73 bus and ask them to put you off at The Church of

Immaculate Conception. Go in and find the pastor. He will know you uncle. Barney might have run to country, but he is a God-fearing man."

Surely Uncle Barney and his wife would remember to pick her up. She felt quite scared at the idea of a strange bus trip and a strange church.

"Missa Daisy, ahm, how much you think that lady selling tamarind ball for?"

President Daisy cocked his head to one side. "Well, I don't rightly know. Mek we ask her. Lady!"

Her stomach lurched. She didn't want the woman to think she was definitely going to buy something. But it was too late. President Daisy was waving his long fingers. The woman swivelled her neck – and tray – to face them. She had been in deep discussion with the sullen man sitting next to her. He looked like he'd swallowed lime juice. The tray of sweets quivered.

"How much fi you tamarind ball?" asked President Daisy.

"Dollar fi three."

"Dis little gyal want three."

Dollar. No. She should keep the money safe. "Missa Daisy – ", but the woman was sorting through the tray.

"Me will give her six fi $1.50. Weh you seh?"

More money, now! The lady was haggling. This was worse. Mary put a hand on President Daisy's arm, but he was grinning and showing his dimples. "$1.70 fe six, throw two icy mint in deh."

"Icy mint ah thirty cents fi one."

"You lie! Since when? Two dollar buy five tamarind, two icy mint, throw in a Busta." President Daisy twinkled. The woman twinkled back. The sour man twitched.

The woman glanced at Mary. "Look how she need fi fat-up! Is only one Busta she want? Five dollar get package deal: two tamarind, three icy mint, two Busta, one gizzada, plus a bag ah Chinese sweetie. Di salt one. Is lunch dat!"

"Lunch? Lunch mean chicken, man! Oxtail!"

They were up to five dollars! This was getting bad!

"Missa Daisy –"

"Me soon come, sweetheart. Mek me just fix dis ooman!" He twinkled some more. "Pretty 'ooman like you, ah try tief a man?"

The woman reached inside her voluminous skirts. "If ah lunch you ah look, me have chicken here. Ten dollar buy some good food. Look like *you* need it. What a man maaga!"

President Daisy roared with laughter. As the woman began to pile out what seemed like huge quantities of food onto the carriage floor, Mary glanced around for someone to help her stop the flow of barter. Maybe the sour man would help. He would have a good-looking face if he wasn't so miserable all the time. But the man looked even meaner now. His face was all puffed up, and his eyes moved back and forth between the woman and President Daisy.

The woman flourished several icy, multicoloured bags above her head. "You want a suck-suck? It hot today, boy!"

President Daisy looked at her and laughed harder. "You ah obeah 'ooman to rass! How you manage keep dem suck-suck cool? You have ice inna you baggie?"

"Eh-eh! Weh you know bout my crotches, boy?"

"All like *him* don't know nothing bout woman!" spat the sour man.

President Daisy fluttered his nails in a dismissive gesture. "Now, Miss Lady, I'm lookin' two box lunch and three dollar sweetie fi me sweetheart, Ezmereleena." He beamed at Mary. "Don't worry, me have money."

"Keep you money, bloodclaaht *batty* bwoy!"

The train froze. The lady clutched at her tray. "Donovan," she whined, "you don't see me doin' business?"

"Shut up you mouth, gyal!" The woman ducked her head, all twinkle gone. Mary thought Donovan's face was even worse than before. It was two times bigger, and his eyes were shining dangerously. His whole body was swelling, chest forward, fists clenching. He wasn't as tall as President Daisy, but he was much bigger. And so *angry*.

Mary looked at President Daisy. His body had changed too. It was as if he'd gotten smaller, just for a moment, like he was wrapping himself deeper into his own skin. But when he spoke, Mary couldn't believe how calm his voice was.

"Boy. Quiet youself."

It was too late. Donovan got to his feet. The sweetie tray teetered. Three tarts fell to the floor. Donovan crushed one under his heel. He was chanting now.

"Batty bwoy. Maama man. Suck hood bwoy. You love dem nastiness don't it, batty bwoy?"

"Ezmereleena," said President Daisy. "Put you fingers in you ears."

She obeyed, disbelieving. The world became muffled. Why was the man being so mean to President Daisy? She could see both men's mouths moving. *I don't want to see any beating,* she thought. She took her fingers out of her ears. Not being able to hear them was worse than waiting on bang-a-lang devils in the train.

"Ah going *fuck* you up, bwoy!" Donovan snarled. He swung. The women in the carriage shrieked.

President Daisy moved faster than anyone Mary had ever seen. He shifted to the right, unfolding himself out of his seat and past his attacker, all in one motion. His tall, red hat remained upright, serene and immovable.

Donovan's fist collided with the window, making a very satisfactory thwacking noise. He howled and cursed, cradling the wounded hand.

"Boy, I don't want to fight you." President Daisy was at his full height now. People stared and clamoured. Donovan's woman croaked a protest. "Leave de man in him personal business, Donovan!"

"Business? How you mean? Him fi *dead*!" Donovan lunged at President Daisy, who sidestepped him again, making him stumble. The carriage lurched. Donovan righted himself, grunted, and tried to hit him again. Mary realized that she was sucking her thumb. She took the offending digit away from her mouth. That was for *little* girls. She gulped, waiting for the meaty fist to connect with President Daisy's face. President Daisy stepped sideways. There wasn't much space, but he seemed able to move around it like a peeny-wally. Donovan roared in frustration. Mary felt like her head would break into little pieces.

Which is when President Daisy reached out and began to tickle the man.

It was the last thing anyone could have expected. First, the silver fingers in Donovan's solar plexus, as his hands went upwards in defence. His eyes bugged out of his head so hard, Mary wanted to laugh. Moving swiftly, his tongue stuck out in concentration, President Daisy danced his hands across his opponent's body, shoulders, stomach, running under his arms, down to his hips, across his neckbones, fingers flying as if he was playing a piano, always two steps ahead before the other man could push them away. Donovan was practically crying in frustration.

"You going to stop play with big man, boy?"

"*Batty* –"

"Alright, then. But if you play with big man, big man will play with you."

"Ease off me, man! Don't touch me –"

"Or what?" President Daisy drew nearer. Donovan writhed and shrieked. President Daisy was holding one of his arms above his head, tickling his armpit. "You *lucky* that woman and pickney deh bout."

Tears streamed down Donovan's face. He began to beg. "Please sir, please…" He had dropped to his knees, but still President Daisy stooped over him, forcing laughter and painful gasps out of him. Mary thought he looked angry for the first time and that was a bit scary.

"President Daisy!" she said, as loud as she could.

"You going back weh, boy? You going stop try frighten pickney?"

"Yeah, yeah!"

"Tell de likkle gyal you sorry. She name Ezmereleena."

Chokes, gasps.

"Me sorry-me sorry-Ezmereleena. Me sorry!"

"Stop, President Daisy, *stop*!" said Mary.

President Daisy looked confused, as if he'd been somewhere else, not there. "What?"

She stared at him. "Stop tickle him now."

It stopped. The American daisy on the hat swayed gently.

Donovan got to his feet, sweating profusely. He looked at President Daisy with something like awe. His sides heaved.

"You… you *touch* me."

"Yes. A battyman touch you. Now go sit down in another carriage and take you woman with you and tell her nice things."

Donovan scrambled backwards. The sweetie woman followed him more slowly. As she passed Mary, she dropped five sweets into her lap. She exchanged a look with President Daisy.

President Daisy nodded. "Yeah."

He sat down. His face seemed sad. Mary looked at him. All those things he said and Donovan said. It whirled around her head.

"Missa Daisy…"

"President." His face looked like he might cry, and she wanted to hug him so he wasn't upset, but she didn't know how. "I'm sorry, Ezmereleena."

She reached out her hand. "You want a tamarind ball?"

They sat, sucking the sweets, spitting seeds into their hands. Mary extricated a lump of sugar from her back tooth. President Daisy rubbed stickiness off his front teeth. The carriage went bang-a-lang. Soon she would be in Montego Bay, and there was nothing she could do about it. She put her hand on her jaw and sighed.

President Daisy looked at her. His face had gone all soft, like cotton. "What happen?"

It came out in a flurry. "My cousin Toby say dat country full up ah duppy and how dem smell bad and dem gwine come get me, an' I know de devil in di train not comin' while you is here, but de duppy going to definitely come for me and eat me spleen and I can't tell Uncle Barney or him wife because dem is church people and all dem going to say is *foooolishness*…" Her lip trembled. She was telling a stranger all this, but he had an American daisy in his red hat.

President Daisy patted her arm. "Don't cry, Essy. Listen to me."

She sniffed and tried to be brave.

428 PEEPAL TREE . CONTEMPORARY CARIBBEAN SHORT STORIES

"Yes," he said. "Country have duppy."

That wasn't what she had expected at all. She put her thumb in her mouth.

"*But*," President Daisy flung out an arm, "when you see them at night time all you haffi do is stop an say howdy. People think seh them bad, but that is a lie.' He grinned at her. "You know, whole heap of people think something bad, but is just because they don't have no experience with that thing. Me have *nuff* conversation with duppy and them never bother me yet. In *fact*, them smell like lady perfume." He sat back with a satisfied smile on his face.

She couldn't believe it. A specialist in duppies!

"So... them not goin' to trouble me?"

"No, man. All you do if you see one is tell dem howdy, and dat you is President Daisy friend."

★

She slept, then woke up when President Daisy shook her to say there were ten minutes left. She straightened her skirt and felt very alone indeed. She thought about how she didn't know Uncle Barney, and even less about his wife. She'd sent Auntie Greenie an Easter bun last Christmas, with sultanas and wrapped in a yellow bow. A woman like that might be nice to her. But she'd also heard that women didn't like strange girls in their houses. Auntie Greenie's friends said so. Trouble was sure to follow when too many hen live in a rooster pen. Her mother had worked as a helper for her American husband before he divorced his wife, so she was already known as trouble. With a mother like that.

The train hissed, slowing.

Maybe Uncle Barney's wife would think she was trouble too.

"No devil came out of the train then," said President Daisy.

"No," she said. But she could feel the tamarinds in her tummy, making her sick.

"Montego Bay, final stop, final stop!" sang out the ticket master.

Silver nails folded themselves over her small hands.

★

Uncle Barney was smaller than she thought he would be, al-

though he did have coolie hair and big eyes. He also had a sign
with her name in big letters: WELCOME! MARY! BROWN! He
was smiling wide.

"Welcome," said Uncle Barney. He pulled her into his arms
and hugged her. He smelt comforting. Like lady's perfume. He
was telling her how brave she was to come on the train by herself,
such a pretty, brave little girl. She looked around. No sign of a
scary wife. She looked up at President Daisy, who was standing
above them both. The cotton wool look was back, so soft and nice.

"This is my friend, President Daisy," she said to her uncle. "He
tickled a bad man on the train."

"Did he now?"

Most of the people who got off the train were gone and the
platform was nearly empty. The air smelled like mango. She
watched a bright green parrot rustle in a tree nearby, then fly to
another, squawking excitedly. She looked back at the men. They
were standing, watching her, smiling.

They were holding hands.

"Her name isn't Mary. It's Ezmereleena," said President Daisy.

She looked at the sign with her old name. It was red, and heart-
shaped, and covered with little American daisies.

OLIVE SENIOR

SILENT

What endured in him was not the remembrance of noise. Not the shots ricocheting in the small room, not the sound of tearing and splintering, not the aftershocks. What remained was the sudden silence that sucked him in and shut the noise out. Only the day before, his teacher had described the eye of the hurricane: that calm, silent centre in the middle of the storm. That sudden stillness before whoosh, from the other direction, the second, more terrifying wind came bursting through. In the heart of this hurricane, he listened for the terror returning, but heard nothing. Not the crack of the door kicked in again, not his father jumping up and reaching for his gun and falling in the very action, not the blasts, the ripping sounds. He thought, in a wondering kind of way, *So this is what it feels like to be deaf*, and inside this new space, he found himself surprised and glad to learn something new, something he could hold on to.

★

Under the bed, where his mother thrust all three of them, his little brother and sister clutch him so tightly they are like warm glue melting against his back. They do not let go even when he begins to crawl to where he can look and see what is happening. Through the space where the pink chenille bedspread ends, a foot from the rough plank floor, he watches the blood pumping out of his father, creeping ever so slowly towards him. He watches the sneakers of the two men dancing around, tossing the place, searching for something, watches as one comes close and lifts a corner of the mattress, bends down to look underneath and sees the bundle of children, his face framed by the metal bedspring in bars of cruel light. In that sudden glare, Joel knows he should close his eyes but he cannot. He knows the men; they are part of his father's posse. After a suffocating moment the man drops the mattress, and when nothing else happens, Joel can't stop himself, he has to crawl out farther to see more of the room, to see his mother.

He sees, first, her toes tightly clenched in her slippers, then as he pushes his head farther out, her hands rigid at her sides. Pulled by the tension of her body, his eyes travel up past her arms, and he sees the gun at her head, her mouth opening and closing. He quickly retreats, closes his eyes tightly, and waits for that final shot. No sound comes.

He has no idea how long he lay there clutching Clive and Jessamine – it could have been days or weeks or years – until he senses someone crawling under the bed, feels his mother's trembling as she locks her body onto them tightly, wordlessly.

After a time, his mother's grip loosens. She raises her body and half turns to face the door as he turns towards her, his chest heavy inside. She puts her finger to her lips and gives him a look that means "Stay here" and gets out from under the bed just as the door bursts in again. Police. He can tell from their boots. His little brother and sister stay silent; not even a whimper, though he can smell them for they have soiled themselves. Him, too. But he knows he needs to be quiet for police are dangerous bad men. Everyone knows.

He watches as they lower their M16s to poke at the body on the floor, which the flies and ants have already colonized in the rising heat. They wipe the congealed blood off their boots on the small rug Miss Simms, his mother's employer, had given her at Christmas and which no one in the family is allowed to touch much less walk on. And though he still can't hear, all his other senses are heightened; sickness is rising in him from all the smells, nasty smells from sweaty bodies, dried blood, bodily waste. As if all the everyday noxious odours of the yard and lane, the entire neighbourhood, the world, are rising up to stifle the air in the room.

He sees the others arrive, the plainclothes men. The first one leans down to get a good look at the man on the floor; he smiles broadly. Others come in to stare at the body, smile and give each other high-fives, strut around and kick with their sneakers and heavy boots at the furniture and possessions strewn on the floor. He can see his mother shaking her head up and down, opening her mouth, turning and moving her body, gesturing with her hands, moving her feet. They take her outside.

He closes his eyes again and drifts back onto the silent island on which they are marooned under the bed, he and his little brother and sister who are now wide awake but silent, too, both with their thumbs in their mouths, still glued tightly to him. He feels as if they will never again be separated from one another. It is as if they are sealed off, hearing nothing of the clamour outside. Nothing from the tenement yard, from the laneway full of curious people, nothing of the everyday sounds, the screams or shouts or curses, the raucous laughter, the music blasting from every doorway, the motorbikes and cars revving up and down the narrow streets and lanes, the scatter of gunshots that near and far pattern night and day like the barking of the mangy dogs.

Then everything happens at once. His mother pulls them out from under the bed, lifts up the baby, and leads them outside through the silently staring crowd to the bathroom where she washes them off, herself too, while he watches the water run red into the hole in the concrete. She rubs them dry and puts them in clean clothes. A policewoman is helping her to dress Jess and Clive and, next thing, the policewoman is taking Jess and the bag with Jess's things and he and Clive are being pushed into the back of a police car.

"Mama," he tries to speak but nothing comes out. She leans inside the car window and puts her hand on his head in that gentle way he loves. "Is alright Jo-Jo. I come to the station and get you later. Look after your brother and sister for me. You are the man in charge."

He opens his mouth to speak but again nothing comes, as if the bullets had been a hand passing across his mouth to seal it. The policeman shuts the car door and they drive off; his last view is of his mother standing there, surrounded by armed policemen, and TV cameras and the street full of curious people. It was a scene so ordinary and everyday in his neighbourhood; he would usually just push through such a crowd on his way to school, even if the bodies were there in full view, not bothering to look or stop to find out who was the latest victim, the whys or the wherefores. He took it to be the way life was lived. He would hear the details at school anyway; the children were always so full of it, playing out the death scene like actors in some gangster movie – Pi! Pi! Pi! At the sound of gunshots, real or imagined, they threw themselves flat, pressing their bodies to the ground. Now in the back of the police car, Joel feels so far away from the scene, from himself, it is as if none of it existed.

He rouses himself when they come to the police station, fully expecting to be locked up in a cell, but in the reception area they sit him and Clive on a wooden bench against a far wall. The policewoman who had taken Jess inside brings her back, sucking on a bottle; she says something and smiles when she hands her over to him.

Just at that moment, pandemonium breaks out at the station. Armed police in riot gear rush in and out; from their movements, he can tell that radios and walkie-talkies are crackling, the station phones are ringing, voices are raised, orders are barked. All the adults are in a frenzy. The children on the wooden bench press themselves against the wall for safety, and are soon forgotten. After a while, Joel moves Jess off his lap and seats her beside him so Clive who is nodding off can lie on the bench and put his head in his lap. Jess doesn't protest as she normally would. She leans against Joel, who puts his arm around her, wondering if she and Clive have also fallen deaf and dumb.

Joel is dying of thirst. His jeans and t-shirt are soaked from the heat of the day and the clammy bodies of his brother and sister. His sockless feet feel slick and damp and uncomfortable inside his sneakers. He contorts his body so as not to disturb the little ones and lifts up first one foot and then the other to take the shoes off, glad he hadn't done up the laces. They are the same make as the sneakers worn by the men the night before, by the plain-clothes detectives – the favoured footwear of all real men, like his father, who'd brought them all new shoes from his last trip to New York, crossing off another thing from his long list of promises – like moving them out of the tenement and into a real house, soon.

Joel remembers how proud he was to wear his new sneakers to school, and at the same time worried that someone would beat him up to steal them. Now they feel like fire consuming his feet. He pulls them off and drops them on the floor, then kicks them hard under the bench. He wriggles his toes. He is dying to lie on the bench and go to sleep. He knows he can't. He has to stay alert. He is the man in charge.

Much later, when things have quietened down at the station, someone notices them. Joel sees the policemen and policewoman looking at them and talking. He wonders where they will take them and if they will shoot them and why his mother hasn't come. He knows she will come, for she has never let him down yet. But when? And if the policemen take them somewhere, how will she find them?

The policewoman comes over and takes them in turn to the washroom, making them use the toilet and wash their hands and faces; talking to them all the while, though he can't make out what she is saying. A policeman takes Jess's bottle and Joel is surprised when he brings it back; he doesn't wait on the policewoman, he takes the baby in his arms to feed her, parading around with her as the other police tease him and laugh. Another policeman comes in with bags from Kentucky Fried. Joel didn't know he was hungry until he catches the smell of chicken and fries. He is pleasantly surprised when the policeman hands a bag each to him and Clive. He didn't know he could get through a large Pepsi so fast.

After this, Clive falls asleep. Joel stays alert, watching out for Jess who the police have taken away into another room. By the time they bring her back, in clean nappies and clutching another full bottle, they have switched on the lights and the little bit of sky he can see outside is darkening. His mother hasn't come and the big policeman in charge is looking at them in a vexed way, talking to the policewoman. Joel knows they are going to move them somewhere or take them back home. But what if his mother isn't there? And the gunmen come back? He is sure they took his father's guns, so he won't have a weapon to defend little Clive and Jessamine.

Then his mother does come in the door, in a rush, followed by a well-dressed lady who he knows as Miss Simms, one of the women she did daywork for. Miss Simms is young and pretty and rich. She is always sending them presents. She and his mother turn and smile at them; but, when he makes to move, his mother signals for him to stay where he is. They talk to the police. Next thing, the police rush them all through the back entrance and into Miss Simms' car, which is parked in the lane, and she drives away in a tearing hurry, not in the direction of home. His mother and Miss Simms don't say a word until they are well out of their part of town – a part that people like Miss Simms never visit.

In the back seat, the three of them sit down low as their mother instructs them, so they can't be seen. She herself is crouched down in the front seat so it looks like Miss Simms is the only one in the car. They travel for a good long time like this before their mother sits up and Joel passes Jess over to her.

After that it is as if Miss Simms, with her long wavy hair and thin brown hands on the wheel, cannot stop driving, as if she is the one that has to carry on, carry them far away from the danger that stalks them, through streets Joel has never seen, past gardens and trees and houses as big as churches, way past where Miss Simms lives. They climb higher and higher towards the mountains he sees in the distance, leaving the city far behind. Through the open windows he feels a fresh breeze, air that is cleaner than anything he has felt in his life. Around them, the land is dark, except for the light now and then of a house in the distance, the occasional car headlights suddenly lancing the night, approaching like monsters before abandoning them to the dark. He has never seen such darkness before, yet he isn't afraid. He is kneeling on the back seat so he can look out the rear window and wriggle his bare toes. From this vantage point, he can monitor the splendour of the dark hills that are closing ranks behind them like guards; witness the purity of the clear skies above, and the embedded stars that are shimmering and pulsing like gunshots – but far, far away. And silent.

JAN SHINEBOURNE

THE GODMOTHER

"Put it in her palm, then she will always have luck."

I did it, just as Mother said, and like magic or luck, the baby opened her palm and took the coin. Then they took it from her and put it with the rest of her money and presents.

★

Now her father was telephoning. His voice was travelling not just through the telephone line but also in my memory. Outside, the English rain is falling. People are passing by but I can still see his face: jovial, happy. A tall, strong, handsome man for a child to idealise.

Am I making him up? Did I use to make him up? He is speaking my name with an accent and intonation that is not a Georgetown voice, not a New Amsterdam voice, but a Canje voice, the one that was too familiar to be mistaken for any other a mile or ten or twenty or seventy or a hundred miles upriver or up the road. He is sounding just like my father, many years dead now and buried where I was born.

When she expected a visit from a special visitor, my mother used to enact laborious rituals of cleansing and cooking. I was witness to this ritual for so many years that I also perfected it. I dust the entire house: ceilings, walls, books, shelves, furniture, wash all the dust away with soap and water then rinse with perfumed water. If we'd had carpets they would have been shampooed, so I shampoo the carpets. The labour of preparation never wearied my mother; it charged her with energy. I still mimic this behaviour, her preparation for receiving people, not just cleaning and cooking, but making something extraordinary happen.

I plan Guyanese food for my long-lost godchild and her parents: calaloo-and-egg soup, pepperpot, ground provisions, salt-fish and boiled eggs in a wash of olive oil with fried onions and tomatoes, fried ochroes, chicken curry and roti, hassa cooked in coconut and rice, chow mien, black cake. From their hiding places, I take precious casareep, rum and cassava bread smuggled into London. Like Mother, I will take out my best china and glasses for these guests. In cooking this meal, perhaps a dream will come true.

I have to travel across London, to Brixton, to buy sorrel, soursop, hassa, mangoes, papaya, wiri-wiri, and ball-of-fire pepper. The journey is familiar. I can close my eyes and find my way round the underground. Usually I check the route on the underground map at the platform while I wait for the train. Sitting in the carriage I read the smaller replica of the same map on the ceiling of the carriage and count the stops when the train pulls in and out of stations. Today I ignore these maps.

Today, my feet, not my eyes and Brixton landmarks, take me to the market. I don't stop in at the Ritzy for a programme or phone Claudia to see if she is in. I don't stay all day shopping in the market with her and eating lunch. I don't visit Cecil's Bakery for salara and pine tarts. I go straight to Evan's and he gives me the sorrel and soursop he says just came from Trinidad and he tells me I am lucky to get the wiri-wiri and thick-leaf thyme from Guyana because he is growing it himself in his own kitchen. The return journey is the same – no maps.

In winter, the kitchen is the coldest room in the house. The draught pours though the door, along the tiled floor, snaps at my heels, and gnaws at my feet. But I am in another world as I cook. In that world, the sun is hot. Naturally, my god-daughter's christening was on a Sunday, at midday.

Sunday was a family day. We would all be together at home, living in slow time with the newspapers to read and lunch to cook and eat at leisure. It is the one day Father and Mother sleep in the afternoon. They sleep outdoors in the hammocks under the mango trees. This memory is very easy to live. I slide into it so easily, like a contented child going to sleep between clean sheets fresh from drying in the sun and fresh air. Sometimes, it is this easy to live in the past and present.

Happy, I begin to peel the onions, boil the water and heat the oil. The clock reminds me I have three hours to cook the meal before the Allens are here. When he telephoned, I could not remember their names. He was Joseph, his wife was Cynthia, and my goddaughter was Yvette. Now their faces in my mind have their rightful names. This brings with it the placing of people to places. The school, the church, the sugar factory, the overseers quarters, the court and police stations – these are parts of the past to dislike because they were places for colonising people.

The christening is as bright as the sun was on that day. I see it as clearly as I see the ingredients of my cooking. The steam from the pots forms a mist. It rises in the air and I see more of the christening. It is very very hot but the men are wearing suits and ties. I pour the boiling water over the salt fish. I toss cloves and cinnamon sticks, orange peel and dark sugar into the hot, scarlet sorrel liquid.

I can see my father's trunk again – an ancient possession of his. This trunk came from somewhere far away. My father always tells me which country, but I always forget. He came from three, or more. He was born in one, one brought him here and several adopted him. I am a child again, struggling to drag it from under the bed. The handle is thin, black metal, very loose in my small hands. Every time I pull it towards me, from under my parents' bed, I think I am pulling a country towards me. I like to pull it out and open it, over and over. I always think I never know what I am going to find. But whenever I open it, there are always the same things there: a strange, shining black suit with a high-collared jacket and a white shirt with a stiff collar and large cuffs. I have never seen him dressed in this suit but he kept it in the best condition. It was not a suit for wearing. It never left the trunk except to be cleaned and aired. When I was no longer a child, someone told me it was his father's suit. My grandfather may have made it, since he was a tailor. There were papers in the trunk that I would secretly play with, because he said they were very important – yellowed, browning paper tied in pink string. He also kept there the letters he and my mother wrote each other when they were courting. Sometimes, my mother kept a dress for best there too, but not for long. All our birth certificates were kept in the trunk and mothballs too, to preserve everything.

We rarely had occasion for dressing up, only for births, marriages and deaths. Then our Sunday best came out of the trunk, out of the mothballs. Special occasions smelt of mothballs, of best soap, talcum, perfumes and new dresses. We always cleaned and washed ourselves – and everything else besides – for the new born, the newly wed and the dead.

The smell of ripe plantain is strongest in the pot of boiling cassava, yam, plantain and sweet potatoes. For the curry, I have to blend fresh pepper and jeera very lightly. The gravy has to be extremely thin. I must use only one fresh tomato and a leaf of thyme. Add water at the very last. I can see my mother dip a spoon into a karahi of boiling curry, trickle the gravy from a height so it cools in the air in its passage to the palm of her hand. I am in her kitchen again. She would never taste from the spoon, only from her palm. I trickle metagee into my palm but taste from hers. I am cooking for ghosts, spirits. The smell of my food is attracting them. For this very reason, there is no cooked food on the day of a funeral. The rituals of cooking, the opening of trunks smelling of mothballs, soap, perfume and talcum powder were part of the christening.

At the christening all the girls are in organza dresses. Mine is the palest colour of pink. I wear a small, white pillbox hat and white gloves. I am not just any child today, I am a godmother. My mother and father are there, and the Allens, and the baby, all the village. I can see the table, full of food. Today, I am cooking the same meal they prepared for the christening.

★ ★ ★ ★

My relatives arrive before my guests of honour. The scent of the food puts them in a good mood, makes them forget the cold weather, and stirs their memory.

The Allens lived in Cumberland all their lives until they went to live in Georgetown, in 1966. People were always leaving the country areas for Georgetown but I never thought they would leave.

"And they never came back to visit?"

"Oh yes!"

"But I never saw Yvette again."

"When they came to visit, you were always at school."

"No one told me when they visited."

"After the race riots, Joseph joined the new government, and stopped coming to Berbice. But he always wrote to your parents, he kept in touch."

"I never knew that. I used to ask after Yvette, and nobody ever told me that."

"There was an English priest who did the christening. Father Mason. He still in Berbice?"

"He was from the North of England. He was a paedophile. Everybody knew about it. I would not have him christen my child."

Secrets are the difficult parts of memory, especially secrets you are still not permitted to know, still not permitted to speak, secrets that were knowledge and power to protect the ones in control. You dare to speak them and they silence you with public shaming and ridicule. Secrets, knowledge and power were for closing ranks, keeping in the ones who never tell and keeping out the ones who do. Father Mason is dead now. We do not live in his parish. Our jobs do not depend on baptisings, christenings, masses, evensongs and funerals. His secret is not important any more. They can tell it now. But God is not dead. God might hear. Be careful. If you say it, say it once, and we will pretend we did not hear. There are places where there are echoes we cannot drown – places of the past, places of the mind, places of the heart.

When the doorbell rings I will open the front door and it will be as if memory is opening. The past and present will be joined.

The doorbell is ringing.

★ ★ ★ ★

Certainly their faces hardly bear a resemblance to the faces in my memory. They greet us with religious words. They are born-again Christians. Their mission is conversion. Before the meal, they say grace. Joseph behaves like a god. He expects women to wait on him, and Yvette and Cynthia do. He is a man of power. He was a policeman. Yvette and her mother hardly eat or speak, only when he prompts them.

Did I expect the ghosts would rise like Lazarus from the dead? Round and round the table goes the conversation. Guyana was now the second poorest country in the world after Haiti and malaria had returned; it was no longer the 'bread basket' of the Caribbean; no longer had the highest literacy rate in the region; our political culture was in ruins; we could not return home. Joseph nods like a president. They ask him questions about Guyana, the kind of anxious questions emigrants ask.

"How are things in Guyana?"

"Oh very good."

"Are the police still killing the opposition?"

"Oh no."

"Has the race politics stopped?"

"Oh yes."

"Are the roads improving?

"Oh yes."

"Has malaria really come back?"

"Oh no."

"Is there still a food shortage?"

"Oh no."

" You are a good public relations man for the country!"

"Oh yes indeed I am. After all I am the Chief of Police in Berbice."

Finally, only the fruit salad and black cake remained – the last fragments of the dream meal. On and on they talk about Guyana – the politics, the power struggles and hatreds without end. Joseph dictated the conversation. They could share no other memory with him.

Before they started on the black cake I had to perform the ritual. I don't know which I was – my mother or my young self. Perhaps both. Perhaps it was something to do with my father's trunk, but although I can see that Joseph did not like it, I went on speaking. I was telling Yvette I was sorry I never got to see her again, and I opened her hand and placed in it the pair of earrings I had bought for her. It was the right ritual. This is what you do for a godchild. You give gifts that last.

Her father spoke directly to her. "Yvette, you are very lucky indeed to have such a nice godmother. I hope you are grateful.

You know, the young people are never grateful. You are very lucky to be born to have such a godmother. Those are good gold earrings, worth plenty. Let me see them."

He does not give her back her earrings. We clear the table. Joseph does not help. He throws his arm over the back of the chair and crosses his legs.

The time comes for them to leave and Joseph asks to speak to me privately. I take him to the kitchen.

"Maybe you live in England too long, and you don't remember. But it is the custom for the godparent to also give a present of money to the godchild father."

"My present is for Yvette, not for you."

I clear away the remains of my dream dinner. I wash the plates, cooker, and walls and surfaces of the kitchen. Yet, I am certain I detect a lingering scent of mothballs in the air.

ELIZABETH WALCOTT-HACKSHAW

HERE

There are so many cars ahead of me, even today, Saturday, it'll be a while before I get the green light and cross the major intersection, so I look to the left for no reason in particular, and I see three boys walking along the side of the highway; the first in what I call cowman boots, black rubber boots, like the ones I wore as a child so that I could pretend to be the man who took care of the cows opposite our first house in the valley; the second boy taller, skinnier, in rubber slippers, his thin tee-shirt billowing in the wind like a sail; the third with blue-black madras skin in torn khaki shorts and an oversized white vest, and all three powdered with fine, white sand. They skin and grin, all the while staying in their single file, Indian file, one behind the other, on their side of the highway, the side with the coconut trees, the wooden huts, the razor grass, the rice grass, and everything so green except for the white mosque, crescent moon and star rising out of the water with the billboard: *Islam, The Fastest Growing Religion In The World.*

On the other side of the highway is the huge milk factory. Outside its tall gates are pyramids of oranges and grapefruit, piles of mangoes and three old, rusty vans full of gutted kingfish, red fish or carite, with bouquets of blue crabs tied to bamboo sticks planted in ice buckets in the vans' trays. In the middle of the highway, lanes of cars move on either side of the embankment like snails towards or away from the sky-high traffic lights against a cloudless, empty blue sky. At this, the major intersection, this *carrefour*, east, west, north and south converge; trucks, tractors, men at work who are forever widening the road, digging holes, filling holes, only to dig and fill all over again. They've been fixing this highway since I was a child.

The boys pass me; the traffic moves and I catch up to them, then they pass me again. They look so light and free, covered with layers of smells from the cars, the trucks, the factory, the fish, the oranges, the pond, and they laugh and chat, as though they have pockets full of 'blues", one-hundred-dollar-bill-blues, silver shoes, and a view of the ocean from their mansion on the hill.

As I get closer to the lights, the vendors begin to swarm. Timing the lights perfectly, they weave between the crawling cars with bags of oranges, limes, corn, pimentos; weigh pawpaws and pineapples in either hand; roll bins of coconut water, Coca-Cola, bottled water or Apple-J; open black boxes of fake gold watchbands, fake gold watches, knives; haul huge market sacks full of small brown paper bags of cashews, peanuts (salt or fresh), or carry nut cakes wrapped and stacked in huge plastic bags. Rain or shine, there is always the Nut Cake Man with the bandana, hat shades and the strong wrestler's body, the Knife Boy, slim, sharp, six-foot-four, wearing a furry Kangol cap and selling made-in-China knives, and dozens of neatly dressed Bobo Shantis selling nuts from their cotton satchels, and wearing long-sleeved shirts buttoned, tucked and belted into pleated pants, and Baptist blue or red, gold and green Irie cloths wrapped carefully around their dreadlocks.

At the lights before this main intersection there are no vendors, only beggars with twisted arms, back-to-front elbows, limps and jagged bodies, and an elderly Indian couple who walk to beg together. My windows are always rolled up, air-conditioner on, radio on; I know what they look like, how they move, but as they tap on the glass, I just shake my head, sometimes an irritated "no", sometimes a "no thanks", sometimes just a flick of the wrist like shooing away flies. It all depends on my day.

But these boys, I've never seen them before. The tallest one, with the cowman boots, is the leader, he must be sixteen or seventeen, maybe even more, perhaps much older than the others, maybe even an uncle (in those families, things like that happen, mother and daughter only fourteen years apart, father and son sixteen, uncles and nephews the same age). The shortest one could be his sister's son; things like that happen in those families, things like that happen all the time here.

They're eating nuts when they pass me again. A Bobo Shanti

must have given a bag to them for free because he knows that even though they skin and grin, on the inside, like the inside of their hollow, broken homes, they are mashed up, hungry, molested and abused. They toss the nuts from the brown paper bags into their half-open mouths and the shells flutter in the breeze like tiny butterflies.

She's asleep in the back seat, never makes it to the traffic light on a normal day, far less on one like today. This morning, while I was dressing her, she asked me, "How long, Mummy? How long?" – and she put up both hands for me to show her, and counting her tiny four-year-old fingers, I say, "Ten days," as though ten days were like two and not a lifetime when she is away from me.

The man in the car next to me is staring. I feel sorry for him, for his ugliness, for his inability to see how ugly he is or how people either take pity on him or are irritated by him because he reminds them of some ugliness they may have. I give him a quick smile because that's my mood today, and that smile is meant to say, I feel sorry for your physical appearance, your God-given looks, your curse, now leave me alone.

Everyday the same route, the same traffic, even on a Saturday. I look at my watch and the clock on my dashboard, turn the radio on, then off, check the time again, see if my watch matches the clock, then I do it all again and again, because getting from one light to another can sometimes take a lifetime. This morning she wanted to look at those noisy cartoons; she pleaded, begged, "Cartoons, Mummy, please," one billion times, and I always give in, here's your damn cartoon, turn on the TV, keep the room dark. I didn't want to start a day I had been dreading for months. And I have lied to her so many times (as I will again and again because without the lies, it's just too hard), it's not ten days, ten little four-year-old-finger-days, but two months. A lie of the imagination to create a want, a need, a wish; I wish she didn't have to go. My answer to her "How long, Mummy? How long?" wasn't really a lie but, as I prefer to call it, an imagined truth.

He wants her for the entire summer – two months, ten days, there's no real difference to a four year old, all it is is time away from Mummy, a lot of time on bad days, but a minute when her daddy gives her everything she wants.

As we inch on, the three boys plant themselves on the pavement at the intersection. I know their story now, they are definitely family, the eldest one is the presumed, appointed leader, the middle one barely a presence, but the third one, because he is the smallest, the apparent follower, will be the most powerful.

At the airport she didn't even realize what happened. I told her she missed the flight, even though we were there two hours before. She even met the flight attendant, pretty with polished, slicked hair, Jackie, Chanel No 5 Jackie, all set to take her from me to him. I hope she doesn't remember all of this, especially Jackie, or breakfast upstairs in that ice box, stinking of frying bacon, fly and cockroach spray (Flit or Baygon?), plane fuel, perfume and black coffee. She wasn't even cold, though dressed only in her jeans, small white Gap top, and Power Puff Girls pink socks and sneakers. Her knapsack held her tiny sweater, her doll Dolly, her notepad and pencils, all set to fly to her daddy. Since she turned four, he's been asking me to send her for a few days, then a week, now two months. I had them all on my side in the beginning, with my stories about his family, the drugs he did in college, the young cousin who had guns under the front seat of his car, the alcoholic aunt, and the repeated hints about their dry-cleaning shops laundering more money than dirty clothes. But perhaps the best thing for my case was the way he just walked out, like a deserter, a coward, abandoning me and our little girl. Maybe that was why the letters between lawyers kept going back and forth and why the judge let me keep her until now.

A father bringing up a little girl is not right, I keep telling my lawyer, Cathy, but all she ever says these days is that he has a right to have her for the two months. That's when I usually hint about his drinking (although he seldom drinks) and that he almost hit me a couple times (he has *almost* hit me but I have always hit him). Cathy usually pretends not to hear; she knows these are my imagined truths, so she just repeats what the judge has decided. But I think of my baby in Miami and how she will be treated because, although she looks light-skinned here, in America she will be black and will have to suffer in ways she would never have to here. Two months will become two years, and then he will take her away from me entirely and I will be the one begging for time. Again, Cathy, my broken record, comes to mind with her "Judge blah, blah, blah". As soon as I get to a phone I'm going to fire her, I'm sick of all her speeches. I'll find someone else, a lawyer with a child, preferably a young daughter, because a woman without a child cannot possibly understand the endless horrific possibilities: Tina dead in a car crash, Tina kidnapped, Tina kidnapped and sold to child pornographers, or Tina lost, simply lost in one of those gigantic Miami malls.

I cannot go home for the rest of the day, but where do I take her? The flight, direct to Miami, is only four hours. He'll be waiting, pacing, checking the flight information, thinking she got on another flight, another airline. But then, I would have called him. Confused, speeding thoughts attack his naturally calm, steady mind. Then it'll begin. The calls to Trinidad from the airline office in Miami, calls to Cathy, to everyone I know. How long will it all take before he realizes what I have done? One hour? Maybe two? In a crisis, time is not the same, there are gaps, pauses, rushing ahead (like these damn traffic lights), always a checking of the watch. The airline people will be nice to him; everyone is always so nice to him. Charming, they say, but not in a slick way; he has honest, gentle looks, a gentle man, for all his charm and the fact that although coloured and Trinidadian he looks like a white, Cuban, anti-Castro supporter with a slight tan. For his looks, more than anything else, those Americans will help him.

On the drive to the airport this morning, I went over Sans Souci Hill (how does that translate? Without a Worry Hill? Carefree Hill?), foolish name for a place where all the residents can barely make ends meet, where most of the young men have no jobs and spend most of the day playing basketball and smoking *zeb,* but she looked so still in the back seat, lying peacefully, eyes closed softly, motionless, hardly a breath. They say that the easiest way to avoid the pain and shock of an accident is to be asleep. Driving over that hill (although I am quite convinced that I could never do it), I have often thought of what it would be like to drive over the edge, straight over the edge; sometimes, I see the car sailing over the valley to another hill or sometimes being held up by the vines that wrap themselves around the heads of the giant trees that grow up from the valley below.

I was his excuse for leaving but he always wanted to go, to Miami, anywhere to get away from us, me, everyone, everything but our Tina. He never liked it here. He didn't want the family, the family business, he didn't want anything to do with home. He left right after we buried my father. That day, supposedly one of the hardest in any life, was much easier than I expected mainly because I was so hungry; I had starved myself for weeks, hoping that denying myself food would make my father stronger. So at the church service, I felt faint, and by the time we got to the cemetery, all I could think about was food. It rained a light thin rain, a funeral rain. Some people had opened their black umbrellas, making it difficult to pass the floral arrangements from the top of the hearse, over the heads of the nuns, in between my father's two spinster sisters, Auntie May and Auntie Winifred, through the rest of the family and friends, to the side of the grave. Everyone came, everyone except my mother. The prayers went on and on, but the hum of the Holy Marys couldn't cover the thuds of the gravediggers throwing heavy clods of damp soil on my father's coffin. He held me and I felt even dizzier because I was so hungry, and the grave, with the candles planted on the moist, dark brown dirt, looked like a delicious chocolate birthday cake.

Father – the word is relative (no pun intended) – my "real" father, my biological father, never really got to know me or even hold me (according to my mother) because she left him, or he left her, before I was six months old. The reasons have varied throughout the years; there have been tales of infidelity, illness, mental illness, abuse, alcohol, but I know that the true reason is probably all and none of these and perhaps just like him (my estranged husband, whose name I refuse to mention), my father didn't like it here. He came back home to be buried, and maybe my soon-to-be-ex will do that too.

★

This morning, driving to the airport, driving over Sans Souci in the dark, I kept thinking about driving over the edge and wondering how I would react at exactly that moment when I knew I had finally done it, gone off the road, into the tops of the trees. I could only pray that I wouldn't suddenly panic, that I would be calm, not wake her and hope she would just sleep through it all.

She's waking up; no, just turning. I'll need to explain what happened at the airport in a way that will make four-year-old sense, in a way she can repeat in front of her daddy, or my new lawyer (I have, at least mentally, already fired Cathy). I could say that daddy changed his mind, which would not be a complete lie, since he has changed his mind many times, even about having his now beloved Tina. In the beginning, he thought it was my trap, to force him to marry me, to force him to stay here. But in the end he gave in; the "why" of it I can only explain by the nature of the gentle beast who would have felt it was the right thing to do, or maybe he knew it was only a temporary measure, a temporary delay, and in three years he would be out. He left us, walked out of the house, just after her third birthday, but he was never really there in the first place.

I am sure he is not alone, although I have no proof, and my Miami spies have only ever seen him with other guys or his old aunts or sisters who fly up to shop in those island-size malls, but I still feel he has someone. A blond Miss Miami whose Cuban parents don't know he has a sister who is darker than I am, with frizzier hair, or a Mandingo Indian uncle. But Miss Miami's parents don't ask, all they see is his charm and his money. They want the marriage, his boat, and the property he will inherit from his father. He will introduce our little girl to Miss Miami who will complement him and enhance his powers to charm others, because she is magazine-pretty, and America rewards such possessions. Tina will worship her and will soon want to look like her and act like her, walk and talk like her. And even though I have no proof of a Miss Miami, I know he cannot be alone; he needs someone to run his home, to take care of his dry cleaning and of my Tina.

My mother married four times. She always says three; that the first one didn't count, whatever that means. Her friends call her the Elizabeth Taylor of the Caribbean. My biological father was her second husband. Sometimes she says she loved him most of all, but for all the reasons (already listed) it didn't work. The other marriages also didn't work because it is hard, according to my mother, to bring "stepchildren" into a marriage. She tries to sound philosophical, general, generic, but she really means *a stepchild*, me. But strangely enough, those stepfathers were kinder to me than my own father who just left a space, a hole, a book full of blank pages to fill with imagined days spent together.

My mother loves the idea of marriage, and she glowed when I brought him home. It was a rare moment of praise for me, she was so proud that I had been able to attract, let alone marry, someone like him. "Startling good looks," she said. "Good-looking" was never something she said about me. I learnt from her that all that rubbish about being "beautiful on the inside" has little to do with getting what you want in life. Thank God Tina is pretty and not too dark.

Finally free from all the traffic lights, my breathing gets worse, not better, becoming more and more laboured, the breaths getting shorter and shorter. I need to stop thinking about where we can go. I cannot go home and I don't want to go home; home has never been, never meant, comfort, safety or peace, so I'll keep driving, farther and farther away from the airport, away from him, but not towards a home. I am determined now he will never have her, not for a month, a week or even a day.

In all these homes, my mother's homes, his homes, our home, quarrels replay in my head. During the day, when I am busy at work, I can turn down the volume, but as I get closer to a home, I hear them so clearly that the shouting gives me a headache. Tina and I are not going home; we will drive to the malls, eat at her favourite restaurant, put off all the calls for at least a couple of hours. I just hope he doesn't call my mother in California because even from that distance, she'll be able to find me, find us, before Cathy, or even the police. Will he call the police? Probably not, his family hates scandals, hates attracting attention.

★

I see an army of *corbeaux* circling in the distance like hundreds of black Vs against a flat blue cloth. We are on the Beetham highway now, home of the national landfill, the dump. As we drive past, the boys who wait at the entrance, barebacked, shredded shorts, soiled, gloved hands, are ready to help you, guide you through the hills of refuse, for a small fee; they seldom wear masks or handkerchiefs to cover their noses; these Beetham tour guides are accustomed to the smells, the maggots, the dead dogs, the brown diapers, the old sinks, fridges and tires; they have grown up in the plywood, milk-box shacks on the other side of the highway, shacks full of dead, rusting cars used to hide in, lime in, screw in or sleep in when the milk box starts to fall apart. A thick grey haze from the fires and burning tires covers that strip of road like a blanket and I drive through as fast as I can.

Heading towards the capital, Port of Spain, I can see the old lighthouse that stands in the middle of the street, now a rounda-bout. "There used to be water here," my mother always said when she was alive, not half-dead as she is now, at least in my thoughts, living in California with her fourth husband. There are no cruise ships today; these floating cities come to this town from Monday to Friday, to this port that tries to hide its ugliness with bougainvillea and alamanda. The cautious tourists walk through the streets of Port of Spain and compare this port, this capital, to others they have seen in the Caribbean, in more beautiful islands with whiter beaches and friendlier locals. The tourists never venture too far away from the lighthouse, they never go lower down the street where there aren't even flowers to hide the thick, black, oily sea filled with ships lying on their side, like dead dogs on the highway. There they would find shanties, standpipes for showers, holes full of crabs, half-naked children, men and women, living no better than those wrecks in that oily sea.

"Let her stay with me," I said to him over and over before the lawyers took over all of our conversations. And before long, we could only speak in fragments, broken phrases, because each word felt like another splinter.

I drive away from that town, Port of Spain, a name I always

loved as a child, linking my little dot to a bigger somewhere, but now the name irritates me, embarrasses me, especially when the cruise ships arrive. No, we don't speak Spanish here, and I'm sure there is nothing here to remind you of your last trip to Spain. I've never been to Spain and this is not Spain's port, Port of Spain, Port of Pain, Sort of Sane.

My old house, I will soon pass one of my old houses where we lived when I was a child, a house that seemed so strong, able to keep it all out, windows shut, doors closed, curtains drawn, until my mother left my father, or my father left my mother, whichever came first. All I remember is that when they left each other, we cleaned that house as we would a dead body (I've never cleaned a dead body, but I imagine they clean it thoroughly). We took everything out, swept, mopped, bleached, "Ajaxed", "Cloroxed" and then put all the furniture back in. But then the cleaning stopped. We let it rot; the furniture cracked, dust settled everywhere, white walls turned to grey, and soon the smell of my mother's perfume could no longer cover the layers of dirt and decay. Uncle Michael, her third husband, who seemed like an angel at first, helped us leave that house, bury it, build another one, but then he left her, or she left him, and we started the cleaning all over again.

I cannot take her home. I cannot face all the calls, the long explanations, the accusations. He will win again, find me and keep her. I have no one on my side, no fathers, mothers, sisters – no more money to waste on bad lawyers. I have wasted so much of my life living it in threes: my mother, my father and me; me, myself and I; replacing fathers with more fathers; replacing husbands with more husbands. I was taught that threes were lucky, good, blessed: the Holy Trinity, the Father, Son and Holy Ghost, three times lucky, La Trinité, the Niña, Pinta, Santa Maria, three in one. How can I take her home?

One day, while on vacation, we were in a rented Jeep. Tina was still in my watermelon stomach and he wanted to drive to the Atlantic side of the island to a beach he had heard about at the foot of a hill. We drove for an hour, passing fishing villages along the way. I saw the sign for the bay so he turned off of the highway onto a sunbaked, rocky dirt road and asked if I was okay. The narrow, broken road took us through a thorny brush then suddenly opened onto a wide, dry field full of gigantic cactus with arms bent upwards in praise, holding huge orange and pink flowers in their prickly palms. It was very windy, the air was salty and you could smell the ocean down below. With so much space and the Atlantic on the horizon, it felt like another place, no longer the Caribbean. But then the trail stopped. Suddenly, we had to find our own way down to the beach. He was driving carefully, even caringly, but the Jeep kept bumping up and down over the cracked ground, so he asked again if I was okay, if I wanted to turn back, but I wanted to get to the ocean, the deep, blue, rough Atlantic and soak both Tina and myself in the water. And then as we turned to go down, we came upon a lone hut, a *case en bois*, with huge holes for windows and a space for a doorway. The *case* had a clear view of the ocean. He slowed down. There were three of them inside the room; two men in their underwear sitting on the ground, and a young boy, barebacked, lying on his stomach in torn shorts on an old mattress, rum bottles scattered everywhere.

The three of them, two men and a boy. The three of us. The men never looked up. The boy turned his face to the wall. So we kept driving to the Atlantic Ocean, the ocean, not the Caribbean Sea, without saying a word about the men and the boy, without saying a word about the three of us.

CONTRIBUTORS

Opal Palmer Adisa is a Jamaica-born, poet, novelist and educator, long resident in the USA. A performance poet and writer, she is the author of twelve books, including from Peepal Tree: *Caribbean Passion*, *I Name Me Name* and *Painting Away Regrets*. The story in this anthology comes from her collection *Until Judgement Comes: Stories About Jamaican Men* (Peepal Tree, 2007).

Christine Barrow was born in the UK, and lived in Barbados for nearly fifty years where she worked as an academic in Caribbean Social Development at the University of the West Indies. Since retiring she has recently returned to live in the UK (Brighton). The story in this anthology comes from her collection *Black Dogs and the Colour Yellow* (2018).

Rhoda Bharath is a Trinidadian born and resident author who teaches and blogs about politics and culture. She completed an MFA in Creative Writing in 2007. Her debut collection, *The Ten Day's Executive and Other Stories,* from which the story in this anthology comes, was published by Peepal Tree Press in 2015.

Jacqueline Bishop was born in Jamaica, has lived mostly in New York and is currently studying in the UK. Her novel, *The River's Song*, two collections of poems, *Fauna*, and *Snapshots from Istanbul*, an art book, *Writers Who Paint... Three Jamaican Artists*, and most recently, *The Gymnast and other Positions*, a collection of short stories, essays and interviews (from which the story in this collection comes), were all published by Peepal Tree. The latter won the 2016 OCM Bocas Non-Fiction Prize for Caribbean Literature.

Hazel Campbell was born and lives in Jamaica. Sadly, she died as this book was going to press. She was a teacher, public relations worker, editor, features writer and video producer. She wrote three collections of short stories, *The Rag Doll & Other Stories* (Savacou, 1978), followed by *Women's Tongue* (Savacou, 1985). The story here comes from *Singerman*, published by Peepal Tree in 1991. A collected edition of her stories will be published in 2019.

Merle Collins grew up in Grenada, which she left after the US invasion in 1983. She teaches at the University of Maryland. Her poetry publications include *Because the Dawn Breaks*, *Rotten Pomerack* and *Lady in a Boat* (Peepal Tree). She has published two novels, *Angel* and *The Colour of Forgetting*, and two collections of short stories, *Rain Darling* and *The Ladies are Upstairs* (Peepal Tree, 2011) from which the story in this anthology comes.

Jacqueline Crooks is a Jamaican-born writer who lives in London where she delivers writing workshops to socially excluded communities. She is the author of a collection of interlinked short stories, *The Ice Migration* (Peepal Tree, 2018), that follow a Jamaican family of mixed African and Indian origins through time and space. The story in this anthology is from this collection.

Kwame Dawes is a Ghanaian-born, Jamaican-bred poet, critic, fiction writer and editor who is currently the Glenna Luschei editor of *Prairie Schooner* and a Chancellor's Professor of English at the University of Nebraska. He is the author of thirty-five books, most recently *A New Beginning*, a cycle of poems written with John Kinsella. The story in this anthology comes from his collection, *A Place to Hide* (Peepal Tree, 2003).

Curdella Forbes is a Jamaican-born, USA-resident novelist and short story writer. She teaches at Howard University. Her fiction includes *Songs of Silence*, *Flying with Icarus and Other Stories* and *Ghosts* (Peepal Tree). The story in this anthology comes from her collection, *A Permanent Freedom* (Peepal Tree, 2008).

Kevin Jared Hosein lives in Trinidad and Tobago. His novel, *The Repenters* was published by Peepal Tree in 2016. The story published here was the 2015 Caribbean regional winner of the Commonwealth Short Story Prize. His work is also featured in the Peekash anthologies, *Pepperpot: Best New Stories from the Caribbean*, and *New Worlds, Old Ways: Speculative Tales from the Caribbean*, and Akashic's *Duppy Thursdays*.

Ifeona Fulani is Jamaican-born, now resident in the USA, where she teaches at New York University. She is the author of a novel, *Seasons of Dust* (1997) and an academic monograph, *Archipelagos of Sound: Transnational Caribbeanities, Women and Music*. Her story in this anthology come from her collection, *Ten Days in Jamaica* (Peepal Tree, 2012).

Valda Jackson is a widely exhibited visual artist and writer. Of Jamaican heritage, she lives in the UK. Her story in this anthology was first published in *Closure* (an Inscribe/Peepal Tree anthology, 2015).

Keith Jardim is a Trinidadian. He teaches at UWI, St Augustine and delivers creative writing workshops. His stories have been widely published in journals, and the collection from which the story in this anthology comes, *Near Open Water* (Peepal Tree, 2011) was longlisted for the OCM Bocas Prize for Caribbean Literature, 2012 and the Frank O'Connor International Short Story Award; it made the Nota Bene list of *World Literature Today*.

Barbara Jenkins is a Trinidadian who lived for a time in the UK, but has been back in the Republic since the 1970s. She is a retired teacher. Her stories have won numerous prizes, and her first collection, *Sic Transit Wagon* (Peepal Tree, 2013), from which the story in this anthology comes, was awarded the Guyana Prize for Literature, Caribbean Award. Her first novel, *De Rightest Place* (Peepal Tree) was published in 2018.

Meiling Jin was born in Guyana, lived in the UK for a time, and currently lives in Canada. She published a collection of poems, *Gifts from My Grandmother*. Her story in this anthology comes from her collection, *Song of the Boatwoman* (Peepal Tree, 1996).

Cherie Jones is a Barbadian writer and lawyer. She was awarded an MA in writing at Sheffield Hallam University in 2015. Her first collection, from which the story in this anthology comes, *The Burning Bush Women and Other Stories*, was published by Peepal Tree in 2004. She is working on a novel.

Helen Klonaris is a queer Greek-Bahamian writer and teacher who lives between the Bay Area, California and Nassau, Bahamas. She is an LGBTI and Feminist activist and an energy medicine practitioner and teaches mythology and comparative religious studies at the Academy of Art University. Her story in this anthology comes from her first collection, *If I Had the Wings* (Peepal Tree, 2017).

Sharon Leach is a Jamaican writer who is a journalist and the literary editor for the *Jamaica Observer*. Her first collection of short stories, *What You Can't Tell Him: Stories*, was published in 2006. The story in this anthology comes from her second collection, *Love it When You Come, Hate it When You Go* (Peepal Tree, 2014).

Breanne Mc Ivor is a Trinidadian writer who co-founded People's Republic of Writing (PROW). Her first collection of short stories, from which the story in this anthology comes, *Where There Are Monsters*, will be published by Peepal Tree in 2019.

Alecia McKenzie was born in Kingston, Jamaica; she has lived in the USA, Belgium and currently France. Her first collection of short stories, *Satellite City*, won the regional Commonwealth Writers Prize for Best First Book. Her novel *Sweetheart* (Peepal Tree, 2011) won the 2012 Commonwealth Book Prize (Caribbean Region). Her story in this anthology comes from her Peepal Tree collection, *Stories from Yard* (2005).

Mark McWatt is a Guyanese who lives in Barbados, where he retired as Emeritus Professor of West Indian literature at UWI, Cave Hill. He has published three poetry collections, *Interiors*, *The Language of Eldorado*, and *The Journey to Le Repentir*. His story in this anthology comes from *Suspended Sentences: Fictions of Atonement*, winner of the regional Commonwealth, and Guyana Prizes. The stories in this collection are written as if the various voices of former school friends, all of whom have left Guyana.

458   PEEPAL TREE . CONTEMPORARY CARIBBEAN SHORT STORIES

Sharon Millar is a Trinidadian writer who teaches part-time at UWI, St Augustine. She holds an MFA (Creative Writing) from Lesley University, Cambridge, Massachusetts. She lives in Port of Spain and is currently at work on a second collection of stories. Her story in this anthology comes from her first collection, *The Whale House and Other Stories* (Peepal Tree, 2015). The title story won the 2013 Commonwealth Prize.

Anton Nimblett is a Trinidadian who currently lives in New York. His work was published in the anthology *Our Caribbean: A Gathering of Lesbian and Gay Writing From the Antilles*, edited by Thomas Glave. His story in this anthology comes from his collection, *Sections of an Orange* (Peepal Tree, 2009). A second collection of stories is due for publication in 2019.

Geoffrey Philp is a Jamaican long resident in Florida. A lecturer and avid blogger, his poetry collections include *Florida Bound*, *Hurricane Center*, *Xango Music* and *Dub Wise*. As well as his novel, *Benjamin, My Son*, he has published two collections of short stories, *Uncle Obadiah and the Alien* and *Who's Your Daddy and Other Stories* (Peepal Tree, 2009), from which his story in this anthology comes.

Velma Pollard is a Jamaican who is the retired Dean of the Faculty of Education. Peepal Tree have published four collections of her poetry, *Crown Point, Shame Trees Don't Grow Here*, *Leaving Traces* and *And Caret Bay Again*, and a collection of short stories, fables and memoir, *Considering Woman I & II*. Her story in this anthology comes from that collection.

Jennifer Rahim is a Trinidadian temporarily resident in Canada. She taught for many years at UWI, St Augustine. She is a poet and short story writer and is currently working on a novel. Her poetry collections include *Between the Fence and the Forest*, *Approaching Sabbaths*, which won a Casa de las Américas Prize 2010, and most recently *Ground Level*. Her short story in this anthology comes from *Songster and other Stories* (Peepal Tree, 2007). Most recently, her collection of linked short stories, *Curfew Chronicles* (Peepal Tree, 2017) won the overall 2018 Bocas Prize for Caribbean Literature.

Raymond Ramcharitar is a Trinidadian poet and short story writer and journalist who currently works as a press officer for the Sagba corporation. His poetry collections include *American Fall* and *Here*. His story in this anthology comes from his first collection, *The Island Quintet: Five Stories*.

Jacob Ross is a Grenadian who was forced to leave his country after the US invasion of 1983. He lives in Leeds and is Associate Fiction Editor at Peepal Tree. He is a novelist, short story writer and editor, and is much in demand as a tutor for writing workshops around the world. His novel, *Pynter Bender*, was shortlisted for the Commonwealth Prize, and his crime fiction novel, *The Bone Readers* was recently sold to Little Brown. His two previous collections of short stories, *Song for Simone* and *A Way to Catch the Dust* were recently collected with new stories in *Tell No-One About This* (Peepal Tree, 2017), from which his story in this anthology comes.

Leone Ross is a novelist, short story writer, editor, journalist and academic of Jamaican and Scottish ancestry. She was born in England and grew up in Jamaica. Her first novel, *All the Blood Is Red* was long-listed for the Orange Prize; her second novel, *Orange Laughter* was chosen as a BBC Radio 4's Women's Hour Watershed Fiction favourite. Her story in this anthology comes from her collection with Peepal Tree, *Come Let Us Sing Anyway* (2017)

Olive Senior was born in Jamaica and lives between there and Toronto. She is a poet, short story writer, novelist, writer of non-fiction, encyclopaedist and editor. Her poetry collections include *Gardening in the Tropics*, *Over the Roofs of the World* and *Shell*; her novel is *Dancing Lessons*; her short story collections include *Summer Lightning*, *Arrival of the Snake Woman* and *Discerner of Hearts*. Her story in this anthology comes from her most recent collection, *The Pain Tree* (Peepal Tree, 2017).

Jan Lowe Shinebourne was born in Guyana and has lived in the UK since the 1970s. She is the author of four novels, *Timepiece*, *The Last English Plantation*, *Chinese Women* and *The Last Ship*. Her story in this anthology comes from her collection *The Godmother and Other Stories* (Peepal Tree, 2004)

Elizabeth Walcott-Hackshaw is a Trinidadian who is a Senior Lecturer in French and Francophone Literatures at The University of the West Indies, St Augustine. Her co-edited publications include *Border Crossings: A Trilingual Anthology of Caribbean Women Writers*, *Echoes of the Haitian Revolution 1804-2004*, and *Reinterpreting the Haitian Revolution and its Cultural Aftershocks* (1804-2004). Her novel, *Mrs B.* was published by Peepal Tree in 2014. Her short story in this anthology comes from *Four Taxis Facing North* (2007, Peepal Tree 2017).